VAULT of STONE

VAULT of STONE

ARCHIVES OF THE WARDEN
Book Two

V. K. DIXON

XHP
xenia house press

Vault of Stone
Copyright © 2023 by Victoria Dixon

Contact Info: www.xeniahousepress.com

Cover Design by : Maria Spada
Sigil Illustrations by : Hannah Fogarty
Editor : Brittany Howard

ISBN: 979-8-9868452-3-4

First Edition: October 2023

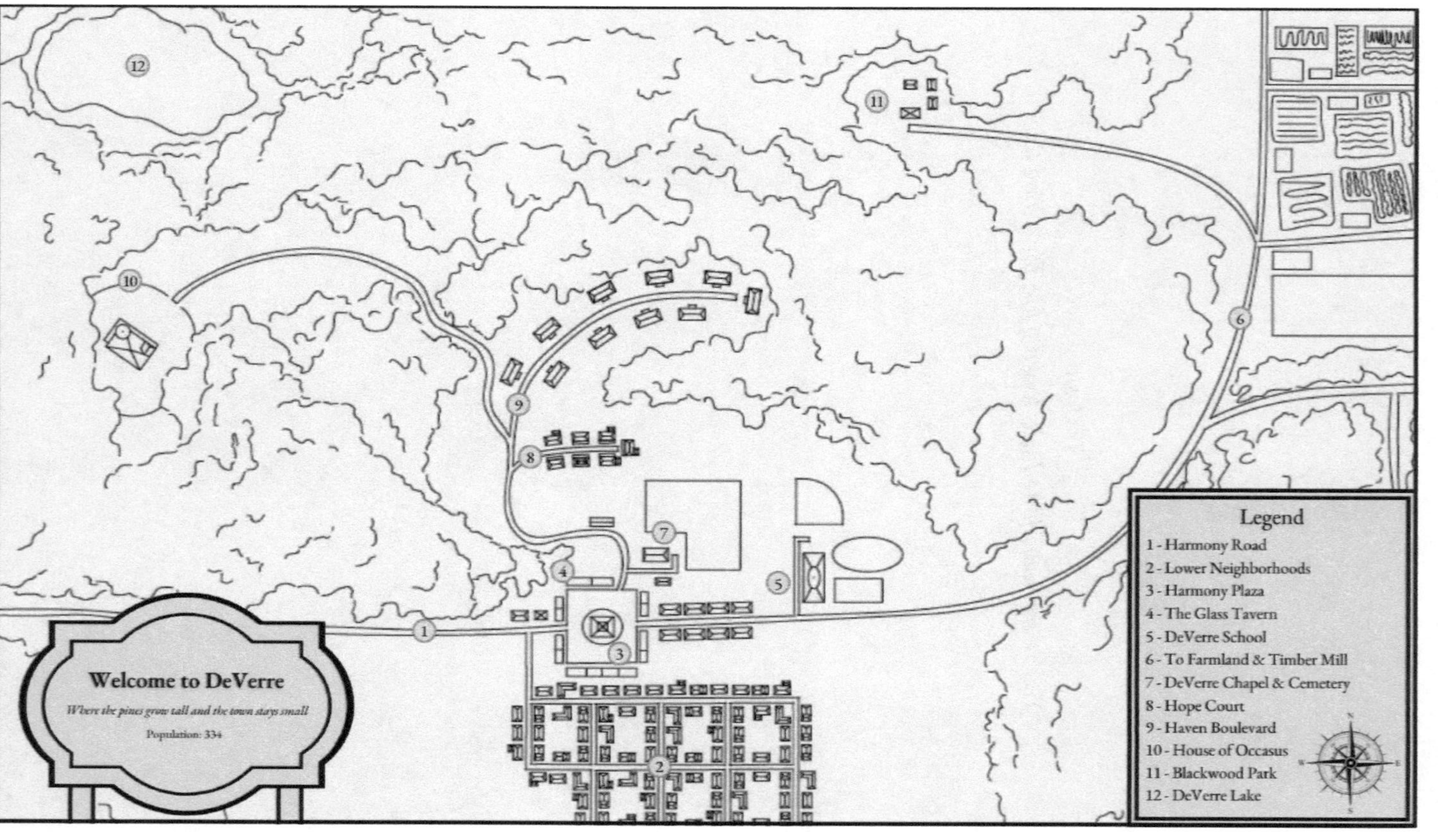

Welcome to DeVerre
Where the pines grow tall and the town stays small
Population: 334
Legend
1 - Harmony Road
2 - Lower Neighborhoods
3 - Harmony Plaza
4 - The Glass Tavern
5 - DeVerre School
6 - To Farmland & Timber Mill
7 - DeVerre Chapel & Cemetery
8 - Hope Court
9 - Haven Boulevard
10 - House of Occasus
11 - Blackwood Park
12 - DeVerre Lake

Table of Contents

Author's Note

The spirit world referenced in this novel is inspired by the truth.
It is not, however, the real truth.
In making the truth fantastic, it is my hope to stir up questions within reality.

One month earlier . . .

Upon an unexpected inheritance, brothers and co-authors Peter and Spencer Collins moved across the country to DeVerre, WA, to pursue their lifelong dream of becoming full-time authors. Excited by the prospects their estranged great-aunt's extensive estate and mansion will bring to them, Peter was determined to make their new home and careers a success. The one wrench in his plan: Spencer.

Unnerved by the sudden inheritance from an old woman they'd never met—who also happened to write about ghosts—Spencer was convinced that the house would be haunted. But Peter wouldn't let his brother's overactive imagination stop them from seeing their dreams come true.

Arriving in DeVerre, the brothers claimed the keys to the House of Occasus and assumed the care of two German Wirehaired Pointers, Anguis and Nex, as well as an inheritance of over four million dollars . . . with one caveat: By the end of the first year, Peter and Spencer must prove their income and show sufficient care of the property and dogs, or the entirety of the estate will fall to Cassandra Clement, Diane's closest and only friend.

Over the next several weeks, Peter and Spencer worked to build a life for themselves within DeVerre. They joined the Sunday services at DeVerre Chapel, attended the games of the town softball league, and became friends with Anna Lambert, a waitress at The Glass Tavern and the town's most well-liked resident.

Yet, even as Spencer settled into his routine, he couldn't shake his nerves. Strange things kept happening around the house—stacks of books fell over when no one was near, coffee brewed when neither brother remembered starting a pot. Things only got worse when he kept noticing a suspicious man wearing a dark green jacket headed deep into the forest surrounding Occasus. Built in the dark woods a mile from town, Occasus's isolation only increased Spencer's paranoia when the brothers learned of increasingly violent animal attacks around DeVerre causing three deaths within the past month.

Despite the town marshal's assurances that it was only a wolf, Peter knew he needed to get proof that DeVerre was a normal, non-spooky town to ensure that Spencer would stick around long enough to see their success come to life.

At Anna's recommendation, Peter visited her sister, Ava, the town's librarian. Though she couldn't tell them much about Diane, she did take the time to inform Peter of the history of DeVerre. Founded in 1884 by Matthias Varon, the town was built in the middle of the Blackwood Forest, and its acreage turned into a lumber mill. For the hundred and thirty-seven years of their existence, the town remained small with only three hundred residents, the founding families maintaining leadership throughout all that time. The Chapelles ran the chapel. The Garniers were the law and order. The Frossards were the doctors. The Raynes—Ava's own family line—were the librarians and record keepers. The Guillaumes were the governing body.

When Peter asked what happened to the Varons—the previous owners of the House of Occasus—Ava informed him of the tragic story of Matthias's great-grandson Michael Varon, an unstable young man who'd murdered his father and committed suicide. The town doctor at the time, Lloyd Frossard, had records of Michael's increasingly concerning condition but was unable to keep the man's presumed paranoid schizophrenia from coming to its disastrous end.

Sure that learning of their home's original owners would cause Spencer's fears to spike, Peter confided in Ava that he worried about their chances of staying in DeVerre. Ava warned him to take Spencer to DeVerre Lake—the town's namesake—showing him it was perfectly normal before he heard the rumors of it being haunted.

Taking Ava's advice, Peter convinced Spencer to join him at the lake. While in awe of the lake's beautiful, serene atmosphere, the trip was ruined by the sudden discovery of the man in the dark green jacket—talking to the air as though in a deep conversation. Freaked out, the brothers hurried home, night falling as they finally reached the back gate of Occasus. As they walked toward the house, they discovered a truck pulling into their driveway, just as growling reached the trees beside them.

To their shock, a hulking shadow crept around the tree, neon yellow eyes glowing in the darkness as a large, black, dog-like creature revealed itself. The creature lunged for the brothers, and they bolted across the grounds of Occasus, running for their lives. In their flight, Spencer clipped his leg on the front bumper of his Jeep, falling to the ground. The creature reared back to tear into him, but a shadow fell over Spencer, blocking him from the monster's path.

A woman stood there, controlling the massive creature as she sent it away in a burst of smoke and shadow.

Lives saved, Spencer and Peter learned their surprising and rather attractive visitor was Diane's friend, Cassandra Clement. She told them the creature that attacked them was a hellhound, a spirit summoned to carry out a task for its master. Then she introduced them to the secrets in DeVerre: There was a spiritual world that ran parallel to the physical; and people like Cassandra could reach into it, harnessing its power. This spirit world held beasts like hellhounds as well as ghosts that could be tethered into phantoms—like the one Cassandra had tethered to Occasus. The brothers then met their heretofore unknown phantom roommate, Gerard Alarie, a DeVerrean from the 1950s.

Cassandra informed the brothers that the spirit world was part of what brought Diane and her husband Liam to DeVerre thirty years ago. But the real reason for their move came from Diane's search for her biological parents. In the 1940s, a mysterious "Mr. F" had delivered Diane and her younger brother Phillip—the brothers' grandfather—to the Collins family for adoption. With years of research, Diane finally discovered that she'd been born in DeVerre and that this Mr. F was a member of the Frossard family.

Cassandra asked for the brothers' help in finishing what Diane and she had started: unlocking the mysteries of the spirit world and discovering their ancestry. Moreover, she was convinced that Diane was murdered.

Sure that it would be wrong to leave Cassandra to face these problems alone, Peter and Spencer agreed to help her. Reviewing all of Diane's old research, they tried to unravel the secrets of DeVerre. At which point they discovered that pages were missing from Diane's draft—a collection of essays about the spirit world from a theologian named Elijah Lawrence.

As their research sent them in never-ending circles, Peter's friendship with Anna turned up their first clue: Ava's husband Owen was the man in the dark green jacket.

After their first meeting, Owen showed up at Occasus the next day offering his help. He admitted to being suspicious of Diane and Cassandra's research but hadn't been confident enough to approach them until now as he was like Cassandra—a Wielder of the spirit world. With his help, they learned far more than anything their research provided. He taught them that DeVerre was founded for the express purpose of protecting the lake, which was a Veil, a pocket of space where the distance between the natural world and the spirit world was thin. The founding families were men and women associated with an organization called the Warden, dedicated to protecting the spirit world from abuse, particularly from their enemies, the Druids, a cult that sought to release the spirit world onto the Earth.

With this new information, Peter concluded that the "wolf attacks" were really hellhound attacks, and they figured out that the Druids were targeting DeVerreans that had ties to Wielders in their lineage. Worried for Cassandra's safety, they agreed to band together with Owen to root out the Druids within the town.

The next day, Ava confronted the brothers, warning them that the Varon estate was more than a landmark—it housed a vault, protected by the spirit world, which held the answers to every secret of DeVerre. Along with her warning, she questioned the trustworthiness of Cassandra, who showed up shortly after Diane became a widow and wormed her way into the woman's will.

Desperate to prove Ava's accusation wrong, but wary of this new information, the brothers went to Owen, asking for his help. Together, they developed a plan for Owen to meet with Cassandra while the brothers searched her family's house. After watching Cassandra's truck and her family's SUV leave, Peter and Spencer snuck into the house. They began their search, finding Cassandra's room—but it wasn't empty.

Inside they found Debbie Mercier, the cousin of Cassandra's mother, searching her desk. Peter connected the dots, realizing that Debbie was the Druid, not Cassandra.

Debbie then attacked the brothers, summoning beasts from the spirit world. Hellhounds corralled them, while tentacled beasts called scylla caught Peter, suffocating him. Busy fighting off a hellhound, Spencer couldn't get to his brother. Debbie was about to end their lives when Cassandra arrived, wielding a powerful arc of light—the essence of the spirit world.

During her rescue, Spencer started a fire in the house, giving Cassandra the chance to bring down Debbie by shattering her soul. They saved Peter moments before his death, dragging him out of the burning house. With hopes that no one had seen them, they escaped back to Occasus, the brothers inviting Cassandra to stay with them now that she was out of a home.

Feeling at fault for not realizing that Debbie was a Druid, Cassandra hesitated to accept. "You're sure?"

Peter raised his brow. "That it wasn't your fault that your mom's crazy cousin turned out to be a Druid intent on murdering us and taking over this town? Or that we want you to live with us?"

"Either way," Spencer said, "the answer's the same."

It took a second, but a slow, appreciative smile spread over Cassandra's face. "It'll be dangerous," she warned. "Not only is there the possibility that they'll try us as murderers, but the Druids will know that we're against them now. They'll see this as an attack. As a start to something."

Cassandra was right, this was only the beginning. And now, the Collins brothers will face far more danger than they ever expected. . . .

PROLOGUE

He couldn't remember the last time he'd been this angry. But then, he couldn't remember the last time someone had challenged him this way either.

They'd held the town uncontested for more than fifty years. None of their people would have ever dared to speak against him or his family.

Diane had been a nuisance, of course. A damn pest that had refused to go away despite how many times they tried to swat her down. However, she had posed no serious threat to them, her prodding a futile effort.

But these boys. . . .

Her death was supposed to make it easier. They'd all agreed. Time was short, and they needed to make their move. They found their way in, and it had been time for Diane to go. She was old; getting rid of her wouldn't rouse suspicion.

Getting Cassandra out of DeVerre and away from Occasus had been a mere detail in the timeline. An easy problem with an easy solution. And securing Diane's death had been as unceremonious as washing one's hands.

But these boys. . . .

They were more trouble than Diane had ever been.

Even more trouble than Cassandra was proving herself to be.

These foolish, tiresome Collins brothers. . . .

It had been a mistake—letting Diane and Phillip go. A closed adoption. A clean slate. A problem solved.

What a joke.

If he had been in charge during those days, he would have taken the children in himself. Trained them and molded them. Used them for their benefit. His grandfather had been soft on the children. The old man had lost his edge with age. He'd been fool enough to try to erase his youthful indiscretion, pretending that traitorous girl was never his. But then he'd grown a conscience, releasing the children into the Collins family's care.

Eighty years later and that indiscretion came back to haunt them in the form of two idiotic, upstart boys.

The Collins brothers had no idea what game they were playing. No clue who they were up against. They got lucky with Debbie; truly, impossibly lucky.

Their luck was about to run out.

He still had use for them—for a short time. For the moment, he'd let them think they were safe. He'd allow them to imagine that they were clever, sneaking around undetected. For an infinitesimal stint longer, he'd let them do the work for him.

But one more step out of line and their search for answers would get them killed. He'd already seen to that. If it happened before they could complete the job, so be it. He wouldn't let them ruin everything his family had worked toward over the past one hundred thirty-seven years. Not even if their meddling led him to answers of his own.

He wasn't a fool.

He wasn't his grandfather.

He'd use this supposed Collins line and then end them once and for all.

These boys. . . .

What did he have to fear from them? What threat did they really pose? They were powerless. They were ignorant.

Whatever disruption they'd caused to his plans, it was a momentary thorn in his side. One he would easily pluck from his skin once he'd finished the job. And in the meantime, he'd let them keep chasing their tails as they ran around in a desperate search for the truth.

A truth that his family had managed to bury eighty years ago.

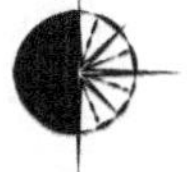

Spencer

The acrid smoke still lingered in Spencer's hair. It didn't matter that he'd already showered twice—once last night and then again that morning. The smell followed him around like a cloud. Burning in his eyes and nose, keeping the memories ever present in his mind.

Over the past hour, Spencer's eyes had glazed as he stared at the blank word document on the laptop screen in front of him. He'd assumed the comfort of writing would distract him, but the escape he sought was as elusive as the words that abandoned him. He couldn't get his brain to focus. Inevitably, his thoughts drifted back to those memories that had kept him awake in the night.

Spencer dropped his head into his hands, elbows resting on the desk. Darkness filled his vision; dots of brown-tinged light erupted as he rubbed his eyes. He could see it all as though it were happening once again.

Heavy shadows clinging to the walls, coiling and writhing as they turned into scylla.

Massive hellhounds bounding out of nowhere, their canines ready to tear through flesh.

Arcing black streaks of the spirit world's essence, slicing through the air toward him.

The terrible pain and loneliness burrowing into his chest, curling into the tight space between his ribs and his heart as an arc reached its target.

The sight of Peter—his brother's face draining of blood as his head lulled to the side, the air choked out of him by the scylla clinging to his body.

Debbie's hand clamping around Cassandra's throat, her pale skin turned yellow in the burning glow of the flames.

Terror flashing in Cassandra's hazel eyes one second before she saved them by shattering the woman's soul.

The lingering scent of smoke as the fire consumed the Merciers' house while they staggered to freedom.

Taking a long, halted breath, Spencer forced himself to open his eyes. He pressed a hand against the tension building in his chest as he stared around the office. Pale light drifted into Occasus, the misty morning casting shadows in the room.

Everything was still and quiet in the house. Tranquil and at peace.

No one stirred within the mansion. Gerard hadn't even shown himself yet; he was likely still brooding over the near death of Cassandra.

It was only Spencer and Nex awake in the early hours of the day. The dog lay sprawled on the rug nearby, his floppy brown ears alert to Spencer's every move.

Spencer had relinquished Anguis to Cassandra last night. The dog had a particular fondness for her, and he knew she could use the company after everything. He hoped the gesture had been of use to her. That she'd managed to get some sleep. Though, with her unsettled gaze and shaking voice as she'd whispered "thanks," Spencer doubted that her night had been any more restful than his.

Despite Nex's calming presence at his side, Spencer hadn't managed more than an hour of sleep. The energy he'd expended in the fight, paired with the amount of smoke he'd inhaled, should have knocked him out cold. He'd even shouldered Peter's weight most of the trek through the woods back to Occasus. His muscles ached, his sprained ankle stinging as exhaustion clung to his body.

Still, Spencer had lain awake, staring at the ceiling as he jumped at every gust of wind, rustle of tree branches, creak of floorboards, and the periodic *thunks* of the heating system kicking on. He had been too on edge to rest; too certain that the Druids would come for them in the night. That they'd exact their vengeance upon learning what the three of them had done.

The early sunlight took far too long to crack through the heavy curtains in his room, and Spencer rose as tired as when he'd lain down last night. He moved groggily for the first hour, soaking in the hot water of the shower for far longer than normal. He stared into the mirror, taking in his bloodshot eyes and hollow expression. He didn't look like himself, he thought. Too old and haggard. Newly hardened and determined.

It didn't matter, Spencer reminded himself. None of it mattered. They were alive. They'd made it home, and he should take comfort in that. As well as the fact that Cassandra wasn't the Druid they'd worried she was.

But even as Spencer dressed, made coffee, gathered his writing supplies, and took a seat at the desk, his thoughts kept returning to the Merciers' house covered in flame and shadow. His body kept reminding him of the pain and the fear, of the death that had nearly claimed them all. His stomach was empty, his shoulders heavy, and his throat raw.

Tired of staring blankly at his laptop, Spencer shut it. He picked up his long untouched mug and rose. Nex's tags jingled as he leaped up to follow. A light rain sprinkled the dining room windows. Though hours had passed since his early start to the morning, he'd gotten nothing done.

Moving to the microwave to reheat his coffee, Spencer forced himself not to scan the kitchen for hidden figures. His habitual paranoia had reached an all-time high. But despite how justified he felt, he refused to indulge in it anymore. He needed to get his head on straight. They had work to do. He had a family to protect. And he would be ready when the Druids came.

The stairs creaked, and Spencer's heart stilled as he whipped his head around, prepared to mount a defense against the intruder.

Anguis bounded down the steps, his copper and white-spotted fur a welcome sight as he rushed toward his brother. The dogs nipped at one another playfully before they pushed through the pet door and ran into the yard. Cassandra descended the final set of steps into the kitchen. Her dark hair hung to her shoulders in messy waves, far more disheveled than Spencer had ever seen. Still, she walked with her shoulders back and chin raised with the confident air he'd come to expect from her.

Spencer hoped it meant she'd regained herself after last night. He hadn't liked how she'd fallen silent as they escaped the fire. How shaken she was. Cassandra Clement was strong, fearless, and unflinching in his mind. And he didn't want to see her any other way.

Catching sight of him, Cassandra smiled. As she'd lost practically all her belongings in the fire, she'd needed to borrow some things. Now she wore a dark green tee and gray pajama pants that were all too familiar to Spencer. "Good morning," she said, voice smooth and controlled.

The microwave hummed as Spencer studied Cassandra, assessing to be sure this renewed sense of self was genuine. It was weird seeing her in his clothes. And it wasn't just that it was the first time he'd seen her wear anything but black, either. They were the same height, so the clothes fit her well, though they were a bit boxy against her feminine frame. It made sense that she'd take his things and not Peter's. But it felt more personal than he liked, and it distracted him enough that he failed to suss out the truth of her demeanor.

"Morning," he muttered as she neared.

Cassandra took a ceramic mug from the cabinet. "Sleep well?"

The microwave timer let out a *beep,* and Spencer jumped.

Cassandra smirked as she poured the coffee. "Guess not."

Managing an amused scoff as he retrieved his own cup, he returned her grin. "Old habits die hard," he joked.

One of her dark, arched eyebrows rose. "Jumping at microwaves is a habit of yours?" she asked, humor lifting her tone. "Seems there are lots of things I'll have to get used to, staying here."

Spencer scratched the back of his head, leaning against the oven. "Not the microwave in particular, but yeah. . . ." He shrugged. "I'm known to be a bit too in my own world at times. How about you? You sleep okay?"

Tipping her head to the side, Cassandra pursed her lips. "It was all right. Kind of weird." She backed away to the kitchen island, taking a seat on one of the stools. "I've been in Diane's room plenty of times, but . . . it's strange—sleeping in there."

"Makes sense."

She eyed him as she took a sip. She wasn't wearing makeup—another new thing. Not that she usually wore a lot of makeup, Spencer reminded himself. Never anything too noticeable. Just enough to make her already elegant features obnoxiously more attractive.

"You don't have to stay in there if you don't want to," Spencer offered, opening the fridge. He stared into it rather than continuing his review of this new, unfiltered version of her. "There's the spare at the back. Pete or I could move back there and let you have one of the bigger ones."

"I'm not going to make either of you move," she replied.

"We don't mind."

"And I don't mind staying in Diane's room."

He chanced a look over his shoulder at her. "You said it was weird."

"Well, yeah," she said, tucking some loose hair behind her ear. "But it's also kind of nice. Diane was—well, she was more of a mom to me than my own mother. It sort of feels like closure, you know? Getting to be in her space like this."

Spencer nodded, then turned back to the fridge. He could understand; better than most. After their dad died when they were kids, Spencer sought whatever means possible to feel close to him again. Whether by sitting in his dad's favorite chair or sneaking out to read in the Jeep. Those were the only places he could pretend that his dad wasn't gone. The only places he could cling to the illusion of connection with him.

It was why he'd begged his mom for the Jeep as soon as he could drive. Why he'd refused to sell it no matter how bad the maintenance bills got. The moment he sat in its beige leather seats, the memories of his dad came back to life, and Spencer could pretend that he was riding along with him.

Finding a bag of bagels and cream cheese in the fridge, Spencer grabbed them and turned back to Cassandra. "Want some breakfast?"

She chuckled softly at his awkward segue, running her thumb over the rim of her mug. "Sure."

Heavy footfalls pounded down the stairs, and Peter emerged in the kitchen, mid-yawn. Though dressed in his usual flannel and jeans, he looked as though he'd just woken—hair a mess, dark circles under his eyes, and lids droopy. But what caught Spencer's lingering attention were the red streaks on his neck.

The collar of Peter's flannel shirt cast a shadow enough to hide the marks, which were in the early stages of bruising. An average onlooker might not even notice them as anything more than the result of an absentminded itch. But to Spencer, they burned like flames—a horrifying reminder of the scylla's nearly successful attempt to kill his brother.

Peter made a sound that somewhat resembled "morning" around his yawn as he ambled over to the coffee pot. "Ooh." Peter nudged Spencer's arm as he spotted the bagels. "Make me one too."

Spencer let the plastic bag twist open in his hands, the tension in his chest lightening with Peter in the room. "How are you feeling?"

"Like I got beat up by a creature from another world," Peter replied. Running his fingers through his wild hair, Peter moved to sit next to Cassandra. He glanced into her mug and pursed his lips, giving her a proud nod. "You take your coffee black, eh?"

"Of course I do," she replied.

"What else did you expect?" Spencer asked, glancing over his shoulder at them. "I was shocked she accepted my stuff last night. That green is pretty bright."

Peter smirked at him. "Fair point."

Cassandra crossed her arms, the dark tee bunching up around the collar. "Excuse me," she said, grinning despite her serious tone. "I didn't realize you two were judging my style this whole time."

"Not judging," Peter assured her, laying a hand on her shoulder. "Just impressed by your dedication. Right, Spence?"

She shoved his hand away, still smiling.

The toaster popped, and Spencer turned back to it, grinning. "Definitely," he played along. "Never been more impressed in my life, actually."

Cassandra's laugh was soft, almost inaudible. "Right, I'm an absolute inspiration."

"No doubt," Peter agreed, lifting his mug for a sip.

Spencer slid the plated and freshly toasted bagel to Cassandra just as her good humor slipped. Her gaze dropped to stare into her coffee as she turned the ring on her right hand. "Cass?" he prompted, confused by the sudden change.

"Huh?" She looked up at him, dark eyes wide.

"You okay?"

"Oh, uh—yeah," she said, failing an attempted grin.

Spencer shared a dubious look with Peter.

His brother tapped her forearm, which rested on the counter. "C'mon, Cass," he prodded. "What's up?"

Cassandra's gaze shifted rapidly between the two of them. She heaved a sigh. "All right, so," she began, "I just—I want you guys to know . . . I don't expect to stay here long term."

Spencer and Peter shared another glance as she continued.

"I really appreciate that you're willing to help me out, but I don't want you to think I'm going to take advantage of your generosity or anything." Her shoulders lifted in a nervous shrug. "At present . . . well, I'm in a bit of a tough spot as I don't exactly have a job."

"You don't?" Peter asked, curiosity tipping his voice up in less of a question and more of a prompting for her to continue.

"Well, I was Diane's assistant," Cassandra explained. "And then Debbie and Mike were helping me out while everything was going on with my mom. But—well, that doesn't matter now."

She took another weighty breath, pushing on before either of them could speak. "I want you to know I'm gonna find a job and get myself a place. And I'll be out of your hair as soon as I can. It might just . . . take a minute or two."

Adjusting the collar of his gray tee, Spencer held Peter's gaze. His brother ran a hand over his mouth; his eyes narrowed as if asking if they were on the same page. Spencer gave him a subtle nod.

Peter sat up straight. "Cass," he said, his tone far more serious than usual, "we're not concerned about that. We offered you a place to stay 'cause you're our friend. You can stay as long as you want."

She hesitated, the doubt clear in the way her eyebrows pulled together. "I don't want to be a bother."

"That isn't possible," Spencer promised, setting the cream cheese and a knife next to her plate.

Cassandra's brow dropped lower. "It's not?"

Something in the weight of her glare made Spencer pause.

Peter frowned, feeling the sudden tension as well.

Setting her jaw, Cassandra drew her shoulders back and folded her hands together on the island counter. "Okay, before we go any farther here, we're gonna take a second to discuss the fact that you two thought I murdered Diane."

Spencer's throat went dry at the accusation. He turned to Peter, who had frozen, lips pressed together and eyes wide.

"Owen told me," she said, watching them both. "When I got to the park, he asked me straight up if I was a Druid. I told him, *truthfully*, that I wasn't. When I asked him why he'd think that, he explained how Ava had convinced the two of you that I was. And not only that, but that it was *me* who was murdering everyone. That I wanted Occasus and that I'd killed Diane to get it."

Peter fingered the handle on his mug, shamefaced, his eyes refusing to budge from the black granite. "Yeah. . . ." He grimaced. "About that . . . we, uh—that's why we went to your place—the Merciers' place."

"I know," she said, the words terse. "That's why *I* came back. I thought I'd catch you two there and confront you about it."

Spencer leaned forward, hoping she'd hear the sincerity of his words. "We didn't want to believe her. We just—we didn't know what else to do."

Cassandra met his gaze, the hurt in her glittering hazel eyes twisting the tension in his chest tighter. "You could have trusted me."

"No offense," Peter cut in, "but we haven't known you that long, Cass. And DeVerre doesn't do a good job of encouraging trust."

"But Ava earned your trust?" she challenged.

"No," Spencer insisted. "It had nothing to do with trust. You told us yourself that we can't trust anyone in DeVerre. That everyone here is lying about something. Even you."

The intensity in her glare died at that, and she slouched in her seat.

"We didn't want to believe it," Spencer repeated. "We didn't want her to be right. But we couldn't risk it either. And . . . I think you'd have done the same thing in our position."

A long, weighted silence hung between them as Cassandra held Spencer's gaze. She twisted the silver ring on her pinky finger as she frowned. But finally, she gave him a single, tight nod. "You're right," she whispered. "I would have."

Spencer felt his shoulders relax, though the tension in his chest refused to release.

Cassandra's expression shifted from wary to disappointed. "I just wish you trusted me."

"Hey," Peter nudged her arm again, "we *do* trust you now. There were questions before, but *now?* If there's one good thing that came out of last night, it's that we have no reason to doubt you again."

Cassandra nodded, eyes trained on her hands.

Though it was clear that she'd forgiven them—or, at the least, accepted their reasons—the tense atmosphere didn't shift. Spencer could feel the darkness clinging to the corners of his body, encroaching on the back of his mind. With the topic of last night broached, there was no going back now.

"I'm sorry," Cassandra whispered.

Peter and Spencer shared a confused look, both drawing up in apprehension.

"For what?" Peter asked.

Cassandra tossed her arms to the side in a shrug. "For everything," she said, exasperation lining her voice. "For getting you involved in this mess. It's my fault—all of it."

"Cass," Spencer leaned over the counter, shaking his head, "that's not true."

"It is," she insisted, meeting his eyes. "It's *my* family."

A heartbeat of silence passed as Spencer racked his brain for ways to refute her claim.

"It's my family," she repeated, giving him a sad smile. "If it weren't for me. . . ."

Peter's chin dipped as Spencer continued to shake his head in silence.

"If I hadn't come back," she whispered, "Diane would still be alive."

"Cass," Spencer objected.

She pushed on, scrunching her nose in apology. "You two wouldn't have gotten dragged into this. You would be safe and back in Norfolk with your family. And none of this would have happened."

"You don't know that," Peter muttered.

A scoff slipped from her. "You didn't hear her," she countered. "Debbie told me—she told me that if I had stayed home. . . ."

Furrowing his brow, Spencer tried to remember exactly what Debbie Mercier had said in those final moments. "She . . . she said that you could have lived," he reminded her.

Cassandra leveled her stare at him. "She said I should have stayed home."

Spencer held her intense eye contact, refusing to back down. "Yeah, but that wouldn't have changed what happened here."

She opened her mouth to contradict him, but he continued without giving her a chance.

"Pete and I would have gotten involved regardless." He nodded toward the office. "Diane and Liam were stirring up trouble well before you came around. We've already determined that her death was due to her own interference in DeVerre."

"And," Peter added, "the fact that the Druids want Occasus means they'll try to get it whatever way they can."

Cassandra's frown deepened. "Wait. . . ." Her eyes drifted between the two of them. "The Druids want Occasus? Why?"

"You don't know?" Peter asked.

Pushing her plate aside, the bagel forgotten, Cassandra leaned against the counter. "Why do they want Occasus?"

"Because of the vault," Spencer explained.

Her confusion was evident by the expression on her face.

Spencer smiled. If they hadn't known she was innocent before, it was an irrefutable fact now. She had no clue about the Druids' intent or the vault of Occasus. Ava couldn't have been more wrong. They had been idiots to believe her for even a second.

"All right, so. . . ." Peter took over, turning to face her. "Apparently there's this vault that was set up by the Varons here in Occasus and it holds all the town's secrets. When that psycho, Michael Varon, went homicidal and ended their line, the way to get into it was lost."

Cassandra shook her head. "That doesn't make sense. The Varon estate sat empty for over forty years. Why wouldn't they have tried to take it before now?"

"Well," Peter sighed, "Ava said that the town's leadership knew about the vault and decided it would be best to forget about it."

"Forget about it?" She scoffed. "It held their secrets. You'd think they'd want to tear down the house brick by brick."

Spencer tugged at the cuff of his sleeve. "It's not that kind of vault."

"What?"

"Ava said it's protected," he explained. "It's somehow linked to the spirit world, and I guess it's got some form of protection from physical destruction."

Cassandra set a hand over her mouth as she absorbed the new information.

"It holds all the answers," Peter added, tapping the handle of his mug again. "To everything, apparently."

Face growing slack in awe, Cassandra's eyes drifted between brothers. "To *everything*?"

Spencer shrugged. "At least to all the answers we've been searching for."

"So. . . ." She paused in thought. "The Druids need Occasus to reach this vault? Why?"

Peter scratched his scruffy jawline. "That's the question, isn't it? If they want in the vault so badly, it means they're looking for something inside it. . . ." He paused and looked at Spencer. His jaw dropped. "Hey!"

Spencer raised his brow. "What?"

Lifting a finger to point at him, Peter grinned. "Debbie," he said as though he'd solved everything. "She was looking for something."

The memory flooded back: *Walking through the Mercier house. Peter pushing open Cassandra's bedroom door. Finding Debbie, the desk behind her, its drawers open.*

Spencer drew his shoulders back, standing up straight. "Yeah . . . yeah, she was."

"What are you talking about?" Cassandra asked.

"When we got there," Peter explained, "we caught Debbie going through your things."

A smug grin pulled at her lips. "Oh, like you two were planning to do?"

"Well . . . yeah," he conceded. "But, unlike your cousin, we were trying to prove your innocence."

"Or my guilt."

"Either way," he continued. "Debbie was looking for something. And when we asked her about it, she wouldn't answer."

"No surprise, I guess." Cassandra crossed her arms. "So, they need something. What?"

Spencer shook his head. "No clue. But she asked us if you'd found the vault. It seems to me, whatever they need . . . it's gotta be in there."

Peter and Cassandra nodded in agreement.

"Which means it's here in Occasus," he clarified slowly, the thought sinking deep into his chest, causing the pressure to bulge against his ribcage. "And they'll be coming for it."

"They're already coming," Cassandra said, her eyes locked on him. "Whatever I did to Debbie—whether she's dead or alive and just . . . broken . . . they'll be coming for me now too."

"They'll be coming for *us*," Peter corrected.

It was a heavy reality—one that Spencer felt a great deal of conflict over. A part of him wanted to stand his ground and fight to save their lives. He wanted to be strong enough to protect his brother and Cassandra. But he also wanted to pinch himself and wake up from this horrible nightmare where they were at war with Druids and monsters and spirits.

If he were honest, he wanted to hop in the Jeep and run from everything surrounding him.

Both Peter and Cassandra were staring at him, watching as if they expected him to break under the weight of his fears. As though he hadn't been the one to step up the previous night and get them all out of the burning building alive.

Hands at his sides, Spencer curled his fingers into fists. A sleepless night hadn't helped his ability to think logically through the terrifying truth that they were in a fight for their lives. His muscles tensed at the memory of the power Debbie had displayed. He flinched as he remembered that power knocking him to the ground and the pain that arced through his entire being, leaving him hopeless and devoid of life. Yet *he* was the one who'd brought them back to safety.

As he met Peter's dark brown stare, then Cassandra's lighter hazel eyes, Spencer stood unshrinking. He wasn't as fragile as either of them thought. And it agitated him that after everything they'd gone through less than twenty-four hours ago, they didn't realize it too.

Spencer clenched his jaw. "How are we gonna stop them?"

Peter smirked, a glint of surprise appearing in his eyes. "Well, I think we need to find out who the heck we're up against," he said. "If we can find them, we can stop them. And then this ends."

"Shouldn't we focus on finding the vault?" Cassandra asked. "If they want it, we need to know what we're supposed to be defending."

Peter lifted his hands in a gesture of surrender. "Hey, I'm just spitballin' here. According to Ava, if we get in there, we get our answers. And I'd imagine that'll give us answers to who the Druids are too."

"So that's our focus then," Spencer agreed, his voice tight. "If we can find the vault and get in, we'll get our answers *and* figure out who it is that we're actually fighting."

"Seems you three are forgetting something," Gerard said, popping into view from thin air.

Peter scowled at the phantom, now standing at the far side of the island. "I don't remember inviting you to this meeting, Gerry."

"I don't wait for invitations." Gerard tugged at the red tie hanging around his neck. After learning of Cassandra's brush with death, the phantom seemed to have taken on a new level of snarky indignation.

Spencer hadn't understood at first. Then Cassandra had informed them that should she die, Gerard's tether to Occasus would dissolve. And the phantom would lose all hope of accomplishing whatever deal he'd struck with her.

Even now, Gerard wore a dark look of focus as he scanned the trio. "You set a house on fire last night and left a woman to die inside of it," he reminded them, his deep voice cutting through their plans like a jagged blade. "DeVerre may be a corrupt town full of narcissists, but they'll care when they find out one of their own has been murdered."

Heart leaping again, Spencer shared a nervous look with Peter and Cassandra. The welts on his brother's neck burned bright red, reminding Spencer of the flames he'd set.

How could they have overlooked something so obvious? They were facing a hidden cult, secrets, lies, and confusion, yes. But more importantly, they were now staring a homicide investigation dead in the face.

"Is there any chance this will come back to us?" Spencer asked, desperate to hear a denial. "Is there any way the marshal will know it was us?"

Cassandra shook her head despite the panic in her eyes. "Only if someone saw us," she insisted. "Otherwise, anything of mine is circumstantial, and you two left no trace."

"We don't know that though," Spencer argued. "There was a fight. We could have left traces of DNA behind and never known it."

"The fire would take care of that, right?" Peter asked, his voice weak.

"Maybe." Spencer shrugged. "If we're lucky."

Holding up her hands to silence them, Cassandra looked back and forth between the brothers. "This is DeVerre, not *CSI: Miami*," she said, her tone tight and serious. "We don't have crack arson detectives working for the police or fire station. If they notice there was a fight, *maybe* they'll dig deeper. But most likely, they'll think it was an accident because they have no reason to think it was anything else."

"But Debbie—"

Cassandra slashed her hand in the air to cut Spencer short. "Debbie excused herself from the practice last night because she said she wasn't feeling well," she explained. "When I left, Mike was double checking to be sure she was okay before heading out to softball practice. He thought she was sick."

Spencer frowned, considering Debbie's husband for the first time. His stomach clenched at the thought of the man returning home to find his wife dead and his house consumed by fire. Then another unexpected revelation hit him. "So . . . Mike isn't a Druid, then?"

Cassandra hesitated. "I guess not."

"He could have been acting," Peter suggested.

"Why bother?" she asked. "It was always the plan for me to leave before them last night. If they wanted to search my stuff, they wouldn't have needed a reason for her to stay home. They had all the time in the world. And it would have been way faster for the two of them to work together."

"All right, so he's not a Druid, and he didn't know she was. That clears one suspect."

"Besides," Cassandra added, her expression softening with relief, "a person who's unwell would be far more prone to accidents. Which makes it unlikely that they'll be looking for a murderer."

"Unless someone saw us," Spencer reminded them gravely.

A loud *bang, bang, bang* reverberated through the halls of Occasus. All three of them jumped at the sound. Gerard disappeared. Peter leaped off his seat, rushing for the kitchen doorway as Spencer and Cassandra followed. They stared down the hall through the dining room and toward the entryway.

Three seconds passed.

Bang, bang, bang.

Gerard reappeared at Cassandra's side, a fierce glare in his dark eyes. "Looks like someone saw you."

"What?" she asked. Panic reappeared on her face as fear pulsed through Spencer's veins.

"It's the marshal."

CHAPTER TWO

Peter

"What?" Peter exclaimed, attempting to keep his panicked tone low as he repeated Cassandra's question. His heart caught in his throat, still raw from the damage done by the scylla.

"What do we do?" Spencer asked, his voice unexpectedly steady.

Gerard shrugged. "I'd suggest answering the door."

"Ahhh. . . ." Peter grabbed hold of his brother's arm. "Okay, Spence, you're up."

"Me?" Spencer's brow furrowed. "Why me?"

"Because he doesn't hate you, and he'll think it's weird that Cass is here."

Cassandra leaned against the kitchen doorframe. "My truck is out front," she reminded them. "He already knows that I'm here."

"Crap, uh. . . ." Peter paused as three more knocks sounded at the door. He began pushing his brother toward the entry. "Spence, you should still answer it."

"Well, someone should," Gerard said, arms crossed. "This is the third time he's knocked."

Spencer shoved Peter away with a glare, then straightened his shoulders, balling his hands into fists at his sides. He gave them all one final look before hurrying toward the door. Peter and Cassandra ducked into the office to peek around the French doors that stood open into the living room. Gerard disappeared again, and Peter envied his ability to listen without making his presence known.

As the marshal began to knock a fourth time, Spencer unlocked the door. From their hiding place, Peter could see the edge of Marshal Tom Garnier on the other side of the threshold. He wore his uniform under a heavy jacket, brown and tan, and sporting a silver badge on the breast pocket. "Mr. Collins," he said, taking in the sight of Spencer. "Good morning."

"Good morning, sir," Spencer said, holding the door only halfway open. "Can I help you with something?"

The marshal leaned forward to glance into the house. Peter pulled back, hand on Cassandra's arm to guide her out of sight. "Yes, actually," Tom said. "I was hoping to speak with Miss Clement."

Peter grimaced as he felt Cassandra tense beside him.

"Uh. . . ." Spencer cleared his throat, then stepped back. "Yeah, uh— come on in."

As the marshal entered Occasus, Peter sprang back from his poor hiding place toward the desk, attempting to appear as though he were nonchalantly at work rather than listening. But Cassandra didn't hesitate to move into the living room as Spencer guided the officer into the house.

Tom raised his chin as he noticed the young woman. Though not much taller than Spencer, something about the authority of the pistol on his hip and the officious nature of his uniform made him appear imposing. Gray sprinkled the temples of his dark hair and his thick mustache never failed to impress Peter. "Morning, Miss Clement," he said, tone heavy despite the average greeting.

Standing between the office and living room, Cassandra gave him a nod. "Morning. How'd you know I was here?"

The marshal scanned her with narrowed eyes. Peter was sure the man's investigator side was taking note of every detail. Including the fact that she was wearing Spencer's pajamas. "Mike told me you had plans with the Collins brothers last night," he explained. "Since you never returned home, it was my best guess."

"Right." Cassandra shifted uncomfortably under his stare.

His eyes flickered back to the office, and Peter busied himself with the papers on the desk. "Care if I take a seat?" he asked.

"Uh, yeah. . . ." Spencer gestured toward the red damask couches. "Please."

"Thank you."

As Tom moved to the nearest couch, he motioned to the one across from him. "You all might want to take a seat as well," he suggested. "I'm afraid I have some bad news."

Peter whipped his gaze away from the pages as both Spencer and Cassandra checked with each other, then him. In their stiffened expressions, he could see his own fears reflected. Whatever news the marshal had come to give, Peter couldn't shake the feeling that they'd be defending themselves soon.

Once the three of them took their seats—the brothers flanking Cassandra—the marshal scanned them again. Unease filled the room from both sides, each of them silent and alert. Rain pattered on the windows as gray shadows stretched into Occasus's living room. The quiet that permeated the room held far too much accusation, the marshal's eyes hard and suspicious as they drifted from Spencer to Cassandra to Peter and back.

Peter's jaw grew tense, a vein throbbing in his neck, sure of their imminent arrest. Would they be convicted, he wondered. They'd done nothing wrong, only defending themselves when Debbie had attacked them. And Cassandra had saved their lives—a second time. Who cared if a house got burned down in the process?

The thought of Debbie Mercier's body left to the flames made Peter's throat go dry. Regardless of the woman's murderous intent, her death was an indisputable weight they'd have to carry for the rest of their lives. A weight that made his skin itch around the collar of his flannel. It had been either her or them, Peter reminded himself. And he wouldn't trade his brother's life for anything.

The unexpected *thunk* of the pet door in the kitchen made them all jump. Tom shifted in his seat as Anguis and Nex came charging into the room, the dogs ignoring the visitor. Anguis stretched out before the fireplace while Nex—fur glossy from the rain—came to sit at Spencer's side.

After watching their arrival, Tom leaned forward, resting his arms on his legs. "I came to inform you, Miss Clement," he began, "that there's been an accident. A fire was started in the home of Michael and Debra Mercier last night. The fire marshal is still investigating the source of the fire, but as I said, it appears to have been an accident."

Cassandra set a hand to her lips as she sank back into the cushions of the couch. Though her response may have been an act, Peter thought her concern was genuine. He didn't doubt the regret she felt. In the late hours of last night, they'd worked hard to convince her that what she'd done had been necessary. Even now, he could see the guilt that lingered in her distant gaze.

"While Mike was at softball practice when it happened," the marshal continued, "Debbie had stayed home, sick . . . as I'm sure you were aware. The emergency response was fast enough to save her from the fire, but. . . ."

Peter's heart lurched, and he glanced at Spencer, whose eyes had grown wide in shock. *Debbie was alive?*

"What—uh, what happened?" Peter asked, feeling they shouldn't leave the silence hanging. "Is she going to be okay?"

Tom sighed. "We're not sure what happened, to be honest. Debbie either tripped and hit her head or . . . something like that. Alex—Dr. Frossard was able to stabilize her despite the severe burns she sustained, but she's in a catatonic state. The doctor and Mike took her to Spokane this morning to place her in intensive care at the hospital there."

Peter hadn't seen Debbie go down. He'd been unconscious when it all happened. But after Cassandra disappeared into Diane's room last night, Spencer filled him in on all the horrors he'd missed. The brothers had stayed up another hour, whispering in the warm yellow glow of Spencer's bedside lamp. Spencer explained how Cassandra had used her powers to tear apart Debbie's soul. That the woman had been a lifeless shell of a human when they'd left her body to the flames.

The shudder of a breath drew Peter's attention to the woman seated between him and his brother. Cassandra's eyes squeezed shut as she took another unsteady inhale. Her hand dropped into her lap as she met the marshal's eyes. "She's alive?" she whispered.

"She is," he confirmed gently. "Though they can't figure out exactly what happened to her. It's not looking good for her recovery."

Cassandra pressed her lips together, chin dipping as her shoulders shook with unshed tears.

"Hey," Spencer muttered, setting a hand on her arm. He slid closer to her on the couch. Nex's gaze followed his movement. "It's okay. It's okay, she's alive."

Moving to sit on the edge of his seat, Tom leveled an apologetic look on Cassandra. "I hate to add more to your plate, but I'm gonna need you to come down to the station to provide a statement," he explained. "And what's more, the fire did a good deal of damage. The house is no longer livable, so I'm afraid you'll have to find somewhere else to stay."

Knowing that this was a problem he could take care of, Peter nodded, drawing himself up. "She can stay with us."

Tom glanced at Spencer and Cassandra, taking note of his hand still resting on her arm. The marshal settled a firm, fatherly stare on Peter. "I wouldn't advise that."

"Why not?"

He raised his brow as though it should be obvious. "The townspeople will gossip."

It took a second for Peter to grasp his meaning.

People would gossip about a single woman living with two bachelors. No matter if things were as platonic as could be, it would look odd. And in a town as religious as DeVerre, it wouldn't go over well.

Spencer's hand dropped back to his side.

"They gossip about me anyway," Cassandra said, voice thin as she raised her head, regaining her confident demeanor.

The marshal stared at her, hands clasped together between his knees. Peter thought he'd press the matter. That he'd insist she listen and either find another place to stay within DeVerre or go home to Spokane.

Instead, Tom rose from his seat. "Miss Clement, I'd be happy to wait for you to make yourself presentable and escort you back to the station to take your statement if you'd like. Or, if you'd prefer, you can meet me there in half an hour."

"My statement on what?" Cassandra asked.

Tom frowned. "Last night's events."

"I was here."

Though it wasn't a complete lie, it wasn't the whole truth. However, Peter wouldn't contradict her alibi. He knew Spencer wouldn't either.

"Be that as it may," Tom continued, "you were one of the last to see Debbie before the accident. I need to do my job and take statements from all parties involved."

"Do you need statements from us too?" Peter asked. "Like Cass said, she was with us."

Tom's hard stare matched the slight twist of disapproval on his lips.

"No," he said. "At the moment, I don't need a thing from you or your brother."

There were few people in the world that Peter actively disliked. He'd never thought much of holding grudges or taking offense. But the dislike that Peter held for Tom Garnier grew as he glared back at the man. "Then you can go back to town," he suggested. "Spence and I will get Cass to you shortly."

Spencer jumped up from his seat, and Nex shuffled out of his way. "I can. . . ." He motioned to the door, suggesting he'd walk the marshal out.

Tom's dark eyes scanned their group as Cassandra rose next to Spencer. In the short, charged conversation, the marshal had never said a word to suggest he suspected them. But his hesitation to leave made it plain: He didn't trust them either.

"I'll expect you in thirty minutes, Miss Clement," he restated, as though she was a flight risk.

Cassandra nodded. "Of course."

Tom's hum of acceptance sounded skeptical. He turned then, his boots clunking against the wooden floors of Occasus. Spencer met Peter's gaze before following the cop.

It wasn't until the door had been shut and locked, and the dim crunch of the marshal's car on the gravel driveway had faded away that the three of them released a collective sigh of relief.

"I—I think we're okay," Spencer marveled, a hand pressing against his sternum.

"Yeah," Cassandra murmured. "Except that I have to give a statement. Which means I have to lie."

The thought struck Peter, and he frowned. "Isn't that a felony?"

"Only if I get caught." She passed him a sarcastic grin. "But I don't have much choice, do I? If I don't, I'll be charged for assault, at the very least. And, worse, I'll expose Owen."

Peter hadn't even thought of that. Cassandra's evening had started quite differently than the brothers'. She'd gone to meet with Owen in the park, only telling Mike and Debbie that she was meeting with the brothers so that no one would know. If she told the truth, Tom would ask why she was spending time with Owen. And Owen's secret wasn't theirs to share.

"Try not to lie," Spencer suggested. "At least, not outright. You were with us last night. We spent the evening at Occasus. Those things are technically true. You left the Merciers' at five-forty and headed to meet up with us. Doesn't matter that the timeline is manipulated. You won't have lied."

"I'll still have left out important facts," Cassandra replied. "And I believe that makes me an accomplice, should the truth come out."

"Should the truth come out," Peter offered, "it'll be Spence who's charged as an arsonist, me as an accomplice, and you'll be charged with the rest of it."

The moment he said the words, Peter regretted them. Cassandra's lips pressed together in instant worry and guilt. Whether or not his joke was true, he hadn't meant to make their friend feel bad for saving their lives.

"Hey," Peter sat forward, arms on his legs, "it's gonna be okay. We're all gonna get through this."

Cassandra's dark hair bounced as she nodded forcibly, as though to assure him that she didn't blame him for his callous statement. "I'm going to, uh. . . ." She took a long, arduous breath and pointed toward the staircase past Spencer. "I better go change."

"Your clothes are in the dryer," Spencer reminded her.

"Right, thanks," she muttered, then stopped after one step in the direction of the kitchen. Her typical confidence had returned, shoulders back as her eyes flickered between them with a slight grin on her lips. Whether it was a show or not, Peter couldn't tell. "You guys don't have to come with me, you know? I can—"

"What are you talking about?" Peter interrupted. "Of course, we do."

"You really don't."

"Did you forget that there are Druids in this town targeting Wielders? Seems to me that you should be under protective custody."

Cassandra drew her head back, a dry smile on her lips. "Seems to me I was the one who kept you both alive last night."

"Cass," Spencer said, his flat tone serious and concerned. Peter turned with Cassandra, surprised at the intent glare he was sending her. "You aren't going alone."

"I'll be fine, Spencer."

There was no response from Spencer. Instead, he continued to stare at her with his arms crossed as he leaned against the doorframe. The forcefulness in his expression reminded Peter of the conversation he and Spencer had shared last night.

Cassandra had panicked after she'd shattered Debbie's soul. *"I had to get us out,"* Spencer had whispered in the dim light of his room. *"She was . . . I think she was in shock. I don't know if she even remembers it. She seemed so out of it. Like she was sleepwalking or something. I think . . . I think if I hadn't given her something to focus on . . . she would have sat there and burned with Debbie."*

If Peter hadn't seen Cassandra last night—eyes glazed over and foot tapping against the pavement as she waited for them—he might not have believed his brother. But he'd watched as her hands shook when she put the truck in gear to drive them the rest of the way to Occasus. He'd heard her voice tremble as she tried to calm Gerard down when he'd found out that she'd almost died.

And as Cassandra stared at Spencer now in the light of the day, Peter thought he saw the same version of her that Spencer had witnessed last night. The one who needed a focus. And needed to know she wasn't alone.

"We're coming with you, Cassandra," Spencer said, his blue eyes almost like ice in the gray light. "We know that you can take care of yourself, but we also know the danger here. And we're the only ones who will keep you safe as if their lives depended on it; because they do. Our lives depend on you, Cass. 'Cause without you, we're just two writers who happened to inherit a house."

It was true, Peter knew. The sincerity in Spencer's words could only come from someone who understood just how desperately they needed Cassandra to stay alive. Though Owen had more experience and power than Cassandra, his marriage to Ava kept him from moving freely. He couldn't even call them the previous evening. He'd had to text to see if they were safe. And if they were to face down more Druids, they needed someone who was *there*. Someone who could keep the two of them from making stupid decisions that would get them killed.

Or, Peter reconsidered, someone to save them from the stupid decisions they'd inevitably make.

And it seemed that Cassandra Clement was the perfect woman for the job.

Their whole lives, Peter and Spencer had been each other's caretakers. Now, Cassandra was taking care of them both. It was only fair that they returned the favor.

"Okay," Cassandra murmured, breaking eye contact with Spencer. She slipped past the couch where Peter sat to head toward the laundry room. Anguis and Nex followed on her heels.

Peter and Spencer waited until they heard her feet pound up the stairs and slow to a steady gait across the hallway above their heads. A door shut, echoing through the halls of Occasus, and Peter met his brother's eyes.

"What'd'ya think?" Peter asked.

Spencer frowned. "About what?"

"The marshal," he explained. "You think he suspects?"

After a long, hesitant inhale, Spencer sighed. "I dunno," he muttered. "But I would if I were him."

"Hm." Peter snorted, shaking his head. "I don't know whether to wish you were or to be thankful you're not."

Spencer didn't say anything but stared out the windows at the lawn.

The gentle rain had turned to sleet in the cold morning, rattling against the panes. Dim light seeped through the heavy clouds. It was as though the world had cast a shadow over itself. As though it knew the somber mood within Occasus.

Peter pressed his lips together, glowering at the weather. Whatever came of this day—whether the marshal decided to arrest them or the Druids tried to retaliate—Peter wasn't about to cut and run. He and Spencer had come to DeVerre for one purpose: To live their dreams. After being attacked by a hellhound, meeting Cassandra, learning of their hidden ancestry, and unexpected ties to the town, that dream had morphed, now a far more complicated vision.

But, in the end, it was the same. And Peter wouldn't let them fail.

All they had to do was make it through the next few hours. After Cassandra gave the marshal her statement, they'd would return to Occasus, find the vault, gather the information needed, and stop the Druids. Then this investigation and the fear for their lives would be moot. Once they could prove that Debbie had been the one murdering people with hellhounds, no one would charge them even if the whole story did work its way into the light.

It would all be fine.

Then, he and Spencer could write their book, figure out who their ancestors were, and help Cassandra learn everything she wanted to about being a Wielder. They'd be a happy, if somewhat odd, family. And life would be perfect.

It would all be fine.

It had to be.

CHAPTER THREE

Cassandra

Sitting on the thin, cushioned chair, Cassandra played with her signet ring. Her mother had given it to her at her high school graduation and she'd worn it ever since. Any time she felt herself getting nervous or falling into deep thought, she found herself spinning it round and round. It had become a comfort to her in the most conflicting way.

Even when she was eighteen, Cassandra knew what the ring meant—she'd always felt the implications it carried. *"You're one of us,"* it said. *"You belong with us."*

Every time she touched the ring it reminded her of its heavy-handed pressure. Every time her fingertips grazed the ridges in the Sauveterre family crest—her mother's family crest, she felt her chest compress under the weight of her family's demands. Every time she could hear them telling her to give up her hunt for the spirit world, to stay home with them.

There were plenty of times in the past eleven years that Cassandra had considered getting rid of the ring. She didn't feel the tie to her family that it suggested. Nothing like the way her brother Isaac felt. He was happy to settle in Spokane with his wife and kids, working as an accountant during the week and hanging out with family and friends on the weekend. He'd never understood why Cassandra wanted to return to DeVerre; why she wanted to seek out the ghosts of the past. He couldn't comprehend why she wasn't happy like he was.

And in the end, Cassandra knew that was the very reason she'd kept the ring. It helped, remembering her family and their disapproval. It kept her on track. Kept her focused.

And right now, she needed to focus.

Tom Garnier clicked on the small metal recorder and met her gaze. "All right, Miss Clement," he said, seated behind his massive brown desk. "Please, tell me about last night."

The DeVerre Police Station was a small, dated place. Despite its good repair, everything looked dingy in the brown and beige that matched the marshal's uniform. From the tiled ceilings, poster and bulletin-covered walls, to the smattering of plastic office supplies on his desk. Several thick folders filled Tom's inbox, and a red light blinked on the phone next to his computer. A smattering of family photos and memorabilia sat on floating shelves above a row of creamy yellow filing cabinets along the back wall.

Cassandra held the marshal's stare. She could easily see the skepticism in his posture—head tilted forward, shoulders drawn in, and hands on the arms of his seat as though ready to leap from it at a moment's notice to stop her from running. His suspicions of her were nothing new. She'd received this same anxious glare from every DeVerre citizen— including him—almost every day for the past four years.

But this time, their suspicions were founded.

Attempting to appear nonchalant while not coming across as indifferent, considering the circumstances, Cassandra let go of her ring and sat up straight. "I'd be happy to tell you," she assured him. "But I'm not sure where you'd like me to start."

"Mike told me that you'd left around a quarter till six," Tom supplied. "Is that correct?"

Cassandra nodded. "A little before that, actually."

"And how would you describe Debbie's state before you left?"

"I didn't see Debbie before I left," she told him honestly. "Mike said she wasn't feeling well, so she was in their room, resting."

"Not feeling well," Tom repeated, taking notes on a yellow legal pad. "In what way? Did Mike give you any particulars of her condition?"

"No. He just said that she wasn't feeling well, so he'd be going to practice alone."

"I see." Tom fell silent, continuing to make his notes. He dotted an I, crossed a couple of Ts, and looked back up at her. "Did you leave before Mike or after?"

Cassandra took a deep breath, sure that this was more of an interrogation rather than a statement. "Before."

"And where did you go?"

This was the question Cassandra dreaded. She knew what answer she needed to give: She'd gone to Occasus. But she also knew that there would be witnesses to the contrary.

When Cassandra had left the Merciers', she'd driven to Blackwood Park—in the exact opposite direction of Occasus. There was no doubt in her mind that she'd been seen on the drive through downtown, past the busy ballfields, and headed to the park. It'd be hard to miss a red truck like hers.

"I went to Blackwood Park," she admitted.

The smallest flicker of surprise pulled Tom's bushy eyebrows together.

Before he could question her, Cassandra offered the information she wanted him to know. "I told Mike I was going to spend the evening with the Collins brothers, but I wanted to go to the park first." She could see the questions rising in the marshal's eyes, so she asked him one first. "Do you know of my past in DeVerre, Marshal?"

Tom drew his shoulders back, chin rising as he surveyed her. "I know what the town says of your past, Miss Clement. My first-hand knowledge is lacking."

"Allow me to clarify." Cassandra arched an eyebrow and smiled at him. "I spoke to ghosts when I was a child."

Tom's eyes narrowed at her admission.

Cassandra hurried to continue so that he wouldn't get her off track. "Since my parents didn't like that, they took me to Spokane," she said. "When I moved back to DeVerre four years ago, it was in an effort to discover if I could still talk to ghosts."

He lifted a hand, drawing his fingers across his mustache.

"I could."

"Mm."

Cassandra crossed her legs, relaxing into the chair. "I went to the park to take a walk. There is a rather large number of ghosts that like to congregate in the woods there. Afterward, I returned to town and spent the remainder of my evening with Spencer and Peter. As I stayed at their place late into the night, they offered Diane's old room to me, and I slept there."

Ending her story, Cassandra swallowed down her last remaining tinge of discomfort. None of it was a lie. She'd told the truth, leaving out only the information that would ruin the lives of her friends and their chances of stopping the Druids.

The unusually long pause stretched on as the recorder's blue light winked on and off every half second. Tom's eyebrows were low over his hooded eyes, chin in his hand as he considered her. Behind him, images of his past mirrored that same fierce stare even as he smiled in the photos. Pictures of him and his wife, following their life from marriage through the birth of both their sons and up until the present featuring their eldest son's graduation from high school. Among them all, there was a picture of Tom in his pine green Jacks baseball tee, standing with his arms around Samuel Chapelle and Alexander Frossard—both of them wearing their royal blue Angels tees—at the softball field.

Cassandra knew Tom like she knew most residents of DeVerre: from a distance. But these images confirmed her instinct to hide the full truth. No matter how dedicated Tom was to the safety of DeVerre, he was too close to too many potential Druids. And he would take their side before he ever took the side of Cassandra and the Collins brothers.

"Hm," Tom murmured again, breaking out of the reverie going on behind those dark, suspicious eyes of his. He sat up straighter, reached for the recorder, and shut it off. "May I make a suggestion, Miss Clement?"

"Off the record, I take it," she remarked, nodding to the recorder back on his desk, its light now extinguished.

The stern, worried look that crossed Tom's face mimicked the one she received from both of her parents every time she went home. Seeing it on the marshal's face nearly made her laugh. "I know you're in a tight spot right now," he began, "but I recommend you find somewhere to stay other than with the Collins brothers."

Cassandra didn't fight the knowing smirk that came to her lips. "Unless that's an offer to stay with you and your wife, Marshal, I don't have much of a choice," she said. "I can't afford my own place, and you know perfectly well that no one else in this town would take me in."

The marshal dipped his head. "To be honest," he muttered, "I would offer. But we don't have a spare room."

"Then I'm afraid I'll just have to stay at Occasus."

"I'm trying to help you out," Tom said, a fatherly edge cutting into his voice at her snarky reply. "Whether those two are the most honorable men in the world or if you have something going on with one or both of them and you just don't care, it doesn't matter. It *looks* bad."

"If helping out a friend looks bad to the people of DeVerre," Cassandra leaned forward in her seat, "they aren't looking at the right things."

Tom held her glare, lips twisted in something between a grimace and a snarl. She was right, and he knew it. The DeVerreans could gossip all they wanted. They could act righteous and pretend they were above the rest of the world. But none of them would be willing to do anything to help. And that made them just as guilty of the misconduct they accused her of.

With a sharp, resigned nod, Tom stood. "Thank you for your time, Miss Clement. If you think of anything else, feel free to give me a call or swing by at any time."

Rising from the uncomfortable chair, Cassandra hiked the strap of her messenger bag higher onto her shoulder. "Of course," she promised with absolutely no intention of following through.

Tom opened his office door for her, the blinds over its window rattling against the pane, then followed her out into the larger, still dull interior of the station. The deputy, Hunter, and the marshal's wife, Stephanie, sat at their desks. Stephanie was talking on the phone but gave Cassandra a polite smile as she passed. Hunter tipped his head to her in acknowledgement alone.

"Have a good day, Miss Clement," Tom offered, stopping beside his wife's receptionist desk.

Cassandra gave him one final, reproachful glance, then pushed through the door and onto the sidewalk of Harmony Plaza. The rain fell in a sheet of icy drops to soak the brick buildings surrounding the old town hall in the center. Immediately before her sat the Jeep, water rippling across its dark green paint.

Peter and Spencer had tried to enter the marshal's office to join Cassandra's interview. They'd promptly gotten tossed out. Cassandra had suggested they wait for her next door at The Glass Tavern, promising that she'd be fine on her own.

The brothers had stared at her, hesitation obvious. They were so similar and yet so distinctive in their own ways. Dark hair that was always a bit messy; Peter's stood on end from his constant tousling while Spencer's tended to fall onto his forehead, ends curling. Thick brows that hung low over their deep set and hooded eyes; Peter's dark brown, Spencer's true blue. They both let their thin facial hair grow in, Peter's patchier than Spencer's. Peter was taller; Spencer was more muscular. Peter's smile tipped up on the side; Spencer's was tempered and even.

And both were treating her like she was a time bomb waiting to go off.

Hurrying to duck under the Kelly green awning of The Glass Tavern, Cassandra thought they might be right. Dressed in her freshly washed clothing from the night before, she wondered if anyone else could smell the smoke left in its knit or if the memories were just haunting her. Clinging to her skin like the cold, damp air.

Rising that morning, Cassandra had sought out company immediately. She needed a distraction to keep her from dwelling on the guilt that welled up inside of her. To keep her from feeling the phantom tingles that raced along her skin, reminding her of when the power had rushed through her arm and into Debbie's chest.

She'd felt it, the rending of Debbie's soul. It ripped through her own chest as though she were experiencing it herself. Yet, she'd been left standing while Debbie crumbled to the ground like a rag doll tossed aside by a disenchanted child. And Debbie's words still rang in her ears: *"You've finally figured it out, haven't you, Cassie? Our power is far more than just ghosts, isn't it?"*

Shoving the memory down, Cassandra entered the tavern, a cheery *clang-clang* ringing out from the bell over the door. The Glass Tavern glowed with welcoming warmth. Dark brown beadboard wainscoting covered the bottom of the walls, while the top half mirrored the rich green of the awning. A handful of patrons sat throughout the restaurant, some enclosed in the leather booths while the rest circled the tables in the middle of the room.

All of them turned to stare at her.

Ignoring the immediate murmur of low whispers and shocked stares at her arrival, Cassandra moved to the bar at the back of the restaurant. The narrow shoulders of both brothers were angled as they turned to watch her approach, a matching look of relief and greeting in their easy smiles. Behind them on the other side of the bar, Anna Lambert stood wide-eyed.

"Hi," the young woman called, the singular word filled with nervous energy.

Wary, Cassandra glanced at Spencer, then Peter, before turning to Anna. "Hi," she returned.

"How are you?" Anna asked, voice infused with a blend of pity, care, and self-consciousness that Cassandra had become all too familiar with three months ago after her mother's car accident.

Cassandra took the empty seat at the end of the bar on Spencer's right. "I'm fine," she replied. "Concerned for my family, of course, but. . . ."

Cassandra didn't care to finish the sentence, and Anna's sympathetic expression assured her that she didn't need to.

Peter leaned forward to see her around Spencer. "That was fast," he remarked.

Tossing another wary glance in Anna's direction, Cassandra didn't think now was the best time to go into the ins and outs of her conversation with the marshal. "There wasn't much to say."

"Right."

The kitchen bell chimed, and Anna jumped. "Your sandwich," she exclaimed, pushing away from the counter.

Cassandra furrowed her brow, realizing both brothers had cups of coffee in front of them. "You got food?"

Peter shrugged in defense. "I was hungry and didn't know how long you'd take."

"I told you it'd only be a minute."

Anna returned to set a plate in front of Peter, bacon and gooey cheese hanging over the sides of the rye bread. "Thanks, Anna," he said, then turned back to Cassandra. "You can get something, too, if you want."

Cassandra sighed. "I'm not hungry."

After taking a swig of his coffee, Spencer scooted his barstool back.

"Come on," he said, grabbing his denim jacket from the back of his seat. "Pete can have his breakfast, and you and I will get the shopping done."

On their way to town, Cassandra had requested to stop by the general store to pick up some replacements for all the things she'd lost in the fire. Neither brother seemed overly excited about a shopping trip, but they'd not balked at it either. They knew how little she owned now.

"Mm, yeah, good idea, Spence." Peter slapped his brother's shoulder and winked. "You two have a merry ol' time."

The instant reluctance that drew Spencer to glance sidelong at Cassandra didn't escape her notice. He reached up to straighten his collar. "We won't be long," he muttered.

Cassandra couldn't help the wry smirk that came to her lips as Spencer avoided her gaze. He tossed a goodbye to Peter and Anna, then headed for the door. Peter was so obvious with his little comments and jokes. He was a peculiar sort of matchmaker and not a discreet one either. She hadn't thought much of it initially; it was just one brother teasing the other. But over the past two weeks, she'd noticed more and more instances of those nervous glances from Spencer. The more Peter teased him, the more Spencer pulled away from Cassandra. As though getting to know her was proof of his interest. As though he had to push away to show he felt just the opposite. And Cassandra didn't like that.

Giving her own goodbye to Peter and Anna, Cassandra hurried after Spencer's retreating form. She followed him into the chilly, gray morning. They rushed through the rain for the Jeep, moving fast enough to avoid getting soaked. The Jeep rumbled on, the mellow rock CD picking up where it had left off when they pulled into the square that morning.

Absent-mindedly, Cassandra's fingers sought her ring again. When they'd left Occasus, she'd sat in the back seat behind Spencer. She hadn't realized her mistake until the pines surrounding the road had broken away to reveal the heart of DeVerre. Through the window to their left, the road curved off onto Haven Boulevard, granting Cassandra the perfect view of the neighborhood.

Mike and Debbie's house stood in stark contrast to the rest of the large white brick and columned houses on the street. Though most of the structure was still standing, the roof had caved in along the far left edge. She could see the window of her old room, the glass shattered and curtains hanging in tatters. The firemen had arrived in enough time to keep the flames that Spencer had started from consuming the whole house. But far more destroyed the house for Cassandra than its physical destruction.

When she'd returned to DeVerre four years ago, Debbie had taken her in as though she were a second daughter. Cassandra's mother and Debbie had been best friends since childhood. They talked every Sunday on the phone. Debbie, Mike, and their two kids—Travis and Rene—had come to Spokane for every birthday and several major holidays each year. After her mother's accident back in August, Debbie had driven down to Spokane at least once a week. And though Debbie took every opportunity to remind Cassandra of how much her mother wished she would return home, the two of them had always had a good relationship.

Now, Cassandra wondered if any of it had been real. If all that time, the woman's kindness had been a guise.

Debbie was going to kill her last night. Actually *kill* her. Like she was a nuisance, a fly to be swatted out of existence.

That was a feeling Cassandra had never experienced before. She didn't even know how to process it. How did you accept that anyone was out to end your life, let alone a trusted family member?

Looking over at Spencer in the driver's seat, Cassandra gave her ring another spin. His eyes were glued to their task, shifting between the road, the mirrors, and back again as he pulled onto the road. He held his hands at ten and two as he rested against the light tan seats.

In the short time she'd known him, Cassandra always had trouble reading Spencer's expressions. He was so serious and absorbed in his own thoughts that it was hard to know when he was at peace or in terror. She had to assume it was the latter most of the time. But he had a better poker face than the average person.

It didn't make sense, Cassandra knew. People didn't make her nervous. Male or female, she could strike up a conversation with anyone. And she'd been alone with Spencer a handful of times. But that was before last night.

Fed up with her obsessive thoughts, Cassandra forced herself to let go of the ring. She reached over to nudge Spencer's arm. "Thanks, by the way," she said.

Spencer glanced at her, mouth slightly ajar in confusion as they turned off the roundabout toward the general store. "For what?"

"For coming with me."

"Oh, yeah." He nodded. "Of course."

Unwilling to let the conversation go, she worked to keep him talking. "It's kind of weird—needing a bodyguard."

A weak laugh came from him as he kept his eyes on the road. "Yeah, I can imagine. Can't say I'm the best choice, though."

"Oh, I wouldn't say that. You managed to tackle a hellhound to the ground. That's a pretty good skill to put on your resume."

She could feel his embarrassment at the compliment in the mere seconds that it took for him to respond. "I mean, I couldn't hold it," he muttered. "If you hadn't come along when you did, neither Pete nor I would be here."

"True," she said, tilting her head to look at him. "But that doesn't make it any less impressive."

Spencer's chin angled toward her as though he wanted to check to see if she was teasing him, but he kept his eyes on the road. "Thanks," he mumbled.

Seeing that her flattery was making his avoidance worse, Cassandra couldn't help the bitter grin that pulled at her lips. She knew that it wasn't his modesty that kept him from truly accepting the compliment. He'd never turned them down in the past. No, there was only one thing that had changed in the past twenty-four hours that could explain why Spencer was so hesitant to be his normal self around her. One act that had taken her from being the spooky ghost whisperer to something altogether more frightful.

She'd become a killer.

Staring through the windshield, Cassandra heard herself whisper, "Do you think we made a mistake?"

They passed the doctor's offices, vet and groomer, hardware, and grocery stores on Harmony Road before Spencer turned into the general store.

"In what way?" he asked.

"With Debbie," she muttered. "With everything that happened last night. Do you think we made a mistake?"

She listened as Spencer breathed in and out as he considered the question. "Maybe," he admitted. "But I think it was an impossible choice."

Turning to study him, Cassandra wondered if he resented her now. She was responsible for bringing Spencer and his brother into this world. A world where their lives were in constant danger. A world where Spencer's nightmares came to life.

If he didn't resent her, she thought maybe he should.

"Thank you," she said, the words almost an apology in their inflection.

His sharp blue eyes flashed to her as he parked the car, the fraction of a smile on his lips. "What're you thanking me for this time?"

Cassandra let out a thin laugh, glad to earn some fraction of friendliness from him. "For helping me."

"We're happy to."

"No." She shook her head as she shifted in her seat to face him. "I'm not thanking you *and* Peter. I'm just thanking *you*."

Spencer's chin dipped, his confusion plain as he scanned her face.

For a moment, Cassandra let herself indulge in the quiet strength radiating from him. She doubted Spencer was comfortable with friendly affection, but right now she didn't care. Cassandra reached across the center console of the Jeep to rest her hand on Spencer's arm, sure that the simple touch would communicate more gratitude than any words ever could.

"Thank you," she said again, keeping her voice as steady and sure as his gaze. "Not for letting me stay with you and your brother. Not for fighting with me against the Druids. And not for sticking around to help me find answers.

"Thank you for taking care of me last night. For telling me to do what I knew. . . ." Her words broke off as the memory resurfaced.

Another phantom tremor caused her hand to twitch, and Spencer glanced down at it, still gripping his bicep.

Cassandra pressed her lips together and removed her hand. She flexed her fingers, the warmth of him lingering.

Clearing her throat, she tried again. "For giving me the strength to do what I knew I had to," she concluded.

There was a look of surprise and wonder on Spencer's face as he stared back at her. As though he was shocked to hear that his actions meant something to her, that he'd been helpful in any way.

He drew a hand up to rub the back of his neck. "Uh. . . ." His expression softened, even as his thick eyebrows remined tensely drawn together. "Yeah, of course."

Such an unpoetic response to her heartfelt gratitude might have come across as apathetic to some. But Spencer's ever-shifting gaze told her it was embarrassment, not indifference, that had caused his lackluster reply.

Letting herself laugh at their awkwardness, Cassandra grabbed her bag, still heavy with Diane's notes. "Come on," she said. "Let's get this done."

Inside the bland interior of the general store, Spencer occupied himself with the small book section while Cassandra perused the women's clothing. Bright white lights glared overhead as she picked through the minimal options. There wasn't much in the way of black items, and even less that suited her taste. But she managed to find enough to get her by for the next couple of weeks. She could take a trip to Spokane to pick up more shoes and fill out her wardrobe later.

The handful of mothers and elderly customers who wandered the aisles all replicated the behavior of The Glass Tavern's patrons, whispering to one another or themselves when they spotted her. Though their disparaging glances weren't a surprise, she couldn't quite find it in herself to write off their attention. Not when they were murmuring about the woman whose soul she'd shattered last night.

A trilling ring cut through the air, startling her. Cassandra gasped, dropping the sweater she'd been inspecting into her cart as she felt her phone vibrate in her jacket pocket. A young woman with a toddler eyed her as she fumbled to retrieve and silence the phone.

The caller ID made her face blanch.

Sucking in a tense breath, she closed her eyes, attempting to steady herself. Then she answered the call. "Hello?"

"Cassie?" The masculine voice landed heavily on her ears.

"What's up, Dad?" she asked, realizing immediately that she knew exactly why he was calling.

"How are you, sweetheart? Are you okay? Are you on your way home?"

The flurry of questions ended precisely where she'd expected. "I'm fine," she promised. "I wasn't . . . I was with friends last night."

"Oh, thank God." Allen Clement sighed, his ever-steady voice continuing quickly. "Mike told us that they've taken Deb to the hospital here in Spokane. He said that she's in critical condition. Travis and his family are on their way over now, and Rene came with them from DeVerre. We're going to go meet them at the hospital. Your mother is . . . she's devastated. Do you know what happened?"

Cassandra leaned against the cart's handle. "No," she murmured the lie, feeling it burn its way out.

"Are you coming home?"

Staring toward the front of the store where Spencer stood reading the back cover of a book, Cassandra pursed her lips. "No, Dad, I—I can't come to Spokane right now."

A second of charged silence passed before Allen's voice came back strong. "Cassandra, this is family," he reminded her. "We don't get to pick and choose when it's convenient for us to be there for them."

"Dad—"

"Debbie was there for us when your mother—" He interrupted his argument with an emotion-filled sigh. "Debbie was there for us. It's only right for us to be there for her."

Cassandra bit back the retort that came to mind and glared at the clothes in her cart. "I understand," was all she managed to say.

"Mike said the house isn't livable," her father continued. "You may as well come home until we figure out what's next."

"I'm staying with some friends, Dad. I need to take care of a few things here and then—"

"Cassandra—"

"Dad. I can't come back right now. I have to take care of a few things first."

A beat of his tense, irritated breath cut through the phone. "All right," he whispered as though it was all he could do not to yell it. "All right, just . . . just come home as soon as you can."

"Okay," she muttered, more to move on than to agree.

"Be safe, please, Cassandra."

"I will."

"Your mother and I love you."

"Love you too." The words tumbled from her lips like she was ripping off a Band-Aid.

Slipping the phone back into her pocket, Cassandra attempted to quell the shaking of her hand. She couldn't go back to Spokane. She couldn't bear to stand in a hospital surrounded by family members mourning the woman who'd tried to kill her. She couldn't pretend to be sorry for Debbie's state. Not when she was the one who put her there.

"Our power is far more than just ghosts, isn't it?"

Glancing up to watch Spencer exchange the novel for another, Cassandra knew that Debbie was right. It was far more. And Cassandra needed to find out just how much more it was.

Otherwise, she feared that she might wind up losing the Collins brothers just like she'd lost Diane.

CHAPTER FOUR

Peter

After their quick goodbye, Peter watched as Spencer shrugged on his denim jacket, rushing forward to open the door for Cassandra even while he continued to adjust his collar. Their dad had trained them to be chivalrous early in life, but Cassandra didn't know that. She gave Spencer an intrigued smirk as she walked past him.

Peter couldn't help the grin that came to his own lips, watching his brother fumble his way through wooing their friend. Whether Spencer knew it or not, he had it bad. Peter had only seen him this flustered by one other girl in the past—when he was seventeen and fell head over heels for one of the college volunteers who helped out at their youth group. A near decade later and Spencer was no more confident when it came to women.

"Looks like you got ditched," Anna teased, leaning against the ice maker behind the bar.

Turning to face her, Peter picked up the sandwich from his plate. "It was bound to happen sooner or later," he said. Then, a realization hit him: He was alone with Anna.

When they'd walked into The Glass Tavern, Anna was hard at work. Peter had smiled at the wispy, dark brown bun that created a sort of halo of curls around her head as she refilled a coffee mug at a distant table.

Then he'd immediately frowned to himself.

While Peter didn't consider himself a coward, he hadn't counted on having to face Anna quite this soon.

Now, Peter took a huge bite of his sandwich to give him plenty of time to think about the last time he'd been alone with Anna. He felt like the world's biggest idiot. What should he say? Could he pretend that it hadn't happened? Would she let him? *Was* he a coward?

Just yesterday, Anna had been trying to thank him for being a good friend, and he'd made an idiot out of himself. A total and complete fool. He'd incorrectly assumed she was putting him in the friend zone, and yet again, he'd ruined a perfectly good relationship.

This scenario was really nothing new to Peter, though. He was practically the poster child for that old proverb about assumptions at this point in his life. He'd lost count of how many times he'd jumped to conclusions, particularly when it came to women. There was no reason to act like a schmuck now.

They were adults, Peter reminded himself. There was only one mature way to handle awkward situations: Ignore them.

Right?

But, Peter wondered, could he risk ignoring his mistake? What if he ruined their friendship so much that it was irreparable? He wasn't sure he could bounce back from this loss like he had in the past. It was rare to find people who appreciated him the way he felt Anna did. Instead of being weirded out by his intense and open personality, she had accepted and befriended him. She called him out when he acted weird, while still appreciating him because of it. That was unheard of in his experience.

Cautiously, Peter looked at Anna. So far, she'd been normal with him today. When he and Spencer took their seats at the bar, she'd immediately set a cup of coffee before each of them and struck up conversation about

Cassandra and the Merciers' situation. Now, she was busy making a new pot of coffee and wiping off the smattering of grounds that had spilled on the counter. Here in the low light of the restaurant, her black-brown curls took on an almost golden shine around the edges.

Peter tried to be kind and courteous to everyone. Yet, when he found someone that he really wanted to be friends with, it was rare that they ever responded to him with the same enthusiasm he felt for them. Anna had never hesitated to be his friend. Even when she didn't trust them at the beginning, she responded to him with the same level of friendship that he offered her.

No, Peter decided, ignoring the situation wasn't the right choice. He wouldn't let another friendship slip away because he'd been stupid.

Swallowing the remains of the bite, Peter tipped his chin toward Anna as she glanced his way. "Good sandwich," he mumbled, pointing to the bread, egg, cheese, and bacon concoction that was dripping sauce onto his fingers.

One of her thick eyebrows lifted in amusement. "Yeah, uh—it's Dylan on shift this morning," she replied. "He's always been our best chef."

Peter cleared his throat. "Cool," he said. "Uh, while I've got you here, I was hoping to talk to you if you've got a second?"

An embarrassed though friendly tilt adjusted her expression. Her eyes darted over his shoulder, checking on the other patrons. "Sure." She waved a hand toward the customers. "They'll keep for a minute. What's up?"

Peter rested his elbows on the bar top, using a napkin to wipe his sandwich-messy hands. "So, uh. . . ." He cleared his throat again and opened his mouth to continue, but she cut him off.

"You don't have to do this, Pete."

Peter's eyes flashed up to hers. "Do what?"

"Whatever *this*—" She gestured to him and his definitively nervous body language, "is."

His chuckle was tense and humorless. "*This* . . . is intended to be an apology," he explained.

Still leaning against the ice machine, a healthy distance up the bar from Peter while remaining within earshot of their quiet exchange, Anna narrowed her eyes at him. She picked up the pendant of her gold necklace, running her fingers over the round edges. "An apology for what? You didn't do anything wrong."

Nudging the plate before him, Peter fought hard to hold her stare. "I made a dumb assumption. And I'm afraid that what I said made our friendship awkward. So, I'm sorry, because I don't want our friendship to be . . . I don't want it to be awkward."

Anna shook her head, a tinge of pink coloring her temples. "Peter, we're not in high school," she mumbled, eyes dropping to the counter between them. "I already knew."

Peter flinched, face growing hot at the assertion. "You knew?"

Anna nodded.

Tugging at his collar, Peter worked down a painful swallow. "Ann, I'm . . . I'm not sure. . . ."

Her eyes locked with his, effectively cutting him off.

Peter stared back at her. She knew? Knew what? That he was interested? But how? He hadn't even been sure of that himself. He liked her—a *lot*. He thought she was cute and fun and amazing—and, yeah, he thought dating her would probably be awesome. But she was taken in her own weird sort of way. And right now, he was far more afraid of losing her friendship than missing the potential opportunity to become her boyfriend.

"Listen, Ann," Peter started over, running a hand through his hair, "I—I'm not gonna lie. I did—I kind of had . . . have? Had? Gah, look." He blew out of a puff of air and held out his hands. "I don't know, okay?"

Her eyes narrowed in confusion.

"I don't know if my—" The words stuck in his throat. He grimaced, then forced them out. "I don't know if my interest was because you're one of the best people I've ever met, or if I actually. . . . But I'm sorry that

I put you in that position. And I want you to know that no matter what, I'm your friend."

There was a long, painful pause as Anna stared at him. The way her eyes remained locked on his face said that she wasn't convinced. She still believed he was more attached to her than he claimed, and his outburst on her porch yesterday afternoon had assured her of that.

Anna dropped the pendant of her necklace and her chin dipped. "I like you, Pete," she said, the inflection in her voice preparing him.

Peter couldn't help the almost inaudible scoff that left his lungs. He knew this conversation all too well. He'd experienced it often over the past fifteen or so years of his life.

She was letting him down easy.

"I really do," Anna promised. "But I just . . . I think you might be too serious for me."

Rubbing his hands together, Peter nodded. "Yeah . . . yeah, I get that a lot."

"It's a good thing, you know?" Anna said, giving him a sympathetic grin. "More guys should be like you. But I'm not—I can't . . . m—move on that. . . ."

Peter shook his head, not needing her reasons. "It's cool, Annie," he promised. "I'm not asking to date you. Yeah, I think you're amazing, but I knew the first time you mentioned him. . . ."

Anna's gaze dropped, and Peter could see that he'd taken a step too far across the line again. He backed away from the subject. "I'm your friend, Ann. That's all I've ever expected to be."

There was another long, tense pause as she fussed with the rows of bartending supplies behind the counter. He wished he could do more to reassure her so they could return to their previous friendship. But he thought saying anything else would only make it worse.

Peter held his tongue and stared at his hands. He considered picking his sandwich back up a time or two. It would be far less awkward to do something while she stood there. But he had the distinct impression that it would come across as inconsiderate or just plain weird of him to eat while she worked through her thoughts.

"He's been texting me," Anna finally whispered.

Peter swallowed past the tension in his throat.

He, being Connor Frossard. The best friend she'd been in love with for twenty years who had just proposed to another woman despite knowing of Anna's feelings for him.

Anna picked at a spot on the counter. "He, uh . . . he said he was sorry for—for not telling me before . . . for not telling me his plans."

Not sure what else to do, Peter watched her out of the corner of his eye. "Oh?"

She nodded. "He texted me five times that night."

Peter raised his brow in surprise.

"I didn't answer, so he called me the next day." She paused and shrugged. "I didn't answer that either."

Now, Peter felt his mouth drop open an inch.

"He's called or texted me every single day since," she said, meeting his gaze again. "I've decided not to respond."

"Really?" he gasped. "Wow, yeah, good—good for you. That's—I mean, that's—you need your distance. For your own sake."

Anna let out an empty sounding chuckle. "Thanks," she said, her expression conflicted. "I've nearly blocked him a few times, but I guess I keep hoping. . . ."

Peter wanted to tell her to stop hoping. That Connor wasn't worth her hope. But he also knew that a twenty-year dream like that—a twenty-year love—couldn't be released after less than a week of effort.

"I'm sorry, Anna," he said instead. "If you need . . . *anything*, I'm here."

A genuine smile came to her lips this time, softening her whole face back into its normal, gentle state. "Thank you, Peter."

"Anytime."

The tension between them eased, the soft murmur of conversation from the rest of the tavern, slow jazz from the jukebox, and the hiss of the kitchen grill providing a background to the prolonged silence between them. Anna may have forgiven him, but Peter wasn't sure if the awkwardness his stupidity had created was fully resolved yet.

Anna's eyes flashed to his nearly untouched sandwich. "You gonna eat that or what?"

An immediate flood of relief washed over him as he looked up to see her rich brown eyes crinkling softy at the edges.

Laughing, Peter nodded. "Yeah," he said. "Yeah, I think I will."

Over the next half hour, Anna refreshed his coffee, and Peter shared his side of hash browns with her in between her rounds to check on her customers. They talked in little bursts of conversation like they had only days ago. And despite his recent mistakes, it felt like nothing had happened. Like Peter had never been an idiot, and Anna had never thought him to have an interest in her. Like there weren't Druids to fight and a vault to find. Like DeVerre wasn't full of secrets, and there was nothing to fear at all.

And though he thought the conversation should have hurt, as it had secured his fate of being just friends with Anna, Peter couldn't quite feel it. They were back to the easy banter they'd had before; he hadn't ruined their relationship. He hadn't lost yet another friend.

Whatever came in the following days and weeks—Druids, beasts, a murder trial—this one thing had gone right for Peter. And he would be grateful for that forever.

~

"All right, how do we find this vault?" Cassandra asked, hands planted on the back of the couch later that day. Upon their return to Occasus, she'd promptly put her new purchases in her room and returned downstairs to meet the brothers so they could begin searching for the hidden Varon vault.

Peter turned to Spencer, who sat on the couch with Nex in front of him. "I guess we just go room by room," he suggested. "You know, check all the walls for seams, look behind all the paintings and mirrors and other stuff hanging on them. Also, the floors." He tapped his toe against the wood planks for emphasis. "There could be a trap door or something."

"That would only work on the bottom floor," Spencer observed.

Peter pointed a finger at him in counterargument. "Right, but there could be a key or something hidden in the floorboards upstairs."

"Maybe you'll get lucky and find a map," Gerard said, the flat delivery of his joke only earning Cassandra's laughter.

"Hilarious." Peter tossed the phantom a disgruntled glance where he sat in the rounded turret of the living room. The phantom lounged in one of the wingback chairs, reading in between bursts of mocking them as usual.

"If we're going to cover the entire house," Spencer said with a sweep of his hand to encompass the building, "I think we should get started. This is gonna take a while."

"Should we split up?" Peter asked, wondering if they'd cover more ground that way.

Spencer shook his head. "We should be together when we find it. We don't know what kind of defenses the Varons set up to protect it."

Peter frowned at the idea. "You think they put some spirit world trap on it? Like, if you try to open it, a whole horde of hellhounds appear to rip your throat out?"

"One can only hope," Gerard muttered, flipping a page.

Cassandra ignored the phantom, crossing her arms. "How would something like that even work?"

"I dunno." Peter shrugged, throwing his arms out to the side. "Owen would probably know, though."

Last night, Owen had texted the three of them in a panic, having seen the fire coming from the direction of the Merciers' house. A rapid burst of messages came through on each of their phones: *"Are you okay?"*, *"What's going on?"*, *"Ava's here, I can't call."*, *"Did you make it out?"*, *"Do you need help?"*

While Spencer was busy digging up a spare set of pajamas for Cassandra, Peter had responded for the trio: *"We're alive. At Occasus. We need to talk."*

Owen's reply had been simple: *"When?"*

Peter had offered for Owen to join them at any point today when his schedule allowed—meaning whenever Ava would be at work, and he could get away unseen. But that morning Owen had texted again: *"Today won't work. The school called. Tomorrow afternoon?"*

"Do we really want to wait until tomorrow to find out?" Cassandra asked.

"I could text him now," Peter offered.

"And say what? 'Hey, do you happen to know if it's possible to create a jack-in-the-box out of beasts?' "

Spencer let out a snort of humor at Cassandra's joke.

Peter sent his brother an annoyed look. "Fine," he conceded. "We go looking for the vault without worrying about whether or not there's some spirit bomb attached to it. Where do we want to start?"

"Here's as good a place as any, I guess," Spencer offered, scratching Nex's head with both hands. He gave the dog a final pat, then stood. "I'll get started on the walls."

Cassandra moved around the couch. "I'll take the fireplace and furniture," she said, giving Peter a sarcastically sweet smile. "You can have the floors since it was your idea, Pete."

With a grumble of acceptance, Peter got down on his hands and knees. Anguis ambled over to him, sniffing his head as though suspicious of Peter's presence in the dog's territory. With an unamused glare at the animal, he began to move from corner to corner in the room, knocking and running his hands along the wood planks and baseboards.

The gray-yellow light of the overcast day soon melted into the rust orange of sunset as they progressed through each room in Occasus. They swept the floors to no avail. They accosted the walls and removed their hangings with no reward. Each fireplace and every bookshelf was scoured for any lever, button, or marking, and they found nothing.

Turning on the overhead light in the upper room of the turret, Peter scanned the corkboard of Diane's genealogical research. His back ached from the hours they'd put into the search. They'd taken turns checking the various areas of the rooms, but he'd never felt so old in his life. Now they were in the last room—their last hope for finding the vault.

The barely-there moon hovered outside the three windows. Millions of stars twinkled down at them. Peter felt their odds diminishing as he ran his hands over the wooden slats of the walls. There were plenty of seams to check, but none were from anything more than natural paneling. Cassandra removed the corkboard from its nail, frowning as she brushed her fingers against the bare wall. Spencer kicked the heel of his boot against the floor, but it all sounded the same. Anguis and Nex sat in the doorway, watching with bored expressions. Gerard had abandoned them long ago.

After rummaging through the tiny desk's single drawer as a last-ditch effort, Cassandra plunked down in the chair. "That's it," she sighed, looking toward Peter and Spencer. "There's nothing here that even suggests a wall safe, let alone a spirit-protected vault."

Peter chewed on the inside of his cheek, frowning at the room around them.

"You're sure that Ava wasn't messing with you two?" Cassandra asked, draping an arm over the back of the chair.

Spencer shook his head, sitting against the far wall where he'd finally given up on checking the baseboards. The dogs snoozed at his side. "She was pretty convincing," he assured her. "Even if she's wrong and there is no vault, she certainly believes there is."

"But what if she doesn't?"

Peter and Spencer shared a confused look.

"What if," Cassandra continued, "she wanted you to believe there was a vault when there was none? What if she intentionally sent you looking for something that doesn't exist?"

"That's a bit maniacal, even for Ava," Peter defended, leaning against the sill of the window behind him.

"She convinced you that I'm a murderer." Cassandra's eyebrows rose. "You don't think she could send you on a wild goose chase?"

"No," Peter insisted.

"Maybe," Spencer countered.

"Dude. Really?"

Spencer shrugged. "I mean, it's possible," he said, holding his hands out before him. "Think about it: Ava wants us to stop searching for answers. What's the best way to be sure we don't get any of them?"

Crossing his arms, Peter scowled, unhappy with the direction his brother's logic was taking them.

Seeing that Peter wouldn't answer the question, Spencer gave the answer himself. "By sending us to look in the wrong places. There's a very good chance that Ava told us about the vault to throw us off track and keep us from getting further into this."

"Sounds likely to me," Cassandra said.

"Of course it does," Peter muttered.

"What does that mean?"

Peter met Cassandra's irritated stare. "It means that you're just as prejudiced against Ava as she is against you."

"I have reason to be!"

"Which is what she'd say about you," he argued.

"Hey," Spencer cut in. "It doesn't matter. Whether Ava was lying about the vault or not, we have other problems on our hands. Like the fact that if Ava *did* lie, she might be a Druid."

Cassandra shook her head. "She can't be."

"Why not?"

"She sent you toward *me* in association with the murders," she said. "If Ava was a Druid, she would have known that you'd find proof to the contrary. And she'd be smart enough to know that sending you in my direction might expose Debbie as well. They've been moving in secret for over a hundred years. Why would she risk giving up any information to you two?"

"That's a good point." Peter pointed a finger in her direction. "Ava has been awfully forthcoming with information in the past. Like, oddly so, at times."

"What do you mean?"

"I mean that when we showed up in DeVerre, she answered every question about Diane and Liam that she could before telling us to talk to you for the rest," he explained. "Then, when I went back to get more information about the town, she told me all about the popularity contest turned power struggle in DeVerre. She said that while the Guillaumes have been the face of the government since the Varons died, they aren't really in charge of anything. They're being controlled."

Spencer ran his hand over Anguis's back absentmindedly.

Cassandra pursed her lips, evidently in deep thought as well.

"Why would she do that if she was a Druid?" Peter added. "If she wanted to lie to us, she wouldn't have told us all that. She would have insisted that everything in DeVerre was fine. That no one was fighting for control."

Spencer squeezed his eyes shut, dropping his head against the wall behind him. "She doesn't get it," he muttered.

Peter and Cassandra waited for him to explain this new theory.

Sighing, Spencer propped his elbows on his knees. "She doesn't get it," he repeated. "She doesn't realize that it's not just a popularity contest. They're *actually* fighting for control over the town because they're fighting for control over the Veil. But she thinks it's just a bunch of narcissists who want to prove they're more important than everyone else."

Tugging at the collar of his flannel, Peter felt at a loss. He wanted to get in the Jeep, go to Owen and Ava's house, and tell the librarian everything. He wanted to warn her that her measly fears about the spirit world were nothing in comparison to the Druids who were trying to take over her town. That there were scylla and hellhounds, and who knew how many other kinds of creatures lurking in the shadows. That there were people who wielded arcs and could shatter souls.

Peter glanced up at that thought. Cassandra had slumped in her seat, her chin resting on the back of the chair. Her eyes were distant, zoned out on some unimportant detail in the room. And, for once, he thought that he couldn't blame Ava for wanting nothing to do with the spirit world.

After all, he'd become an accomplice in a murder because of it.

No, Peter reminded himself, that wasn't the truth. Debbie was the murderer. They shouldn't feel remorse for their choices last night. If anything, they'd saved the town from one more threat to their safety.

Looking over to where Spencer sat with Anguis and Nex at his side, Peter determined not to question their fight with Debbie Mercier ever again. Whatever came, he only had one goal: to protect his brother and their future. Everything else could burn in the wake of it.

The only problem was Peter *hadn't* been the one to protect his brother. Spencer and Cassandra had done that themselves while Peter was busy dying on the floor.

"We have to find that vault," Peter said, more to himself than to the other two. "Whatever Ava does or doesn't know, she had no reason to lie about that."

Spencer nodded, and even Cassandra pressed her lips together in acceptance.

Peter stood up straight, giving the room one last scan. "If it's not *in* Occasus, then maybe it's outside," he suggested. "Either way, we *have* to find it. Because if we don't. . . ."

Casting a resigned glance in Spencer's direction, Peter shrugged, letting his hands slap against his thighs as they dropped back down. "Well," he scoffed. "I'd rather not consider what'll happen if we don't."

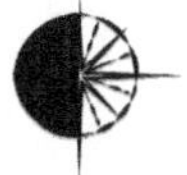

CHAPTER FIVE

Spencer

Walking the perimeter of the brick and iron fence surrounding Occasus, Spencer couldn't help eyeing every crack and chink in its façade. He kept hoping to spot some hidden door or grate that would lead them to the vault. Perhaps a shimmering tremor in the air like the ivory halo that glowed around Cassandra's arc.

After their failed search the previous day, the trio had gone outside—to the delight of Anguis and Nex—to search the grounds of Occasus that morning. They searched for any sign of a secret cellar or basement, combing the entire property. But they'd had no more luck outside than in. There weren't any overlooked or secret entrances in the dried-up grass. None in the trunks of the pine trees sprinkled across the yard.

Now, in the bright afternoon sunshine, Spencer walked with the dogs through the forest around Occasus. He'd woken more well-rested than the day before, his exhaustion finally getting the better of his wild imagination. But his thoughts had kicked back into overdrive the second he'd drifted into consciousness.

In the immediacy of their need to find the vault and the anxiety that had risen with the marshal's appearance at their doorstep, Spencer hadn't gotten the chance to process what exactly had happened to them two nights prior. They'd nearly died. They'd ensured their position as enemies of the Druids. And now, they were in a race against an unknown clock as they attempted to find the answers to the ever-mounting number of questions in their lives.

Nex brushed up against Spencer's leg. He reached down to scratch the wiry fur on the dog's head. He should want to run, he knew. With the weight of everything around them, he should want to pack his bags, force Peter and Cassandra to get in the Jeep with him, and drive away from DeVerre and the spirit world it was meant to protect. But something inside of Spencer stopped him from giving the idea any real consideration.

The moral dilemma of leaving the town to its own devices wasn't the primary reason for his hesitation. He knew it would be wrong of them to choose to save themselves over the lives of three hundred others. If they left, it would mean abandoning the whole of DeVerre to whatever terror the Druids had planned for them. Staying was the right choice—and that made his decision far easier to defend.

However, a deeper, purer, and more selfish reason had coiled tight in Spencer's chest and taken up residence right where Debbie Mercier's black arc had struck him. One that he wasn't sure even Peter would understand.

Spencer knew why his brother wanted to stay in DeVerre. Peter was an addict; he liked problems, and he enjoyed difficulty. They were like games to him. Opportunities for him to prove himself. Chances for him to show the world just how capable he was. And DeVerre—a town of liars, murderers, and Druids—was the perfect place for him to feed that addiction.

And Spencer? He was an addict of his own sort. One who craved perfection and safety. Above anything else, Spencer wanted to live in a world where everything was exactly as he liked it. Calm, slow-moving, and completely controlled. A peaceful, orderly life where he could live in his imagination and be separate from the demands and wishes of others. He wanted a home where he could be free and secure without worrying about how his actions would impact others.

The House of Occasus was ideal for this dream of his. It was equal parts cozy and creepy. It was inspiring and haunting. It was warm and chilling. And Spencer had fallen in love with it.

Peter had been right when he said Occasus was the perfect home for writers like them. There was no doubt in Spencer's mind that he and his brother could be happy in DeVerre, writing their novels and building a life.

With Cassandra as a part of that life now, he could already sense it becoming richer. He liked having her steady and level-headed presence around the house. She was the perfect middle ground between him and his brother. A sensible but playful woman who brought out the best in them both.

The singular wrinkle in this idealistic tapestry being woven in Spencer's imagination was the influence of the spirit world now lurking in the background.

A sharp pang shot through Spencer's ankle, reminding him that he'd been out too long for his still recovering sprain. He sighed, irritated at having such a minor injury. It was one more reminder of what stood in the path of that impossible, self-indulgent dream.

Rounding the corner to the front of Occasus, Spencer stopped next to the large wrought iron gates. Though simple and elegant in design, the black metal twisted into a coiling pattern near its crown. Since moving into the mansion, they'd never closed the gates. Large and heavy as they were, they'd be a constant nuisance to shut and reopen. But even as they hung apart, Spencer noticed another coiled pattern, more intricate in design, at the center.

In the clear division of the pattern, Spencer managed to fit together the pieces in his mind. A circular emblem of stars, a heraldic banner housing the Latin words *omnes pro Christo*, and what he thought was a dagger centered at the hollow of a V.

The Varon family sigil, he assumed.

All for Christ, the Latin read. Spencer wondered at the family's dedication to the spirit world. They'd left everything to follow the prophecy that led them to DeVerre. And in the end, it wound up getting them killed.

Anguis and Nex trotted past Spencer as he lingered at the gate, the dogs heading for the porch. The large, gothic house looked like something out of a novel. In the late autumn, most of the foliage surrounding the house had wilted and lost its leaves. Only the pines smattered throughout the yard remained intact. The weathered brick of the house looked like cinnamon in the overcast morning. On the far right, the rounded, turret-like section jutted out onto the porch.

Scanning the house, Spencer tipped his head to the side. Somewhere inside, a vault held all the answers to every question they had. What had happened in DeVerre all those years ago? How did the spirit world work? How could they defeat the Druids? And so many more that he was sure they hadn't even asked yet.

Spencer slipped his hands into his jacket pockets as the cold wind blew past him.

They needed to find that vault. It wasn't just the solution to their problems; it was the key to unlocking the door to the world he'd always imagined. If they could get into the vault, they could stop the Druids, subdue the spirit world, and save DeVerre. Then he could satiate that all-encompassing desire for a haven, untouchable by the outside world.

"Afternoon," a voice called a few feet behind Spencer.

Jumping around, Spencer scoffed at himself when he saw Owen making his approach on the road. "Hey," he said, tipping his chin up in greeting as he berated himself internally. He really needed to stop being so anxious.

Owen came to stand at his side, as calm and collected as usual. He wore his hunter-green jacket over a cream button up and slacks. Of all the people in DeVerre, Spencer thought he was the one who paid the most attention to his appearance. Never a blond hair out of place or a careless tuck to his shirt. In the short time they'd lived there, Spencer hadn't seen anyone—not even Dr. Frossard or Reverend Chapelle—wear slacks outside work or church functions.

"You looking at anything in particular?" Owen asked, nodding toward the house. "Or just admiring the architecture?"

"Neither," Spencer admitted. "Just reminding myself why I'm here."

"Mm. Yes, I've had to do that a lot over the years."

"But . . . you have Ava."

"I do," Owen agreed, a knowing grin on his lips. The action emphasized his small, round eyes. "But sometimes I have to remind myself why I'm lying to her."

Spencer sucked in a breath of awkward understanding. He eyed the man cautiously. "Do you ever think you're doing the wrong thing? Lying to her?"

"All the time."

"So why do it?" he asked. "You're as religious as the rest of this town, right? Surely you believe that lying is wrong, no matter what."

Owen didn't hesitate to shake his head. "Not at all. I believe we are to be cunning and wise, like snakes. We are also not to throw our pearls before swine. If we have the truth, but it would be trampled upon or mishandled by those we give it to, we should keep it to ourselves. Some truths the heart isn't ready to receive. We must first prepare the soil of the heart before we sow the seed of truth within it."

Spencer raised his brow, trying to take in everything Owen had said. "You should have been a preacher," he suggested. "You like to talk in metaphors a little too much."

Owen's grin widened. "Ava agrees with you."

They both chuckled and began walking up the gravel drive toward the house. Spencer brushed his fingers along the shiny, dark green lacquer of their father's old Jeep. It contrasted heavily against the bright red of Cassandra's vintage truck sitting next to it.

Furrowing his brow as the rest of Owen's words finally connected, Spencer turned back to him as they stepped onto the porch. "Did you just call your wife a swine?"

Owen's laugh was warm and full. "I guess I sort of did." He pulled in a chagrined breath. "Seems I'll have to apologize to her later."

"She won't know."

He shrugged. "I like to apologize even for the things she doesn't know."

"Like the fact that you aren't the man she thinks you are?"

"Just like that."

The two shared a thoughtful look before Spencer opened the door, letting Nex and Anguis slip into the house before them. He and Owen shed their jackets, hanging them in the coat closet before heading into the living room where Peter and Cassandra were talking.

Peter was gesturing emphatically as usual as they talked while Cassandra propped her chin on her hand, elbow resting on her thigh as she sat cross-legged on the opposite couch. Gerard was lounging at her side. The group exchanged greetings as Spencer and Owen joined them, the previous conversation dying down.

"How's it going, man?" Peter asked, watching as Owen took the empty chair that they'd pulled from the turret corner in preparation for their meeting.

"Well enough," Owen said, his inflection far less enthusiastic than Peter's. "I've taken on Debbie's classes at the school, so that will take up a lot of my time over the next several weeks. Or however long it'll take them to find a new teacher."

As Spencer settled into his seat next to Peter, he glanced at Cassandra to see her gaze drop to her hands, which now rested in her lap.

"Why not just hire you?" Peter asked.

"He's not a Sauveterre," Gerard offered.

Owen dismissed the idea with a wave. "I don't care to work there full time. I substitute for them, and that's more valuable to them in the long run anyway.

"Now," Owen leaned forward, resting his arms on his legs, "how about you three explain exactly what happened on Tuesday night?"

An hour later, they'd run through Peter and Spencer's entrance into the Mercier home, finding Debbie in Cassandra's room, the scylla and hellhounds she'd summoned, Cassandra's arrival, Peter's near death, and the fire that Spencer had started. Cassandra had also added her conversation with the marshal to the list of events in the past forty-eight hours of their lives.

After laying it all out for Owen to digest, the man sat with palms pressed together and his fingers held to his lips as he thought for a long, *long* time.

Spencer squirmed in his seat, knee bouncing. Owen was only a handful of years older than him—likely less than two or three older than Cassandra. And yet Spencer felt like they were children waiting for the discipline of their parent after admitting they'd been the ones who'd burned the house down. *Literally.*

Finally, Owen sighed, ran his hands over his face, and gave them all a nod. "All right," he murmured. His usually flat voice held an edge of uncertainty. "All right, this is good. All in all."

"Good?" Peter scoffed. "Dude, the marshal suspects us. And now we've got *all* the Druids about to charge the house for this vault."

"We don't know that," Spencer objected.

"You don't know much," Gerard commented.

Owen passed the phantom a dismissive glance, then turned back to Peter. "It's good because we know now that we were right: There *are* Druids operating in DeVerre. Someone summoned the hellhounds that committed the murders. Our theory of them targeting potential Wielders makes sense. It answers a lot of questions."

"And gives us a dozen more," Spencer lamented.

Owen shrugged in acceptance.

"So, what do we do now?" Cassandra asked.

"Dig around some more?" Peter suggested.

She tipped her head to the side in worry. "We need to be careful. Tom may not have arrested me, but I could tell he was suspicious."

"Yeah, I noticed that too." Peter ran a hand over the welts on his neck. They'd darkened overnight, turning from a pinkish red to deep stripes of brownish maroon.

Spencer gripped the edge of the cushion underneath him. His memories kept replaying the moment that Peter's face had gone white, and his pulse had eluded Spencer's search for six painstaking seconds. He'd been sure that Peter was dead in those seconds. Sure that he'd lost the only person left on Earth that he trusted.

But they were here, alive if not exactly well, in Occasus's living room with the late autumn sunshine streaming through the windows as though they'd never had a near-death experience at all.

"How do we find more information without looking suspicious?" Spencer asked, desperate to keep his brother safe.

"Didn't you already have this discussion?" Gerard said, arm across the back of the couch. In the bright room, his muted pigmentation appeared even duller today. The only sign he wasn't a normal human. "I thought you'd finally figured out that the only thing that works on the people of DeVerre is becoming one of them."

"He's right," Owen said, almost begrudgingly. "The plan hasn't changed. You three need to make connections, and we'll keep our eyes open for anything suspicious in the meantime."

"That's not super proactive," Peter grumbled.

"Proactivity is not our goal," Owen countered. "Protecting the Veil is. Everything else is secondary. Answers, uncovering the Druids, even keeping our lives—those things won't mean anything if the Veil falls into their hands."

Spencer, Peter, and Cassandra all shared a questioning look. Though Spencer was sure that Owen was right, he couldn't help wishing that he wasn't. And that whatever intentions the Druids had for the Veil weren't as nefarious as Owen seemed to think. Perhaps then they could ignore it, stepping out of the Druids' way and going on to live their lives in peace.

Remembering the hollowness that welled up within him when the arc that Debbie Mercier sent his way had struck, Spencer pressed a hand against his ribcage as he cleared his throat. He set his arms against his thighs, leaning forward. "How do we protect it then?"

Owen's round eyes lingered on Spencer's face as he hesitated. "We follow the plan," he said, finally. "And while you three ingratiate yourselves with the town and prod for answers, I'll keep an eye on the lake. No one will suspect me if I go to the lake regularly. Ava knows that I like to go out there. And few other people ever see me. If I notice the ghosts acting strangely or if I see any suspicious activity, I'll alert you, and we'll revise the plan. Until then, we stay the course and keep doing what we've been doing."

The weight of this responsibility pressed against Spencer's shoulders, making him slump forward. How had this fallen to them? They'd come to the town to write; that was all. And now they were somehow wrapped up in a deadly battle for control of a town and a power they didn't even want.

"Well," Peter said, drawing Spencer's eyes to him. His brother sat with his shoulders back and his chin held high as he surveyed the rest of them. "Seems to me that if we're gonna enter into this town's popularity contest and attempt to save it all at the same time, we need to strategize a bit."

"You're going to strategize?" Gerard asked, his dark eyebrows raised. "You can't even stick to your own serial's plot lines."

Peter pursed his lips but otherwise ignored the phantom. "I created a list," he said, reaching forward to grab his notebook from the coffee table. He lifted it to show them all before opening to a dog-eared page. "It's got everything we need to do on it."

"You made a to-do list?" Cassandra asked, sarcasm thick in her raspy voice.

Peter shrugged. "Yeah."

"How organized of you."

"Hey, Spence may be the smart one, but I'm not a complete idiot."

Spencer shook his head, perfectly aware that Peter was, in fact, the smarter of the two of them. He just hid his intelligence behind his jokes and carefree persona so that no one knew how scared he was of looking foolish. But Spencer didn't bring attention to that fact, knowing that Peter would be against it.

"Let's hear it," he prompted instead.

Adopting an officious air, Peter tapped the page in front of him. "First," he began, "find the vault. That's not going so well, so I guess it's sort of an ongoing thing."

They all nodded in agreement.

"Next, figure out who the Druids in this town are." Peter let the notebook hang before him. "As we just discussed, we'll stick to the plan and get people to trust us and start talking. But I was also thinking," he turned to Owen, "didn't you say that you know of some people who are aware of the spirit world?"

Owen frowned, his lips pursed in thought. "I don't know of anyone specifically," he answered. "Ava has her theories about who knows what around here, of course. I've never personally seen any evidence to support those theories, though."

"But she suspects certain individuals?" Spencer asked, following his brother's lead. If nothing else, a few names would give them a head start.

"Yes," Owen said with a sigh, then continued. "She most often mentions the Chapelles, saying that their relationship with the Varons almost guarantees it. She also thinks that the Garniers and Frossards are probably involved in their own way, though she has far less to support either of those claims. Particularly regarding the Frossards, in my opinion.

Their involvement seems highly improbable based on what little she's told me."

Gerard shifted in his seat, catching Spencer's attention, but the phantom remained silent.

"You really think the marshal could be in on it?" Peter asked, brown eyes wide at the idea.

Owen tipped one shoulder up in a shrug. "I have no idea," he admitted. "It's just a theory that Ava's had for a while. Though, I'm not sure she particularly suspects Tom. More likely, it's that the Garniers, being as close to the Varons as they were, had to have had *some* inkling of what they dabbled in."

"Hm." Peter stared at the notebook in his hands.

"If we're trying to figure out who is a Druid and who isn't," Cassandra interjected, "we should probably investigate the Sauveterres first."

They all looked at her—Peter and Spencer with far more confusion than Owen or Gerard.

Cassandra's hazel eyes shifted from brother to brother as she explained. "Debbie's maiden name was Sauveterre. They came to DeVerre with Matthias Varon and started the school. It would make sense for the Sauveterres to be involved with the Druids. And . . . it could be the answer to why the town ended all contact with Harmony."

"What do you mean?" Spencer asked.

"If the family—if *my* family are the Druids," she took a deep breath after the thought, "then they've been here since the start."

Owen nodded, picking up where she left off. "And they may very well have been working from the inside to overturn the Warden's hold on the town all this time."

"Exactly."

"So, what? We need to befriend the Sauveterres, then?" Spencer asked.

Peter held up a finger to point, first at Cassandra, then at Owen. "Didn't you say that the Sauveterres run the school?"

"They founded the school," Owen corrected. "But it's run by the town now."

Gerard scoffed, adjusting the waistband of his trousers. "Unless things have changed—which I doubt—the school may be funded by the town but it's the family who has the final say in everything done there."

"It's a public school," Owen countered. "The government determines all curriculum and funding allotments."

"Who's the principal these days?" the phantom returned coolly.

Owen took a deep breath, leaning against the arm of his chair. Spencer could see a spark of satisfaction light up his blue eyes as he replied, "Neil Alarie."

Gerard's typical expression was somewhere between smug and glowering. His heavily hooded gaze turned down at the corners, and his bushy beard kept his thin lips well hidden. The thick hair that hung along his sharp cheekbones stood in contrast to the standard of his birth era—a sign of whatever grief he refused to speak of, Spencer thought. Locked in time as he was, he always looked the same. So it was rather shocking to Spencer when he caught the way Gerard's whole face lost all feeling at Owen's calmly spoken words. As though he had been stunned into emotionless silence.

Cassandra seemed to notice this change as well. She angled toward the phantom, her head tilted in interest. "You know Neil?" she asked.

With a quick shake of his head, Gerard rested against the back of the couch again as if to return to his customary lazy attitude. "Not personally," he said, running a hand through his long brown hair. "But he's a relative, technically."

Owen narrowed his gaze, scanning the phantom carefully. "How do you know about him? You were dead for thirty years before he was born."

"Ghosts can haunt the town if we want to," Gerard said, his tone flat and bored. "It isn't exactly easy. We're bound to the lake. The farther we drift from the water, the weaker we become, and the stronger its pull on us grows. But from time to time, it's considered worth the trip to escape the monotony of the woods."

"So, were you checking up on your family, then?" Spencer tried to be casual as he asked the question. He dug his thumb into his palm, watching closely for Gerard's reaction.

The phantom flashed his signature smirk. "Wouldn't you like to know?" he rebuffed.

"Gerard," Cassandra warned, raising her sharp eyebrows, her tone demanding a real answer.

With a lazy glare, Gerard's cocksure demeanor didn't dim. "He's Franklin's grandson," he said as though that explained everything.

Cassandra's chin tipped up in understanding. "Ah," was all she said before moving on. "Regardless of who's in charge of the school, I don't think we need to worry about befriending any of my extended family. They don't like me. Debbie only took me in because of my mother. Well. . . ." She huffed. "I'm not even sure that's true now."

"You think she was keeping an eye on you?" Spencer guessed.

"Probably."

"Mkay." Peter rapped his fingers across the page of his notebook in thought. "Does that mean we ignore them?"

"I wouldn't *ignore* anyone," Owen said. "But I wouldn't prioritize the Sauveterres either. We know there is a strong likelihood that they're part of the Druids. Keep an eye on them and be wary of people connected with them."

Peter nodded, turning to give Spencer a thorough scan. Spencer could feel the brotherly probing, Peter testing him for any signs of anxiety or fear. The regular check-ins typically didn't irritate him, but he was getting tired of his brother assuming he was going to crumble under the pressure of their newfound responsibilities.

Stilling his bouncing knee, Spencer motioned toward the notebook. "What's next?" he asked, keeping his voice strong and sure.

Peter shrugged. "Solve Diane's murder."

Cassandra perked up at that, but Owen's forehead furrowed. "Now you're sounding like Ava," he said, leaning a forearm against his leg as he turned toward them. "Why do you think someone murdered Diane?"

"Because she was," Gerard said.

Owen's head swiveled to look at him. "You have proof?"

"She was fine in the morning when she woke," Gerard explained. "I went for a walk, and when I returned, she was ill, lying on that couch there." He nodded his head toward where Spencer and Peter sat. Spencer felt a trickle of discomfort rolling down his spine, but he refused to let it show.

"An hour later, she was dead," the phantom concluded.

Owen ran a hand over his jaw in thought. "That's not evidence."

"But it is suspicious, isn't it?"

Owen's grim expression admitted as much.

Glancing back to where Cassandra sat on the far side of the room, Spencer remembered when they'd met her. While seated in this very room, she'd asked for their help to catch Diane's murderer. They'd read Diane's old research and drafts, checked books out from the library, and done everything they could to figure out who had killed the woman for nearly two weeks to no avail. Their only lead in all that time had been the missing pages of Elijah Lawrence's essays.

Spencer felt his lips part as the revelation dawned on him. "Her murderer was a Druid," he said, then realized how obvious it was. "We've always known; we just didn't have a name for it until Owen came around."

Cassandra met his gaze, a gleam of comprehension in her eyes. "That's why they took the pages."

"The pages?" Owen prompted.

"Diane had collected Elijah Lawrence's essays," Cassandra explained. "We were trying to decipher them, but someone stole them from her draft after her death."

Owen's brows shot up, his eyes growing wide. He heaved a massive breath as though a weight had landed on his back, knocking the air from his lungs. "I'd say that's pretty adequate proof of foul play," he muttered.

Gerard let out a smug snort.

"However," Owen continued. "I don't see any reason for the Druids to take Elijah's essays. They have no use for them."

"Cass said they're sort of like a how-to book," Peter offered. "Maybe they need instructions for something."

Owen shook his head. "Druids pass everything down through oral tradition. They don't believe in written instruction," he explained. "Besides, Elijah lived at the start of the Warden's knowledge. While I've never read his essays, I'm aware that his works were far more theological and basic in terms of his understanding of the spirit world. Druids would have no cause to research his work."

Spencer looked to Peter, pondering this conundrum. "If the Druids had no use for the pages, why would they take them?" he asked.

"The only reason I can think," Owen offered, turning to Cassandra, "is to keep them from you."

"Me?" Cassandra's nose scrunched up, the small hollow in her cheek making an appearance. "Why? I could hardly understand them *with* Diane's help."

"They don't know that," he reminded her. "And even if they did, it wouldn't change the fact that *you* are their most formidable adversary. Considering that they don't even know about me, at least. Leaving a how-to book on the table isn't a smart move."

Cassandra nodded slowly, understanding seeming to dawn on her.

Spencer smiled at her encouragingly. "See," he teased. "We were smart to put you in protective custody."

She met his attempt to lighten the mood with a smirk. "I suppose you were."

"Do we think that's why they killed Diane, though?" Peter asked, bringing them back to the moment. "Just to get the essays away from you?"

She shrugged, her black sweater bunching with the motion. "I doubt they even knew about the essays. We never talked about them, and we only read them here in Occasus. It was probably a last-minute decision, taking the pages when they saw them on her desk after they murdered her."

"Maybe." Peter ran a hand over his scruffy jawline. He looked at the notebook on his lap again. "This is kind of a decent segue into the next topic on the agenda: We need to figure out who the heck we are."

Owen's eyebrows pulled together in confusion, but Spencer and Cassandra both nodded.

Gerard huffed, picking at his nails. "In the grand scheme of things," he said, voice a low growl, "do you *really* think your ancestry is as important as finding a murderer and staying alive?"

"What if it helps us to stay alive?" Peter countered.

"How would lineage help you stay alive?"

There was no answer to that.

"All right, fine," Peter conceded. "It's still something to do, but—admittedly—it's not super high on the priority list. However," he held up a finger as though about to wow them all, "these next two *are* the most important."

Spencer didn't get his hopes too high, knowing his brother's penchant for dramatics.

"First," Peter said with a direct look at Cassandra, "we need to talk with the Chapelles."

Cassandra narrowed her eyes while Spencer scratched the back of his neck. "Why?" he asked.

"Because!" Peter exclaimed. "We know they know *something*. They told Cass's parents to take her away from DeVerre simply because she saw ghosts. And Ava's sure they know about the spirit world as well. They should be our prime suspects."

"I don't know about considering them as suspects," Owen cut in. "But I would say they're persons of interest, at the very least. Ava has talked with Sam on several occasions, trying to get him to be open with her about what he's doing to protect DeVerre from the spirit world. He's never taken the bait or said anything to confirm that he knows what she's talking about, but she's convinced that he's hiding something."

Peter extended his hand toward Owen, eyes wide as he looked at Spencer as though to emphasize his point.

"Yeah, okay." Spencer knocked his brother's hand out of the air.

"Also," Cassandra added, "Juliet Chapelle saw her boyfriend get killed by a hellhound. There's a good chance the Chapelles are neck deep in this."

"Be careful," Owen warned. "If you do talk to the Chapelles, mitigate how much of your knowledge that you expose. As I said, Ava has tried to have conversations with Sam before, and it hasn't worked out. If you press too hard, you'll wind up as much of a pariah as she is."

"Or maybe you'll make another friend like the marshal," Gerard snickered.

Peter glowered at the phantom, preparing to snap back. But Spencer was ready to get to the last task on their list. He nudged Peter's arm, nodding to the page. "And the final task?"

"Ah." Peter shut the notebook and tossed it back on the coffee table. "Last but not least, we need to befriend the Frossards."

The group raised their brows dubiously, but it was Cassandra who spoke. "Wait, why?" she asked.

"Ava said something to me a while back," Peter explained. "That if the Frossards approve, the town approves. And Anna also told us that everyone looks up to them. They seem like the best place to start to me."

Cassandra narrowed her eyes. "And your opinion has nothing to do with the fact that you'll need to spend more time with Anna to get close to them?"

Peter shot a nervous glance in Owen's direction, but Owen showed no sign that he held any particular feeling toward the suggestion in Cassandra's accusation. "No," Peter insisted. "But I'll be honest, it helps that we're already friends with her. Gia seemed really fond of her. And she's best friends with their son."

"They're not talking right now," Owen said.

Spencer frowned. "Really? Do you think that'll be a problem? Like, will his parents take offense because they're . . . what? Breaking up?"

"They were never dating. I told you that," Peter reminded him.

Owen shook his head. "I'd rather not discuss the specifics of their relationship," he said, holding out a hand to stop the conversation. "But if you're concerned about Gia or Alex losing their fondness for Anna because of their son's stupidity, don't be. They've been like a second set of parents to her since she and Connor were five. Alex and Gia Frossard adore her. Their son's engagement won't change that."

"So, you think Anna can arrange an invite to their house?" Cassandra asked. "Dinner, maybe? Or at least something to give us an excuse to talk to them."

"I don't appreciate the idea of using my sister-in-law as a means to an end," Owen replied, his usually flat tone now thick with agitation.

"She's not a means to an end, Owen," Peter assured him. "She's our friend. But she also happens to be friends with people who may know a lot more than they're saying. They might even be able to give us the answers if we can get them to trust us."

Remembering the mysterious Mr. F in the baby picture of Diane and their grandfather Phillip, Spencer knew that Peter was right. The Frossards weren't only the heart of DeVerre; they also held the secret to their own family's past. Even if the man in the photo was dead—which he almost certainly was—there was a chance the family had kept records of *why* he'd taken the two children to Norfolk for their adoption. And why it had been kept quiet.

But there was one other man who could help them.

Spencer looked across the room at Gerard, meeting his dark stare. "You said that you knew the Frossards in the '50s?"

"I did," the phantom confirmed.

"Is there any information you can give us that will help?" he prodded. "Anything that would give us some connecting point or a way of understanding them better? Anything that would make them like us more?"

Gerard grunted with his typical, mocking amusement. "They'll hate you regardless," he said. "And there's nothing much you can do about that."

"You're a fount of knowledge, Gerry," Peter grumbled.

Cassandra seemed to share Peter's irritation. "Gerard, there has to be something that you know," she pressed. "Something that will help us."

"I *am* helping you, Cassie," he returned. "The Frossards are elitists. They run this town with their money and popularity, and they are used to being pandered to. *You* might've had a chance had you not tied yourself to Diane when you returned a few years ago. Being a natural-born DeVerrean would have been acceptable to them. Living on Haven with the Merciers would have given you a leg up. But these two?" The phantom scanned the brothers with a scathing look. "They're outsiders. And the Frossards don't like people outside of their own blood."

The rest of them were silent, contemplating that statement. Spencer held in the urge to insist that he and Peter were DeVerreans too. Whether the town knew it or not, they had just as much DeVerrean blood as the rest. Though, he realized that wasn't entirely true.

Diane and Phillip had left DeVerre two generations prior in secret. They'd both married outside of DeVerre. Phillip had one son—their father, David. And David had gone on to marry Mallory Joseph, another non-DeVerrean. Which now made Peter and Spencer only a quarter DeVerrean at best.

And they had no proof that their grandfather was from DeVerre to begin with.

"There are Frossards in the forest," Owen said, bringing Spencer back to the living room. The bright afternoon light was starting to dim, its rays hanging low over the trees outside. It made Owen's hair glow far blonder than usual.

"What do you mean?" Peter asked.

"Ghosts," Cassandra offered.

Owen nodded. "I've tried to speak with them several times, but they don't like to talk."

"I've done the same," Cassandra added.

"We could try again," he suggested. "Now that there are two of us, they might be willing to at least offer advice."

Spencer pressed his hands to his mouth, fingers entwined together. His heartbeat rose in his chest as his anxiety built. The idea of talking to ghosts would creep him out on a good day. Now that they were slogging through the disaster that was DeVerre's paranormal activity, he felt a tremor of fear welling in his chest. One that made him want to leap up, open his laptop, and write about worlds that weren't real, just to remind himself that there was something he could control.

"Spence?" Peter prompted. "What'd'ya think?"

Knowing there wasn't much else to do, Spencer dropped his hands between his knees and nodded. Discomfort meant nothing. If they could end the fight for DeVerre, he and Peter could have the home they'd always wanted.

"I think it's a place to start," Spencer said, glancing at Cassandra. "And that's the best we can ask for right now."

"Cool." Peter reached over to slap Spencer's shoulder, then nodded to Owen. "Should we talk to some of those ghosts, then?"

CHAPTER SIX

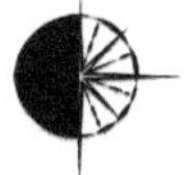

Spencer

arm mug of coffee in hand, Spencer moved through the kitchen toward the office. As their previous meeting with Owen had gone late into yesterday afternoon, they'd made plans to visit the lake—and the ghosts who resided by it—today when they had more time and Ava wouldn't be around to find her husband's absence suspicious. But as Owen had returned to the care of Debbie's classes at the school, they now had to wait most of the day for him to join them.

And while part of Spencer felt ridiculous for considering it, he refused to let another day slip past him without writing. They might be in a fight for their lives, but that didn't mean writing was any less important. After all, they had the serial to keep up with *and* a career to build. Druids or not, they couldn't keep Occasus without the support of their writing.

Used to being the first one awake, Spencer jumped, sloshing hot coffee over the rim of his mug when he entered the dining room to find Cassandra already seated at the far end of the table. He stifled a curse under his breath, and she looked up. A slow smirk grew across her lips as she surveyed him.

"Good morning to you too," she said, capping the highlighter she held.

Finding the ability to laugh at himself, Spencer set the coffee on the table. "Sorry," he muttered, then held up a finger. "Hold on a sec."

Spencer hurried into the kitchen to rinse off his hands and grab some paper towels. When he returned to dry the splashes on the wooden floor, Cassandra was waiting patiently.

"I didn't expect you to be up," he admitted, kneeling.

Cassandra leaned to the side to watch as he cleaned. "Apparently not." Humor laced her tone. "You're the early bird, I take it?"

"Of Pete and I, yeah. I think working at a coffee shop ruined me for sleeping in."

"I always forget that you were a barista. You don't strike me as a latte type of guy."

"Can't say I am," Spencer said as he rose, separating the dirty rags from the clean ones. The mess hadn't been as large as he'd anticipated, so he wound up with a wad of unused paper towels in one hand and a smaller, damp one in the other.

"I bet you were into pour-overs," she teased.

With an amused scoff, Spencer shook his head. "Nah, those requests were always annoying. Kind of like Pete and his special cocktail, you know? A hassle you really don't have time for when you're busy."

Cassandra smiled, tapping the highlighter on the open page of the book in front of her. Spencer glanced at it, noting that it was her Bible. He didn't know why it surprised him. One of the first things she'd told them about herself was her dedication to her faith, and he'd caught her reading the Bible the previous morning as well. But that was the weird part about it, he supposed. He couldn't remember the last time he or Peter had thought to crack open their Bibles. Not that they didn't care to; they just never had the time.

The hollow appeared in Cassandra's cheek—the not-quite-dimple that made her look mischievous and scheming—and made Spencer acutely aware of how awkward he looked standing there with wads of paper towels in his hands.

"I'll, uh—I'm gonna toss this," he said, hurrying to throw half away and set the other half on the counter.

When he returned to retrieve his coffee, Cassandra had her head bent over the page, having exchanged her highlighter for a pen. He watched for two seconds as she began to write in the margins, a vague memory flashing into his mind. One he wasn't sure he'd ever thought about until that moment.

It was one of those memories that lacked detail, the sort where there wasn't even a setting. But he distinctly remembered his dad doing that same thing when he was a boy. Marking up his Bible with notes and lines to remind him to pay attention the next time he read the same verse.

Shaking off the memory, Spencer backed away to the office. Watching Cassandra focus on her morning devotionals made him feel guilty for neglecting his own. Like he wasn't as good of a Christian as her. It wasn't like he didn't want to read his Bible. He'd like to. But how was he supposed to find time for it? He'd had way too much to do in Norfolk, working two jobs, trying to write as much as possible, and maintaining relationships. Here in DeVerre, it was even worse. With Druids after them, a vault to find, and a town to save, time was a precious commodity.

Spencer pushed off his momentary shame and opened his laptop. He sipped the bold coffee as he waited for it to boot up. He had to get a good start on the next episode. They couldn't afford to lose any of the minimal fan base they had cultivated through the blog if they wanted to make their lives in DeVerre a success. That was the thing, Spencer knew. Staying in DeVerre wasn't just about fighting off Druids and stopping the spirit world from being unleashed. If they didn't get their book published and start making money, he and Peter would lose their chance to stay in the house they'd inherited, and the millions of dollars that came with it.

He had to stay focused. He had to get the work done.

Over the past month or so in DeVerre, Spencer and Peter had managed to write a solid plot line for the end of the blog. Knowing that they wanted the book to pick up where the serial left off, they had no reason to continue it once the book was released. And since they knew the general start of the book, they were ready to bring the serial to a close.

They'd both agreed: *Wenzel & Frankly,* the serial, was going to be complete by the end of the year. They had four more regular episodes to write, and then they'd publish a special edition, series wrap-up to announce *Wenzel & Frankly,* the novel. But there was still so much to do.

So, Spencer pulled up his word processor and began a rough outline of his episode for the next week.

The hours whiled away, like they always did for Spencer when he wrote. His vivid imagination took him into Frankly's world of 1880s New York. He could see the cobbled roads, feel the cold and foggy air, and hear the characters talking to one another as he built the world. His own heart raced in time with Frankly's as he wrote about the inspector's narrow escape from a monster of Peter's design. He couldn't help the small smile that pulled up the edges of his lips as he worked in the new character he and Peter had determined to introduce as the propellant toward the book.

Serene Verlice would be Wenzel and Frankly's introduction to the new villain of the story—the cult behind all the mayhem of monsters within the city. They'd always known that something more was at play beneath the surface, but they'd never taken the time to figure out what it was. And now they were finally going to give their true villains a name.

During their planning, Peter and Spencer had determined that Wenzel and Frankly needed a catalyst that would bring them face to face with the ultimate villains. And they'd settled upon bringing in Serene, a woman searching for her missing brother, who held secrets of her own. Attempting to find her brother, Wenzel and Frankly would be introduced to the new storyline. And it was Spencer's job to introduce Serene in the next episode.

However, he couldn't help but deviate from the plans he and Peter had made as he wove in the woman's appearance.

Spencer glanced up from his laptop into the dining room. It was empty now; Cassandra had left an hour or more ago and hadn't returned. Nor had Peter shown his face yet. Aside from Nex, who lay curled by the fireplace on his right, he was completely alone.

"What do you think, bud?" he whispered to the dog. "Will this get me in trouble?"

Nex's amber eyes drifted up to meet his gaze. The dog blinked lazily.

Spencer smirked. "Yeah. Yeah, you're probably right."

He turned back to the computer. "I'm gonna do it anyway."

~

The morning passed in a blur of activity for Spencer. With well over two thousand words under his belt, he rose an hour before lunch to get to the gym. His ankle was still sore, tender from how he'd rolled it on the Merciers' stairs, but he was determined to exercise despite it. He knew life was far from normal—what with Druids on the prowl—but he refused to lose even a fraction of his strength and condition. Not when he might need it to defend himself, his brother, and Cassandra.

Though Peter initially balked at Spencer going out on his own, they'd all agreed: The brothers needed to behave as though everything was normal. Until the marshal closed his investigation, there could be nothing in their daily routine that appeared suspicious to the residents of DeVerre. So Spencer would go to the gym and take his walks while Peter did the grocery shopping and visited the tavern. And one of them would *always* be at Cassandra's side.

When Spencer returned to Occasus, Peter had sandwiches ready for lunch. The trio ate together, Peter offering wild theories about which residents were Druids and who they might be able to trust. After lunch, he suggested they search for the vault once more.

The endeavor greedily consumed the rest of the afternoon. They swept through the lower floor but had only managed to get into Peter's room once more when Spencer glanced at his phone and caught sight of the time.

"We'd better get going," he said. "Owen said he'd meet us in five minutes."

Peter pushed the small bookshelf in his room back against the wall. "Yeah, okay," he muttered, moving to his nightstand.

"What are you doing?" Cassandra asked when he opened the drawer.

Pulling out two metal objects, Peter carefully tucked the smaller of the two in his back pocket. "I'm thinking ahead," he said, then showed them the unloaded handgun they'd recovered from Diane's desk weeks ago. Spencer realized the smaller object had been the clip. "If I had thought to bring this along when we went to check out your place, I never would have gotten these." He gestured to the bruises on his neck, now a dark bluish brown that made Spencer's skin crawl.

Cassandra pursed her lips, a cynical glint in her eyes. "You that good of a shot?"

Peter shrugged. "I'm all right."

"Our Uncle Matt took us to the shooting range now and then," Spencer explained, watching warily as Peter slipped the small weapon into the holster they'd ordered, then concealed it in the waistband of his jeans. "Pete's actually pretty decent at it."

"Hm." Cassandra didn't sound impressed. "Did you get a license to carry?"

"Not yet," Peter replied.

"Then you can't carry it."

While Spencer tended to agree with Cassandra, he couldn't help but feel the same exasperation that echoed in Peter's sigh.

"Look," Peter said, holding his hands out, "if it means the difference between us living and dying, I'll take a misdemeanor. Besides, it isn't even loaded."

"Then why carry it?"

"I have the clip, if I need it."

Cassandra shook her head. "Fine. Just don't get caught, okay?"

"Yes, ma'am." Peter tipped an imaginary hat to her, then flashed Spencer an amused grin.

Hurrying down the stairs for their jackets, the three stepped onto the porch. Peter locked the door as Spencer and Cassandra watched the dogs bounding across the yard. Creamy clouds smeared the blue and gold sky, the sun beginning its early descent in the afternoon. With their late start, the odds were that they wouldn't return to Occasus before nightfall. The memory of their last trip to the lake flashed behind Spencer's eyes—the night when the hellhound attacked. The night that brought them Cassandra and the spirit world along with her.

Peter led them down the steps, Cassandra a few strides ahead of Spencer. He watched her black boots as they disturbed the gravel drive. Anguis and Nex hurried to pad at her side. Her fingers reached down to scratch each dog behind the ears as they went.

Sometimes Spencer thought he should be upset with Cassandra for coming into their lives and bringing all this chaos with her. She'd said it the other day—it was *her* family involved with the Druids. Yet he didn't feel even the slightest tinge of regret at her presence in their lives. Having her around felt natural. Like there had always been something missing, and she was the only one who could fill that gap.

Passing through the front gates, Spencer told the dogs to stay on the property. They both plopped their butts down, ears tucked in forlorn disappointment at being left behind. Spencer smiled at their wiry brows, sure that the dogs were frowning back at him.

The thick pine trees surrounded the road, its flat black macadam a stark relief in the middle of the woods. And up the side of the pavement,

Spencer saw Owen walking toward them. He raised his hand in greeting as the three of them headed his way.

"Afternoon," Owen called as they drew near.

Spencer tipped his chin up in greeting, but Peter spoke, "Do you have something against cars, Professor?"

Owen grinned in that mild manner of his. "I'm a substitute teacher, not a professor," he corrected. "And no, I don't have anything against cars. But I also don't have much need for them."

"I've experienced the hike from Occasus to town and back, and trust me," Peter scoffed, "it requires a car."

"Then I doubt you enjoyed your journey to the lake either," Owen replied, moving for the forest.

Spencer couldn't help chuckling at the memory of Peter attempting to trek through the woods with him the first time they visited the lake. Though Spencer worked out to stay in shape, Peter didn't see the necessity of exercise. And that resulted in him huffing and puffing his way through the tree roots, moss, rocks, and mud.

"Is it a long hike?" Cassandra asked, a concerned expression pulling her eyebrows low.

Their feet ground the pine leaves into the hard-packed dirt as they began their journey, summoning a sharp scent of earth and greenery.

"About half an hour," Owen said, taking the lead. "Have you never been there?"

"No," she admitted.

"Really?" Spencer asked, glancing over his shoulder at her.

Cassandra lingered at the back of the party, moto jacket hanging open over her black knit sweater. "Never had a reason to go."

"Except that it's freakin' beautiful," Peter exclaimed, turning to walk backward as he spoke. "Seriously, it's one of the coolest places I've ever been."

Spencer slapped Peter's back, alerting him just in time to avoid tripping on a jutting rock.

"So—" Peter spun around. "What do you do when you're not substituting, Owen?"

Hands tucked in the pockets of his bomber jacket, Owen walked at an easy pace. "I work primarily as a writer."

Spencer felt his eyes grow wide. "You're a writer too?"

"Yes. Although, I write articles and essays for academic and religious websites and publications rather than fiction."

Spencer supposed the man fit the job. "So, you're a freelancer?"

"In a manner of speaking."

"I used to do that too. In Norfolk."

Owen angled back to look more clearly at Spencer. "You wrote articles?"

"Uh, no," Spencer corrected. "I mostly freelanced as an editor. You know, copy edits and proofreading? But occasionally, I got jobs writing copy for people."

"Did you enjoy it?"

"Not as much as what I'm doing now."

Cassandra's shoulder bumped into Spencer's as she walked past him. "Fighting Druids?"

Spencer chuckled and rubbed the back of his neck. "Writing full time."

"Right," she replied, sarcasm obvious in the singular word.

And Spencer supposed he saw her point. Today was the first time he'd written in what felt like forever.

The group fell silent as they traversed a particularly steep climb. As the first to the top, Owen reached down to help Cassandra up. The pines around them were wet with the cold rain of the previous night. Some of their needles remained frozen from the dropping temperatures. While Owen helped Peter next, Spencer crested the hill by himself. He shivered and pulled his denim jacket tighter, taking a second to roll out his tightening ankle.

"So," Cassandra said as they started again, "now seems as good a time as any for you to tell us more about the Warden."

Resuming the lead, Owen let out a long puff of air. "Where do I start?"

"Why don't you just start with their founding?" Spencer suggested. "What their purpose is, and who they are."

Owen sidestepped a large root. "That's an awful lot to explain," he muttered. "The Warden was founded in the late 1560s by John William Lawrence. You know about him, right?"

"A bit," Spencer confirmed. Cassandra had mentioned John William when she'd first told them about the spirit world. He turned to her for clarification. "Didn't Diane and Liam study his essays or something?"

Her dark brown waves blew across her cheeks in the cold breeze. She reached up a hand to tuck them behind her ear. "That's how they found Elijah's works," she confirmed.

Owen held back a large branch for the three of them. "Right. John William founded the Warden in response to the discovery of the Druids. He lived in Amesbury, UK, near Stonehenge, where he studied the spirit world along with Heinrich Schwarz. They'd heard of ghost sightings and other strange happenings in the area. Schwarz was certain that there was some theological relevance to the phenomenon, so they moved there to investigate, hoping to make a connection to the spirit world referenced in the Bible. While there, Schwarz passed on, and Lawrence continued his legacy. However, they didn't anticipate that their studies would draw the attention of others who wanted to access the spirit world."

A chill ran up Spencer's spine to the base of his neck. He felt sure he already knew Owen's next words.

"In 1567, there was an attack on Amesbury, and the Druids tore the Veil located at Stonehenge."

"Wait," Peter gasped. "There's a Veil at Stonehenge?"

"There *was*," Owen corrected.

"Was?" Spencer repeated.

"It's moved since then."

"They can move?"

Owen shrugged. "I'm not sure how, but yes. According to my understanding, they can move."

As Spencer stared down at the muddy earth, Owen returned to his story. "Lawrence lost most of his friends and family due to the beasts that the Druids released in Amesbury. From that day forward, he knew this study of his and Schwarz's wasn't just some academic or theological pursuit. The world was at stake—these Druids were attempting to find the Veils and unleash the power inside of them. So, he created the Warden to bring their efforts to an end."

"Wow," Peter muttered, meeting Spencer's shocked expression. They both turned to Cassandra, who shook her head in wonder.

Spencer felt like a million new questions had sparked in him but settled for the one at the front of his thoughts. "And that's what you and the Warden do? Work to stop the Druids?"

"That was the original intent, yes."

Spencer narrowed his eyes at the cryptic reply. "And do you follow that intent?"

"Me? Absolutely," Owen insisted. "I've given everything I am to the work of Lawrence. Being raised in a Warden town by Wielder parents taught me early on that our faith isn't just for us. It's for the world. We have a duty and a responsibility to take care of each other. To take care of even those who don't believe what we believe. And I will do everything I can to live up to that charge.

"However. . . ." A dark look crossed Owen's face as he stared through the trees. "Not everyone has the same dedication as my family. And there are Warden members who prioritize their work differently."

"What do you mean?"

Owen hesitated as they walked. Spencer wasn't sure if he was ordering his thoughts or if he didn't want to answer. When he did reply, his tone was tighter than usual, sharp and flat. "The Warden is like any organization. We have passionate members and others who are dispassionate. Ones who value our founder's values and ones who have created their own twist to his words. We have zealots among our ranks, as well as those who treat their membership lazily.

"It's how the human condition works, I suppose," he concluded. "Some of us hold fast to the teaching of our youth, and others wish to use only the parts that suit their personal desires. So, yes, a vast majority of the Warden believes wholeheartedly in pursuing the purpose of our cause. But others are less . . . stalwart in their faith."

Spencer frowned, conflict pressing against his chest. He couldn't help glancing at Cassandra walking at his side. After seeing her dedication to her daily devotional time and hearing Owen speak so profoundly and reverently about their faith, he couldn't help feeling called out. He didn't doubt his beliefs, but he did doubt he was as committed as either of them.

Clearing his throat, Peter seemed to reflect a similar discomfort. "So why isn't all this common knowledge, huh?" he asked. "I mean, we've been in the church our whole lives, and I've never heard about ghosts or phantoms or the Warden or any of this stuff."

Owen grinned. "I wouldn't imagine you had. Neither Lawrence nor Schwarz were looked upon kindly by their fellow theologians in the 1500s. They were labeled as kooks or worse, as heretics. People didn't respect their writings and studies. They thought their work was blasphemous, dealing with witchcraft, necromancy, and other evils."

"Sounds like someone I know," Cassandra muttered.

"Like Ava?" Peter returned.

She gave him a dry grin. "Her too."

A faint scoff came from Owen. "Yes," he sighed. "This dismissal of their work created a gap in history beyond those within the Warden. Everyone who didn't respect them wrote their work off. Most even made sure to ban it from all Christian literature. There grew a staunch line of division between those who listened to Schwarz and Lawrence and those who didn't. And that's why it's so hard to find any information on the Lawrences, the spirit world, and the Warden itself.

"Every bit of information is now held tightly within Warden hands," he explained. "We prize knowledge. Almost to a fault."

"To a fault?" Spencer repeated, confused by his words.

"The Warden is so protective of our history and discoveries that they tend to hoard it," Owen said. "It makes for secure records, but it also means that we aren't good at sharing. Even with our own people at times."

They all paused as they reached the crest of the hill that led to DeVerre Lake. Owen surveyed the area as though seeking out the ghosts they'd come to find, and Peter leaned against a tree catching his breath. However, Cassandra gazed open-mouthed at the view. Spencer couldn't blame her; it was as beautiful as he remembered.

While Spencer gave his aching ankle a rest, he scanned the scenery. Still, serene, and perfect. A gentle fog rose from the glassy surface in the cold late autumn air, mixing with the infinity of pine trees around its edges.

A tug in Spencer's gut pulled him a step closer. There was something about the lake that drew him to it. Something in its atmosphere that created the permeating sense of calm soothing over him, he thought. Its undisturbed perfection. It made him want to walk right up to the water's edge and dive in headfirst, as though the water could drench him in its peace and surround him with its security.

Owen stepped around them, heading closer to the water's rocky bank. "Some of us think it's a problem," he continued. It took a second for Spencer to realign his thoughts to the previous conversation regarding the Warden's secrecy. "There are others who disagree, believing it's better to keep the spirit world confidential and contained. They think that by keeping it controlled in our small circles and towns, we can keep others from exploiting it."

Hearing the disapproval in his tone, Spencer tucked his hands into the pockets of his denim jacket. "But you don't agree?" he asked, falling in line with Peter and Cassandra.

Owen shook his head. "I think it's dangerous. The fewer people who know, the fewer there are to stop the Druids. That's exactly what's happening here in DeVerre."

Peter scrambled over a huge tree root, its tip extending out to disappear under the surface of the glass lake. "That's the point of this, right? For you to teach us so we can help you stop the Druids."

There was a pause as Owen scanned the lake. "True. But I'm not the most qualified for the position."

"I mean, you *are* a teacher."

"You have to know the information to teach it," he returned. "And due to the Warden's secretive nature and hierarchy of trust, there are gaps within my own knowledge. Not every member is allowed full access to the Warden's information. That sort of trust comes with years of service. The longer your family has been in the Warden, the more information they give you. My family moved to Harmony three generations ago, which only gives us fifty years within the organization."

Spencer gaped at him. "Fifty years isn't enough to secure their trust?"

Owen raised his blond eyebrows. "They've been around since the 1500s, Spencer. Most of the families can tie their ancestry back to the Lawrences themselves. Fifty years doesn't prove your loyalty when they've all got centuries."

"These people sound like DeVerreans," Cassandra remarked, crossing her arms.

"Trust me, I'm not in favor of it," Owen said with a hint of bitterness. "As I said, I think it's dangerous. We must be sure that *all* our people can effectively defend against the Druids and protect the Veils. Like this one."

Owen motioned to the pristine, slate-blue waters. Spencer turned toward the lake. It was a Veil, a curtain that led to the spirit world. But how? It was a body of water, as natural as the trees surrounding them and the dirt beneath their feet. How could it house the power of the spirit world?

"You said that the Druids tore the Veil in Amesbury." He looked at Owen. "How?"

The man gave him a mirthless grin. "That's above my pay grade."

"Hm."

"Was it a lake too?" Cassandra asked.

"I don't know that either, to be honest," Owen admitted.

"What do you know?" Peter joked.

Owen chuckled. "Not as much as I'd like." He shifted, beginning to walk around the rest of the water. "I *can* tell you that while I disapprove of the secrecy in general, I do understand the Warden's reasons."

"You do?" Spencer prodded.

"Of course, I do. Not everyone in this world has pure motives. And that includes some of our own members. Beyond that, there are differing opinions amongst our people. Some of our members want to wipe out the Druids altogether. Others believe we should give them a chance to renounce their paganism and join us. They are still created in God's image, after all. But then comes the question of what happens if we give them the chance and they destroy us from within?"

Owen sighed. "That . . . well, that almost happened," he explained, "about eight years ago in a town called Porthaven. I'm not supposed to know about that either, but . . . people talk."

Spencer huffed, thinking of the way news traveled in DeVerre.

Owen tugged down the back of his jacket as he continued. "Porthaven is a perfect example of the Warden growing too confident in their powers and things getting out of hand. A cautionary tale, I suppose. But there are all kinds of debates for and against trying to redeem the Druids. Porthaven is a particularly strong case against it.

"Then, to add to the debates. . . ." He paused to gesture to the lake again. "There's the fact that not everyone holds the same views on how we should handle the Veils. Some believe, as Ava does—that they're too strong and dangerous for us to leave them free. They want them kept a secret and locked away where it's harder for people to access them. Which was the very point of DeVerre in the first place.

"Then, there are people like me," he continued, "who believe that the

Veils serve a purpose. That God didn't put them on Earth for us to ignore. We should use them and channel them for good. For *His* good. Otherwise, we're blatantly disregarding what He's given us."

"So, you think we should be using this Veil?" Cassandra asked, the surprise in her tone mirroring Spencer's internal reaction.

"In a manner of speaking. We don't know enough about the Veils to know how to use them accurately," Owen said. "I believe we should study them. We need to know their purpose so we can put them to proper use."

Spencer nodded, the idea a blend of logic and danger that only increased the conflict he felt in his chest.

"And, of course, there are people who range between those two sides," Owen said. "Wielders or not, most people within the Warden are uncomfortable with how little we know and how much it seems the Druids know. Again, I think that's a flaw in our design. While the higher-ups know a great deal, they don't share it with the rest of us. And that leads me to question if they truly know as much as they're letting on."

"You think they're lying?" Spencer asked.

"I think they're as in the dark as the rest of us." He paused thoughtfully. "At least, most of them. Some say . . . there's a town—I don't know where, but it's the epicenter of Warden knowledge. And it's where our leaders reside."

Spencer narrowed his eyes as Peter spoke. "But you don't know where it is?"

Owen grinned. "That's above my pay grade too."

"What isn't above your pay grade?" Spencer smirked, then ran his hand over his hair as he processed all the information. "Sounds like secrets aren't exclusive to DeVerre."

"Unfortunately, no."

"But you trust them? The Warden?"

"I believe in their cause if that's what you're asking," Owen confirmed. "And yes, I trust most of the members I've interacted with. But there are far more whom I've never met. Including the leadership."

"You've never met the leaders of your own organization?" Peter asked, his expression incredulous.

"Did you ever meet the leaders of Norfolk?"

Peter acquiesced to that defense.

"But you know who they are, right?" Spencer pressed.

"A couple of them."

"And they live in that secret town?" Cassandra asked.

"From what I know."

Pressing his knuckles into his palm, Spencer looked at the water's edge. "How many Warden towns are there?"

"Oh, uh. . . ." Owen huffed, the puff of air turning to fog in the cold. "I'm not sure I've ever heard an exact number. In North America, I'd guess . . . twenty or thirty, maybe. There are several in Europe and a handful throughout the rest of the world, too, from my understanding."

Spencer turned back to him in shock. "There are that many Veils?"

Owen's eyebrows tugged together in confusion before he shook his head. "No, no. There aren't nearly that many. At least, not as far as I know. Just because it's a Warden town doesn't mean a Veil is present. Harmony itself has no Veil. As I mentioned, the Varons brought the Warden to North America via Canada in the 1600s. Their instructions were to spread, so that's what they've done."

"Why spread?" Cassandra prodded him, arms crossed. "What's the point of it?"

"Presumably, to ensure the spirit world's safety," Owen offered. "The Varons received a prophecy telling them to go to Canada, and more than two hundred years later, they learned it was to found DeVerre and protect the Veil. Most of our towns are just places our people can go, and rest assured knowing there are like-minded individuals surrounding them."

"Like communes?" Peter asked.

Owen laughed. "I don't think DeVerre would qualify as a commune, do you?"

"No," Peter agreed with a grin. "So, that Porthaven place: Did it have a Veil?"

The dry lift of Owen's brow told them everything they needed to know.

"Right," Peter chuckled. "Above your pay grade."

Owen shrugged, reaching to tap Cassandra's arm before gesturing to the trees behind them.

As Cassandra followed his direction, so did Peter and Spencer. Thinning branches and the gray trunks of the pines were all Spencer saw even as he narrowed his gaze. "What are we looking at?" he asked.

"There's a ghost there," Owen explained, nodding to the spot in the trees.

Spencer whipped his head around as though he'd suddenly face a ghoul sailing through the air to harass him. But only the trees and fog met his eyes. "Huh," he mumbled, trying to shake off the way his skin crawled at the knowledge of a ghost's presence.

Cassandra nodded, confirming the sighting. "I've talked with him before."

"Me too."

"Is this the same ghost you were talking to the day we caught you up here?" Peter asked, eyes glued to the trees.

Owen turned to Peter, a look of hope in his eyes. "Can you see him?"

"What?" Peter gasped, taking a step back. "Oh, no. Nah, I'm just . . . trying to, I guess."

"Mm, I see. Well, it's not too surprising," Owen said. "While I'm sure both you and Spencer will start seeing them soon, it typically takes time for people to develop into Wielders. Even after they've gone through what you did a few nights ago."

Attempting to slow his heart rate to its normal rhythm, Spencer rolled his shoulders back. "Is that all it takes to become a Wielder? Having experiences with the spirit world?"

Owen shook his head. "Sometimes it doesn't even take that. It's about the measure of faith, not experience. Now, the experience will often help develop our faith. But people like Cassandra—they never need to experience the spirit world. They were born with the faith already implanted in them.

"People like you and Peter?" He tapped his chest. "People like *me*? We need a more personal experience to awaken us to the faith we bear. You'll both become Wielders; of that, I have no doubt. It'll just take some time."

"Do you think. . . ." Spencer looked at the glassy water once more before lifting his eyes to meet Cassandra's copper and jade gaze. He turned back to Owen. "Do you think Cassandra didn't need the experience because she lived near a Veil as a kid?"

"It's possible," Owen admitted. "I don't know how it all works, honestly."

Spencer scrunched up his nose, feeling that the past hour had done little to give him answers. "Doesn't it frustrate you?" he demanded. "Having all these questions? All these things you don't know?"

Owen's response was patient. "That's life, Spencer. Life itself is a mystery. If we can't learn to appreciate that, we will never find the joy within it."

CHAPTER SEVEN

Peter

They stayed at the lake until the sun had sunk low on the horizon. The shadowy forest grew to a haunting level of creepiness. While Owen and Cassandra attempted talking with the half dozen ghosts they came across, Peter and Spencer stood watching. It was weird enough that their friends could see things the brothers couldn't, but hearing them carry on their one-sided conversations while the silence of the frosted forest permeated the lulls in their exchanges made Peter question his sanity.

"You really think they see something?" Peter whispered to Spencer as they hovered a few feet back, leaning against a large tree near the lake.

Spencer shrugged, his eyes glued to the duo and the supposed ghost. "We trust them, right?"

"I guess."

Spencer threw a perturbed glance his way.

"Okay, yeah, fine. We trust them." Peter released a sigh. "But this is freakin' me out."

"Me too."

After each short talk with the ghosts, Owen and Cassandra returned defeated.

A fact that didn't appear to phase Owen. "This is how it always is," he explained. "I've only met two ghosts in all my time here that have been willing to carry on a conversation that lasted longer than two minutes."

"Who were they?" Cassandra asked.

"Glen Alarie and Clarence Mercier."

Peter's brows shot up in recognition of both last names. "Any relation to the other Alaries and Merciers we know?"

Cassandra took a deep, knowing intake of air. "Glen was Gerard's father," she said, eyes drifting through the fog as though looking for him. "He wasn't a very kind man. Talkative, though."

"He's the one I was talking to a few weeks ago when you saw me up here," Owen explained, motioning to Peter and Spencer. "Glen isn't particularly knowledgeable about the town, but he does like to exchange information. He died young—when his youngest was only two. Glen is interested in knowing what happened to his family. I tell him what's going on in the town, and he tells me stories about DeVerre in the early 1900s."

"And the Mercier ghost?" Spencer prompted.

"Clarence," Owen reminded them. "He's a different story. He knows about the spirit world and the fact that people are involved in it. However, he doesn't know much beyond that. And he's an angry sort of man. He wanted to destroy the spirit world if he could."

Cassandra shifted uncomfortably from foot to foot, chewing on her bottom lip. Her eyes were on the dirt at her feet. "Clarence was Mike's father's name."

"Mike?" Peter gasped. "As in Mike Mercier, Debbie's husband? The guy you lived with, and we decided couldn't be a Druid?"

Cassandra nodded.

"Are we sure he's not a Druid?" Spencer asked, an almost imperceptible shiver shaking his shoulders. Whether it was from the cold or the conversation about ghosts, Peter didn't know. He'd popped up the collar of his denim jacket to block out the wind, but it was so ratty that the corners flopped helplessly.

Owen shook his head at the idea, his light eyebrows pulling together. "It's not likely," he said. "Clarence was clearly *not* a Druid. And if Mike learned anything from his father, I doubt he would have approved of Debbie's activities."

"If he knew about Debbie's activities," Cassandra muttered.

Peter wondered at that. Was it possible for a husband not to realize that his wife was a murderer? Could he have been that blind?

But then Debbie had hidden it from Cassandra. And Owen hid that he was a Wielder from Ava. Perhaps lying to your family wasn't quite as hard as he anticipated.

"Do you still talk to Clarence?" Spencer asked.

"No," Owen said. "I learned what he knows, and while I offered to visit him from time to time, he either stays away intentionally, or our paths simply don't cross anymore."

"What if he's found peace?" Cassandra suggested.

"It's possible but not likely. He told me he can't let go until the 'demons' are removed from his town."

Peter gaped at him, but it was Spencer who gasped out, "Demons?"

"He didn't know the term Druid," Owen explained. "And he'd heard enough stories to determine that whoever wielded the spirit world was dabbling in dark works. His inaccuracy didn't matter much to him when I remarked on it."

"Hmph." Peter sagged against the side of the tree beside him. "So, what? The rest of the ghosts just aren't willing to help?"

"No," Owen said while Cassandra shook her head.

"Why?" Spencer asked.

"My best guess?" Owen tossed a hand to the woods around them. "They're all Druids."

"What?"

"To my understanding, which is admittedly limited, Druids *always* become ghosts. It's part of their dogma, I believe. They hold onto the world because they believe it is their eternal home. They can't move on because to do so would mean giving up their eventual reincarnation."

Peter grimaced. "Sounds like a fun group of people."

"But they could name the Druids for us," Spencer said. "We don't even need them to tell us. If we just find out their names—"

"Most won't give us their names," Cassandra interrupted. "Every time we try to talk to them, the only thing they're willing to say is that we should give up, stop looking, find someone else to talk to, or all of the above."

"Some of them have told me I'm in over my head," Owen added. "Which is probably true. But the real problem is, regardless of their names, we wouldn't know who were Druids and who were people like Ava and Clarence: against the spirit world entirely on principle. Until they answer us, we can't jump to conclusions."

"Great," Peter grumbled, then rose and stretched. "Well, should we head back, then? It's gonna be a pain to get back to Occasus in the dark."

"It's not like we haven't done it before," Spencer retorted.

Peter shoved his shoulder in reply.

The hike home left Peter with the distinct feeling that he'd never be warm again. Despite the activity and energy required to keep their footing as they climbed the rocks and rises of the forest, the impending winter had firmly sunk its teeth into DeVerre, unwilling to let go. As the sun made a final descent behind the trees and only a small wash of orange still stained the horizon, even the physical exertion couldn't keep them warm.

The sight of Occasus's wrought iron gates brought a sigh of relief to Peter as he shivered again. He, Spencer, and Cassandra all made for the gate, but Owen stopped at the edge of the road. "I've got to go," he said, tossing a thumb in the direction of town. "Ava's expecting me home for dinner."

"Right." Peter nodded, reaching to give Owen's arm a slap of gratitude. "Thanks for everything, man. Let us know if you have any other thoughts or suggestions."

"Actually," Owen scanned them purposefully, "I do have a suggestion: You three need to go to the game tonight."

"The game?" Cassandra asked, frowning.

Owen zipped up his jacket, the cold finally reaching him. "It's the final softball game of the season. If you don't show up, people will be suspicious. And it'll give you a good start toward making more friends in this town."

"Ah, yeah. Makes sense, I guess." Peter turned to Spencer and Cassandra to see if they were up for an evening of socializing. He couldn't say he felt like attempting to investigate tonight, but he was growing tired of hanging around Occasus as they had the past two days. As little as he cared about sports, Peter thought the idea of the game sounded fun. They could sit on the bleachers with Anna and Haley, grab some nachos, and forget about their troubles for a little while.

But the frown creasing Spencer's forehead didn't reflect the same optimism. "Uh, Pete?"

"Sup?" he asked, surprised by the worry in his brother's expression.

"I don't think you can go."

"Why not?" he demanded.

Spencer tapped his own neck. "People will notice."

Peter's hand rushed up to brush the bruises there. He'd noticed them when he rose that morning. They looked like bands wrapped tightly around his throat; they felt that way too. But they didn't stop at his neck. They twisted across his arms and torso all the way to his legs. Their deep bluish-purplish-brown hue made him want to gag at the memory of the scylla's tentacles choking the air out of him.

A heavy sigh escaped Owen. He moved toward Peter. "Let me see," he ordered.

"What?" Peter asked.

"I can fix it."

"You can, what?" Spencer gasped.

Cassandra looked no less awed. "You can heal people?"

Owen moved slowly and carefully as he moved Peter's collar out of the way. Peter flinched as the man set cold fingers on his neck. The bruises were tender, and Peter couldn't help instinctively tensing as Owen prodded him.

"Relax," Owen said, eyes on the bruises instead of Peter's face.

"Dude, your hands are around my neck," Peter grumbled. "It's kinda hard to relax under these conditions."

A mild grin crossed Owen's face, gaze focused on his hands. A small flash of amber energy erupted around Peter's neck, curling between Owen's fingers. He'd barely seen it, but Spencer and Cassandra's gasps told him it hadn't been a trick of his eyes.

"Holy crap," Spencer muttered, stunned as Owen backed away from Peter.

Cassandra pressed both hands over her smile. "That's amazing," she whispered, the words muffled beneath her fingers. "Can . . . can anyone . . . ?"

Peter's hand went reflexively to his neck, the sharp sting he expected at the touch shockingly absent.

"Like I've said before—" Owen looked over at Cassandra, hands back at his sides. "Technically, yes, anyone *can*. But this is a far more advanced ability."

The three stared at him in awe as he began to back down the road. "Have a good night," Owen said. "And let me know if you learn anything."

"Thanks," Peter called.

Owen dipped his head in a humble nod. "Anytime."

~

It didn't matter how many times he saw it, Peter kept stopping in front of the mirror to stare at the spotless skin on his neck. He knew it shouldn't surprise him. He'd seen so many crazy things over the past couple of weeks, why should something as simple as healed bruises be a shock?

Still, as Peter changed out of his muddy boots and exchanged his thin Henley for a thick thermal, he kept checking his reflection, expecting the dark welts to have returned.

Between the chaos of Cassandra's statement at the station, searching for the vault, getting Owen up to date, and talking to ghosts, Peter had done quite a good job forgetting that he'd almost died. He'd let the distraction of their planning keep him from remembering that terrifying reality. Now the immediacy of distraction had faded.

As Peter stared into the mirror, he couldn't stop the flashes that sprang into his mind. The memory of rushing for Debbie. Pushing her to the ground as she thrust her hand forward, commanding the scylla to attack. The way their tentacles snapped out, wrapping around his legs, then coiling across the rest of his body with impossible speed. Flexible limbs with painful, sucker-like protrusions attaching themselves to his skin. The pressure tugging at his flesh through the fabric of his clothing, creating massive bands of bruises across his chest, arms, and legs.

Once the scylla's tentacles had wormed around his neck, they'd twisted to cut off his air. As they squeezed his chest to clear his lungs, Peter realized he was going to die.

A shiver shook Peter out of his stupor, and he forced himself to turn away from the mirror.

They were gone now; all the bruises had disappeared entirely.

Yet even once he'd fully dressed, precisely mussed his hair, and hidden the gun safely in his waistband, he couldn't stop himself from standing in front of his dresser to once more stare into the vintage mirror and investigate his neck just in case.

The shadow of dark brown stubble that he really should clean up was all he found.

Despite the bruises' disappearance, Peter could still feel the phantom itch they'd left behind. That was why he couldn't stop checking. It felt like the bruises were lying under the surface, hidden but still creeping under his skin.

They were gone, Peter assured himself. Truly, completely gone.

Peter tugged on the now too-tight collar of the crew neck. It rubbed the base of his neck raw, constantly reminding him of his near death.

Grabbing a heavy flannel on the way out of his room, Peter shrugged it on as he hurried down the staircase. Spencer was already sitting on the couch with his ratty denim jacket, spinning the keys around his finger as he held a book in the other hand. His eyes focused on the page, feet propped on the coffee table.

"Where's Cass?" Peter asked, peering into the living room to see Gerard on the far sofa, lounging as he read his own novel.

"Upstairs," Spencer muttered.

"Still?" Peter exclaimed as he took his jacket out of the coat closet. "We're gonna be late."

"It's a softball game." Gerard tossed him a superior glare. "No one will care if you're late."

Peter set his hands on his hips, leveling a return glare at the phantom. "You haven't been out in a while, Gerry, so forgive me if I don't take your advice on social awareness."

"You're one to talk about social awareness," Cassandra said, appearing behind him in her moto jacket. A thick, knitted scarf hung around her neck.

"What's that supposed to mean?" Peter asked, brow pinching together.

"Don't worry about it," she said, patting his shoulder as she turned to Spencer. "Ready to go?"

"Yep." Spencer tucked a bookmark into the pages of his novel, then dropped it on the coffee table.

The cold November air hit them with full force as they stepped through the front door. Peter zipped up his leather jacket, rushing for the Jeep. "Why do they still play softball this late in the year?" he grumbled.

Cassandra shrugged, following beside him. "First, the cold doesn't bother us like it does you Southerners."

"We're not Southern," Peter argued. "We're from Virginia."

"That's the South."

"We don't even have accents."

Her smirk as they climbed into the Jeep said she disagreed. "Second," she continued, leaning forward between the front seats to look at him. "It's DeVerre's only form of entertainment. As long as there isn't any snow, they find a way to play."

"When does it start to snow?" Spencer asked, backing up to turn and drive out of the gates.

"Any day now."

Peter tucked his hands under his arms. "I think I'm gonna need a heavier jacket."

The softball field sat next to the school on the far side of Harmony Plaza. So many vehicles filled the parking lot that Spencer had to pull the Jeep to the side of the road along with several other vehicles. Townspeople wandered from their cars, trucks, and SUVs to the field, cutting it as close on time as the brothers and Cassandra. A handful of other families arrived after them, clusters of people working their way across the sidewalk and frosted grass to the ball field.

Jostling their way through the crowd, Peter scanned the field. The players were finishing their warm-up drills, a handful wearing hoodies over their t-shirts—blue for the Angels, black for the Ravens. He caught sight of the reverend, Samuel Chapelle, as he tossed the ball with the town doctor, Alexander Frossard. Their two biggest suspects.

Samuel and Alexander looked little alike, Peter thought, his eyes on the men as they neared the field. In fact, with his ruddy complexion and reddish-brown hair, Samuel stood out like a sore thumb amongst the rest of DeVerre. He was on the shorter side of average, near Peter's height, and a good ten years younger than the doctor across from him.

And Alexander? Well, he looked just like his son—the jerk who'd broken Anna's heart. Not unexpected, he supposed, with the perfect genes that got passed down through the family. Even at fifty-something, Alexander had maintained his golden blond hair that now shone under the stadium lighting. He was broad-shouldered, muscular, and had the firm jawline of a Greek god. Beyond that, Ava's report on how the town looked up to Alexander and his family could have easily been literal as well as metaphorical. The man's towering height made him easy to spot in the crowd.

Packed bleachers caused the spectators to crowd the walkways with camping chairs and fill the grass with blankets. Though everyone had bundled in sweaters, beanies, and scarves, no one paid much mind to the cold that nipped at their noses. Groups bunched together, chatting and greeting newcomers as they waited for the game to start.

Despite the sense of anticipation, this gathering was nowhere near as enthusiastic as the previous games that Peter and Spencer had attended. The chatter was a hush rather than its usual rumble. No one moved with any sense of excitement or pep. And when people caught sight of Peter, Spencer, and Cassandra making their way up the sidewalk, they instantly fell silent and began nudging their neighbor.

As they drew near, a handful of the onlookers passed them somber smiles. A few muttered condolences to Cassandra, although no one moved to engage in actual conversation with her.

Pressing closer to Spencer, Cassandra returned each person's sympathy with a polite nod and appropriately solemn expression. The chatter rose as they progressed closer to the center of the crowd, nearing the field as more and more people took notice of the trio.

Spencer slipped his hands into his jacket pockets, chin tucked. Peter knew that all this attention bothered his brother. Spencer wasn't a fan of large social gatherings on a good day; this would be even worse. The way everyone was staring at them, Peter felt the tension rising in his own shoulders.

But instead of recoiling from it, he held his head high. They couldn't let the people of DeVerre think they had any reason to be uncomfortable in the spotlight. As far as the town was concerned, they'd had nothing to do with Debbie's accident. And they needed it to stay that way.

"Hey, Peter," a familiar, cheery voice called, drawing the trio's attention to their left. Anna waved at them from the bleachers, Haley at her side.

Peter smiled, tapping Spencer's arm in a command to follow before he headed for the women. "Hey! You got room up there for a few more?" he asked, looking up to where they sat near the top of the metal seats.

Anna scanned the people surrounding her on the bench, and Peter did the same. Haley sat to her left, curly blonde hair puffing out from under her white beanie. There were several others whom Peter didn't recognize farther down the row, but nearest him on Anna's right was a pretty brunette he thought he'd met before. Her thick, black-brown hair draped around her shoulders, accentuating her light, tawny complexion.

While Haley and Anna asked for people to make room, Peter turned to the young woman. "Hey, we've met, haven't we? Danielle, right?"

Large brown eyes met Peter's as the woman stared back at him in surprise. "Uh . . . yeah," she replied, her voice soft.

"You're in Anna's Bible study?"

"Uh-huh."

"We went bowling together. I'm Pete; this is Spence."

"I remember."

"Cool." He motioned back behind himself. "That's our friend, Cass."

Just then, Anna waved for Danielle to scoot down so the three of them could climb up. However, when Danielle stood, it was to jump down from the bleachers. She was so short she hardly reached Peter's shoulder. "That's all right, Anna. I'll sit on the end," she said, then turned her kind smile on the three of them and gestured to the seats. "After you."

Though surprised by her offer, Peter decided not to ignore it. "Thanks," he said, hoisting himself onto the bleachers to take his seat next to Anna.

Gentleman that he was, Spencer graciously let Cassandra go up before him, which left him to sit next to Danielle. Peter felt slightly bad for the girl, knowing she'd be stuck with little conversation far from her friends and with only Spencer for company. But she'd chosen her lot.

No sooner had they exchanged their greetings and taken their seats than Samuel stepped onto the pitcher's mound in his blue uniform. Everyone fell silent as he faced the crowd, the autumnal wind sweeping up some of his bright hair when he removed his ball cap. "Good evening, DeVerre," he said, wearing a compassionate smile as he scanned the people. "We start every game with a prayer, but tonight's will be a bit different."

Cassandra squirmed next to Peter, and he nudged her arm with his elbow in encouragement.

"In light of the unfortunate events on Tuesday night," the reverend continued, "we'd like to take the time to offer up a prayer for the Mercier family. Would you all bow with me?"

The crowd did as instructed. Peter, Spencer, and Cassandra followed suit a fraction of a second later.

Peter stared at his hands between his knees the whole prayer. It bothered him, pretending to pray for the woman who'd tried to kill them—twice. Who'd almost succeeded—twice. It was wrong, wasn't it? They were praying for a woman to recover when she was actively trying to destroy them all.

Or maybe, he thought, not all of them.

Maybe the Druids were here tonight.

It seemed likely.

Muttering an amen that he didn't feel, Peter worked to relax as he looked up. Everyone around them kept glancing over at Cassandra, but she didn't return their stares. Instead, she kept her eyes on Samuel as he returned to the dugout.

Attempting to ignore the onlookers, Peter turned to Haley. "What's Aaron up to tonight?"

Her ever-joyful smile beamed as bright as the lights overhead. "He's hanging out with Owen and Ava," she explained, then looped her arm through Anna's, huddling closer in the cold.

As opposite as they were, Haley and Aaron were one of the best couples Peter thought he'd ever met. Talkative, bubbly Haley never seemed to mind that Aaron Lambert was a hermit who preferred cars and video games to everyone but his own family. Peter often wondered at how friendly the young man was to him and Spencer. It was as though once Anna had chosen to befriend Peter and Spencer, the rest of the family decided that perhaps the Collins brothers were worth a careful consideration as well.

And that boded well for their mission, Peter thought. Anna had a way with people. She was good at making them feel cared for and important. And if she had been able to make her standoffish older siblings give Peter and Spencer a chance, then the odds of her getting the Frossards to do the same looked favorable.

After all, Peter reminded himself, Giana Frossard had said herself that Anna's endorsement was the best in town.

The game went on at a leisurely pace, and Peter tried not to shiver each time the wind blew through. Giana was sitting at the base of their stands, surrounded by several other middle-aged women as they cheered on their husbands. Soon the Angels were leading 5-0, and those women were practically ecstatic with pride.

As Alexander came up to bat, Giana called out, "Hit it out of the park, Alex!"

Her husband turned around, winked at her, and took his place in the batter's box.

Peter scowled at the display. Whether or not they needed to earn the couple's approval, he couldn't help the intense dislike that settled into him whenever he saw the Frossard family. Maybe it was the overly perfect façade they put forward. Or maybe it was how they seemed to have the whole town wrapped around their fingers. Perhaps it was because of their family's strange connection to his own.

He told himself that it *didn't* have anything to do with their son or the inexplicable urge of competition he felt toward him.

When Alexander did, in fact, hit it out of the park, the bleachers erupted around them. Peter stayed in his seat, clapping in concession as even Anna jumped up beside him. Giana turned around to give Anna a high-five before hugging the brunette woman beside her. It was utter nonsense.

Yet, as Anna sat down, Peter thought this might be his chance to take a stride toward their goals. Dropping his voice, Peter leaned closer to Anna as she took her seat. "Hey, if it's none of my business, feel free to tell me, but. . . ."

Her dark brown eyes met his in confusion.

"You doing okay? You know, being friends with the Frossards and not. . . ."

Anna's smile faltered, but she recovered quickly. Several curly wisps of hair danced around her face as she nodded. "Yeah, I'm fine, Pete," she promised in a whisper. "Gia and Alex have always been wonderful and I—I can't be mad at them for. . . ."

"That's awfully mature of you."

She let out a huff. "I don't know if it's maturity. More like horrified embarrassment."

Peter bumped his shoulder against hers. "There's nothing for *you* to be embarrassed about."

"I guess not."

Though Peter typically would have taken the time to assure her that in no way was she in the wrong, he felt the urgency of their situation pressing in on him as the final inning approached. He needed to do something to further their connection to the Frossards, to ask Anna to introduce them to Alexander after the game. They'd met Giana in the past, but maybe Anna could draw them all into a conversation together. But how did he make a request like that sound natural?

"By the way," Anna said, voice still low. "There's an afterparty at The Glass Tavern for the winning team."

"So, for the Angels," he surmised with the now 7-0 score giving the Ravens only one more chance to bat.

She smiled. "Yeah. Gia told me to invite whoever I want if the Angels win, so . . . if you guys want, you should join."

"That sounds great," he exclaimed, thrilled to receive an invitation to hobnob with DeVerre's elite with almost no effort of his own.

Suddenly, laughter burst out from Peter's right. He whipped his head around, shocked to hear his brother's deep, full laugh blending with another of a far more feminine quality.

At the end of the bleachers, Spencer and Danielle were practically doubled over from whatever it was they'd found so amusing. She had her hand on his arm, trying to speak again through her laughter. "Hold on," she gasped. "Hold on. You're not serious."

"I am," Spencer insisted.

Frowning, Peter turned to Cassandra, who was sitting ramrod straight on the bench between him and his brother. "What's happening over there?" he whispered to her.

Cassandra turned an irritated smirk his way, her dark eyes full of something he was sure couldn't be anything other than rage. "Spence has found your biggest fan," she replied, tone as hard as her glare.

"*My* biggest fan?"

"No. Yours. As in both of you."

"What are you talking about?"

"She reads *Wenzel & Frankly.*"

"Oh." Peter looked at Danielle with renewed interest.

The young woman and Spencer seemed to have regained their composure once again. She was listening with rapt attention—both hands back in her lap—while he explained something about his personal writing process to her.

"Huh," Peter muttered. "I guess that's cool."

"Yeah, it's splendid."

An unintentional chuckle escaped Peter at the jealousy in her tone.

He thought about telling her not to worry about it. Spencer wasn't interested in Danielle any more than any other girl. But as he glanced down at his brother, he got a distinct impression that maybe he was wrong. After all, Danielle did have a dark and mysterious attractiveness that resembled Cassandra's. And she'd managed to get his typically quiet brother chatting as though they were old friends.

No, Peter thought. There was no way that Spencer had suddenly found the gumption to flirt with a girl when Cassandra was sitting right next to him. Absolutely not.

Peter frowned, turning back to the game. At least, he certainly hoped not.

CHAPTER EIGHT

Cassandra

After being stared at the entire softball game only to be subjected to the disdainful reception of DeVerre's elite at the afterparty, Cassandra couldn't help the feeling that the town was watching her. As though they were all waiting for her to slip, giving them a chance to point their fingers at her as the cause of the fire, the cause of Debbie's catatonic state.

The paranoia curled in her chest like a cat, snuggling up next to the guilt that had made its home there four nights ago.

Cassandra hated it—the guilt that came with killing someone. The feeling that if people found out, they'd see her as a murderer. A monster. All for saving the lives of her friends.

Even Spencer had admitted that he thought they may have made the wrong choice, impossible as it had been. If he thought she'd done the wrong thing, then there was no doubt in her mind that the whole town would judge her for her crime far before they heard her case. But the problem was, she couldn't blame them.

Still holding onto life or not, Cassandra had killed Debbie. The use of her power had ripped the woman's soul to shreds. No matter if her body breathed on, the woman was not there.

Ever since that night, Cassandra had wondered if that's what Debbie would have done to them. Would she have left them like that? Soulless. Lifeless. Hollow shells of dust and atoms held together but void of life.

The more Cassandra learned, the more she realized how twisted up in this world her whole family was. How high the odds were that she was fighting her own flesh and blood. And she couldn't help wondering if this was who she'd been born to be. If the Sauveterres were Druids, then what about the Clements? Did her parents know? Was that why they'd taken her away? Because they didn't want her to be like the rest of their family?

In the soft yellow and gray light of the partly cloudy morning, Cassandra stared at herself in the oval bathroom mirror. Like everything else in Diane's house, the gilded golden frame of the mirror was an antique specially chosen to restore the mansion to its former glory. It hid the fact that its owner was as unsure of her identity as Cassandra was.

Was it worth it, Cassandra wondered, getting answers if it led to this? If it led to her becoming a killer?

Frowning at her own image, Cassandra tightened her jaw. She was a killer already, wasn't she? If she kept going, it was likely to be only the first of many deaths by her hand.

A fact that even the bystanders of DeVerre had seemed to suspect last night.

Cassandra had learned how to read people over the years. Their subtle glances and body language said far more than words ever could. Actions proved feelings—not words. And the actions of DeVerre were haughty, dubious, and damning.

Those sentiments had come through most clearly when Anna led them to where Giana Frossard stood talking with a fellow Angels' wife. Cassandra recognized the woman at Giana's side but could no more place a name to her face with its sleek brown hair and rich tan than she could

90% of the room's occupants. She'd been five when her parents took her from DeVerre; she didn't remember the names of anyone she'd known then who weren't direct family members. And when she'd moved back, she only spent time with Diane—which meant additional relationships were as unlikely as they were unwelcome.

While Giana nodded politely in greeting toward Peter and Spencer, saying, "pleasure to see you boys again," she'd turned hard, calculating blue eyes on Cassandra. "Yes, it's nice to officially meet you, Cassandra. I was so sorry to hear about your family. Have you heard any news? How is Debbie?"

The inquiry sounded perfectly innocent, but it rang false in Cassandra's ears. "As good as can be expected, it seems. Still in a coma," she replied. Her father had called her again that morning to give her an update and make another request that she come to Spokane to be there for her mother and Debbie's family.

"I suppose that's good news," Giana remarked, glancing at her friend with a sorrowful smile. Then she resumed her glare. "Your mother's accident also resulted in a coma, didn't it?"

"It did."

"And how long did that last?"

"About two months."

"Is that usual? Do the doctors believe Debbie will require that long to recover as well?"

Cassandra pulled in a long breath as the interrogation continued. "I honestly don't know."

"Mm. Well, our whole family is praying for her and the rest of your own family, dear," she promised, an artificial glimmer in her icy eyes. "Do you have any plans to go home?"

That made Cassandra's back go rigid. "I'm not sure. Possibly."

"Good," Giana said, emphasizing the word. "I'm sure it would mean the world to your family."

She delivered the words kindly enough, but Cassandra got a distinct impression that it was a threat. The same sort of threat that brought Debbie's words back to her. *"You could have lived if you had just stayed home."*

"I'm sure it would," Cassandra managed to reply, working not to grind her teeth noticeably.

But Giana didn't notice. In fact, she dismissed Cassandra and the Collins brothers altogether then, turning to talk with Anna, a glow of admiration on her face as she rubbed the young woman's arm. She seemed all charm and support to the Lambert girl. A tarnish on Anna's otherwise impeccable veneer if Cassandra had been asked.

The rest of the party had continued in a similar fashion. Peter seemed to enjoy himself, hanging out at Anna's side most of the night and working hard to schmooze the high society members of DeVerre. He seemed to do a decent job of it.

With no interest in getting involved in the conversation around her, Cassandra stuck with Spencer at the start of the party. Which proved to be the worst decision she could have made.

Danielle MacDonald had effectively locked down Spencer's attention, constantly talking about *Wenzel & Frankly*, asking him questions about the writing process, and even asking after Anguis and Nex. It turned out that Danielle was one of the churchgoers who'd volunteered to take care of the dogs while Diane's will was in probate. It was the most Cassandra had heard Spencer talk in all her time of knowing him. Which was admittedly not long. But still. The guy hardly ever said a word, and now he was chatting with this stunning brunette who hung on his every word like they'd been best friends forever?

Cassandra didn't like it. She might not have known many of the townspeople by sight, but she knew their names well enough to know that the MacDonalds had ties to the Frossards. Both through loyalty and through marriage. And she didn't like the way Giana kept staring at them from across the room.

When Danielle excused herself to use the restroom, Cassandra had taken the opportunity to warn Spencer. "Be careful," she whispered.

"What?" Spencer asked, hands comfortably tucked into his jacket pockets.

"She's a MacDonald."

His bushy eyebrows drew together. "Why is that a problem?"

"The Frossards and MacDonalds are very close."

Spencer leaned nearer, dropping his voice even lower. "I thought we wanted to be close to the Frossards too?"

"Only so much as it proves whether they're innocent or guilty."

"I still don't see what that has to do with anything."

"Spencer." She frowned at him, sure that he should be smarter than that.

"What?"

"Be *careful*."

"With what?" he demanded, the question as tense as it was quiet.

Cassandra could feel that her smirk displayed her absolute bewilderment. "Why do you think she's talking to you?"

"Oh, come on, Cass." He scoffed. "You sound like Peter."

Pressing her lips together, Cassandra wanted to punch him for being such a clueless idiot. But she didn't get a chance for any sort of rebuttal since Danielle had returned just then.

Uninterested in listening to the two of them continue to flirt like school kids, Cassandra excused herself to get another drink. She wound up choosing to sit at the bar with her second old fashioned rather than get involved in another conversation she wanted no part of. The solitude didn't last as Samuel Chapelle stepped up to the bar, a half-drank pint of beer in his hand. "Mind if I join you for a moment?" he asked, motioning to the barstool beside her.

Cassandra scanned the reverend. Still dressed in his uniform from the game, the royal blue of his shirt made his cool gaze even brighter. A pleasant expression kept his presence unthreatening in nature. But she knew from past experience that the reverend had little desire for her to stay in DeVerre.

Feeling that she had no choice, Cassandra gave him a nod.

Samuel took his seat, setting the pint glass on the counter. "I won't bother you long," he promised. "I just wanted to check in. How are you? Have you spoken with your family recently?"

"I have," she admitted. "And I'm fine. Considering everything."

If Samuel was put off by her terse responses, he didn't show it. "I'm glad to hear that. Is there anything I or my wife or the church could do for you? We'd like to be a help in whatever way we can."

Holding the reverend's steady stare, Cassandra couldn't help considering it to be rather impassive. He was doing his job here. He didn't actually care if she needed help. If he did, he would have helped her and Diane years ago.

Cassandra gave Samuel a polite, if dismissive, smile before turning back to her drink. "I appreciate it, Reverend. But I'm perfectly taken care of."

Accepting her rejection, Samuel muttered a cordial condolence along with his farewell. And Cassandra was alone once again.

For the remainder of the evening, she listened as the large crowd of people gossiped and chattered behind her. The night reminded her of her earliest days in DeVerre. The days when she sat with Debbie and Mike at church but really didn't participate in any other social events.

Now in the freshly dawned morning of the next day, Cassandra walked out of the en suite bathroom and into Diane's room. She hadn't lied when she'd told Spencer she liked being in the woman's space. It felt nice, living where Diane used to live and sleeping where she used to sleep. As if she was residing in a constant hug from the wonderful old woman.

Diane Larkin was the first person Cassandra had ever met who knew what it was to be a true outsider in the world. And being without her made her feel as though she were drifting out into the void of isolation once again.

When she'd first returned to DeVerre, Cassandra had begun looking for answers on her own. She'd gone to the library, earning herself a lecture from Ava when she'd requested books on the supernatural within DeVerre. Though they'd not been open with one another about *why* it was that Cassandra was researching the subject, she'd sworn off trying to befriend the librarian or her family from that day forward.

And after several failed attempts to cultivate friendships with anyone else who might have an interest in the spirit world, Cassandra had determined to take one last shot at getting something out of the reverend. As it had been Samuel Chapelle's father who told Cassandra's parents to take her from DeVerre in the first place, she'd been dubious of his help. And she'd been right.

When she tried to ask him about ghosts within DeVerre, he'd quickly shut her down, insisting that ghosts weren't real. He'd quoted the Bible to her and emphatically encouraged her not to seek out darkness. But she'd heard all that and more from her theology professors in college. And she wasn't about to give up just because they hadn't had the same experiences she had.

Cassandra had earned a bad reputation within her first couple weeks back in DeVerre. People avoided her. They called her crazy—albeit in whispers, but she still heard.

One Sunday morning, Diane approached her at the church. Evidently, the older woman had heard rumors about her in a similar manner to the rumors Cassandra had heard about Diane. Despite how long she'd lived there, the DeVerreans still carried on their wild gossip about the reclusive woman who wrote about ghosts.

"Good afternoon," Diane had said when she'd stepped up to Cassandra's side after the church service. "I'm Diane Larkin. I hear that you have an interest in ghosts. Is that correct?"

Peter and Spencer reminded Cassandra of her friend. They weren't exact replicas by any means. But there were enough similarities that made her smile. Like their hooded, intent gazes, their thin-lipped smiles, and pale, but rosy complexions. Diane was trim like the brothers as well but with a far more willowy frame. She even shared those bright blue eyes that Spencer had inherited.

Cassandra's instinct was to assume that everyone wanted to talk her out of her beliefs. But she'd heard enough about Diane to feel certain that wasn't the woman's agenda.

Standing in the sanctuary those four years ago, Cassandra had stared at Diane, wide-eyed. She wondered why she hadn't thought to go to her in the first place. "Uh, yeah," she'd said. "Yeah, I study them."

A warm, knowing smile spread across Diane's face at that. The lights above created a halo-like effect on her white hair, which she'd pulled back in a tight, low bun. She wore a dark gray dress with handkerchief-like layers under a lighter gray cardigan. A tiny golden brooch of the sun was pinned to the cardigan, and a trio of multi-metaled chains hung in layers around her neck. She was nothing if not eclectic. And somehow the most sophisticated person in DeVerre.

"So do I," Diane had said, her voice as comforting and calm as her gentle gaze. "I'd love to discuss the topic with you sometime if you have an interest."

"That'd be amazing," Cassandra hurried to say.

"Wonderful. Why don't you come by Occasus for lunch soon?"

"Sure, that—that would be great. Does tomorrow work?"

Diane's soft laugh was infectious. "Yes, that works just fine."

And that was the beginning. Diane and Cassandra met weekly at first, discussing the less serious aspects of ghosts and their sightings. It took almost two full months of their meetings before Diane admitted to knowing about Cassandra's past, having heard the gossip about the little girl who talked to ghosts.

"I remember your parents taking you from town," Diane had said. "I wanted to say something. To stop them. It didn't seem right to me—them taking you from your home. But Liam was worried that it would bring trouble our way, and he talked me out of saying anything. I've regretted that for some time now."

Cassandra had told her everything after that. And Diane did the same.

She'd introduced Cassandra to what the spirit world really was. She'd shown her Elijah Lawrence's essays, as well as her and Liam's research from over the years. It was like Cassandra's eyes were suddenly opened after over twenty years of being blind. She finally understood so much about who she was, and yet she still knew so little.

Over the following three years, Diane had become more family to Cassandra than any Clement, Sauveterre, or Mercier ever had been.

And now, Diane was gone.

Cassandra eyed the bed on the far side of the room. Its four grand posters stretched high toward the vaulted ceiling within the alcove of the turret. Cloudy light poured in from the windows on all sides. This room held so many memories of Diane. Journals and research. Pictures and trinkets. Gifts from Liam and letters from the Collinses in Norfolk.

Moving to the dresser, Cassandra ran her fingers over the golden tray, three glass bottles glinting on its surface. She lifted the perfume to her nose, breathing in the soft scent of gardenia and tuberose. If she closed her eyes and imagined hard enough, she thought she might still hear Diane's voice. Perhaps she could even feel her presence in the room with her.

But it wasn't Diane's presence that she felt.

It was no one.

The geometric ridges of the perfume bottle bit into Cassandra's palm as she gripped it tighter to keep her hands from shaking. A slight ringing of silence cut through her ears. A reminder in the emptiness of the room of what she'd lost.

Then there was an extra pressure on the cold, thread-like sensation that sat at the base of her skull. An unspoken request—almost a knock— on the back of her mind from Gerard. She could always sense when he was near. Or wanted to be near. And this was his way of asking to make an appearance.

Cassandra set the perfume bottle back on the tray, the glass tinkling against the metal. She felt Gerard's arrival behind her. She didn't bother turning to acknowledge him. Instead, she reached for the earrings on the dresser—the only pair she had left.

"You seem irritated," Gerard remarked.

Cassandra slipped the back of her earring in place, eyes fluttering up to look at him through the mirror above the dresser. "What makes you say that?"

He smirked. "Your sunny disposition."

Cassandra returned the amused grin. "I could lighten up, couldn't I? Just because my family is filled with murderers and Druids doesn't mean I have to take up the family business. I can just be a murderer."

Arms crossed over his chest, Gerard leaned against the black marble fireplace. "I've known plenty of murderers in my time, Cass, and trust me when I say you don't qualify."

Cassandra didn't care to debate definitions with the phantom. Not when her mind kept reeling back to the fear that Debbie had been right; maybe she should have stayed home.

Next to the tray of perfume and lotion rested an antique jewelry box of porcelain and gold. Cassandra lifted the lid, peering in at all Diane's brooches, necklaces, and bracelets. The woman had liked to accessorize, so the box nearly overflowed with all the pieces. But there was one small velvet square that held a singular, sacred piece of jewelry.

Careful not to touch the tiny golden bracelet lest she tarnish it, Cassandra ran a finger along the cream velvet tray it sat in. It was a simple piece, a child's trinket. *My mother gave it to me,* Diane's memory reminded her. *She called me her sunshine.*

Cassandra stared at the small pendant dangling from the thin chain. A little sun charm, beaming brightly. She smiled forlornly at the bracelet. "Diane always was obsessed with the sun," she whispered.

"She named her house after it," Gerard muttered.

Cassandra nodded but didn't look up from the bracelet. "You know it was murder?" she asked for what felt like the millionth time. She had to get confirmation. She had to know she wasn't pursuing a false sense of justice.

Gerard's deep voice rumbled to her. "I can't lie to you, Cassandra. You know that."

Taking a deep breath, Cassandra shut the jewelry box. She did know that. It was one of the first rules she'd given him—he couldn't hurt anyone, he had to listen to Diane, and he couldn't lie to Cassandra. She'd never doubted any of Gerard's words because she knew the phantom was incapable of withholding the truth.

Cassandra turned then, moving to the chair beside the fireplace where she kept her messenger bag. She paused, standing at Gerard's side before looking up at him. "Thank you," she said. "For being with her when I couldn't be."

Gerard had been with Diane in her final moments. He'd told Cassandra how the woman fell ill, complaining of stomach pains and nausea first, then in the final few hours of a tingling that spread throughout her limbs. She'd lain on the couch while Gerard sat on the coffee table. The tether to Occasus allowed Gerard to touch inanimate objects, anything devoid of life. But in Diane's final moments, he'd not even been able to hold her hand.

Gerard's dark brown eyes locked onto hers as he took a measured breath in and out. "Little good it did."

"I'm sure it did more than you know." She went to pat his arm before remembering his immaterial form.

Gerard caught the gesture and quirked his brow.

"Sorry," she said with a scoff. "I don't know what I was thinking."

"In the past three years, you've never made that mistake," he said, his voice gruff and unyielding. "What's the one thing that's changed since then?"

Confused by his accusatory tone, Cassandra scrunched up her nose. "What are you talking about?"

"Those boys are making you soft."

An incredulous breath escaped her. "Excuse me?"

Gerard stepped forward, pointing a finger to his chest. "You made me promises, Cassandra."

She dropped his gaze, the accused realizing her guilt.

"When was the last time you looked for my family's murderer?" he demanded.

Staring at the Turkish rug, Cassandra reached for her ring. Somehow the woven swirls of gold, orange, and blue wool beneath her feet gave her a distinct impression of condemnation. "I've been distracted," she whispered.

"I know."

"I haven't forgotten."

"This is a two-way street, Cassandra," he reminded her. "You help me, and I help you."

"I haven't forgotten," she repeated, hardening her tone as she met his glare once more. "And I *will* find them. But surely you understand that a seventy-year-old cold case isn't really priority right now."

Anger flared in his eyes.

"No one is going to get you answers if I die," she snapped.

"And you think those boys are going to protect you?"

She shrugged in confirmation. "They've promised to."

"They can't even protect themselves."

"Seems to me they've done a decent job up until now."

"You're the only reason they're alive, and they know it," he spat. "They don't care about your protection. They care about their own."

Cassandra glared at him but couldn't find a retort to throw back. Not when he was speaking the truth that she'd so blatantly tried to ignore for the past four days.

"You heard what that one said," he mocked, leaning down toward her. " 'Without you, we're just a couple of writers who happened to inherit a house.' "

Her jaw clenched as he echoed Spencer's words back at her.

"They know," he hissed. "They know that the second you die, they die. Just like me."

Cassandra crossed her arms, taking a step back to free herself from the oppressive cloud of Gerard's bitterness. But it didn't help. His words wormed their way into her head, confirming what she already knew.

"They don't love you any more than they love me," he growled, head angled down toward her. The shadows from the cloudy morning caused his angular face to appear even sharper and his dark eyes even deeper. "Those boys only care about each other and their damn stories. If they have to throw you to the wolves to keep each other alive, they will."

Shaking her head forcefully, Cassandra tried to push away his warning. "Don't be ridiculous."

"Have you forgotten how quickly they betrayed you? That they believed that shrew of a librarian over you?"

Cassandra's breath caught in her throat. He was right. It hurt her, the way they'd lost faith in her so quickly. But she couldn't blame them for it, could she? Not when she knew better than to trust anyone in DeVerre. Even them.

"I understand your situation, Cassie," Gerard said, his tone softening as the fury faded in his eyes. He looked truly compassionate as the corners of his mouth turned down, his long, dark hair hanging around his face. "Of all people, I understand. Seventy years of isolation can make a man do things he never thought himself capable of. I know you lost Diane. I know that it's hard. But if you let your loneliness allow you to forget that those boys have brought more danger into your life than answers, then you *will* die next time."

Unable to hold his weighty stare, Cassandra dropped her eyes to the rug again. His words cut her deeply. She *was* lonely. She'd been lonely for the past twenty-four years. And only Diane had brought her respite from her solitude.

And then the Collins brothers had come to DeVerre.

In the midst of losing Diane and fearing the plunge back into isolation, Peter and Spencer appeared in her life. They'd given her hope. As foolish as it might have been, she'd instantly felt drawn to the brothers. Not only were they a reminder of her lost friend, they were better in some ways. They were her age. They were funny. They were friendly. Less mentors and more peers. The feeling was startling for someone who'd not had true friends most of her life.

It was immediate, the connection she'd felt to them. Peter naturally felt like a brother to her. More so than even Isaac. He was protective, caring, and affectionate in his own weird way.

And Spencer . . . well, he felt like something Cassandra had been looking for, for a long time. Like someone she could rely on. Someone who made her feel seen. Someone who made her feel strong and good and needed.

The thoughts made Cassandra's fingers twitch, desperate to grasp her ring and twist it round and round for eternity.

"You're already getting too comfortable with them," Gerard warned, his tone sharp once more. "You're teasing them and cuddling up to them and pretending they're your family. But they aren't."

"Then who is?" Cassandra demanded, eyes flashing up to his. "You?"

He blinked.

"I can't even call my own relatives family anymore." Her voice came out in a low hiss. "Debbie tried to kill me. My parents took me from DeVerre with full knowledge that I belonged here. Clement, Mercier, Sauveterre—whatever the hell else I am, none of my 'family' is anything of the kind."

Cassandra tossed her hand back toward Diane's bed. "The one person I could trust is dead. And I'm more alone than ever." The words tore out of her with more emotion than she knew she'd been holding. Painfully, they ripped through her throat as tears welled in her eyes. "If I can't trust those brothers, who can I trust?"

Her question was met with silence.

Gerard had no more answers than her.

Dropping her hands to her sides, Cassandra allowed the emptiness and hopelessness of the last three months to crush her. Her mother's accident and extended coma. The repressive stint of living in Spokane while she recovered. The news of Diane's death. The inability to properly mourn her closest friend. Her whole family begging her not to return to DeVerre. Finding a hellhound chasing Peter and Spencer. Saving their lives. Meeting them. Discovering the missing pages. Meeting Owen. Learning about the Warden and the Druids and the fact that her very life was in danger. Killing Debbie.

It was too much.

And it wasn't going to stop.

Cassandra sighed, reaching down to grab the messenger bag from the chair beside her. "All right," she said, turning back to Gerard. "You're right, I haven't been holding up my side of the bargain."

Gerard's eyes narrowed.

"You interested in doing some research?" she prompted.

"Have I ever wanted to research?" he countered.

"No, but I thought you might this time."

"Why would I?"

"Because I'm going to research your family."

The phantom raised his head. "Why?"

"I thought you wanted to know who killed them."

A slow, sly grin spread over Gerard's face. "Well, look at that." His deep voice lost its usual gravelly undertone as his eyes lit up. "You gonna stop flirting with that boy long enough to get me some answers, Cassie?"

Knowing the jab shouldn't sting as much as it did, Cassandra returned his good-humored smile. "I'm just following through on my promise. Besides," she walked to the door, "I can always flirt with him later."

Opening the bedroom door, Cassandra came face-to-face with Peter. He stood with a hand in the air, primed to knock. He looked like a kid caught in the act of sneaking a cookie before dinner, mouth hanging ajar and eyes shifting from a look of joy to horror as he saw her face.

"Ah, hey!" Peter snapped out a pair of finger guns and chuckled nervously. "I was, uh—I was just coming to talk to you."

Cassandra refused to let the heat building in her neck reach her face as she wondered how much he'd heard through the old, not-so-well-sealed doors of Occasus. She leaned against the doorknob, holding his gaze with a confidence she didn't feel. "What's up?"

Peter's eyes drifted beyond her to where she was sure Gerard was hovering in the background before landing on her. "I, uh—well, the, uh—the marshal is here."

A cold tingle swept down from Cassandra's crown as the blood rushed from her head. "What?"

"Yeah." Peter wore a grimace as he glanced toward the staircase. "He said he needs to talk with us."

There was a pause as Peter tugged at his collar. His worried brown eyes met hers. "All of us."

Cassandra

The marshal sat waiting with Spencer in the living room, a steaming cup of coffee in his hands. His dark brown jacket draped over the arm of the couch. He turned when Cassandra and Peter entered, mouth set in a determined line.

"Miss Clement," Tom greeted with a nod.

Cassandra couldn't find any words to reply as the question of *why* he'd come back to Occasus rang in her head. Had he figured it out? Had someone seen them at the Merciers' and stepped forward? Was he here to arrest her?

Still, she managed a nod in return, taking a seat next to Spencer. The scene practically replicated the events of Wednesday morning. Tom was on one couch while Spencer and Peter sat on either side of her. She could even sense Gerard in the room as well; his hidden presence hovered somewhere in the office at her back. But there was something different about the way the marshal eyed them today. There was a fresh air of assertiveness about his shoulders as he sat upright, a clarity in the way his gaze scanned them.

"You said you needed to talk with us?" Spencer prompted, his voice unusually rigid.

Tom continued to study them, his dark eyes flickering to Spencer. They darted back to Cassandra.

Raising her chin, she stared back. Even as her heart pounded in her chest, she knew she couldn't look away. She couldn't give him any reason to think she was guilty.

"Yes," Tom finally replied. He took a sip from the ceramic mug, then rested it on his thigh. "The investigation of the Mercier housefire and Debbie's strange condition has taken an unexpected turn."

The breath caught in Cassandra's chest, but she refused to show any sign of fear. Instead, she held the marshal's stare, leaning forward to show her surprise and attention.

"Unexpected, how?" Peter asked, instantly belligerent.

The marshal barely spared him a glance, his attention solely focused on Cassandra. "It appears there was a struggle."

"A struggle?" Cassandra repeated, the words heavy on her tongue.

A single nod. "A fight."

"A fight? Between whom?"

"That's an excellent question," he said, his inflection like the words were an accusation themselves.

To her right, Spencer's knee began to bounce. "I'm confused," he said. "If you don't have the answers, why are you here? Are you looking for suspects? Our thoughts on who may have wanted to hurt her?"

"No."

"Then why *are* you here?" Peter demanded. "Just to make Cass feel bad about her family's situation?"

Now, Tom turned to level an annoyed glare at Peter. "Because I need more information, Mr. Collins. If there was an attack at the Merciers' residence, it means someone caused Debbie's condition—whether accidentally or otherwise. And it means the fire itself *wasn't* an accident."

In her periphery, Cassandra caught the way Spencer's jaw tightened. If the brothers had one flaw, it would be their inability to lie.

Tightening her own poker face, Cassandra tried to draw the marshal's attention back to her. "Why would someone attack Debbie? Or start a fire?"

"To cover up her murder?"

Cassandra blinked. "But she's alive."

"Maybe they thought she was dead," Tom suggested. "Perhaps in the struggle, Debbie fell and hit her head. Perhaps the assailant thought she was dead, and in their panic, they decided to burn the house around her, hoping it would deter a murder investigation."

"When did you notice signs of a struggle?" Peter asked abruptly.

Tom narrowed his eyes. "What?"

"When did you first notice signs of a struggle?" he repeated like he was talking to a child.

The marshal's lips curled up in irritation. "When we searched the crime scene and collected evidence."

"So . . . Tuesday night?"

There was a beat of silence as Tom considered the question. "Yes."

"And you're just now informing us that you're suspicious of foul play?" Peter shook his head, a sly grin on his lips. "The math doesn't add up, Kojak. Are you here to accuse us or not?"

The marshal's thick mustache twitched. "You're a disrespectful pain in the ass, you know that, right?"

"I've been told that from time to time."

Tom continued to glare at him, fire in his eyes. "I am here," he spat with a great deal of anger despite his steady voice, "to ask for your help."

Cassandra was sure none of them had expected this turn of events.

Spencer's knee stopped bouncing and he sat up in surprise. Even Peter's jaw dropped open as his eyebrows shot up.

"There are questions coming up," Tom continued as they all stared at him dumbfounded. "Questions which make it clear that this goes deeper than I want it to. I'm beginning to suspect my friends and . . . I don't like that. I want answers."

"What makes you think that *we* can get them for you?" Spencer asked.

Tom swallowed what looked like an impossibly large pill. "Because you're the only ones that I can trust."

Everyone but the marshal froze. Cassandra wanted to scoff at his words. The marshal trusted *them*? Why? What could make them more trustworthy than the people he'd grown up with? The town filled with his friends and family? How could he ever think *they* were the ones he should trust?

A conversation she'd overheard last night in the dimly lit tavern drifted back to Cassandra. Two men had stood at the bar waiting for their beers. They hadn't paid attention to Cassandra as she sat scrolling through the latest episode of *Wenzel & Frankly* on her phone. But she'd listened as they'd grumbled. And it hadn't been the first time she'd heard the same complaints that night.

"I understand why you're here," Cassandra said.

Tom looked perturbed but didn't respond.

"Last night, I overheard several men talking at the tavern," she explained. "They were complaining about what a poor job you're doing. Saying you can't even catch a rabid wolf to keep the town safe. They suggested getting someone else to do the job."

Now Tom looked irate. But he didn't direct the anger at her. It wasn't news to him. He knew that the townspeople were after his job, and *they* were the recipients of his fury.

"You're afraid to lose your job, so you're coming to us for the answers you can't find."

Her words seemed to be all the invitation the marshal needed. He sat forward, plunking the coffee mug onto the table before him. "I need to know how many of you are Wielders," he demanded.

An intense silence fell over the room. A fierce autumn breeze hummed in time with Cassandra's pulse, thudding in her ears. Occasus creaked as clouds covered the morning sun.

Cassandra glanced at Spencer, then Peter. Both mirrored her shock. The marshal knew about Wielders? Did that mean he knew about the spirit world too? About the Veil? Was he a Druid? If so, why would he ask for their help? Why would he reveal his knowledge? If he was their enemy, he could easily kill them and cover up the crime.

"What are you talking about?" Cassandra managed to eke out.

Tom didn't appear fazed by their surprise. "Don't play stupid with me. I know at least one of you is a Wielder, and I need your help."

"We offered to help you weeks ago, man," Peter returned. "You didn't seem to appreciate the gesture."

The marshal glared at him. "I had no reason to accept your help before."

"What reason do you have now?" Peter countered. "We don't even know what you're talking about. What's a Wielder?"

Tom slicked back his dark brown hair, revealing large patches of gray at his temples. "Listen, I don't care about your pride, son," he shot back. "I'm not in the business of catering to narcissistic boys who don't know when to grow up and be a man."

Peter bristled, and Spencer placed a hand over his mouth to cover an irritated grimace.

Cassandra set a forestalling hand to Peter's arm, eyes still glued on the marshal. "What do you want from us?" she asked, tone even and controlled.

"You asked three days ago if I knew anything about your past in DeVerre. Well, I do," he said, holding her stare. "Sam is my best friend. His father was the one who told your parents to take you away."

"I remember."

"Do you also remember that Sam didn't approve?"

Cassandra felt her eyes go wide.

"I know what you are," he continued when she gave no reply. "I've known since your teacher caused that uproar twenty-five years ago."

She considered denying it, playing dumb to the whole idea of Wielders, but she didn't see a reason anymore. "Then why ask?"

"Because I wanted to give you a chance to be honest with me."

"Because you wanted to test me," she argued.

"In a way," he admitted, tilting his head in acknowledgement. "But the fact is, I already know you're a Wielder. What I don't know is if these two are." He swept his finger toward Peter and Spencer.

Sitting up straight in her seat, Cassandra didn't speak, and the brothers held their silence along with her.

Tom heaved a sigh. "Fine." He tossed a hand in their direction like he was dismissing their refusal. "But let me make myself perfectly clear: I've known for months now that those wolf attacks were nothing of the kind. And I know that you three couldn't have orchestrated any of them. How do I know that? Because you two," he pointed to Peter and Spencer, "weren't here for Taylor's death. And you," he shifted to Cassandra, "weren't here for any of them. No matter how much this town would like to blame you three, there's no way you could be involved."

For the first time since Debbie's betrayal, Cassandra felt a glimmer of hope as the marshal scooted to the edge of the couch, his brown eyes pleading with them. "Something is going on in DeVerre," he insisted. "Something that's been going on for far longer than any of you three have been alive."

They stared back at him in shock.

"Hell," Tom added. "It's been goin' on since before *I* was born."

This was the moment they'd been waiting for, Cassandra realized. A moment of connection that would finally give them the insight into this town that they so desperately needed.

"What do you know?" Cassandra asked.

Tom met her gaze. "What do *you* know?"

She gave him a dry grin. "You may say that you trust us. But I'm afraid we don't trust you, Marshal."

Tom's thick caterpillar-like eyebrows hung over his eyes as he inspected them. He was still suspicious despite the little trust he'd given them. He had to be. It was his job to suspect everyone.

But Cassandra was patient. And she was just as suspicious as him. He hadn't had a trusted family member attempt to kill him four days ago. He hadn't learned that Druids filled his family tree. He hadn't had to become a killer himself.

At least not to Cassandra's knowledge.

With a dip of his chin, Tom conceded. "My father taught me everything I know," he explained, "just as his father taught him. It isn't much, but . . . it's enough for me to take care of our people."

He sighed, running a hand over his face. Cassandra could see in the dark circles under his eyes that this was weighing on him more than he let on. His hard exterior was cracking under the pressure of unknown forces.

"It *was* enough," he restated, the words a heavy admission. "It's not anymore."

Tom paused, eyes distant from the internal debate he was considering. He looked straight at Cassandra. "This town was once full of people like you," he said, voice heavy. "People who could reach into the spirit world and use its powers. My father explained that a century ago, the citizens of DeVerre stopped trusting those people. They chose to fight against them, banning their powers from the records and histories to eradicate it. No one was supposed to teach their children about the spirit world anymore, helping the truth to disappear. And to rid the town of the powers altogether."

Cassandra gripped the side of her thigh, too familiar with the methods of DeVerre when it came to eradicating connections to the spirit world.

"Some people didn't listen," Tom continued. "Some of them—like my great-grandfather—passed the knowledge down as a means of protection, knowing that should the powers ever resurface, there needed to be people who knew how to combat it. Others must have continued using it for personal gain. People, I suspect, like Debbie Mercier."

Heartbeat spiking, Cassandra struggled not to reveal her emotions at this admission of the marshal's.

"I don't know what they're up to," Tom said. "And I have no clue who else she was working with, but . . . *something* is going on. And I want to make it stop. But I need help."

A tense silence hung in the room as Cassandra checked with Peter and Spencer again. The brothers were staring around her at each other, a silent conversation passing between them. It seemed too good to be true, too easy to have a founding family member come to them asking for an alliance.

"Why?" Peter finally asked, turning back to Tom. "Why trust *us*? We're outsiders."

"That's *why* I trust you," Tom said. "You're all outsiders in your own ways. People don't associate with you here, which tells me that you aren't working with those other Wielders, mucking everything up.

"Miss Clement was right." He gestured to her. "The town is getting restless. Three deaths from a wolf that we can't seem to find? Sam's daughter crying werewolf? Now Debbie's terrifying condition and the fire? They're scared. And they're starting to lose faith in me."

Peter brushed his thumb against the bridge of his nose, the look on his face suggesting that he might agree with the citizens.

Cassandra didn't share the sentiment. "You realize that some of them are the ones doing this, right?" she prodded. "Your own family and friends could be the ones murdering people."

"Yes," Tom insisted, nodding. His eyes were wide, and his brow furrowed in worry. "That's why I'm here. I can't trust anyone anymore, and I hate it. I don't want to think that the people I care about could do this. But . . . my suspect list is only growing. And I'm running out of time."

His eyes shifted back to Cassandra. "I know you're a Wielder," he repeated. "I don't know exactly what that means, but I know it means you have more insight than I do. And I also know that whatever happened to Debbie was caused by a Wielder."

Cassandra's heart thumped double time.

"It's unnatural," he continued, "the way she . . . well, her condition. But I don't know who did it."

With a slow sigh, Cassandra met his gaze. "I did."

Peter and Spencer shot each other looks of horror at her admission.

Tom's eyebrows pulled into a straight line.

"It was me," Cassandra admitted once more. "You're right. There is way more going on in DeVerre than you understand. And Debbie was one of the ones murdering people."

The seconds ticked slowly as Tom ran a hand over his mouth, tweaking his mustache.

Spencer inched closer to Cassandra's side as the marshal watched them, as if he were going to leap up to defend her if Tom tried anything.

But Tom stayed in his seat. "Like I said, I was suspicious of Debbie."

"She wasn't alone," Cassandra said.

"I didn't think it would be just one," he said, nodding. "Does that mean that Mike . . . ?"

"We don't think so."

"How?"

Cassandra shrugged. "She lied to me my entire life. Why couldn't she lie to her husband too?"

Still brushing his mustache in thought, Tom's eyes went blank. "Who then?"

"We don't know."

He waved a hand toward Peter and Spencer on either side of her. "They're helping you?"

She nodded.

"You're both Wielders, then?"

The brothers shared a look.

"Not yet," Peter admitted.

Tom dropped his hand to his chin. He seemed to be fighting against his next words. Like he knew he needed to say them but didn't want to.

A small grimace tugged on his mouth before he asked, "Will you help me?"

Peter and Spencer turned to each other, then to Cassandra. They were following her lead now. She'd revealed them, choosing to trust the marshal when he'd suggested his distrust of Debbie. It was a risk, she knew. One that could very well get them killed. But it could just as easily save their lives.

"Yes," Cassandra said, meeting Tom's desperate brown stare. "So long as you help us."

That confused the marshal. "I assumed—I did expect it to be a sort of . . . partnership. Us working together."

"Yes, but the fact is," Cassandra tipped an eyebrow up, "just like you need to know the things we know, *we* need to know the things that you know."

"Specifically, the history of DeVerre," Spencer jumped in upon the marshal's lingering confusion. "We need to know why the town chose to cover up the spirit world and the existence of Wielders and . . . all of it. We need to know everything that your family has kept secret."

Tom raised his chin, understanding sinking in. "Yes, of course. It's a lot of information, but I can make time now if—"

Spencer shook his head, cutting him off. "Not now."

"Why not?"

Cassandra's thoughts echoed the marshal's words.

Spencer met her and Peter's questioning gazes. "We have a friend," he explained to Tom, "and he would be very interested in hearing this too."

Peter reached around Cassandra to pat Spencer's shoulder. She smirked, realizing his forethought. Owen would jump at the chance to get the answers he'd been searching for over the past decade. They couldn't exclude him from the conversation with the marshal.

"You've got a friend?" Tom asked, the tilt of his brow dubious.

"Shocking, isn't it?" Peter retorted.

"Could you come back Monday afternoon?" Spencer asked.

"You remember me saying I'm running out of time, don't you?" Tom tossed a thumb over his shoulder in the direction of town. "The longer I wait to get answers, the more opportunity I give people like Tony MacDonald to turn everyone against me."

The name of MacDonald made Cassandra purse her lips and toss Spencer an "I told you so" look.

Spencer didn't seem to catch her ire. "While I'd love to say that our exchange of information will change everything, I doubt it'll be that simple," he admitted.

"And Monday is the soonest we can meet?"

"I'm afraid so."

"Fine," Tom sighed. He slapped his hands to his thighs, beginning to rise.

Peter and Spencer followed his lead. Cassandra watched from the couch.

Tom eyed them a moment longer as he pulled on his jacket. He cleared his throat, hand resting on his thick work belt. "I'd be remiss if I didn't say thank you," he muttered, voice low and tense. As though he didn't like displaying gratitude. Or he just didn't like feeling grateful to the Collins brothers. But he met their gazes in turn, the sentiment plain on his haggard face. "So, thank you."

As Spencer walked the marshal to the door, Cassandra kept her seat, hands in a white-knuckled grip on her lap. The relief of having law enforcement on their side hadn't kicked in yet, nor had the excitement that they'd finally get some answers.

Staring at the signet ring, barely visible in her death grip, she knew why: It didn't matter what information Tom Garnier was able to give them. Her family was involved. The problem was that she didn't know just how involved they were. And she was afraid to find out.

The hall on the top floor of Occasus had only one small, hexagonal window by the stairs. It let little light into the narrow passageway, allowing the shadows to cling to the corridor even at its brightest.

Cassandra walked to the door at the far end of the hall, Gerard following at a close, steady stride. After Tom left and the brothers decided to take the time to discuss plot lines for *Wenzel & Frankly*, she'd taken the opportunity to return to her earlier task—getting answers for Gerard.

Now Cassandra rested her hand on the handle of the spare room on the third floor of Occasus, hesitating before she depressed the vintage latch. The room was another reminder of Diane that caused her memories to flash and her emotions to rise.

Diane had shared everything with Cassandra, including the details of her search for her parents. Yet, she'd kept this room a secret. And each time Cassandra asked to help her with the search, Diane had shaken her head, giving her a small, forlorn smile. "No, dear," she'd say, the words often accompanied by a pat on the hand. "I'm afraid this is a personal journey. One that I must walk alone."

Entering the small, rounded room, Cassandra thought she finally understood Diane's need for privacy. She felt similarly hesitant admitting to Peter and Spencer that she was sure her family knew something about the Druids. And she knew that this research into Gerard's past had little to do with keeping her promise to the phantom at all. She knew that digging into his history would help her find answers about her own. The Alaries were as old as the Sauveterres; following his family line would give her an excuse to track her mother's line simultaneously.

Ignoring the boxes piled off to the right of the room that held information about the Collins family, Cassandra approached the simple wooden desk sitting against the far wall. She took a seat, slipping her messenger bag from her shoulder. Pulling the binder and laptop from its main pocket, she set herself up for her research.

Gerard shut the door before beginning to pace behind Cassandra. Since he was dead, she knew he wouldn't get tired or his feet sore. But it still felt strange to have him wander the room instead of sitting at her side as Peter or Spencer would.

With no other chair to offer him, Cassandra kept the thought to herself. "All right," she said as the computer booted up. She lifted the stack of papers off the desk—the list of residents from the 1950s that Diane and Gerard had worked up. "So, we're looking for your brother."

"No," he corrected. "We're looking for evidence that my brother killed my wife and child."

"Well, we aren't going to find that on a list of names, Gerard."

"Then what are we doing up here, Cassandra?"

She threw him an annoyed frown, unwilling to admit the selfishness of her search. "We're trying to find out if there are any connections between your brother and the rest of the strange stuff going on in DeVerre. We're looking for a motive."

"And looking at a list of names will help us find motive?"

"Possibly. If nothing else, it'll give us an idea of the people he spent time with, and that will give us an idea of whom he might have confided in."

Gerard crossed his arms. "If you're trying to figure out if my brother was a Druid, you don't need that list. I can tell you: He was."

Cassandra spun around in her seat. "He was?"

"Yes."

"And you didn't think to share this information with us before?"

Gerard shrugged. "I didn't know their moniker until that Warden man showed up."

"His name is Owen."

He shrugged. "I don't like him."

"Why? Because he can break your tether?"

"Because he reminds me of all the other sanctimonious bastards I grew up around in this town."

Cassandra frowned at him. "Owen is a good man. And he's helping us. When Peter and Spencer were suspicious of me, *he* came to me. He *trusted* me."

"Doesn't mean I have to like him."

"Fine," she replied. "Don't like him. You don't like anyone anyway."

"I like you," he contradicted. "I liked Diane."

"How sweet of you."

"Are you going to find my evidence? Or did we come up here to discuss whom I do and don't like?"

Turning to the desk, Cassandra shifted through the research pages to find Gerard's brother's name. "You're sure Franklin was a Druid?"

"As positive as I can be without him having said so to my face," he confirmed. "And if you're looking for motive, I have that answer for you too."

"You do?"

Gerard came to stand by her side at the desk. It was odd having him so close. She knew he was a phantom, but he looked so real that she always expected to feel the warmth of a human radiating off his form. Instead, she could only feel the thread of his spirit coming from the tether she'd created to bind him to the house.

Reaching forward, Gerard flicked his brother's name on the paper, and it snapped between her fingers. "He wanted me to join them," he said.

"He wanted you to join the Druids?"

"That's not how he said it, but yes, that's what I'm assuming they were now. He said that we were powerful, that our family was powerful, and we'd denied our ancestry for too long. Letting the 'elite' of DeVerre treat us like dirt under their nails while we had just as much right to power as them." Gerard scoffed. "That we could show them just how powerful we were. Together."

Cassandra frowned, having felt the direct disapproval of the DeVerre nobility herself the previous night. Were they the same elite that Franklin had referenced? It seemed likely. The Frossards, Chapelles, Guillaumes, and MacDonalds were all part of the governing influence of the town. And, as far as Cassandra knew, they had been for years.

Returning her thoughts to Gerard's explanation, Cassandra looked over at him, where he hovered at her shoulder. "And you didn't care to join him?"

"No," he growled. "Our whole lives, my family faced the ridicule and scorn of the same people who shared ancestry with the Alaries. And he wanted to buddy up with them so he could be just like them. I had no interest in their false sense of prestige. I was happy—small and pitiful as my life might have been."

Cassandra never knew quite what to say when he spoke to her about his family. He was always careful with his words, never fully speaking their names or referencing them. He mainly ranted about what he'd lost and demanded revenge—justice, he called it.

Sighing, Cassandra tried to reconcile this new knowledge with all the other information she'd learned. "All right, so Franklin was a Druid, and he wanted you to be one too. Why is that motive?"

"Because I said no."

"And you think he killed your wife and child because you rejected him?"

He leveled her with a hard glare that she knew was the only answer she'd get.

Chewing on the inside of her lip, Cassandra turned back to the papers. "How do we prove it?"

"I spent two whole years trying to figure that out, and it got me here. I don't need any more proof. I know it was him. Now I need justice."

"I can't get you justice without evidence, Gerard. And what are we going to do with that evidence anyway? It isn't like Tom can arrest your brother when he's six feet under."

A strange quirk tugged on Gerard's lips, like he was trying not to smile. Or the expression might have been a suppressed snarl, Cassandra thought.

Instead, he set a hand on the back of her chair, leaning down by her ear, his next words whispered in a fierce snarl. "I want *justice*, Cassandra," he demanded. "And as I'm dead, it's now a justice only you can give me."

Turning to look at him, Cassandra thought she should have flinched from his nearness. But she didn't feel any inclination to draw away from him. Instead, she held his glare, sure she knew what he was suggesting. "You said it this morning, Gerard: I'm not a murderer."

"It isn't murder if it's revenge."

She frowned at him.

"And you've already killed once."

She scoffed as she turned away, the comment cutting deep. "That's some twisted sense of ethics you have."

"An eye for an eye, Cassandra. Your own Bible says that. I've read it many times."

She shook her head at the suggestion, knowing that all her theological arguments would fall deaf on his ears.

"A life for a life."

Her head snapped back to glare at him. "I'm not going to kill an innocent person for you, Gerard."

He was silent and still, only his right eye giving a single twitch.

Cassandra held his furious glare with equal fervor.

"They aren't innocent," he finally replied, voice cold. "They're his children. His blood. Druids, like him."

"Do you know that?" she demanded. "Do you know that his children became Druids?"

"If he killed my family because I refused to become one, do you think he'd give his children any other choice?"

"I'm not killing someone to satisfy your own perverted sense of justice."

"You promised me, Cass."

"I promised that I'd help you find the truth."

"You promised me *justice*."

"Justice isn't murdering someone who had nothing to do with your wife and child's death!" She spat the words, rage bubbling in her chest. She worked to keep her voice from rising wildly. Whatever madness of Gerard's she was fighting to combat, she couldn't let the brothers hear her below. She couldn't lose control—no matter what sort of monster Gerard wanted her to become for him.

"I will help you find out if Franklin killed them," she promised, anger warping her raspy voice. "I will get you evidence. But I will not murder for you!"

He continued to glare at her but pushed away and returned to pacing.

Cassandra knew his mind hadn't changed. He was only biding his time now. Working to find another way to convince her. To manipulate her into doing his bidding. She trusted Gerard not to lie to her, but that didn't mean she believed in his goodness.

Letting him brood, Cassandra scanned for Franklin Alarie's name on the page. The paper shook as her hands trembled from the residual anger that burned within her, so she laid it on the desk, flattening it with her palm so she could make sense of the typed lines. Diane had scribbled a couple of notes next to his name: *G's brother — teacher*.

With a jolt of hope, Cassandra felt her emotions begin to cool.

Franklin had been a teacher.

Tossing the papers aside, Cassandra pulled up the document tab on Diane's computer. Her friend had created her own list of DeVerre's genealogy on her laptop based on Gerard's information, and she knew the information she needed would be there.

The document was easy to find, and she scrolled through its first few pages before she found Gerard's family tree. She took note of Diane's tracking system—names, dates of birth and death, marital status and spouse name, and number of children. She glanced at Gerard's name along with his wife's, but her curiosity about them didn't hold long as her eyes snagged on a familiar name.

Cassandra twisted her ring. "Your mother was a Sauveterre?"

"Hm?" The sound of Gerard's pacing came to a stop. "Oh, yes. She was."

She turned to look at him. "We're related?"

"Very distantly. My grandfather was your great-great-grandfather's brother."

"We're family?"

He rolled his eyes like it was more of a nuisance than anything. "I'm family with most people in DeVerre. Trust me. It isn't that special here."

Frowning, Cassandra turned back to the computer. "Is that how your brother became a teacher? Your mother's family got him the job?"

"Mm," he confirmed. "It was his first step to discard his tainted connection to us lumbermen."

Eyes drifting back to his brother's name, Cassandra's eyes caught on another familiar name. "And . . . his wife was a Frossard?"

"Like I said," he grumbled. "We're related to everyone."

She glanced over her shoulder at him. "I thought your grandfather also married a Frossard."

Gerard grinned snidely. "Yes, Franklin and Sadie were distant cousins. It wasn't quite as strange in our day, but even then, I thought it was distasteful. However, Franklin wanted a wife who would give him notoriety, and he knew a Frossard could do that for him."

Wary of the connections emerging in Gerard's family, Cassandra twisted her ring in another revolution around her finger. Sauveterres and Frossards. Their connection could be a coincidence, but it could also be their first clue to the identity of another Druidic family.

Perhaps Peter had been right; using their connection with Anna

Lambert to get closer to the Frossards might be the best way to discover the family's involvement.

Cassandra's eyes drifted to the corkboard above the desk. The picture of Diane and Phillip hung in the center, the sticky note labeling the man in the corner as "Mr. F" now drawing her special attention.

Mr. F.

Either Lloyd or Lee Frossard, Diane had determined.

But what she hadn't figured out was *why* either of the Frossard brothers would have taken her and her baby brother to meet with the Collinses in Norfolk, VA, back in December of 1940. The idea that one of the men had been their father Gerard had quickly negated, assuring her that both men were too loyal to their wives to carry on a lasting affair. Though Cassandra had always wondered how he could be so sure, she remembered his words from the other day: "*. . . the Frossards don't like many outside of their own blood.*"

Though there was a chance of some form of relationship to the Frossard family, Cassandra thought Gerard was correct. Be it Lloyd or Lee in the picture—the Frossards wouldn't allow anyone to threaten their family. Not even one of their own.

But that might be the answer. The Frossards may have ensured the safety of Diane and Phillip because they felt it was the right thing to do. Diane could see ghosts like Cassandra. Her powers hadn't developed past that, but odds were the two of them had shared more in common than their abilities alone.

They may well share a Druidic ancestry.

And the Frossards might have sent Diane from the town like the Chapelles had sent Cassandra away.

To rid the town of any connection to the spirit world.

The etching on her ring rubbed Cassandra's fingertips raw. This discovery confirmed it. There was one connecting point between her family and the Druids, and it was within the Sauveterre line.

Cassandra's mother's family was involved with the Druids. There was no doubt in her mind. Debbie's involvement could have been a fluke. But with Franklin Alarie's strange connection to both the Druids and her family, she had serious questions. Ones that she was sure her mother could answer.

Cassandra's throat tightened at the thought. "Well, that decides it, I guess," she muttered.

"Decides what?" Gerard's voice caused her to jump, having forgotten he was there.

Releasing her ring, Cassandra shut the laptop. "I have to go home."

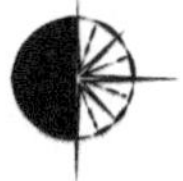

CHAPTER TEN

Spencer

Stepping into the warm interior of DeVerre Chapel the next day, Spencer shook off the last of the cold morning air. For the past several weeks, a subdued and sorrowful atmosphere had filled the church services due to the wolf attacks. This Sunday was no different.

Against the overcast, rainy sky, the light that filtered through the arched windows added a gray tinge to the walls. If it weren't for the white LED fixtures overhead, the weather would have cast the room into shadow. As it was, the chapel's gothic design lent itself to the gloomy weather and atmosphere, giving the room a decidedly moody air.

Just as they had at the softball game and then the party at The Glass Tavern, people stared at the brothers and Cassandra as they moved through the foyer and down the aisle for a seat. Not that it surprised Spencer. The populace of DeVerre had always looked at them with a distrusting glint in their eyes. Now with Cassandra at their sides, the stares had become cautious and regretful. No longer glares but sidelong glances cast out of the corners of their eyes.

Spencer couldn't decide whether it was an improvement or not.

Making their way down the center aisle of the chapel, Spencer scanned the sanctuary. The dark wooden pews reflected the gleaming lights as people murmured around them. The people of DeVerre seemed to have assigned themselves seats, taking the same ones each week. Alexander and Giana Frossard sat in their usual spot, in the second row from the front—heads high and demeanors relaxed as they quietly conversed with Samuel's wife on the front row. Five rows back, Anna, Aaron, Haley, and Ava sat together, surrounded on either side by other congregants.

Spencer glanced over his shoulder to see Owen sitting in the production booth, manning the PowerPoint and soundboard. Though tucked away from most of the room's line of sight, the man merely gave him a simple nod in greeting as their eyes met.

Despite the rest of DeVerre's seating assignments, Peter and Spencer hadn't received their own. And Cassandra had always sat with Debbie and Mike near the front. So, now they scrambled, trying to find a place for the three of them to sit together.

"Spencer," a soft voice called to his right. Not so loud that it caused the whole chapel to take notice, but as Spencer turned, so did all the people in the pews surrounding the voice.

Spencer looked down in surprise. "Oh, hey, Danielle."

Half-rising from her seat, Danielle smiled sweetly in Peter and Cassandra's direction before turning back to Spencer. The moss green sweater she wore emphasized her rich tan skin and warm chocolate eyes. "Did you guys need seats?" she asked, volume appropriately reverent in the chapel even as she hurried to speak. "We have plenty of room. Scoot down, guys. Come on in."

Staring at the length of the thin, blue cushion Danielle and her friends had cleared for them, Spencer felt an immediate twinge of disappointment. He looked over his shoulder at Peter and Cassandra as if for help. They merely glared at him. He wasn't sure what they wanted him to do about it. It wasn't as if they had much choice in the matter. To say no would be rude. And in their pursuit of cultivating friendships within DeVerre, they couldn't afford to refuse anyone's offer.

With a sense of resignation, Spencer turned back to Danielle and moved to take a seat. She kept smiling at him as he sat next to her. His stomach twisted, hoping she wouldn't see his anxiety in the smile he returned to her.

It wasn't that Danielle wasn't nice. And she certainly wasn't unattractive. He found her extraordinarily pretty with her deep brown eyes, strong yet elegant features, and petite frame. After spending most of Friday night with her, he'd come to learn that they were close in age, had many of the same interests, and shared a similar sense of humor.

No, the problem wasn't with Danielle.

Spencer just didn't want to give Peter any ideas about him and the woman.

For the first half of the softball game, Spencer had sat in almost complete silence, eventually pulling out his phone to take notes when he thought of ideas for *Wenzel & Frankly*. It wasn't until Danielle shifted awkwardly on the bench beside him, rubbing her hands along her black jeans, that he realized his impolite behavior. He'd stashed the phone back in his jacket pocket, cleared his throat, glanced at her out of the corner of his eye, and muttered, "Is anyone you know on the team?"

He'd realized how stupid the question was when she turned to him, almond-shaped eyes narrowed and full lips lifting at the corners. Everyone in DeVerre knew everyone else. With the exception of him, Peter, and Cassandra, of course.

"Right," he had mumbled. He'd met Danielle once before, he remembered. Back when Peter and he had gone bowling with Anna's Bible study. Danielle had been there. And she'd not said a word to him the entire night. So why should she want to talk to him now?

But unexpectedly, Danielle did talk to him. "My uncle is on the team." She pointed to the field. "Tony. The shortstop."

Spencer had followed her direction, spotting a massive brute of a man standing on the rust-colored dirt of the ball field. Tony MacDonald looked only as tall as Spencer on the field, particularly next to Alexander Frossard, who played at third base. But what the man lacked in height, he made up for in muscle and breadth.

"So, I have what might sound like a weird question," Danielle continued.

Spencer looked at her, realizing he had to look down to meet her eyes, which was an odd sensation for him. At his height, he didn't often get a chance to look down at people, not even girls. Especially not while sitting.

When he didn't respond, the young woman continued, "How are Anguis and Nex?"

"Oh." Spencer cocked his head, taken aback by the question. "Uh . . . they're good."

She'd smiled. "Good! I'm glad to hear it."

"Yeah?"

"Yeah. I was one of the people who watched them."

Spencer nodded in understanding, remembering that Nicole Descoteaux—the lawyer who oversaw Diane's estate—had mentioned that a handful of residents had volunteered to care for the dogs while the will was in probate. Danielle was the first volunteer he'd met. "Oh, cool. Thanks for doing that."

"I was happy to," she said, her voice friendly. "They're great dogs. I kind of got attached."

Spencer had found himself smiling at her politely, thinking the conversation would end. But it didn't.

Danielle had tucked some of her thick brown hair behind her ear and glanced sidelong at Spencer. "You and your brother write *Wenzel & Frankly*, right?"

Spencer's jaw dropped. "Uh, yeah."

Her smile beamed, though she wouldn't look at him. "Yeah," she murmured. Her hands fidgeted nervously in her lap. "I'm kind of . . . well,

I know it probably makes me sound ridiculous, but . . . I'm a huge fan! I've loved your stuff for a long time now and when Anna told me that you guys had moved here, I couldn't believe it."

"Really?" Spencer had asked, feeling somewhere between terrified and excited. In all their time as writers, he couldn't recollect meeting a fan who wasn't a family member or a friend. To meet one in DeVerre, of all places, was unprecedented.

Danielle finally met his gaze again at that. "Yeah, it's amazing. I know I sound like a crazy fangirl or something, but I've read every episode at least two or three times now. When I first met you, I was too nervous to say anything—which makes me sound even crazier, I now realize. I'm an adult, and I don't know how to talk to a guy? How weird is that? But—it's just super cool to meet you guys."

In the cold Friday night air, Spencer smiled meekly, the lines beginning to blur in his mind. Was she just a fan, or was she, God forbid, interested in him? He didn't know what to do.

But he didn't think he could rebuff her either.

Spencer wound up talking with Danielle for the rest of the evening. Which was fun, for the most part. People usually only asked polite, anecdotal questions about their writing. Things like: What do you write? How long have you been writing? Do you have anything published?

But Danielle had asked him questions about his favorite episodes, how they developed their ideas, and what he liked best about each character. Things that he actually wanted to talk about; things that *got* him talking.

And he had enjoyed himself.

Until Cassandra had gone and confirmed his suspicions, warning him to be careful of Danielle's attention. He didn't want her to be right. He didn't want Danielle to be interested in him. Because in his life right now, there was only one person he had time to take care of: Peter. If he got himself a girlfriend—which he didn't even want in the first place—he'd be abandoning his brother. And he could never do that.

An unexpected predicament which still astounded him two days later. And now Spencer felt stuck.

Sitting in the pew with Peter on his left and Danielle on his right, Spencer clenched his jaw. There seemed little he could do about the situation now. If Danielle had taken an interest in him, he just needed to be careful not to encourage her further. He wasn't entirely certain how to do that, though, when he also didn't feel safe rejecting her friendship either.

Cassandra had been right about another thing. The MacDonalds were close to the Frossards. And there was a chance that a *platonic* relationship with Danielle might get them even closer to the family than Anna's friendship alone.

However, as the church service went on, Spencer kept his eyes off Danielle just in case. He wanted to be sure he didn't give her any signal that he was especially aware of her. Or of the way her arm brushed against his every so often.

When Reverend Chapelle bowed his head for the final prayer, Spencer followed suit, along with the congregation. He'd memorized the closing prayer over the past month and a half. In every service, Samuel closed with the same lines: "Draw us to the heart of your Son, inspire us by your Holy Spirit, and teach us to see the unseen."

It wasn't that strange of a prayer. In fact, Spencer thought it was poetic. He wouldn't have taken much notice of it if they'd said a similar prayer at their church in Norfolk.

But they were in DeVerre. A town where the unseen *was* seen.

Looking up as Samuel said, "amen," Spencer felt like he was taking the man in with new eyes. Was it possible for the reverend to speak those lines every week and not know about the unseen world in his own town?

Reflexively, Spencer massaged his thumb against his palm as he watched Tom Garnier rise several rows in front of them. Instead of his uniform, he wore his Sunday best—a button up and slacks. Still, the marshal carried a sense of intense suspicion as he scanned the room.

Tom had told them that Samuel opposed the decision to take Cassandra from town. What he hadn't said was *why*. Had Samuel disapproved due to moral grounds? Or for a different, more personal reason? One connected to the unseen he referenced in his prayers?

As the congregation rose to leave, Danielle immediately asked Spencer how his Saturday had been and if they had any plans for the rest of their weekend. He felt his palms grow sweaty, unsure how to break away from her without hurting her feelings. He thought to nudge Peter, hoping for a rescue. When he glanced over his shoulder, he found his brother and Cassandra talking with Anna, Aaron, and Haley in the center aisle as though they'd forgotten that Spencer even existed.

Well, Spencer realized, not all of them were ignoring him. Cassandra glanced at him with a taunting smirk before turning back to Anna.

Frustration welled in Spencer's throat. He didn't want to talk to Danielle. He really didn't want to talk to anyone. Not when he had so many questions rolling around in his head. Over the past couple of days, Spencer had tried to research the Warden. He'd come up empty—which he supposed he should have expected—finding nothing but video game and literature references on the surface and unrelated groups or topics when he'd tried digging deeper.

But Spencer was desperate for the information that Owen was clearly unable to give them.

When Danielle asked if it'd be okay to get his number so that they could work out a time for her to come by to see the dogs again, Spencer had to suppress a grimace. His gaze swept over the sanctuary nervously as he gave her the number, and she texted him hers. "Well," Danielle said, "I should probably get going. But hopefully, I'll see you soon?"

"Sure." Spencer nodded, not feeling the grin of farewell that he gave her.

"Bye, Spencer."

He waved, unwilling to say anything else as Danielle slipped past him and headed for the exit. As she paused in the foyer to grab her coat, she said goodbye to Samuel, who was slipping a scarf around his neck. Most of the sanctuary had cleared out, only a couple of groups like Peter, Cassandra, and the Lamberts lingering to chat. The reverend's copper hair caught in the bright lights above as he pulled his coat from one of the pegs on the wall.

As he put the coat on, Samuel looked over the chapel. His eyes landed on Spencer, and Spencer realized how awkward it was to be caught watching him. But the reverend gave him a smile—which Spencer returned—then zipped his coat and turned to the door.

Before the idea could fully form in his mind, Spencer rushed around the pew, squeezing past Peter. He almost tripped on his brother's feet but caught himself before doubling his stride. "Reverend," he called, thankful that the chapel was small.

Samuel paused to look over his shoulder. He held one of the doors cracked open. As he caught sight of Spencer, he let go and the door fell back in place with a soft *whoosh*. "Yes?"

"Uh. . . ." Spencer rubbed his hands together, the chill that had seeped in through the door casting a frigid tinge into the entryway. "I'm sorry to hold you up. I assume you were heading home?"

"Yes, I was," Samuel confirmed, clasping his hands in front of him. "But that's all right. Was there something you needed?"

Spencer licked his lips nervously, realizing just how little he'd thought this through. "You're, uh—you don't lock up?" he managed to ask, unsure what he'd wanted from the reverend in the first place.

"There's really no reason to lock the chapel," Samuel explained, his eyebrows raised. "And I like to leave it open in case someone might like to come by for prayer or time alone with God."

"Oh." Spencer rubbed the back of his neck, still not used to the way small towns never seemed to lock anything.

"Is that all you needed?" Samuel asked with a good-natured grin on his lips. As if the thought that Spencer was concerned for the security of the chapel amused him.

A thin laugh escaped Spencer. "Uh, no, I—I was actually wondering if it'd be possible to meet with you?"

The reverend's chin lifted as his gingered eyebrows pulled together.

"Like, I just had a few questions, and I thought that—well, you might be able to answer them for me."

Samuel nodded, his expression of surprise reducing to that amicable grin once more. "Of course, I'd be happy to meet with you."

"Great! Maybe tomorrow morning?'

"How's Tuesday? Mondays are my Sabbath."

Tempering the disappointment that he wouldn't have any additional information to offer when the marshal came over tomorrow afternoon, Spencer nodded. "Right, that makes sense. Tuesday sounds great."

"Excellent," Samuel said, stepping toward the door. "Does 10:30 work for you?"

"Yeah, that's fine."

While the reverend left, Spencer tried to decide whether he felt more nervous or excited about the meeting. He hoped they'd have a whole slew of their questions answered through the marshal and the reverend by Tuesday. Though, he couldn't help the pessimistic thought that both meetings would probably reveal a whole other group of questions that would need answers too.

Secrets upon secrets.

That should be DeVerre's new motto, Spencer decided. The town of duplicity and hidden agendas.

But then, Spencer thought that was a recurring theme right now, not only with DeVerre but also with the Warden. Even Owen, a member specifically tasked to uncover the truth within the town, didn't know half as much as Spencer thought he should. He didn't even know the leaders of the organization he worked for. Whether he knew the names of a couple or not, it was hard to trust the people you were working for when you didn't know who was in charge.

Spencer wondered what the other Wardens towns out there were like.

Were they as secretive as DeVerre? He imagined they'd have to be if the Warden's policies were any indication.

What was the name of that town that Owen had mentioned? The cautionary tale. Port-something. Portland? Porthampton?

A hand clamped onto Spencer's shoulder, causing him to jump. "Calm down, Columbo," Peter said, squeezing his shoulder. "Just me. You ready to head home?"

Spencer sighed, taking his jacket from Cassandra as she stepped into view. "Yeah," he said, swinging the jacket around to slip over his arms. "Let's go."

~

The second they returned home, Spencer texted Owen to ask for the name of the town he'd forgotten.

"Porthaven," Owen replied.

At his desk with Nex and Anguis flanking his chair, Spencer searched for every Porthaven in the United States. There was only one.

"Well, that was easy," Spencer muttered to himself, clicking on the town's website first.

Located at the top eastern corner of Maine, the small town of Porthaven didn't seem so small compared to DeVerre. It had over a thousand residents, a thriving tourism industry, and was—as the name denoted—an active port. Seafood being its main export, fishing was the highest recorded career for its residents.

Spencer scanned the whole website but found nothing that referenced the Warden. He turned to the wiki page next. There he learned about their highly attended fall festival, the state championship their high school had won eight years back, and the old brick church that was the town's prized location.

It gave him nothing.

Rubbing a hand over his face, Spencer wondered what he'd been hoping to find from Porthaven that their search from DeVerre hadn't given them. It was clear: Warden towns were as shrouded in mystery as the organization itself. Trying to unveil the enigma did nothing more than frustrate him.

"Hey—oh, sorry, am I. . . ." Cassandra's voice drew Spencer to look up. She stood in the doorway, frozen upon seeing him with his head in his hands. "I can come back later."

Spencer dropped his arms to the desk as an embarrassed chuckle worked out of him. "No, no, it's fine. I was just. . . ." He motioned to the laptop, then thought better of trying to explain. "What's up?"

Though she lingered at the threshold a moment more, Cassandra resumed her path and headed for the desk. Anguis sat up as she approached, tail wagging. She gave his head a scratch before leaning against the left side of the desk. She smirked at Spencer, the hollow forming in her cheek. "Two things," she said, crossing her arms. "First, I have a question."

He gave her a chin-up gesture in acceptance.

"Did you make me a character in your serial?"

Spencer felt his stomach drop. "What?"

Cassandra's brow arched as he stared at her with a dumbfounded expression. How did she know?

"Serene," she prompted. "She's me, isn't she?"

"How do—Serene hasn't even been introduced yet," he sputtered, unsure how to convince her that the truth she'd already figured out wasn't actually the truth.

"Pete sent me the draft you sent him for approval."

Spencer ground his teeth. "It wasn't finished."

"He told me." She smirked. "Is Serene based on me?"

"No," he lied.

"So you just happened to create a female character who controls monsters, has dark brown hair, hazel eyes, and a mysterious past coincidentally?"

"Serene is twenty-two."

Cassandra let out a snort of laughter. "Right, she couldn't possibly be inspired by me, then."

Growing more irritated at Peter by the second, Spencer shook his head. "She's not inspired by you, Cass," he insisted.

"You're sure?" she asked, those hazel eyes that had inspired Serene's flickering over his face.

"Yeah," he promised.

She didn't seem convinced.

Spencer didn't feel like convincing her. "What was the second thing?"

Cassandra sucked in the corner of her bottom lip, scanning him. He wasn't sure why, but she appeared to be checking his mood. He wondered if it was because he'd been so frustrated upon her arrival. Or that he'd shut down her teasing too bluntly.

Straightening his shoulders, Spencer tried to relax back into his chair, hoping to show her that he was at ease.

Her lips lifted in a knowing smile. Reaching into her pocket, she kept her unwavering stare locked on him. "I found this," she said, proffering the object she'd retrieved.

Spencer raised a hand to take it, realizing what it was before he'd even gotten a clear look. He recognized the faces in the photo too quickly for him not to connect the dots.

Fighting the way his chest tightened on instinct, Spencer took a deep breath as he held the photo cautiously before him. Taken almost fifteen years ago, it was one of the last pictures of him, Peter, and their dad before the accident. At eleven and thirteen, there weren't many differences between him and Peter then versus now. Peter's hair was an unruly mess as usual, and his overdramatic, toothy smile bright. Spencer, small and shy, leaned up against his dad's side, tucked under his strong arm. And David Collins, with his clear blue eyes, lean physique, and calming smile, embraced his sons like they were the greatest and most dear treasures in the entire world.

"I thought you'd want it," Cassandra said, her raspy voice soft as it brushed over him.

Spencer tightened his jaw, steadying his rush of memories before looking up at her. "Thanks."

She nodded. "It—I was organizing Diane's stuff in her room, and it fell out of one of her journals," she explained. "I scanned the pages, and I think I found where it belonged. She was talking about her plans to leave the house to you two. She'd said something about intending to leave it to David, but . . . then her adopted brother, Oliver, told her about you guys."

"Oliver?"

"Yeah, they were the nearest in age, so they stayed close. He was her primary source of information until he died."

Setting the picture on the desk, Spencer furrowed his brow. "I figured my grandfather would have been the one to talk to her."

"Oh, well . . . I guess you wouldn't know." Cassandra took a deep breath. "Phillip and Diane had a falling out. It's why she never went to Norfolk. She wanted to meet you guys—she talked about it all the time, but . . . visiting wasn't much of an option."

A dozen arguments popped into Spencer's head at once. Their grandfather, Phillip, had died more than a decade ago; if Diane hadn't wanted to come because of him, she could have at least made it to the funeral. And what about after that? Why wouldn't she make the trip after he'd passed to try and smooth out the wrinkles of the past to begin a relationship with them?

But knowing how all-encompassing the past month of their life had been, Spencer's spike of irritation dissipated. He couldn't remember the last time he'd called his mom, and they hadn't even had a falling out. "What happened between them?" he asked.

Cassandra shrugged. "She came out here."

Brows lowered, Spencer frowned. "That's it?"

"Diane was searching for their biological parents," she explained. "Phillip . . . well, he felt it was a betrayal to the Collinses. Ronald and Helen had been wonderful parents. And Phillip felt she was abandoning them when she decided to leave home.

"They argued about it so many times that. . . ." She pressed her lips together and sighed. "Diane finally decided that it wasn't worth it. She wouldn't give up her search, and Phillip wouldn't let her get through even one conversation without demanding that she come back."

Spencer remembered his grandfather Phillip. He hadn't had near the relationship with him that he had with his dad, but he always remembered him being a kind, tenderhearted man. He struggled to see that side of the man his memories shaped for him.

Cassandra's compassionate smile grew sardonic. "It's a feeling I can relate to."

Conversations from the past rose in Spencer's mind. "Your family does that to you?"

"Every time," she confirmed.

"I'm sorry."

She scrunched her nose in a look of dry humor. "I'm used to it. But, anyway, I understand why Diane never went back. It's easier to avoid the place that makes you feel like you've betrayed the people who love you the most."

Running his finger along the thin edge of the photo, Spencer looked back at his dad. To the proud gleam in the man's eyes. He hoped that he was proud of them even now. That he was watching over them as they put themselves in harm's way, all to achieve their dreams.

"Can I. . . ." Cassandra began but cut herself off.

Spencer looked up in time to see her wave a hand through the air, brushing away the unsaid words. "What?"

"Nothing. Forget it."

"Cassie." He reached over to nudge her elbow. "What is it?"

Lips parting, Cassandra stared at him with a wary glint in her eyes. "I . . . I was just going to ask. . . ." She paused again, her uncertainty beginning to make him nervous. "You don't have to tell me, all right?"

Spencer shifted, uncomfortable under her intense stare. "All right."

Her gaze softened as she smiled gently. "How did your dad die?"

The question hit Spencer with its usual sting—like a paper cut, deep and welling with blood. He avoided discussing their dad as much as possible so that people wouldn't ask questions. He didn't mind thinking about his dad, but he hated talking about him. It caused his mouth to dry up, trying to get the words to pull free of his throat.

Breath catching in his lungs, Spencer worked his jaw back and forth. He hadn't attempted this conversation in a long time. And he didn't look forward to trying it again. "It was, uh . . . one of those . . . freak accidents, you know? Should have never happened, but . . . it did."

Cassandra twisted the ring around her finger, watching him silently. Something in the steadiness of her stare, the unflinching way she listened, encouraged him to sit up straighter.

"He was a mechanic," he explained. "He preferred working on cars— the Jeep was his pet project. But, uh . . . he worked for the navy. On the boats, mostly. And there was this . . . this job that, uh. . . ."

As the words failed him, Spencer clasped his hands together on the desk. He couldn't quite bring himself to break Cassandra's stare, but he couldn't manage to speak either. The rest of the story built up in his chest, entwined with the memories of the hellhounds, scylla, and Peter's near death less than a week ago.

David Collins's death felt like a hundred years gone by and yesterday at the same time to Spencer. He could remember every emotion he'd felt when the officer had shown up on their porch with the news; how his entire world had shattered, and he'd felt like he'd been torn to shreds in its jagged shards. He remembered their mother's tears as she crumbled. He remembered how Peter had managed to hold back his own tears whenever either Spencer or their mom were present. He'd caught his brother many times with tear-stained cheeks, but fourteen-year-old Peter had never shown his grief in public. Not even at the funeral service. And Spencer had always known it was his effort to prove that he was strong enough to take care of his mom and little brother.

What Spencer couldn't remember were the important details. The facts that people always wanted: What had caused the explosion that blew the engine into sharp knives of metal and severed his father's artery? Which artery was it? Had he died instantly? Who was at fault? How often did things like that happen?

Spencer had none of the answers to those things. And he didn't really care to know them.

Looking down at the picture, Spencer pulled in a deep breath. "He was a great dad," he whispered.

The warmth of Cassandra's hand on his arm drew him to meet her ever-steady gaze again. Her look wasn't of pity but of compassion. Of tenderness that smoothed over him as her thumb brushed against his shoulder. "Thank you," she replied, her tone soft like her smile. "For telling me."

Though Spencer didn't think he could respond as the pain in his chest grew, he nodded anyway.

Cassandra released him and stepped away from the desk. "I'm gonna go do some more research."

He continued to nod.

Anguis followed as she backed into the hallway. Her smile turned playful. "It wouldn't be the worst thing, you know," she teased.

"What wouldn't?"

"If you used me as your inspiration for Serene," she said, a sly hint in her voice smoothing out its usual raspy edges. "I'd be flattered."

While Spencer tried to think of some smart retort, Cassandra turned and disappeared around the corner.

Spencer rubbed his palms together, sucking in a deep breath. He didn't have time to think about the potentially perilous consequences of creating Serene Verlice in the likeness of Cassandra. He'd already dreaded what Peter would say once he found out what Spencer was planning for their characters.

His eyes drifted to his dad's face once more, the photo reflecting the yellow light of the desk lamp. Fourteen years and it hurt no less. A pain that only Peter could understand.

Losing their dad had broken Spencer as a kid. Without Peter at his side, he doubted he would have ever recovered. After almost losing Peter, too, Spencer knew he couldn't go through that again.

He *wouldn't* go through that again.

Turning back to the laptop, Spencer resumed his research. He had to find some answers, some fragment of knowledge that would give them an edge. Anything that would keep his brother alive.

CHAPTER ELEVEN

Peter

Monday morning came in the blink of an eye.

Peter practically leaped out of bed, threw on a Henley and jeans, and burst down the stairs. His anticipation for their meeting with the marshal that afternoon had him buzzing. But there was one thing that hadn't escaped Peter's notice yesterday morning at church, and it held all his attention now. It didn't matter whether Spencer was too busy chatting up that Danielle chick or if Cassandra had intentionally ignored it. While Anna, Aaron, and Haley had greeted them, Ava had brushed past without a second glance.

Peter had seen it, the clear and intentional dismissal in her eyes. No one else seemed to find it troubling—how obviously set against them she was. But Peter felt the weight of it. They'd gone too long without confronting Ava, and now she was shunning them for choosing to work with Cassandra.

But she didn't know the truth. She thought Cassandra was a danger to the town and her way of life. And despite their own initial reaction, they now knew that couldn't be farther from the truth. Cassandra and Owen, together, were the only things keeping the Druids from unleashing the Veil, destroying the town in the process.

And if they were going to succeed in saving DeVerre, Peter was convinced they needed Ava's help.

A fact he had intentionally kept off their checklist, knowing Cassandra wasn't likely to approve.

Now, as the morning grew misty outside, Peter hurried into the kitchen for a quick cup of coffee before he headed out. He'd peeked into Spencer's room but didn't find him there. Which he supposed he should have expected. Even his "early" morning was late to Spencer.

Peter rounded the corner into the dining room on his way to the office. But he found the desk chair empty as well.

Frowning, Peter turned around to Cassandra, who sat at the far end of the dining table. "Hey," he called, then grimaced as she looked up, and he realized she'd been reading her Bible. "Sorry. You know where Spence is?"

Cassandra tucked some of her dark hair behind her ear. "He took the dogs for a walk. Said something about working out an idea."

"Ah, gotcha." Peter nodded, used to his brother's reflective process—whether regarding writing or reality. "Well, dang. I was gonna ask him if I could borrow the Jeep."

"Isn't it your Jeep too?"

"Technically, no," Peter explained. "Spence convinced Mom to give him the Jeep when he got his license. So, it's officially *his*. I sold my car when we left Norfolk, so I don't actually have one."

"I see." She capped her highlighter. "Well, he left about twenty minutes ago, so I'd imagine he'll be back soon."

He scoffed. "You obviously haven't lived with Spencer long enough. His walks are my hikes."

Cassandra gave a light chuckle at that. "If you don't want to wait, you can take my truck."

"Really?" Peter perked up. He'd secretly hoped to drive Cassandra's truck ever since he first saw it. He'd never tell Spencer, but he thought her vintage truck was even cooler than the Jeep.

The thought of betraying their dad's Jeep sent a pang of guilt through him. "Ah, no," he said, waving the idea off. "I'm sure he won't care. I just like to ask."

"That's nice of you," she replied, playing with the highlighter.

The reminder of his interruption caused another flicker of guilt. He motioned to her Bible. "Sorry to interrupt you. I'll let you get back to it."

Waving a dismissive hand through the air, Cassandra smiled. "I don't mind. And I am in a public space."

Peter furrowed his brow. "Why are you out here? Not that I mind. Like, you can totally do whatever, wherever. But, I mean, people typically read their Bible in private. You know, to keep focused."

"Yeah, I know." She shrugged. "And, sure, it can be distracting down here, but it doesn't bother me. I like being around people. And . . . well, really, it's because this is where Diane used to do her devotional time each morning. As we got closer, she invited me to join her. I'd come over pretty much every day, sit there," she motioned to the chair to her left, "and we'd read our Bibles, take notes, discuss our thoughts, and most of the time, we'd pray together. It was nice. And doing that here again makes me feel like she's still with me."

Scanning the table with what felt like new eyes, Peter ran a hand over his neck where the memory of the bruises still itched. The concept of personal Bible study wasn't foreign to him. He'd just never done it himself. Reading the Bible was hard enough. Taking notes and having time to discuss it was impossible. And to do it daily? Forget about it.

But since Cassandra started living with them, he'd noticed her ritual. She sat at the table with a cup of coffee, her Bible, a notebook, and a little canvas bag filled with pens, highlighters, and sticky tabs. The edge of her Bible looked like an Ivy League student's textbook with muted tabs sticking out all over the place. He'd gotten a glimpse inside of it, too, and he knew that handwritten notes covered the pages to the point where the margins hardly remained.

"That's, uh. . . ." Peter scratched the back of his head. "That's cool. It's nice that you get the chance to relive those memories."

Cassandra smiled but didn't respond.

"How do you find time for it?" he found himself asking.

She laughed. "I *make* time for it. Like Spencer makes time to go to the gym. Like you make time to visit Anna."

"I don't visit Anna *that* much."

Her grin said she disagreed.

"I get your point, though."

"You can join me if you want."

Peter raised his brow, surprised. "Oh, uh—thanks."

The tilt of her head said she knew why he hesitated. "No pressure, though."

Peter held her gaze, not sure if the judgment he felt came from her or himself. From the goodness of her tone, he was pretty sure it was self-inflicted.

Running a finger along the side of his mug, Peter pressed his lips together. He should join her. Both he and Spencer should. Not only was it the right thing to do, but the daily practice would also help in the fight for DeVerre. Owen had said faith was the key to unlocking the ability to wield the spirit world. And if the two of them could manage to access it, their chances of survival would go up exponentially.

But it was a lot of work.

Like, a *lot* of work.

And he wasn't sure there was time for it.

"Thanks," he said again. "I may just take you up on that."

Cassandra nodded, though her grin didn't show confidence in his response.

Taking a large gulp of coffee to help his expeditious retreat from Occasus, Peter glanced at their new roommate again as he headed back into the kitchen. It was odd having a woman living with them. Of course, they'd lived with their mom for twenty years, but that was a whole different beast. She was their *mom*.

Cassandra was nothing of the sort. She was their age, cool, clever, and downright gorgeous. If he wasn't so sure that she was the perfect woman for Spencer, he might have considered making a move at some point down the line. But even that made things weird. He didn't know if or when Spencer might make a move. And what would happen if he did?

Living with a woman they weren't related to complicated things. They had to put more foresight into everything. Showering was a planned event with her in the house; he wasn't about to walk through the halls in a towel. Getting a midnight snack was a mission of stealth, making sure he tiptoed through the house and didn't wake her up. And he found himself questioning his words these days, unsure what kinds of jokes or language she was comfortable with.

If Spencer and Cassandra started dating, then things would get even more complicated.

But then, Peter had to be honest with himself, neither Spencer nor Cassandra had shown much interest in being in a relationship. In fact, he couldn't say that either of them had shown much interest in each other at all. Of course, that was par for the course with Spencer. Even when he did have crushes on girls in the past, he always played it so cool that the girl never knew. Heck, Peter barely ever knew.

As far as Cassandra was concerned, she didn't seem to give Spencer any special attention either. She was just as friendly with Peter as she was with his brother. Any jokes or physical contact she paid to one, she also paid to the other. And Peter could never say he'd gotten anything but sisterly affection from Cassandra Clement.

Placing his empty mug into the dishwasher and heading for the door, Peter decided he needed to do some recon on the pair of them. There were questions to answer regarding his brother and their roommate, but he would figure them out later. For now, he needed to get to the library.

Even with his jacket on, Peter shivered in the Jeep. Washington was already colder than any winter they'd experienced in Norfolk. And with the thick freezing raindrops, on the cusp of turning from sleet into snow, it was only getting worse.

As the rain picked up, Peter leaped out of the Jeep and dashed into the library. He shook some of the dampness from his hair before straightening his shoulders, lifting his chin, and tugging his jacket straighter around him. He wanted to appear confident and calm when he approached Ava. He couldn't give her any reason to see him as unsure.

Weaving his way through the plant and book-covered shelves, he pulled in a deep breath of the herbal blend that permeated the library. Ava always had some pot of tea going, giving the place a distinct sage-like atmosphere. Today the sharp scent of cooling mint crisped the air.

When he turned the corner, Peter saw Ava sitting at the table that she used as a desk. But instead of her usual relaxed and lounging manner, she sat slouched over a large book on the table. Head down, her black-brown braids tumbled over her shoulders, a few pooling onto the table.

"What do you want?" Ava asked, eyes locked on her book.

Peter wondered if she knew it was him or if she would have greeted anyone in the same fashion. He took cautious steps up to the desk. "Hey, I, uh—I just wanted to swing by and talk."

Tucking some of those long braids behind her ear, Ava scoffed. "What could we possibly have to talk about?"

Peter shifted from foot to foot. "Well, I mean, the last time we talked, you accused our friend of being a murderer, so I thought it would be a good idea to clear that up."

She raised her chin, looking up at him with a bored stare. Her high cheekbones and arched brows always reminded him of Anna. The Lambert sisters were both beautiful; there was no doubt about that. But Ava was of a more striking, unique beauty, while Anna owned a softer, feminine look. And the elder sister was far more capable of making a man feel like an idiot with just one glance.

Ava leaned back in her seat. She pulled each side of her chunky cardigan closed as she crossed her arms, resting them on her stomach. "There is nothing you could say that would *clear up* anything."

Tightening his jaw, Peter could see the conversation heading in the wrong direction. He had hoped to get Ava in a good mood. Maybe then she'd be gracious enough to discuss everything in a level-headed manner. He thought she might listen then, and he could help her see that her fears—while somewhat founded—weren't as relevant as she thought.

But with her immediate hostility, he didn't see much point in hoping anymore.

Peter took another step forward, setting his hands on the back of the chair opposite of her. "Listen, Ava, I know that this all scares you—"

Her eyes narrowed at that.

"But I think you might find that you're being a little narrow-minded if you gave me five minutes to explain."

"Narrow-minded?" Her sardonic smirk said she didn't find the suggestion all that amusing. She gestured to the seat, then rested her arm over her stomach again. "By all means, take five minutes and explain to me how dealing with the dead is a good idea."

"It's not—" Peter cut himself off, hearing that the words were already too reactive. He took a deep breath and tried again, softening his tone. "We aren't dealing with the dead."

Her brow cocked, and he realized that wasn't altogether true. They were living with a phantom, for goodness' sake. And they'd taken a special trip to the lake with Owen to talk to ghosts.

"Well. . . ." He shrugged. "We aren't doing anything evil."

"Oh, well, that's fine then."

Peter pulled the chair out and plunked down into it. "Look, I get it. It's freakin' weird, okay? All of this. But it isn't like Spence and I asked to get dragged into it. Neither did Cass, for that matter."

"So, walk away from it."

"We can't."

Ava laid her arms over the book, leaning toward him. "Why not?" she demanded. "What could possibly be so serious that you're messing around with spirits and demons?"

Peter jerked back at the final word. "Demons?"

She scoffed, shaking her head. "And you wonder why I say you should leave it alone." She pierced him with her dark glare. "You don't even know what you're involved in. This isn't some fun little quirk to our town. It's a mark on our heritage. The founding families of DeVerre were stupid enough to mess with things they had no business touching. Thankfully, they came to their senses and eliminated that behavior. When the Varons died, it finally died with them. And it wasn't until your friend Cassandra returned to town that things started getting weird again."

Knowing that Cassandra had been more than exonerated from Ava's accusations, Peter shook his head. "That's not true."

"How would you know? You've lived here for a month. I've lived here my whole life."

"That doesn't make you the authority on the area."

Her laugh was harsh and caustic. "No, that would be because my mother taught me the entire history of DeVerre. And, furthermore, because I'm in charge of keeping all the records."

That intrigued Peter. "*All* the records?"

She slammed the book shut in front of her. "I've already told you and your brother far more than either of you should know. Far more than I'm even supposed to know. You have more than enough information to make it clear that you should leave the spirit world untouched. *And* that you shouldn't associate with Cassandra Clement."

"You're right." Peter nodded. "I have plenty of information on both Cass and the spirit world. Even more than you."

She smirked. "Yet you didn't know about the demons?"

The word cut through Peter again, a chill running down his spine. "Are you talking about the hellhounds?"

Ava rolled her shoulders, resetting her jaw as she stared at him. "Is that what she calls them?"

Peter shrugged. "Well, it's not just her, but yeah, we did learn the term from Cass first."

"Not just her?" Ava repeated, lips parting as she glared at him.

Realizing the dangerous ground he was treading, Peter recalculated. He couldn't veer too close to telling her about Owen. He wouldn't be the one to reveal the man's secret. But he needed her to know that Cassandra wasn't the only one with powers in DeVerre. And he needed her to trust him, to take his words seriously.

"Ava, we aren't pursuing this blindly," he promised. "And we aren't doing it selfishly, either. We're trying to save the town."

"Save it from what? By dabbling in the spirit world, you will bring it upon the town. Your attempt to save us, is going to destroy us."

"You don't understand—"

"No, Peter, *you* don't understand!" Her words were biting. "You and your brother can believe that witch's lies all you want, but I will not be pulled into her trap."

"She's on your side!"

"She *can't* be! Everything she wants to do, I'm against. If you insist on working with her, you must know you are working against me."

Peter shifted in his seat, fighting every urge to spit out a hundred arguments with just as much fury as her.

"And I will not help you," Ava added, her tone final. "Not when you're bringing demons and monsters into my home."

"They aren't. . . ." The words caught in Peter's throat. Were the beasts demons? He couldn't be sure.

His hand flew to his collar on instinct, remembering the scylla. Their inky black forms and slitted neon yellow eyes flashed in his memory. His heart kicked up a notch as his skin tingled.

Were they demons?

Cassandra insisted that she'd never tried to summon a beast. She was afraid of what it would do to her to have that sort of contact with one of them. She could control them and send them away, but she had no interest in interacting with them.

And what about Owen? He'd never mentioned the idea of conjuring a beast. Peter couldn't imagine the man would have anything to do with something he thought was demonic. But if the spirit world produced those demons through the same means as those arcs they wielded, why would Owen have anything to do with it at all?

Ava took advantage of his prolonged silence to regain control of the conversation. "Why did you visit my husband the night the Merciers' house burned down?"

Blood draining from his face, Peter felt his whole body run cold. His brain rushed at a million miles an hour to come up with an answer to that question. What could he say? What had he said to Anna when she asked? It had been days ago. He'd told her that it had something to do with their writing, right?

"Uh, we, um. . . ." He tried and failed to swallow around the lump in his throat. "Spence and I wanted him to . . . help out with our book."

"Why?"

"Huh?"

Ava gave him a disappointed look, which said he should be smarter than that. "You met my husband *one time*," she reminded him. "And you acted like a nervous fool the entire night. You didn't learn anything about him. I doubt you even know what he does for work."

It was true. While Peter had learned that Owen was a substitute teacher part-time and a freelancer writer full time, he'd only learned that during the meet-up that they'd intentionally made sure Ava knew nothing about. And if Peter was honest, he didn't know much more about Owen other than his two jobs, his city of origin, and the names of his family members. He wasn't even sure of his age.

"Why would you and your brother ever think to ask Owen to help you with your writing?"

The panic inside Peter rose. He couldn't give it away. He wouldn't. But what could he say?

Ava's eyes watched him like a scientist observing a specimen. She zeroed in on him, taking in every detail. And he knew she would use all the data she found to form a brand-new theory, no matter how right or wrong it ended up being.

"We needed help," Peter said honestly.

"Owen's help?"

"Yes."

"Why?"

Peter drew his brows together, frowning at her. "Because you scared the shit out of us, Ava," he spat back, angrier than he'd been in a while. He didn't know whether it was his panic or the build-up of the last several days coming to the surface. "You made us second guess the woman who has become one of our closest friends. The woman who will inherit our house if we decide to pack it up and head back to Norfolk. And it freaked us out. The only person we could think to talk to was your husband."

Drawing back, a look of uncertainty crossed Ava's face. "You went to ask him if he supported me?"

Realizing how sketchy that sounded, Peter shrugged. "Kind of."

"What did he say?"

Now he was on seriously dangerous ground. "Uh . . . well, he said he didn't know."

Ava's fingers tapped on the cover of the giant book.

Peter glanced at the gold filigree of the title. But he only caught a glimpse of one word before she slapped her hand over the rest of it.

"He didn't know?" Her words came out in a tense monotone.

Tugging at the collar of his shirt, Peter shrugged again. "Yeah."

Ava's eyes dropped to the table.

In the silence that followed, Peter wondered if he'd made a mistake coming to her and trying to get her on their side. They needed her, didn't they? She kept the records of DeVerre. She knew everything about the place. Or, at least, most things. And as they still couldn't find the vault, they needed answers.

"Get out." Ava's voice cut through his musing.

Peter gaped at her. "What?"

Her dark brown eyes flared as they met his. "Leave."

"Ava—"

"Peter," she returned. "I don't want you coming back here."

He opened his mouth to speak, but she kept going.

"I won't help you anymore. I won't answer any questions, and I won't give you any advice." There was no emotion in her voice. It was flat and even. And that was far more frightening than if she'd yelled at him.

"I tried to help you," she continued. "And you ignored me. Worse, you tried to turn my husband against me. And now you're living with the woman attempting to destroy everything I stand for.

"Don't come back here," she said. "Don't come to my home or try to talk to me. As far as I'm concerned, while you and your brother are associated with Cassandra Clement, you are not welcome in DeVerre."

Peter felt like he'd taken a punch to the gut. What could he say to that? How could he convince her to listen when the only means of telling her the truth was revealing Owen's secret?

"Ava, please, listen to me," he tried again.

"Goodbye, Peter," she said, then stood, gathered the book into her arms, and walked through a side door to what he assumed was the storage room for the library.

Peter sat at the table, staring after her.

What had he done? By trying to fix their problems, had he just made things a dozen times worse?

Knowing that anyone could be a Druid was a problem. But having Ava officially mark them as enemies to the town was dangerous. Even if most of the townspeople took exception to her coarse demeanor, she still held influence. She was the record keeper, after all. The gatekeeper of their history. She knew things that no one else did. And the powers that be would listen to her long before they'd listen to the brothers.

To make matters worse, Peter knew he'd caused a rift between Owen and Ava. If she hadn't been suspicious of her husband's activities before, she certainly was now.

He had to warn Owen. He had to admit what a monumental mistake he'd made.

Curling his hands into fists, Peter glared at the door Ava had disappeared behind.

No, he promised himself. He didn't have to admit anything. He just had to fix it.

And he would.

One way or another, Peter would find a way to uncover the secrets in DeVerre. And he'd put a stop to them once and for all.

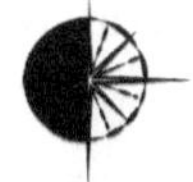

CHAPTER TWELVE

Spencer

Weighty stares were passed back and forth in the overcast afternoon, only the glow of the lamps supplying any warmth to the room. They sat around the dining room table. Cassandra at the head, Owen to her right, and Peter and Spencer to her left. And at the opposite end of the table, Tom had taken his seat.

Owen had left school early to arrive before the marshal. His dark blue eyes were distant now, and he fidgeted in his seat. Spencer had never seen him so unsettled.

"We're sure we can trust Tom?" he'd asked when he joined them at the table.

"Sure?" Spencer tilted his head to the side as he weighed the idea. "Probably not. But I'd say we can trust him more than anyone else right now."

"He was pretty convincing," Cassandra agreed, placing a cup of tea before Owen. He muttered a thank you before she continued. "I don't see any reason to doubt Tom's honesty. He seemed too relieved to have help to be using us."

"Hm." Owen began to rub his hands together in worry. "All right, well . . . I trust your judgment."

"Do you?" she challenged, gesturing toward his hands.

He paused, glancing down at his white-knuckled grip. A tense chuckle puffed out of him as he pressed his hands flat on the tabletop. "Yes," he promised. "I do. It's just that I've gone a long time keeping my abilities hidden from everyone in this town. Revealing myself to you three was one thing. None of you are close enough with Ava to cause concern."

Peter adjusted abruptly in his seat, bumping into Spencer's chair. "Sorry," he mumbled.

Owen continued, unaware of their exchange. "But Tom . . . well, he's known her longer than I have. And whether they're friends or not . . . I worry that this will lead to her discovering the truth about me."

"Wouldn't it be a relief, though?" Peter asked, his words rapid. "You wouldn't have to hide anything from her anymore."

Owen nodded, though he heaved a heavy sigh. "It would be a huge relief to be open with her. But . . . I know my wife. And I know that if she doesn't have a change of heart before she finds out . . . that'll be it for us."

"She's your wife!" Peter scoffed, a clear look of indignation scrunching his face. "You guys made vows. She can't be petty enough to break them for her own prejudices."

"I've lied to her," Owen countered, "for over eleven years—our entire relationship—about the thing she fears the most. There is no chance that she'll forgive me for that if she doesn't accept the truth about the spirit world before she finds out."

Spencer understood that. Better than the rest of them at the table. He'd come to DeVerre for his brother only to find himself face-to-face with his greatest fears. Though he felt he had coped with a reasonable level of competency, his own response to it wasn't too different from Ava's at the end of the day.

They both wanted to remove the threat and make their home safe.

Ava just happened to misunderstand who the threat was.

When Tom arrived, Spencer led him into the dining room as Anguis and Nex followed, sniffing their visitor. The marshal slowed as he caught sight of Owen. Older than all of them by more than a decade, Tom looked his age in the dim light of the encroaching mist. His wrinkles grew deeper as he furrowed his brow and narrowed his gaze.

"Owen," Tom said, hesitation and confusion in his tone. "You, uh . . . you're with them?"

His strong nod defying his prior anxiety, Owen held the marshal's stare. "I am."

"Does Ava know?"

"No."

Tom took several seconds to consider the news. "You're a Wielder?"

"Yes."

"Damn," the marshal huffed. "She's gonna be pissed if she finds out."

"Which is why I'd rather she didn't."

"She won't hear it from me." Tom reviewed the other three, then turned back to him. "No one will. What happens here is between the five of us."

Anguis and Nex slipped under the table as Tom took his seat, and Spencer moved back to Peter's side. He pulled out his chair, glancing at Owen, then Cassandra. He caught a slight smirk on her lips as she ran a finger over the rim of the glass of water before her. Spencer only had to guess what amused her for a split second.

It wasn't just the five of them here, he realized. Gerard was invisible somewhere, listening in.

As he wondered how the cop would take the revelation of the phantom in their home, Tom settled into the chair in front of him. "All right," he said, loosening the tan collar of his button down. "So, I guess you want to hear everything I know?"

"That would be great," Owen replied.

"Mm . . . okay." He let out a long sigh. "Well, I'll tell you what my father told me. I'll warn you, it isn't much. The facts got watered down through each generation. I'm not sure if that was intentional or just a bad game of telephone. But I imagine it wasn't easy—trying to remember all those facts and details and having no one to talk to about them."

"Anything is helpful," Owen assured him.

Tom nodded, and Spencer rested his arms on the tabletop in anticipation. The marshal brushed his fingers over his mustache and cleared his throat. "So . . . back when the Varons, Chapelles, Garniers, and . . . all the rest of 'em came to DeVerre, it was to protect the lake.

"Apparently," he tossed a hand in the air as though it were a fantastic notion, "it's associated with the spirit world. Can't say I understand how any of that works, but—well, that's not why we're here. The founders were all Wielders is my point. They were able to access and harness the spirit world. Not that I understand that either."

Spencer cast Peter a worried glance out of the corner of his eye. They knew all this stuff. Between everything that Gerard, Owen, and Cassandra knew, they'd pieced it together easily. And now he worried that Tom didn't have much more information than they already did. Would this meeting be just another waste of time?

Tom rested his elbows on the table, holding his hands out in the air before him. "The Varons had the most power of them all, so they headed up the founding of DeVerre, earning them the primary position of authority," he explained. "However, not all the men and women who signed up to settle here were of the same . . . persuasion."

That was *slightly* new information.

Spencer felt one of the dogs lay their head on his foot. He spared a glance down, seeing the white blaze between Anguis's brows. With a grin, he accepted the dog's comfort, his eyes unconsciously drifting toward Cassandra. He'd found himself doing that whenever Anguis paid him particular attention. And now he found Cassandra sitting forward in her seat, eyes locked onto the marshal with rapt focus.

"The founding families kept the knowledge of the spirit world safely guarded from the others," Tom said. "It wasn't the sort of thing you shared with the general populace, you know? Some might've been too afraid to settle here. And others may have wanted to claim the power for themselves. It was potentially dangerous. And they were cautious about the people they shared it with."

"Seems smart to me," Peter said.

It sounded like typical Warden behavior to Spencer.

The marshal huffed. "Yeah, it does, doesn't it? However, one can be too cautious. And most were *so* careful that they were even hesitant to share the information with their own children. Over the years, less and less of the family members learned anything about the spirit world, which meant less and less of them became Wielders."

"Wait." Spencer leaned forward, interested. "Why would they stop teaching their children? They came here to *protect* the lake. The fewer Wielders they had, the fewer people able to protect it."

"Obviously, I wasn't there," Tom replied. "But my guess is that they were either too confident or too scared. Maybe both."

"Those are sort of conflicting feelings," Cassandra remarked.

"Not necessarily. They feared the spirit world but also had confidence in the Varons."

"Because the Varons were in charge?" Spencer prodded.

"Because they were *always* strong," he clarified. "The Varons didn't approve of waiting to train their children. From an early age, they began to teach them how to interact with the spirit world and keep it at bay. This . . . well, this did lead to some disagreements within the town. But all in all, no one challenged the Varons because they knew the family would protect them."

The marshal paused, gaze dropping to his hands. "At least . . . that's how it was for a long time."

Spencer leaned more heavily on the table as he felt Peter angling toward him. This was it. They were going to get the answers they'd been looking for.

Tom took a deep breath before starting again. "Back in the early 1900s—my father wasn't sure of the exact timeline—there was a . . . an incursion, I suppose you could call it. Somehow, the spirit world broke free of its—its bindings or . . . whatever it is that holds it back, and it ended poorly. Several people died, and there was unrest in the founding families.

"No one knew how it happened," he explained, "but the blame got pushed onto the Varons. They were supposed to keep the spirit world at bay and protect the town. And they'd failed. Some thought they were slacking on their duties. Others . . . well, others thought they'd done it themselves."

"They thought the Varons had done it intentionally?" Owen set his elbow on the table, resting his chin in his hand. "Why?"

"The rest of the families were worried about how powerful the Varons had grown compared to the rest of them. There was concern that they'd become greedy with that power and that they'd reached into the spirit world to access more."

Owen narrowed his eyes dubiously but nodded for the marshal to go on.

"Many families tried to talk with the Varons and learn what had happened, but they maintained their innocence and insisted that they had the spirit world under control."

"Did they?" Peter asked.

"How should I know?" Tom tossed his hands out before him in a shrug. "However, the Garniers and Varons were close. My great-grandfather believed that the Varons weren't responsible for the attack. As the marshal at the time, he was working to solve the case. He was convinced they were being set up. Yet he had no evidence."

Tom took a deep breath, then blew it out in an exasperated sigh. "The rest of the families held a secret meeting to discuss how they might handle the situation. My great-grandfather went intending to steer the meeting toward finding the truth rather than controlling the Varons. But the rest of them didn't care to hear his opinions. They felt enough was enough. They'd seen the dangers of the spirit world, and they had no interest in passing that fate onto their children."

A heavy sense of foreboding ate at the back of Spencer's brain. Something about that meeting didn't sit right. The marshal had said that the Varons held the confidence of the whole town. That they'd trusted them. How had one event caused all of the founding families to turn on them?

"Aside from my great-grandfather," Tom continued, "every single person at that meeting wanted to see an end to the spirit world. They wanted to remove all contact with it. There was a vote and, of course, their side won. So, they issued an ultimatum to the Varons: End all contact with the spirit world or lose control of the town."

Spencer rested a hand over his mouth, still working to puzzle out this sudden flip.

Peter leaned into his periphery. "But the Varons were the most powerful of them all, right?" He shook his head. "If the rest of the town had lost most of its Wielders, they couldn't pose much of a threat. How did they get the Varons to listen?"

"It was simple, really," Tom replied. "They were going to vote them out of office. It wouldn't matter if they had supernatural powers, then. Charge of the town would pass to someone else, and that would remove the Varons' voice from everything."

"I'm surprised they didn't fight back."

"The Varons weren't a vindictive family," the marshal said, his tone almost disappointed. "They . . . well, they could see when they'd lost, and they were smart enough to take the wins they could. I think they were playing the long game. Hoping to get back in control once things had calmed down."

"So that was it?" Cassandra asked, her voice tinged with frustration. "They just gave in?"

"They did," he confirmed. "The town buried all connection to the spirit world. They removed all traces of it from the records, the history books—anything else that could lead to it."

Cassandra let out a sigh, and Spencer couldn't help but share her frustration. After everything he'd heard about the family, he was surprised to hear that they'd let the others win so easily.

"However—" Tom held up a finger to stall their letdown. "The Varons weren't happy about any of it. And my family wasn't thrilled either. Despite their promises, the Varons and Garniers kept their children aware of the spirit world. My family didn't pass on all the information— as I said, there are a lot of gaps in my knowledge. I only know enough to ensure that I can protect the town from the lake. And from people like Debbie Mercier and whomever she was working with."

A flicker of humor tugged at the side of Spencer's mouth hearing the unspoken in the marshal's words. "But the Varons passed it all on, didn't they?"

"They did."

"And your family worked closely with them up until they died?"

"From what I know."

"So," Peter cut in, drawing their attention to him. His brows arched high on his forehead. "You're a Wielder too?"

"What?" Tom drew his head back in surprise. "No! No, I have—I don't know the first thing about magic."

"It isn't magic," Owen said, his ever-steady gaze studying the marshal's face. "You said, 'people *like* Debbie.' You don't know what their proper name is, do you?"

Tom's eyes went wide. "I wasn't aware they had one."

"They're called Druids," Owen said, his voice flat and deadpan as though they were having a perfectly normal conversation.

The marshal's face twisted up in confusion. "Like . . . like those crazy nature worshippers?"

"A sect of them. It's their goal to release the spirit world into the Earth."

"Oh, God." Tom gasped. "It's worse than I thought."

"What did you think it was?" Peter asked, a hint of superiority in his tone. "Just a handful of creepy weirdos terrorizing the town?"

Though he passed Peter an annoyed frown, Tom raised his brow. "More or less."

"So, you're completely unaware of the Druidic people?" Owen asked.

"I mean, I've heard of 'em." Tom scoffed, exasperated. "But I always thought they were a bizarre cult that only existed in Ireland."

Owen cocked his head to the side. "Well, they are a cult, but they're not that isolated."

The marshal brushed his mustache again nervously. "And you think they've come to DeVerre to, what? Use the lake to release the spirit world?"

"That's my best guess."

Tom grimaced and shook his head. "But Debbie and Mike are natural-born DeVerreans. Her family built the school with their bare hands, and they've run the place ever since."

"The Druids have been here from the start," Cassandra said, drawing their attention. She sat with the window at her back, face cast in shadows, and eyes darker than pitch. "My mom's whole family is from DeVerre. Debbie's family. They came to DeVerre as founders."

Spencer's stomach dropped.

Owen let out a hum, a small sound of revelation. "They made their way into the inner workings of DeVerre and are waiting for the right time to strike."

Tom's brows pulled together in doubt. "You think they've been waiting for over a century?"

"They're patient people."

"No one is that patient."

"They are," Owen insisted. "The Druids see death as a means to bring on their true form in the spirit. While they'd rather experience that form here in the present, they have no problem waiting until after their death if it helps achieve the 'grand design.' They believe that once the spirit world has overtaken the natural world, the divine forms of their spirit will release with it, and it will be as though they never died in the first place."

Peter and Spencer gaped at him along with the marshal.

"And these people have infiltrated the town?" Tom asked, a thread of panic in his heavy voice.

"Seems that way."

"This is *far* worse than I thought."

"But you have suspects, right?" Peter asked, desperation in his tone.

"A few," Tom confirmed, though he didn't appear confident. "They're more like hunches. People acting off and the like. Nothing concrete. And nothing that convinces me enough to make an arrest."

"Who are they?" Spencer prompted.

Shifting in his seat, Tom reached down to pull a folded envelope from his back pocket. "Here," he said, pushing it toward Spencer. "This is a list I've worked up over the past month and a half. I've included everyone I've ever suspected, regardless of my current opinions. Being so new to town, you may not know most of the names, but Owen will."

"Any we should pay particular attention to?" Spencer asked, pulling the bundle of papers from the envelope. Staring at the ink on the lined pages, he realized the marshal was right; he knew many of the last names listed, but only five or six belonged to people he actually knew.

Tom scratched his jaw in thought. "The Ozannes have always been territorial and standoffish. But it's one of theirs that died first, so I thought that counted in favor of their innocence. The MacDonalds are a strange bunch, too, but they haven't been around since the start. I've never liked how Tony made his way onto the town council, though. It struck me as suspicious."

Spencer did his best not to look Cassandra's way at the mention of the MacDonald family. He could well imagine her smug grin, knowing she'd been right to be wary of them.

"And now," Tom went on, "I've got a great deal of suspicion about the whole of the Mercier and Sauveterre families. No offense, Miss Clement."

"None taken," she assured him.

"As far as the rest of that list. . . ." Tom paused and scowled. "Well, now I'm second-guessing every founding family in this town. They're all there too. Including my own. Barring my wife and sons, of course."

Peter let out a grunt, staring at the list over Spencer's shoulder. "Looks like our suspect list includes the whole town."

"Not quite," Tom muttered.

Owen pushed back his chair. "I hate to leave prematurely, but Ava will be getting off work in the next hour, and I have to walk home. But first, we need to discuss the equinox."

"The what?" Tom demanded.

"The Druids believe in celestial patterns affecting the spirit world," Owen explained. "They think it's stronger when the heavens are in alignment."

"You don't believe in that mumbo jumbo, do you?"

He shrugged. "Can't say I'm convinced either way. Whatever the case, we do know that *they* believe it. And that means they're likely waiting for a celestial event to do whatever they've been working toward."

"And we're sure it's the equinox?" Spencer asked.

"I'd say we're not sure of anything," he admitted. "But only three major celestial events are coming up aside from the regular moon cycle: the partial lunar eclipse, total solar eclipse, and the winter solstice."

Peter raised his brow, a grin tugging up the right side of his mouth. "You did your homework, didn't you?"

A small, imperious smile spread over Owen's face. "That I did."

"All right," Tom said, shifting forward in his seat. "What's your theory then? Which event are they waiting for?"

"Could be any of them," Owen said. "However, I'd guess it's the solstice. The solar eclipse will only be visible in Antarctica and parts of South Africa. And the lunar eclipse isn't as impactful, being partial. An equinox is a major catalyst of change. It marks a new season. If I were looking for an impactful event, that's the one I'd choose."

They all nodded, agreeing with his assessment.

"But, of course," he said with a shrug, "I could be completely wrong."

A tight laugh escaped Cassandra. "We're quite the team," she muttered.

Unable to help but feel similarly cynical, Spencer made sure to keep the sarcasm from his own voice. "So, we prepare for the equinox but stay aware of the eclipses?"

Owen nodded. "I'd also suggest staying watchful during any new moon as well."

"And we work on making connections within the town in the meantime?"

"Exactly."

"And if we find any Druids," Peter added, then pointed to the marshal, "we call you?"

"Seems that way," Tom muttered, exasperation tingeing his voice. "In the meantime, I'll go over my suspect list with this information in mind. If the Sauveterres are involved, I'll keep a sharp eye on them."

"And most importantly," Owen said, looking over all of them, "remember what we're trying to do here. This isn't about keeping the town safe, or finding murderers, or pursuing personal agendas. This is about protecting the Veil. We must keep the lake out of the Druids' hands. If they get the chance to release the spirit world, all of this will be for nothing."

Spencer's breath caught in his chest. Everything they were facing—all their plans—it was all to protect the Veil. But how?

A hundred years ago, the people of DeVerre decided they didn't trust the very people who led them there. The people meant to do what they were attempting now: Protect the Veil. And from the start, they'd faced the doom of Druids waiting to take over. It was no wonder they couldn't figure things out—the Druids had been planning their coup from the start.

The truth of the revelation hit Spencer in the gut.

The Druids had been planning it from the start.

They knew so little about being a Wielder, Spencer realized. And they were facing an enemy who knew everything. An enemy who had the town of DeVerre under complete control.

There was so much more to the spirit world than summoning beasts and wielding arcs. So much they'd need to know to stay alive.

Spencer pulled his hands into fists underneath the table. They were getting answers. Slowly but surely, they were finding the truth. First, with Owen. Now, with Tom. And tomorrow, Spencer promised himself, he would get the truth from Samuel Chapelle.

CHAPTER THIRTEEN

Peter

If Ava had hoped to discourage Peter, she'd done just the opposite.

Waking the next morning, he felt refueled, as though energized by her opposition. He could admit that she had a point about the dangers involved in the spirit world. But he'd already known that. It was impossible not to know that at this point.

But he wasn't afraid—of Ava's threats or the Druids.

Peter had heard someone say once that bravery and stupidity were often one and the same. And while he didn't know whether or not they were right, he thought he had the necessary amount of stubbornness to offset whatever intelligence he lacked.

After barreling down the back staircase into the kitchen, Peter poured himself a cup of coffee before following the sounds of Spencer and Cassandra's voices around the corner. Finding the pair in the office, Peter tipped his chin up in greeting. "Sup?"

Spencer sat in the desk chair, laptop open before him, while Casandra sat on the edge of its surface, nearest the open doorway. "Morning." She smiled. "I was just telling Spence about my plans to head to Spokane today. But he doesn't want me to go."

Spencer crossed his arms. "It isn't that I don't want you to go. It's that you aren't supposed to be alone."

"I don't need a bodyguard outside of DeVerre."

Peter furrowed his brow. "Why're you going to Spokane?"

"A couple of reasons," she replied, too cryptically for his taste.

Nex and Anguis padded into the room from the kitchen, their fur damp from the morning rain. They went right for Spencer, who reached over to scratch each of their ears as he spoke. "It'd be nice to know your reasons."

Smirking, Cassandra's eyebrows rose. "You two are like mother hens. I'm a big girl. I can handle a drive into the city."

"It's not about that," Peter argued. "Why are you going to Spokane?"

"I'm not doing anything that'll get me hurt."

"So. . . ." Peter drew the word out in exaggeration. "What *are* you doing?"

Tightening her jaw, Cassandra hesitated. Finally, she gave an indifferent shrug. "DeVerre's general store didn't have everything I needed, so I'm going shopping."

"Oh." Peter frowned, disappointed by the mundane trip.

Spencer drew his head back, satisfied with her answer. He lifted his mug and took a sip.

Cassandra gave her ring a single twist. "Then I'm going to swing by and confront my parents."

Spencer choked on his coffee while Peter's eyes went wide.

Setting the mug on the desk, Spencer brushed the back of his hand over his mouth. "What?"

"Why would you do that?" Peter demanded.

Cassandra's stare was far too calm for the conversation. "Because they've been lying to me my whole life, and I think it's time for them to tell me the truth."

The brothers shared a dubious look.

Spencer rested his arms against the desk. "Do you really think that's the best idea?"

"Why wouldn't it be?" she asked. "My parents clearly know something. Or, at least, my mother does. She and Debbie were best friends. There's no way that she wasn't aware of the Druids. And if that's the case, she'll be able to give us the information we need to know."

Peter couldn't refute the plan. And he wasn't sure how they hadn't thought about it before now. "All right, yeah. That's smart."

"Thanks."

"But you're not going alone."

Spencer nodded in agreement.

Cassandra sighed. "I'll be fine."

"Maybe." Peter raised his brows. "But maybe the Druids will see it as the perfect opportunity to run you off the road."

She gave him an amused grin. "And you coming along would stop them from doing that?"

"There's a chance."

Cassandra tossed a hand through the air. "Fine. You both gonna join me?"

Peter couldn't help the excitement rising in his chest. This plan would be good. It would get him out of the house and give him something to do. Finally, a task that would result in some answers. And it would be fun to go on a little road trip. After the weightiness of the past week, they could use a break from DeVerre. "Yeah, let's do it!"

"Oh, uh," Spencer cut in, rubbing a hand along the back of his neck. "I can't go."

Peter and Cassandra both frowned at him.

"Why the heck not?" Peter demanded at the immediate let down.

Spencer gave them an apologetic shrug. "I made plans to meet with Reverend Chapelle this morning. I'm supposed to be there in half an hour."

"You're meeting with the reverend? Alone?" Peter didn't like the sound of that.

Neither did Cassandra. "It's dangerous, Spencer," she warned, sharp eyebrows lowered over her eyes. "Sam may be a religious man, but that doesn't exempt him from our suspect list."

"I'm not going to do anything stupid, Cassie," he promised. "I'm just going to get a feel for what he knows. See if there's anything to learn from him or if he's as innocent as he seems. I'm not even going to bring up the spirit world."

She hesitated but wound up giving him an approving nod.

Feeling no less cautious, Peter leveled a serious stare at his brother. "You sure this is a smart play?"

"Don't worry, Pete. I'll be careful."

Peter sucked in a deep breath, trying to decide if that was true. He'd known that he was overprotective of his brother before they'd moved to DeVerre. But since moving to the small, secluded town, a whole new world of danger had opened itself up. And he didn't like the idea of leaving him to investigate the reverend alone. Not when the same Druids who could attack Cassandra might see it as their chance to come for his brother.

"We could wait," Peter suggested. "Surely this meeting won't be that long."

"It's already ten o'clock."

"So what?"

Spencer frowned. "Even if the meeting only lasts an hour, it'd be after eleven by then. And Spokane is, what? Two hours away?"

"A little less," Cassandra said.

"So, we'd get there around one-thirty," Spencer concluded. "It'd be better if you two go now and get it taken care of. Then, if Cass's family *does* have information, you can come back at a reasonable time, and we can figure out what to do with it. Otherwise, you'll just be waiting around for me when you could be getting stuff done."

Peter frowned at the logical suggestion. "Fine," he grumbled.

"Also," Spencer added. "While you're shopping, I think it'd be a good idea for you to pick us up some winter stuff. My jacket's not really cutting it anymore."

Peter nodded. "Yeah, mine's not doing so great either."

Cassandra smirked as she turned to him. "Looks like we'll have a little shopping day, Pete."

"Thrilling."

Within ten minutes, the two of them had gathered their things, slipped on their jackets, and headed out to her truck. The cherry paint of the vintage Ford held just the right amount of dinginess, its age muting the shine of the silver handles, side mirrors, and embellishments. Peter loved it.

"I can drive if you like," Peter offered.

Cassandra brushed the idea off with a quick wave while she headed for the driver's side. "Nah, that's all right. I like to drive."

Peter tried to squelch his disappointment. "Well, if you need a break or anything, let me know."

The two of them climbed into the truck, the plush, cushioned bench seat accepting their weight with ease. As immaculate as the Jeep, the truck's dustless dashboard and clean seats marked it as well cared for. A pine air freshener hung from the rearview mirror, softening the musty scent of age.

Glancing over as he clicked his seatbelt in place, Peter caught the small, contented smile that came to Cassandra's lips as she rested one hand on the steering wheel and the other turned the key in the ignition. He couldn't help snickering in immediate recognition of that look.

As the truck revved to life, Cassandra looked at him. "What?"

"Nothing."

Pulling the gear shift down into drive, Cassandra passed him an annoyed, though slightly amused, glare.

"It's nothing," he repeated, smirking as he looked over to the Jeep parked on their right. "Just . . . you two and your cars."

The gravel crunched under the tires as they pulled around the drive. It gave way to the smooth macadam as they passed through the large, wrought iron gates of Occasus.

"Us two?" Cassandra's words came out like an accusation. As though she already knew who he was referring to but didn't appreciate the connotation.

Peter nodded. "I'll never understand it. Don't get me wrong; I like the Jeep. It's a nice memory. But it'll never mean as much to me as it does to Spence."

"And what makes you think I'm as attached to my truck as Spencer is to his Jeep?"

"The way you sit in it."

She tossed him a confused glance.

"It's like it's your safe place," he said, picturing how his brother transformed whenever he got in the Jeep. Shortly after their dad's death, there was a night that Spencer went missing. Peter and their mother had looked everywhere for him. They'd searched the entire house, gone to the neighbors, and called family.

After hours of searching, Peter had finally figured it out. He went to the patch of dry grass on the far side of the driveway where their dad used to work on the Jeep. When Peter had looked in the windows, he'd found twelve-year-old Spencer curled up in the backseat, asleep with a book at his side. When he had woken his little brother, Peter asked Spencer what he was doing out there. Spencer replied, "I just wanted to be near Dad."

The memory brought a smile to Peter as he finished his thought. "You're relaxed here," he explained. "Spence is the same way."

Cassandra didn't reply but tightened her grip on the steering wheel, convincing him that he was right. Though, he couldn't figure out why she held the same sort of attachment. It was a cool truck and all, but she hadn't lost either of her parents. And after everything she'd said, he doubted she'd cling to something inherited from one of them anyway.

"What makes this truck so special?" Peter asked.

The way she hesitated—jaw tight as she shifted uncomfortably—made him wonder if he was pushing for something he hadn't earned the right to know. But she let out a lightly humored scoff. "It's just . . . it's just a truck," she muttered. "But about four and a half years ago, I wanted to start over. I was tired of trying to make Spokane work when I just wanted to be in DeVerre. So, I sold my stuff, bought this truck off a little old lady whose husband had died a few years prior, and loaded up the back with everything I had left. Then I came here."

As they drove through the roundabout of Harmony Plaza, Peter smiled at Cassandra. "I get it," he said. "When we left Norfolk, I did the same thing. It's like a fresh start. A chance to change your life. And leave behind everything that everyone else thinks about you."

Cassandra glanced at him as she pulled onto Harmony Road and headed west. A surprised but pleased smile lit her face. "You know, Pete," she said, voice light and laced with humor. "You and I are a lot more alike than I originally thought."

Chuckling, Peter returned her grin. "Why? 'Cause we both like Spencer better than anyone else?"

Though her glare looked annoyed, she couldn't hide the laugh she tried to twist into a scoff. "No," she said. "Because neither of us is willing to let people tell us what to do."

Tipping his head to the side, Peter smirked. "Yeah," he admitted. "And it constantly gets us both in trouble."

The winding drive on the backroads of Washington State would take up most of their trip before reaching the highway that led south to Spokane. The sun shone above them in the late morning, making the frosted pine trees glitter as they whizzed past. As he surveyed the landscape, he noticed Cassandra's eyes regularly drifting to the rearview mirror. At first, he'd thought it was mere proper driving etiquette. Then he recognized the tension in her shoulders with each glance. As though she was worried that they were being followed.

After a glance in his side mirror and one to the road around them,

Peter confirmed that the backroads of Washington remained clear of all travelers but them.

Taking it upon himself to distract her, Peter began searching through Cassandra's collection of old CDs in the center console, asking her about her favorites. She had good taste in music, he decided, selecting one of the classic rock albums to pop into the outdated stereo system.

Even as they talked music, Peter couldn't get the comparison between him and Cassandra out of his head. Were they really that alike? He hadn't thought so. She was rather snarky, and he'd often heard how he overdid it on the sarcasm as well. She was headstrong like him. She was willing to take risks—leaving everything behind to pursue what she wanted. And she was fiercely protective and loyal.

All good things in his book.

All things that Spencer needed in his life.

Peter knew it was abnormal—the way he constantly played the unwanted wingman for his brother. Some people might find it odd, even. But he didn't care what they thought. He knew his brother better than anyone.

Many times in their life, Peter had irritated Spencer by meddling in his love life. Spencer told him to back off and to forget it—that he wasn't comfortable with the idea of dating; sometimes, he claimed that he didn't want to get married at all. But Peter had never listened because he knew the truth: His brother was just afraid, as always. And if Peter didn't find Spencer a wife, he'd never find one himself.

If Peter was perfectly honest, it wasn't an entirely selfless pursuit. He'd promised to take care of Spencer. And his brother couldn't live life alone. If Peter went off and got a wife himself, then Spencer would be on his own. That wasn't an option. So really, Peter's matchmaking was all about practicality. Get Spencer settled and married to someone who could take Peter's place so that Peter could go and start a life for himself.

Adjusting the collar of his leather jacket, Peter settled deeper into his seat as he chatted with Cassandra. Yes, he thought, the ghost-whisperer might be the most unexpected choice for his brother, but that exact quality also made her the perfect match for him. He was afraid of everything. She was afraid of nothing. She could take care of him. And Peter could be content knowing that his brother was safe and happy.

"So," Peter said over the music. "You think your mom is a Druid?"

Cassandra laughed at the sudden subject change. "No, not really," she said. "I don't see her leaving DeVerre if she were. But I think she knows about them."

"And you're planning to just ask her about it straight out?"

Taking a deep breath, Cassandra hesitated. The hum of the road beneath the wheels blended with the electric guitar trilling through the speakers.

"I don't know," she said, finally. "She's probably still in rehab, so I don't know what condition she's in."

"Oh, right." Peter grimaced, having forgotten about her mother's accident. Cassandra hadn't told them much about the situation other than that her parents had practically begged her to move back home, and she'd refused. "Sorry, I forgot about all that."

"It's fine." Her voice was monotone and dull, as though she had mentally checked out.

Unsure if he should ask her about it or if she'd rather he left it alone, Peter ran a hand through his hair. "Then . . . you're just gonna play it by ear?"

"Yep."

"Mm."

Tapping her fingers on the steering wheel, Cassandra stared at the cracked and faded yellow lines on the road.

Peter cleared his throat, trying to find a way to lighten the mood. "It's, uh . . . it's kinda weird," he said. "Goin' to meet your family."

She smiled at that. "It's weird bringing you to meet my family."

Feeling encouraged, Peter nodded. "I feel like you brought the wrong brother."

There was a single beat of silence. "Trust me, meeting my family isn't that exciting," she said, not taking the bait. "They're normal, and they like it that way. It'll be like meeting anybody else."

"Like being back in Norfolk, just colder?" he suggested.

Cassandra chuckled. "Yeah, just like that. And just so you know, I'm planning to shop first. That way, we can leave as quickly as possible after we talk with them."

"Do they know you're coming?"

"No."

Peter shifted in his seat, draping an arm over its back. "You're just gonna surprise them?"

"No, Pete, I'm not. I'll give them a call when we're done shopping."

"And they'll be cool with that?"

"Probably not. But since they like taking every opportunity possible to tell me to come home, they'll be pleased I'm giving them a chance to do it again."

"Mm." Peter eyed her, unsure if talking about it was helping or hurting the situation. But after ten minutes of staring out the window at the never-ending forest of pine trees, he'd gotten bored. "You have any siblings?"

Cassandra glanced at him. "Yes."

The abrupt reply made him sure that was the wrong topic to choose. "You don't have to tell me about 'em," he assured her. "We can talk about something else."

With a long, drawn-out sigh, Cassandra smirked. "I have a brother."

"Seriously," Peter insisted. "You don't have to—"

"I don't mind, Pete."

"You seem to mind."

"No, it's—" She cut herself off with a scoff. "No one ever asks me about my family. Whether because they already know them or because they don't care. And I'm not really used to it. But I don't mind."

Trying to decide if he believed her, Peter decided to test it. "All right," he muttered. "What's your brother's name?"

"Isaac."

"And . . . he's younger?"

"No," she said, tone lighter than before as though she were settling into the conversation. "Ike is older."

"Really?" He pursed his lips in surprise. "I pegged you for the older sibling."

She laughed at that. "Why?"

"Because you're protective and self-contained. The older sibling has to be that way to take care of the younger one."

Cassandra glanced at him again before turning back to the road. "Yeah, well . . . I probably just come across that way because I'm the outcast in my family. Ike is the perfect son. He's done everything right; he got a secure job, married an amazing girl, and has two adorable little boys. *And* he stayed in Spokane."

"You have nephews?" Furrowing his brow, Peter had trouble reconciling the idea with his knowledge of Cassandra.

"I do."

"You're an aunt?" Peter shook his head, unable to imagine such a domestic version of her.

She smiled but didn't reply.

"But that's it, then? Just you and your brother?"

"Just us," she confirmed, then cocked her head as though thinking better of it. "Well, and Sandy, my sister-in-law."

"Right." He nodded. "Are you close with either of them?"

"Not really," she said, the detachment back in her tone. "Ike and I were closer when we were kids, but we grew apart in our teens. Different crowds and things. And while Sandy is nice, and we get along fine, she isn't my kind of person."

Peter scanned her, curious. "What is your kind of person?"

She tossed him a grin. "People like Diane."

He returned the grin, eyebrows rising. "Wielders."

Cassandra tipped her head toward him though she kept her eyes on the road. "People who aren't satisfied with the status quo. People who want more." Her smile grew. "People like you and Spencer."

Unable to help the warmth spreading in his chest, Peter reached over to nudge her shoulder. "Color me flattered."

She shook her head at his teasing tone.

"In all seriousness, though," he added, "it does mean a lot. And we like you too. It's been nice having you around."

Cassandra muttered a thanks.

Resting back in his seat, Peter stretched his legs out in front of him, ready to do some digging to uncover the truth about his brother and the ghost-whisperer. "In fact. . . ." He inflected his voice with as much seriousness as possible, though he didn't think it did much good at covering his amusement. "I'm pretty pleased with how everything's turning out. It's been a good little test run, in my mind."

She scrunched up her nose. "A what?"

"Test run," he repeated. "I was concerned, you know? About what it might be like once Spence found someone. But now I know I don't need to worry anymore."

Cassandra sucked in a sharp breath as he continued.

"You fit right in. And I've gotta admit—" He smirked at her. "I've always wanted a sister."

Cassandra shook her head as she glared at the road ahead of her. "You've gotta stop that, Pete."

"Stop what?"

She huffed, throwing the glare his way. "You have to stop saying things like that."

Peter narrowed his eyes at the frustration radiating off her, seeing his plan take effect. He knew he was making her uncomfortable. He knew he was pushing too hard. But sometimes, you had to back people against the wall if you wanted the truth.

"We have to work together, Peter," she continued, her words choppy and irritated. "We have to be a team. The more jokes like that you make, the more Spencer will think it's real. And if your brother thinks I'm trying to date him, he won't want anything to do with me."

Peter knew his grin was smug but couldn't find it in himself to care. "That's not true."

"It's already happening," she shot back. "He can hardly look me in the eye most of the time."

Peter rolled his eyes. "Yeah, well, that's just 'cause he's Spencer. He's scared of everything. Including attractive women."

"Well, he can't be scared of me," she insisted. "Not if we want to live through all of this. You have to stop it!"

"All right!" He held up his hands in surrender. "All right, I get it. I'll keep it to a minimum."

Cassandra threw another fierce glare his way in the split second she looked away from the road.

"I'll *stop*," he promised. "But I won't like it."

"You're so ridiculous," she muttered, the words like a smack. Her next words were louder. "Why do you even make those jokes? It's like you're fifteen or something, making fun of your brother for having a crush. Even when he *doesn't* have a crush."

Peter grunted at her overly defensive reaction. Which only further convinced him that she *was* as interested as he suspected. "He *definitely* has a crush, Cass."

She glowered at the road ahead. "If he has a crush on anyone, it's on Danielle. I've never seen him so chatty."

Hearing the jealousy in her tone, Peter couldn't help sniggering. "Yeah, I did notice you weren't a big fan of Danielle."

"For your information, I'm not a fan of Danielle because she's a MacDonald. Even Tom told us that he was suspicious of her family. But clearly, Spencer doesn't share my hesitancy, and that's fine. He can have a grand ole time dating the girl as far as I'm concerned."

"Oh, come on," Peter said with a huff. "You can't tell me you don't see it."

"What?"

"It's so obvious, Cass. He likes *you*."

She shook her head.

"But I know my brother," he continued. "And I know he won't do a thing about it until someone else makes him. He's too scared to take the risk."

"Peter, stop it," Cassandra insisted. "I don't see Spencer that way, and I don't want to. So, keep your jokes to yourself."

A long, weighty silence spread between them as Peter watched her, and she watched the road. Cassandra tucked a stray strand behind her ear, her silver ring catching in the sunlight. When her hand hit the top of the steering wheel, the other shifted up to rest next to it. She began to twist the ring.

Peter smirked. He'd noticed her nervous tic over the past few days— one that sprang up most often when Spencer was in the room.

The conversation between Cassandra and Gerard that he'd accidentally stumbled upon the other day rang back through his head. *"You gonna stop flirting with that boy long enough to get me some answers, Cassie?"* Gerard had asked, confirming what Peter knew. *And* that he wasn't the only one who had seen it.

Unless, Peter thought, the phantom had not been referring to Spencer but to Peter himself.

With a grimace, Peter glanced at Cassandra. She was still playing with her ring, but her shoulders seemed to have lost their rigid stance. He wasn't blind; he'd noticed that she was attractive the minute they'd met. But for some reason, the idea of taking an interest in Cassandra Clement had never even crossed his mind.

Playing with the zipper on his jacket, Peter pursed his lips as he stared at the woman. Was there any chance he'd been wrong? That he'd misjudged her actions as flirtations with Spencer when she'd meant to direct them toward him? He certainly hoped not. He'd already relegated her to being his brother's girl, and to think of anything else felt wrong.

Cassandra caught him staring as she looked both ways before turning onto the highway. "What?"

"Nothing," he mumbled.

"Peter."

He didn't respond but narrowed his eyes on her face as she glanced back at him again. Her dark eyes scanned him, and she scrunched up her nose.

A snort of laughter escaped Peter. That one look told him all he needed to know.

"What is wrong with you?" she demanded.

Peter shook his head. "I see the way you look at him, Cass."

He could practically hear her suck in a breath to argue, but he cut her off. "And it's not the same way you look at me or anyone else."

"Peter," she said his name again, but this time it was like a threat.

"I don't mind." He kept his words light with humor. "I'm certain that Spence doesn't either. In fact, I guarantee you that he's thrilled."

Her hands gripped the wheel tighter.

"I'll let it go after this," he promised. "But I want you to know something first."

She waited, silent.

"He's my brother. And if you hurt him, it's not gonna go well between us."

Cassandra pressed her lips together as she glared at the road. For a moment, Peter thought she'd yell at him for his presumptions. That she'd tell him to back off. That he was wrong.

Instead, a slow, dry smile brightened her face as she tapped her fingers against the wheel. "You are the most annoying person I've ever met."

"I get that a lot."

The look she passed him was far softer than her prior ones. "But you're a good brother," she said. "A better one than I've ever had if I'm being honest."

Though the sentiment made him feel proud, Peter couldn't help the sadness that accompanied it. He knew how important a good brother was. He had the best brother in the world—which made him uniquely qualified to understand just how awful life would be without a brother like that.

To lighten the mood, Peter gave her his best lazy grin as he reached over to slap her arm the same way he would Spencer's. "As far as I'm concerned, Cass," he said. "I am your brother at this point."

Her eyes narrowed, though her smile didn't falter. "You've known me for less than a month, Pete."

"And you've already saved my life multiple times. If that doesn't make us family, what does?"

She laughed, the sound bright and hopeful. "Family is a strange thing for me. My family is filled with Druids and liars."

"Hey!" He spread his arms wide. "Spence and I don't know who the heck our family is at this point!"

She shrugged as though accepting that they had equally questionable backstories.

Peter leaned forward to ensure that she understood how serious he was. "I don't care how long we've known you, Cass. We promised to take care of you, remember? You're our family now. And nothing's going to change that."

Cassandra turned from the road to study him for a long moment. "Don't make promises you can't keep, Peter."

"I always keep my promises, Cass."

The tires hit the rumble strip, jarring them back to their location. She veered back onto the road, a tight but appreciative laugh puffing out of her. "Well, maybe hold onto that promise for a bit longer," she said. "You might want to take it back after we talk with my parents."

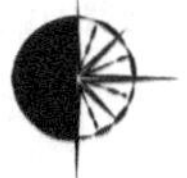

CHAPTER FOURTEEN

Spencer

S pencer arrived at the chapel promptly on time, the sun disappearing behind an oncoming rain shower as he pulled into the lot. November's cold air cut through his denim jacket, even inside the Jeep. If it weren't for the fact that Aaron had fixed up the whole vehicle a few weeks ago, he would have considered getting the heater checked out.

Glad to know that Peter would pick up some thicker coats for them while he and Cassandra were in Spokane, Spencer couldn't help feeling somewhat jealous of his brother. He wished he could have gone along with them, if just for the chance to get a glimpse into who Cassandra truly was.

In the week they'd lived with Cassandra, it had become clear to him that there was one side of herself that she showed and another that she kept in isolation. Even though she was easy-going and open, he was starting to realize that was only the version she wanted people to see. She hid a huge portion of herself behind layers of jokes and indifference to keep people at bay.

Spencer understood. His reserved demeanor served the same purpose. As did Peter's overly friendly persona. Spencer couldn't fault her for being careful with how much of herself she gave to people. And with all they'd been through over the last month, he couldn't blame her for not trusting them either.

But it would have been interesting to see a version of her that wasn't in DeVerre. A side of her personality and character that only family could bring out.

And, of course, Spencer wanted to know what her family had to say in response to her questions. The idea that they might have information about the Druids made the Clement family and their departure from DeVerre even more mysterious. Spencer wasn't sure whether to hope the Clements could give them everything or, for Cassandra's sake, that they knew nothing. He supposed it should be the latter.

Before his disappointment could grow, Spencer reminded himself that there was a reason he hadn't gone. And he was ready to get information of his own.

After turning off the Jeep, Spencer did up a few buttons on his jacket before opening the door. The rain and wind were like ice. He shut the door with a *thunk* before rushing to the thick, wooden chapel door. Tugging on the slick metal handle, he slipped through the heavy door.

Warm, yellow light filled the chapel's interior, glowing against the white walls and modern furnishings. The sanctuary was empty, but to his immediate left, the reverend's office door stood open.

Samuel Chapelle sat behind a desk almost as cluttered by books and papers as his own in Occasus. "Hello, Mr. Collins," the reverend said as he stood. He held out his hand as Spencer walked in.

Standing on the other side of the modest desk, Spencer accepted the handshake. "You can call me Spencer."

The reverend smiled. "Then you should call me Sam." He motioned to the brown leather chair beside Spencer. "Have a seat."

Settling in, Spencer scanned the office. The room was small. Nothing grand or overly designed. But it was cozy, with lots of full bookshelves, pictures of the reverend's family, and crayon art that was evidently from his daughter's early years.

The rain pelted against the windowpanes behind Sam. "So, how can I help you, Spencer?"

For the first time, Spencer realized the error he'd made in requesting to meet with the reverend. Alone, he didn't know what to do. So used to having Peter around to start the conversations and prompt his own questions, Spencer felt like a fish out of water trying to take charge of a fact-finding mission like this.

Spencer swallowed down his discomfort and met the reverend's kind eyes. "Honestly? I'm not sure."

Sam rubbed a hand over his coppery beard, a slow smile spreading over his face. "You did ask to meet with me. Surely you had something you wanted to discuss."

Nodding, Spencer tried to think of how Peter would dive into the matter at hand. His brother was brash at times, but he was also tactful when he needed to be. He appealed to the person's interests before pursuing his own. Often it did the trick. So, he would try the same.

"I'm just sort of confused, I guess," Spencer said, resting his arms on his thighs as he leaned forward. "I've grown up in the church, but . . . well, I've just never been surrounded by so many people who were so devout."

Sam's left eyebrow rose in intrigued humor. "Devout? Hm. Yes, I suppose you could say that DeVerre is more dedicated to their faith than the average town. But why does that confuse you?"

Knowing he couldn't give the whole truth to the question, Spencer unhooked the buttons on his jacket as he considered the best way to get around it. He didn't want to lie to the reverend. He didn't like lying in general. Not only was he sure it wasn't ethical or a Christian-like behavior, but he also didn't think he was very good at it.

Why was he confused? Beyond the Druids professing a faith they surely didn't believe in, what about DeVerre tripped him up? What could he tell the reverend that was true?

What confused Spencer?

A thin, self-deprecating scoff slipped from him as he dropped his eyes to the dark carpet beneath his boots. There was one thing these days that confused him to no end: Cassandra. Her and her strange ability to be so fearless. The way she could get up each morning and take thirty or more minutes to spend time with God even though they were facing death and innumerable questions.

"I guess. . . ." Spencer stopped, raising his head as he worked out his next words. "I guess it's making me wonder about my own faith."

That made Sam's light eyes grow wide for a second. "How so?"

Realizing how that could sound, Spencer shook his head. "Not that I'm questioning my faith," he assured him. "Trust me, I'm solid on that."

"Then what are you unsure about?"

Spencer wrung his hands. "Well . . . I guess, I'm just not sure that I'm a very good Christian."

"What makes you say that?"

"I don't know."

Sam tipped his head to the side. "You say that you're sure of your faith?"

"Yes."

"But you don't think you're a good Christian?"

He grimaced. "Maybe . . . maybe it's more that I'm not a good *enough* one."

"Because you're comparing your own faith to the faith of those around you?"

Spencer shrugged. "I suppose."

Taking a deep breath, Sam leaned back in his leather chair. He studied Spencer as his hand brushed over his beard several times. "In most cases, I'd suggest that comparing our faith with someone else's is a dangerous game to play. We can become so focused on the *doing* of the faith, and not on the *living* of it that it becomes more about ourselves and less about the cross.

"However, it doesn't sound like that's your problem. You said the devout confuse you. Why?"

Processing the question, Spencer wondered what he'd gotten himself into by coming here. He hadn't intended to have a theological discussion with the reverend. At least, not of this sort. He'd wanted to learn about the history of DeVerre's faith. Not how to reaffirm his own.

"I don't. . . ." Spencer sighed. "I don't know. I just . . . I see how they live, and I just—I wonder if I'm missing something."

"I'm not sure I understand."

"How do they do it?" he asked, hoping the man might have a real answer for him. "How do they live every day as though they don't care if it'll be their last? How do they not care that the worst could happen any second?"

Sam's demeanor shifted at that, less confused and more compassionate. He tucked his chin as he surveyed Spencer. "You're afraid of dying?"

Spencer blinked at the oversimplification of his fears. "No, not—not *dying* so much as. . . ." Throat going hoarse, he paused again. "I'm not afraid of my own death. I don't look forward to it, by any means, but . . . no, I'm not afraid of dying."

The reverend nodded. "You're afraid of those you love dying."

Again with the oversimplified truths. Spencer rubbed his hands along his thighs. "I guess."

"And why does that scare you?"

"Why wouldn't it?"

Sam gave him an understanding smile. "We all die, Spencer."

"I know."

"It doesn't make it any easier though, does it? Knowing?"

"No."

A heavy silence fell in the room.

Spencer felt like a failure in more ways than one. He'd come to the chapel with the intention of securing information. And instead, he'd opened himself up to a whole slew of uncomfortable revelations and thoughts. He didn't want to think about his fear of losing the people he loved. He didn't want to recall the memories of his childhood that made him more afraid than anything else ever had.

Living in a haunted house, searching out secrets, and fighting off Druids should be the things that scared him the most. But instead, something far more mundane terrified him.

"I'm not afraid to die," Spencer said to the carpet. "I'm afraid of living and being alone."

Raindrops pattered louder in the following beat of silence before Sam sighed and sat up straighter. "You do realize, Spencer," he said, "that fear is a sign of faulty trust?"

Meeting the man's gaze, Spencer narrowed his eyes in confusion. "What do you mean?"

"Fear is a lack of trust. We only fear when we don't trust that the outcome will be good," Sam said. "That the One taking care of us will *make* it good."

Tightening his jaw, Spencer tried not to bristle against the church rhetoric. He knew all this. Just like he knew everyone would die. Just like he knew that his fears were irrational. Knowing did nothing to remove the fear, though.

"Yeah," he muttered. "Yeah, I know that."

"So, you don't trust God?"

A wry grin came to Spencer's lips. "See what I meant? I'm not a very good Christian."

Sam smiled. "We all have something that God is working on with us. It's part of being in a relationship."

Nodding, Spencer rubbed his hands together. Again, something he knew. And something that made him feel guilty.

Sam adjusted in his seat, drawing his attention. "May I ask you a question?"

"Sure."

He hesitated, a cautious glint in his eyes. "I hope you won't take offense, but . . . I feel a responsibility to ask," he said. "Cassandra Clement is living with you and your brother now, isn't that correct?"

Spencer raised his chin, knowing what the reverend was getting at. He hardened his jaw, prepared to defend their situation. "Her family's home burned down."

"I'm aware it's a difficult situation that she's in," he said in what Spencer assumed was supposed to be a respectful tone. "Are you or your brother . . . involved with Miss Clement?"

"No." The word came out hard and more aggressive than Spencer intended.

Sam cocked his head at the tone. "Is there any chance one of you might be in the future?"

Pressing his lips together around the irritation he felt building, Spencer took a deep breath. He didn't want to say anything that would prevent the possibility of him gleaning whatever information he could from the meeting, but he wasn't in the mood to discuss the topic with the man.

"I'm sorry, but I don't see the relevance of that question," Spencer said, sure the flat edge to his voice made his frustration clear. "If you're asking because you feel single men and women shouldn't live together, then it wouldn't matter if we were dating, or not. But let me be perfectly clear, I may struggle with certain aspects of my faith, but my concept of morality isn't one of them."

An apologetic smile tipped up Sam's lips. "And that concept of morality doesn't include premarital sex?"

Spencer glared at him. "Even if Cassandra and I *were* involved, no. That would not be an option. And it wouldn't be for Peter either."

Raising a hand, Sam dipped his chin down. "I can see your sincerity," he said, calm despite Spencer's agitation. "And I appreciate it. I only ask because some people in town feel that your situation at Occasus is . . . questionable."

Spencer scoffed. "What would you like us to do? Kick her out? No one else would take her in."

There was a flicker of embarrassment in Sam's eyes. "I understand. And I appreciate your honesty with me. It's good to know that—well, I'm glad to hear you and your brother hold so fast to your beliefs."

Spencer let out a sardonic laugh as he crossed his arms. "Believe me, even if we didn't, Cassandra's a better Christian than either of us. She wouldn't put up with that crap for a second."

Sam looked up at him in surprise. But he shrugged, and the expression relaxed. "Good for her." He shifted forward in his seat. "I do hope you didn't take offense at my asking. I just wanted to be sure I'd done my due diligence. But I'm happy to hear it. And I'm glad you and your brother are part of our congregation. Any time you want to talk, my door is open."

"Thanks," Spencer muttered, then sucked up his discomfort in exchange for the reason he'd asked to meet. "But that's why I'm here, actually. I had some questions."

"Right." Sam nodded and gestured toward him. "Please, go ahead."

Taking a few seconds to regain his composure, Spencer worked his jaw back and forth. He wanted to blurt out all his questions, get the answers, and leave. But he knew that he needed to take a more socially appropriate approach. Which meant he had to move slowly and get the simplest answers before trying to earn the more complicated ones.

Spencer began, "Like I said, I grew up in the church. But while there are similarities in the services I'm used to and the ones here at DeVerre Chapel, there are some things I'm not used to."

There was a clear look of confusion on Sam's face. "Such as?"

"Just the way the service is run," he explained. "It's not quite

Catholic—not that I've ever actually been to a Catholic church, but I know about the liturgy and things they use. And while you guys use some similar liturgical . . . facets in the service, it's clear that you aren't Catholic."

Sam's smile turned amused. "No, we aren't."

"But you're not quite evangelical either."

"Well, we are Protestant, which is really all evangelicalism is."

"But you're a reverend," he countered. "And you utilize—well, you use some form of liturgy, don't you? Whether it's of your design or someone else's."

"I suppose I see what you mean. Personally, my only experience with the average evangelical church was during my years in seminary, so I'm not as versed as some on the topic. However, I do know that our denomination is quite different from that of the average church."

Spencer raised his chin. "And what denomination is DeVerre Chapel, exactly?"

Leaning forward, Sam rested his arms on the desk as he settled in to give his answer. "*Technically?* We're a variant of Lutheranism."

That sparked a memory in Spencer. He couldn't remember whether Owen or Cassandra had mentioned Lutheranism to him. But he was sure it had something to do with the Warden.

"However," Sam continued. "Our particular denomination stems from a theologian shortly after Luther's time named Heinrich Schwarz."

Spencer ran a hand along his stubbled jawline. That reference, he *knew,* had to do with the Warden. Schwarz was the man who'd mentored John William Lawrence, the founder of the Warden and the father of Elijah Lawrence. And Elijah was the man who'd written the pages stolen from Diane's draft.

Sam folded one hand over the other on the desktop. "Schwarz dedicated his life to making a difference in the church. Luther's dedication to Christ and the Church as a whole, inspired him to follow in his footsteps. He wanted to do something for the Body of Christ. He wanted to leave a legacy.

"So, he spent his whole life seeking out ways to improve the Christian's walk with God." The reverend shrugged. "He came to the conclusion that the best way to be in a relationship with God was to focus on the Spirit of God."

"Like, the Holy Spirit?"

"Yes, that is my understanding."

Spencer hesitated. From everything he knew about Schwarz and the Lawrences' studies—little as that was—he doubted it was as simple as that. Owen said the Warden's purpose was to protect the spirit world from the Druids' influence. That Lawrence spent his whole life dedicated to Schwarz's research, which meant that Schwarz knew about the spirit world. At least in some capacity.

"And DeVerre Chapel is based on Schwarz's theology?" Spencer asked.

"Again, *technically*, yes. However, it's quite different from the typical denomination in that Schwarz never created his own church. We base most of our theology on his research and findings, but we are not Schwarzians like there are Lutherans or Calvinists or Wesleyans, and so on.

"We focus our theological studies on the Bible alone," he concluded. "And Schwarz's teachings merely inform our opinions and how we structure our services."

"Is that where the prayer comes from?"

Sam raised his brow. "I assume you're referring to the prayer at the end of each service."

"Yes."

A dry grin lifted his whole countenance. " 'Teach us to see the unseen,' " he quoted.

Spencer nodded. "I've never heard anyone else pray that. Or, at least, not that specifically. And certainly not at every service."

The reverend sat back in his seat. "It was Schwarz's personal prayer. He prayed it every day during the final decade of his life." He shrugged.

"It's a good prayer, altogether. Longing to be drawn to Christ. To be inspired by the Holy Spirit. To see the unseen. It's very Biblical. So, we pray it in honor of him and to keep our focus on it."

Spencer drew his brows together, studying the reverend. He couldn't tell if he knew of DeVerre's secret spirit world or not. Was he sussing out Spencer as much as Spencer was testing him? Could he see the unseen? Did he even believe it was possible?

Cassandra was sure the Chapelles had some understanding of what was going on. And while Tom had dropped the bombshell that Sam opposed his own father's suggestion to remove Cassandra from DeVerre, it didn't mean Sam himself knew. That may have been the very reason he disagreed; while his father might have known, there was a chance that Sam wasn't aware that they were sending away a little girl who could talk to ghosts. The Garniers may have passed on the knowledge of the spirit world to their children, but had the Chapelles?

Spencer was tired of working around the secrets of DeVerre. He wanted to ask Sam outright if he had any involvement. But the patient gaze of the pastor made him hesitate.

Taking a deep breath, Spencer glanced at one of the pictures on Sam's wall. The silver frame contrasted sharply against the pine trees in the background. There, in the center, stood Sam with his wife and daughter. The women both had dark brown hair and deep olive complexions, while his ruddy skin tone and reddish hair stuck out like a sore thumb. They were all smiling in the image—a happy, loving trio.

Next to it was another photo of the young Juliet Chapelle. And along with her was a teen boy with sandy blond hair, wearing a lopsided grin. His arm hung loosely around Juliet's shoulders as they posed for the picture. After all the talk, Spencer had no doubt that this young man was Brendan Descoteaux, the last victim of the hellhounds and Juliet's boyfriend.

Spencer set his jaw. The pictures convinced him. Samuel Chapelle wasn't a Druid. There was no way he'd have sent a hellhound after his daughter and the young man he'd openly mourned a handful of weeks ago. Whatever he did or didn't know, he couldn't be on the Druids' side.

Meeting the reverend's eyes again, Spencer felt the pressure in his chest release. "I have one more question for you if you don't mind?"

"Of course."

"Do you know anything about the Varons?"

The flicker of surprise in Sam's eyes made Spencer wonder if he'd asked the wrong question.

Quickly working to clear up any mistake he might have made, Spencer held his hands out before him. "I know they used to own our house," he explained. "But I know little else about them. I—I heard that the Chapelles and the Varons were related, so I thought . . . could you tell me anything about them?"

After a single beat of silence, Sam rose from his seat. "I'll do you one better. Come with me."

Though surprised, Spencer practically leaped out of his seat, excited to see what the reverend would show him. He'd asked about the Varons on a whim—a wild grasp. He hadn't even intended on asking about the family, but now he didn't know why he hadn't thought about it in the first place.

Sam opened the door to the rain that fell in sheets. "Ah." He glared at the sky, then ducked back inside to grab a heavy rain jacket from the coat rack inside the door. "Sorry, it's not going to be a pleasant time, but . . . well, if you want to know about the Varons, this is probably the most information you'll find on them these days."

Spencer waved off any concern, promising he didn't mind the rain. His heart kicked up as they walked out of the church, not caring one bit that he'd wind up drenched. This was exactly what he needed. All the information on the Varons. Possibly just what he needed to help him find the vault.

Turning left outside the chapel, Sam led him down the sidewalk toward the back of the building. He took the veering path that led to the cemetery a short distance from the chapel. For DeVerre's small size, the cemetery was surprisingly large. Though, Spencer supposed that over a century of residents had come and gone from this life within its existence.

A short, wrought iron fence kept the cemetery enclosed and protected from wild animals. Sam unlatched the gate, gesturing for Spencer to enter first.

Throat going dry at the thought of entering a cemetery, Spencer forced himself to push through the gate without pause. He knew better than to let his foolish imagination get the best of him. He'd faced hellhounds and scylla and a murderous woman a mere week ago. He could handle a graveyard.

The gray sky lent an eerie atmosphere to the graveyard, the steady rainfall pattering on the short and unassuming headstones. Small, simple markers with old carvings worn down with age lay scattered across the yard.

Sam walked around Spencer and led him past the first few rows. "My brother is the mortician and looks after the cemetery," he began. "As our uncle had no children of his own, Gabe took on the job. Our uncle passed all the stories down to him, so he's much more knowledgeable than I am on the history of the individuals here.

"But," Sam continued, "I can tell you what I know about the Varons and show you their plots."

Hair already plastering itself to his skin, Spencer brushed at the clumps that hung on his forehead. "That'd be great. Thanks."

Sam smiled and ushered him down the fifth row of headstones. "Here," he said, gesturing to the first two, "are Matthias and Cecile Varon. You may have heard that it was Matthias Varon who founded DeVerre back in 1884. He was our first mayor, and by all accounts, he was a great and generous man. I believe my three-times-great grandfather and he were inseparable.

"Which is why—" He moved down a few plots. "The majority of my own family is buried within this row with them. Matthias and Frederic were like brothers. The only reason Frederic wasn't interred here is due to his wife's death shortly after the founding of DeVerre. You'll notice that we organize the cemetery by the date of death first and, on occasion, by family name second. Our ancestors valued the sanctity of marriage, so they made sure to keep a plot open for any spouse who outlived the other."

Spencer suppressed a shiver from the cold rain as he listened.

"Next to Matthias is his grandson, Matthew. And next to Matthew is his wife, Nathalie." The reverend led him farther down the row as he explained the family history. "Nathalie died quite early in life, so Matthew was moved up here rather than down by his father, which I'll show you next."

Scanning the gravestones as they walked past, Spencer took note of the name and dates on each one. There were seven Chapelles all in a row before they came to the next Varon. He started to do a double take of the Chapelle headstones, noticing the last few death dates were all within the same year, but Sam began talking once more.

"Here is Matthias's son, Marcus, and his wife, Lena. And just two more plots over rests Matthew's son, Michael Varon."

Prickles ran along Spencer's skin as his eyes landed on Michael Varon's headstone. He knew plenty about the man. He'd been the last living member of the Varon family—the one who'd murdered his father and committed suicide just after.

At least, according to the town.

Cassandra said that Diane hadn't been convinced by the claim. Meaning that Cassandra wasn't convinced. Spencer had yet to pick a side.

"Michael was. . . ." Sam sighed, passing Spencer a sad smile. "He was a troubled man. There were signs that he was mentally unstable, and it ended with both his and his father's death. Michael was unmarried, so he was the end of the Varon line."

Tucking his frigid hands into his jacket pockets, Spencer couldn't tear his eyes away from Michael Varon's name engraved into the headstone.

"I've often wondered what happened to him," the reverend said, his own stare locked on the grave.

Spencer glanced at the man. "You have?"

He nodded. "My grandfather grew up around Michael. There was a bit of an age gap between them, but he remembered playing together as kids." His light eyes remained affixed on the headstone. "Despite their age difference, my grandfather said Michael was always kind and attentive to him and the other kids in town. He said that you could tell that he had a good heart."

Looking back to the headstone, Spencer pressed his lips together at this contradictory description of the man he'd come to know as a psychotic killer. The etching on Michael's headstone was as simple as the rest with his name and year dates, but along with the other members of the Varon family, it bore another inscription: *Virtus, devotio, et cor.*

Spencer found his eyes locked on the grooves of the Latin words carved into the ashen stone. "How did someone like that grow up to be a murderer?" he muttered.

Sam gave him a spare glance before he tugged the hood of his jacket higher over his head, raindrops running down the sides. "I try not to ponder on evil too long. It's better to study goodness, righteousness, and love when you want to know the truth. However, Michael's story tends to be a common subject of gossip here in DeVerre, which makes it hard to escape. And, as I said, I've always wondered what could change a kindhearted kid into a murderous man."

Spencer shifted uncomfortably as the reverend returned his gaze to the grave. "Did you ever come to a conclusion?" he prodded.

"No," Sam admitted. "We all have the potential for darkness in us. It stems from our own selfishness. But no, I've never felt right about any of the theories that sprung to mind."

A long, weighted silence hung between them as they both stared at Michael Varon's resting place.

As his heart dropped, Spencer couldn't believe that he'd learned nothing new—nothing that could help them. He'd only discovered more questions, as usual. Hanging his head, Spencer fought the sigh that wanted to escape him.

"I know that's not the most detailed of answers," Sam said, his tone apologetic. "But I'm afraid that's all that I know. And I don't think many other people in town will be able to tell you much more about the Varons either."

The reverend's light eyes flickered to the graves they'd passed before, then back to Spencer. "The Varons became something of a point of contention within DeVerre back in the early 1900s. There was a . . . parting of the ways, I suppose you could call it, between them and the rest of the founding families. Even my own ancestors separated from them. I can't tell you why exactly. But what I do know is that the Varons became power-hungry. I suppose that happens when you let someone take charge with almost no checks in place.

"But after that time, few people associated with the Varons anymore. There was a heavy prejudice against them. And that makes it difficult for the truth to filter through the opinions after some time."

Spencer frowned. "You think that people are lying about the Varons?"

Sam quickly shook his head, flecks of water flying off his hood with the movement. "No, no," he said. "Not lying so much as misinterpreting information. When you have a bad opinion of someone, it colors everything you think and feel about them. It wouldn't matter if they did a wonderful act of kindness; you'd find a way to make it come across as selfish and detestable in your own mind.

"I don't believe for a second that the people of DeVerre ever intended to lie about the Varons," he insisted. "I just think that they let their personal feelings color their view of them. And I think that makes it difficult to know what's true and what's opinion."

Spencer thought he understood. That's how most of DeVerre felt to him. A vague image that changed depending on whomever he talked to that day. "Thanks," he said, though he didn't fully feel the sentiment. "You've given me a lot to think about."

Sam took a step to lead him to the front gate. "I'm glad. And if you think of any more questions—about your faith or DeVerre—please, don't hesitate to come to speak with me."

Finding no hint of falsity in the reverend's voice, Spencer smiled. "Thank you," he said again. "I'll do that."

Parting with the man when they reached the sidewalk, Spencer jogged to the Jeep while Sam hurried back into the chapel. He hated to get into the Jeep soaked as he was, but he didn't have another choice. Shivering as he turned the key, he looked thoughtfully at the chapel door.

Had the meeting been a total wash? Had he really learned nothing of value? Was there any point to it at all?

Spencer huffed. Probably not.

The white, wooden cross above the door stood out through the sheets of rain. Spencer tipped his head to the side, remembering Schwarz's personal prayer.

To see the unseen.

The theologian who inspired DeVerre's chapel was the man who had mentored the founder of the Warden. And it seemed to Spencer that Owen's presence suggested the Warden still held a strong interest in DeVerre. Its existence may have dissipated from the populace, but considering how closely the town held to its faith, there had to be a few remaining who knew of the organization. Even if they were all Druids now.

Someone had stolen Elijah Lawrence's essays from Diane's draft. Someone didn't want Cassandra to have access to them. And they needed to know why.

Putting the car in drive, Spencer headed back to Occasus. He may not have learned anything new, but the conversation *had* given him a direction. He needed to find those pages.

CHAPTER FIFTEEN

Cassandra

They arrived in Spokane while the sun was still high in the sky. The city always made Cassandra nervous, as though she were willingly walking back into the trap that her parents had set for her. As though she would be stuck there forever.

But with Peter at her side, the nerves didn't cling quite as strongly as usual. He'd been good to his word and left her alone about Spencer, exchanging the conversation for less consequential and perfectly distracting things. Things that helped her forget she was going to confront her mother and father and the tension rising in her chest the closer and closer they got to her home.

It took them all of an hour to get their shopping done. Not long enough for Cassandra's tastes, but it was what it was, she supposed. Might as well get the confrontation over with.

Sitting in the truck with a handful of paper bags between her and Peter, Cassandra pulled her phone out. Her fingers twitched as she pulled up her father's contact number, and she forced herself to press the button while Peter watched her with a patient, encouraging look on his face.

Two rings buzzed in her ear before the call connected. "Hello?" Her father's deep and even timbre hummed through the speaker.

"Hi, Dad," Cassandra replied, fidgeting with the steering wheel since she couldn't twist her ring. "How are you?"

"I'm all right, Cassie. How are you?" The question held weight to it. His surprise had merit. She never called her family. Not unless she needed something or felt guilty. And after the past week of him plaguing her with calls and text messages, he likely assumed it was the latter this time.

Cassandra tried not to sigh audibly as she resigned herself to the hollowness in her stomach. "I'm fine. I'm in town, and I thought I'd swing by to see Mom if that's okay. I know she's got rehab and everything, but—"

"No, no, rehab is only three days a week now. We'd both love to see you, sweetie. It'll be good for her. She's . . . well, she's been having trouble the last few days with the news about Debbie and everything. You're in town now?"

A jolt cut through Cassandra, and she choked back the urge to let out a terse huff. Of course, her mother would be devastated about Debbie's catatonic state. She should have expected that. She should have prepared for it.

She told herself not to feel sorry for her mother. Not when Debbie had tried to kill her. Not when her mother might have been aware of Debbie's role with the Druids this whole time. She shouldn't feel ashamed of defending herself when her own family was lying to her.

Despite her convictions and the knowledge that she should be pleased that her father was so welcoming, Cassandra couldn't help wishing he'd tell her to stay away. "Yeah."

"We're at the hospital now. Do you need directions?"

Cassandra's heart stuttered like an electric arc had flashed through her body. "I thought you said she didn't have rehab today?"

"She doesn't—oh, no, we're with Mike and Rene. Travis had to return to work, but. . . ."

Her dad's voice trailed off into a hum of noise as he kept talking. Cassandra couldn't take in whatever else he was explaining to her. She could only stare at the white-knuckled grip she had on the steering wheel.

They were with Debbie.

They wanted *her* to visit Debbie.

She nearly dropped the phone, then shook herself out of the panic, catching the end of her father's words. ". . . you could come by?" he asked.

"Um, did you ask when?" she managed to mumble out.

"Yes."

"Well, how much longer are you planning to be there?"

"Another few hours, I think." His voice dipped as though he didn't want others to hear him. "Mike refuses to leave her side, and Rene is a wreck. We're trying to stay with them for as long as we can before returning home for dinner."

Dinner? Cassandra looked at the clock on the dash. With her parents' typical schedules, dinner wouldn't be for another three hours.

"Can you stay for dinner too, Cassie?"

Hearing how rapidly her breath was coming out, Cassandra refused to glance Peter's way, sure she'd see concern on his face. "No, I—I can't stay that long. Uh, Dad?"

"Yes?"

"Why don't I just meet you at the house?"

There was a long, tense pause.

"You should *really* come to the hospital, Cassandra."

Cassandra *really* didn't want to.

The steering wheel grew slick under her clammy palms. "Okay. I'll be there soon."

He sighed contentedly. "Sounds good, sweetheart."

"Bye."

"Love you."

Cassandra flinched. "You too."

Hanging up the phone, Cassandra released the heavy sigh she'd held the whole call. It hurt to talk to her parents, knowing they didn't approve of her. That they wished she'd be more like them. Their smothering nature was difficult on a normal day.

This would be a million times worse.

Knowing what she now knew—aware as she was that they'd been lying to her and that they'd hidden the truth her entire life—cut deep. It was like feeling her family's rejection for the first time.

Peter cleared his throat, reminding her of his presence. "You, uh . . . you forgot to tell him you were bringing a friend."

The truck hummed pleasantly as Cassandra shifted into first gear. "I didn't forget. I chose not to tell him."

Peter's eyebrows drew together. "Oh. Why?"

"Because they'd ask why you were with me, and I'd rather not have that conversation over the phone."

"I guess that makes sense."

"I should warn you about a couple of things," she said, pulling out of the parking lot. "First, my mom's accident left her with several injuries. She's recovered from most, but there are scars."

"Uh, okay, yeah, I'll be . . . I won't be weird about it."

She passed him a sardonic grin. "Thanks."

"What's the other thing?"

With nothing else to do but tell him, Cassandra kept her eyes on the road. "We're going to the hospital," she explained, "to see Debbie."

~

The elevator's *ding* was harsh and ominous. Neither Peter nor Cassandra was ready to face what awaited them in the large white hospital. Carrying the burden of your actions was an oppressive weight on its own. Being forced to visit the consequences of them was like being forced to touch the flame you started.

Still, they managed to walk through the dingy halls, their boots echoing off the ceramic tiles. Nurses in bright scrubs passed by on their way to check on patients. A low, whispering din of voices—some worried, some placating, some calm—buzzed in tandem with the fluorescent lights above their heads.

By way of the nurse's station, they found their destination but stopped short of entering the room when they saw the group of people sitting in the waiting area. People Cassandra had known her entire life, and yet they felt far more unknown to her than the man who walked at her side.

In a huddle of chairs was her family. Mike held his head, fingers entangled in his brown mop of hair. He'd always been a big, burly man. But sitting in this hospital, he looked small, pallid, and fragile. At his side was Rene Mercier, his and Debbie's daughter. A couple of years older than Cassandra, she looked uncannily like her mother, her light brown hair cropped to her shoulders, wearing a loose, floral dress and one of her mother's old cardigans. Cassandra recognized it as the one Mike always kept in the car because Debbie complained about it being too cold everywhere she went.

The daughter had her hand on her father's shoulder, her crystal blue eyes on the faces of Cassandra's parents as they spoke. Allen Clement was the same as ever, in a red pullover on top of a plaid button up with his work slacks. During her mother's coma, he'd taken time off work from the accounting firm. The company still understood when he needed to be with his recovering wife. Now, he'd taken the afternoon to be with her extended family, as well.

Allen's arm rested comfortingly across the adjoining chair where Julianne Clement sat. A light pink sweater warmed her slim shoulders where her dark brown waves hovered. Even from a distance, Cassandra could see the noticeable thinness to her mother's cheeks; she otherwise appeared recovered from her own time at the hospital, her light skin warmed back to its usual undertone.

But there were the deep, brown-red gashes marring the left side of her face. Three scars of varying lengths, caused by her head slamming into the shattered car window. Wounds that the doctors promised would heal, despite the scars they'd leave behind.

What wouldn't heal was the sight in her mother's left eye.

It was Rene who saw them first. Her eyes grew wide at the sight of them—eyes with the same upturned corners as her mother's.

Cassandra's heart stopped beating as she and Peter approached the group, her gaze locked with Rene's. Did she know that it'd been Cassandra who'd taken her mother's life? That she was the cause of all of them being here? Was that why her mouth gaped open, and her eyes began to blink rapidly?

No, she couldn't know, Cassandra reminded herself. No one knew but her, Peter, Spencer, Gerard, Owen, and now Tom. A list she had no intention of adding names to.

But Rene's surprise dissolved into tears as she rose from her seat and opened her arms. "Hey, Cass," she murmured, taking slow, weary steps to pull Cassandra into a hug. "Thank you for coming."

Cassandra did her best not to tense as she returned the hug. "Of course," she murmured.

A flurry of greetings followed Rene's, all of them equally heart-wrenching. First, Julianne rose, unsteady as Allen helped her up—still unused to seeing out of just one eye. Her mother's hug was brutal. Frail arms squeezed around her neck as tears welled in her eyes. "Oh, Cassie," she whispered in her ear. "I'm so glad you're here, sweetie."

Her father's hug came next; weighty and demanding, just like his insistence that she come to the hospital.

Then Mike rose, tears unabashedly staining his cheeks. He didn't even speak. He just pulled Cassandra into a hug as though she was in as much pain as him.

Every ounce of Cassandra's being begged her to drop to the tile, curl up into a ball, and disappear from the world. Four faces stared at her with such sorrow and pain. Trauma that she'd caused.

Cassandra's hands trembled as she stared back, unsure she had the strength to speak. Then she saw all four sets of eyes flicker behind her. Glancing over her shoulder, Cassandra found Peter hovering in the background, lips pressed together and hands in the pockets of his jeans. He rolled back and forth on his heels, his gaze averted as though aware he was an interloper.

"I didn't realize you were bringing a friend," Allen said, his dark eyes sharp and astute as he took in the unwelcome addition.

"Yeah, sorry," she hurried to say. "I didn't even think about it. Everyone, this is Peter."

Hearing his name spoken, Peter's gaze snapped in their direction, his mouth agape. "Oh, hey." He took three rapid steps to close the distance, holding out his hand. "How's it going?"

Her family stared at him for a full, awkward five seconds before Allen removed his arm from Julianne's shoulder and accepted the handshake. "Hello," was the only reply he gave.

Mike's eyes narrowed. "You're one of those Collins boys, aren't you?"

"Dad," Rene muttered in rebuke. Then she smiled at Peter. "It's kind of you to come."

Peter nodded as though unsure what to say. He edged backward to stand partially behind Cassandra while the rest of her family stared like he had two heads.

Cassandra sighed, hiking the strap of her messenger bag farther onto her shoulder. "Is there any news?" she asked.

Mike's shoulders drooped, and Rene set a hand on his arm. "The doctor is with Mom now," she explained, her meek voice weary. "He should be done soon."

Julianne reached out a hand, fumbling with her impaired vision before she found Cassandra's fingers. She adjusted her grip, taking a solid hold of her daughter. "Why don't we have a seat?" she suggested.

Her mother tugged on her hand, drawing her to the old, uncomfortable-looking chairs just as a door behind them opened. A man in navy scrubs and a white lab coat stood in the entry, clipboard in hand. "Mr. Mercier?" he called.

Mike practically sprang forward. "Yes?"

"I've finished my examination if you'd like to come in for a moment?"

Rene clung to her father's arm, their matching blue eyes wide with what looked like equal parts fear and hope. Mike set his hand over hers, then looked to the Clements. "Julie, would you like to . . . ?"

He didn't need to finish the question. Julianne dropped Cassandra's hand and rushed to take Rene's as the trio hurried into the room after the doctor. The door shut behind them with a firm *click* that resonated in Cassandra's chest.

Debbie was behind that door. Or her body was. And there would be no good news from the doctor.

Meeting Peter's wary stare, Cassandra wondered if he felt like as much of a fraud as her, being here.

Allen cleared his throat, drawing both of their attention to him. Under the humming white lights overhead, he looked gaunt and worn out. "Cassandra, could I speak with you for a moment?" he asked.

Furrowing her brow, Cassandra hesitated, fearing what he could need to say with such immediacy now that the others were gone. "Yeah, sure."

His dark eyes flickered over her shoulder. To Peter.

"Oh, right." Peter snapped his fingers, recognizing the dismissal. He pointed toward the corner, in the direction of the elevator. "I think I saw a vending machine back that way, so I'm gonna. . . ."

Cassandra pressed her lips around the grin that fought for control as he let the sentence hang to hurry away. Her humor evaporated the second she turned back to her father.

Allen stood there, arms crossed over his pullover and his dark eyebrows drawn low. "Really, Cassandra," he muttered, voice muted. "You brought a boy to a family matter."

She arched her brow. "He's twenty-eight, Dad," she said, taking a seat. It turned out the chairs *were* as uncomfortable as they looked. "He's hardly a boy."

Allen stared down at her, disapproval plain on his face. "So, you are dating him?"

A spark of irritation flickered to life in Cassandra. Less than five minutes back together, and he was already making assumptions.

"No," Cassandra said, the single word tight in her throat.

Her father nodded haughtily. His shoulders notably relaxed, and he let his arms uncross to settle his hands imperiously on his hips. As though assuring himself that he should have known better than to assume his daughter was stupid enough to get involved with someone like Peter.

An impulsive reaction sprang from Cassandra before she knew what she was saying. "I'm dating his brother."

Allen's jaw nearly hit the floor. He held her gaze, his dark eyes a near replica of her own.

Cassandra knew she shouldn't lie. Especially since the idea would mortify Spencer. But the look of shock and indignation in her father's tightened jaw gave her a sense of vindication. He could judge her all he wanted, but he didn't know Peter, and he sure as hell didn't know Spencer.

Drawing his head back, Allen eyed her as though trying to test her lie. "That's Diane's nephew, isn't it?" His chin angled in the direction that Peter had disappeared.

"Great-nephew technically, but yes, Peter is one of them."

"And you're dating the other one?"

Cassandra settled into her lie. "Yes."

"Why?"

Leveling her father with an annoyed stare, Cassandra didn't care to give him further reasons to judge her. "Dad, I didn't come here to discuss my love life with you. When I'm ready to talk to you about Spencer, I'll bring him instead of Peter."

"Spencer?"

"Yes, Spencer." She crossed her arms. "Now, I can't stay much longer, but I hoped to talk to Mom before I head home. Would it be all right if we went back to the house soon? I'd like to get back to DeVerre before dinner."

Allen's thick brows pulled closer together as he inspected her. The bright fluorescent lights glinted off the large patches of silver at his temples amidst the dark brown hair. "Why did you bring your boyfriend's brother with you?"

"Because we both had things we needed to pick up in town. I didn't know I would be joining you at the hospital."

"You weren't planning to come to visit Debbie?"

The surprise in his voice cut at her. Of course, he would be surprised. They didn't know she wasn't grieving the same way they were. "I just didn't know you were here," she rectified. Then she tried to course correct to a less difficult subject. "Why does it matter that I brought Peter?"

"It doesn't."

"You're acting like it does."

"That's because I'm confused, Cassandra," he said, dropping into the seat next to her. "You went back to DeVerre less than a month ago, and now you come back with a boy—a young man—and then you tell me that you're dating his brother? Why didn't he come with you too?"

Cassandra sighed. "He's busy. Dad, please, once we get the news, can we go back to the house? I need to talk to Mom before I go home."

Allen sat back as he began to scan her suspiciously. "Deb and Mike's home burned down."

"I'm aware."

His glare asked the question for him.

But the door opening again saved her.

Rene stood in the doorway, tears openly running down her cheeks as the doctor slipped past with an apology. "Allen. Cass," she said, her voice a tremulous, hollow sound. "Would you—" The question died out as her nose scrunched up, and she lifted a hand to her lips.

Allen hastened from his seat, hand tapping Cassandra's arm in a summons.

Standing on shaky legs, Cassandra stared at the open doorway. Yellow lamplight blended with the brown edge of shadows in the corners. Rene and Allen passed farther into the room. She watched as her father stepped to Julianne's side, putting his arm around her. Cassandra's mother curled into her husband's side, burying her face in his chest.

A tremor ripped through Cassandra's hand as it hung at her side, a haunting of the arc that had torn Debbie's soul. She didn't want to go in. She wasn't even sure she could get her feet to work.

But Allen turned to stare back at her, gaze sharp and demanding through the door.

Edging forward, Cassandra fought down the fear rising to close off her throat. She could do this. She *had* to do this.

Walking through the door felt like stepping into the maw of a beast. It swallowed her whole, accepting her into the bowels of agony and despair. Mike sat by the hospital bed, with Rene crouched by his side. Both shed perpetual tears. In his hand, he held Debbie's, the IV affixed to her wrist.

Cassandra came to a halt several feet from the bed, but it was close enough. Her heart hammered, her throat was on fire, and her hands shook so badly that she had to curl them into fists, pressing them into her sides. Her nails cut into her palms, but she accepted the pain as she stared at the woman she'd fought one week ago that very day.

Debbie's body lay there, functioning properly. Her chest rose and fell with steady breaths. The heart rate monitor beeped in rhythm despite the feeding tube in her mouth. She could have been faking it if it weren't for her skin, bubbled and scarred from the flames Spencer set blazing. But the truth shimmered in Debra Mercier's gaze.

As rich a brown as ever, but dull, empty, and completely lifeless.

Whatever state her body was in, Debbie was dead.

And Cassandra had killed her.

~

They stayed at the hospital for another hour. Peter had managed to escape having to enter Debbie's room, seeing her soulless body. But the image would stay with Cassandra for the rest of her life, a permanent scar upon her memory and heart.

Once her parents finally agreed to leave, Cassandra's lungs constricted anew as she pulled into the driveway of her childhood home in the early evening glow. The whitewashed wooden slats, deep blue shutters, and overflowing flower boxes should have given her a sense of comfort. Those brick steps and wrought iron rails should have brought back lovely memories. Instead, they made her feel the most profound sense of loneliness.

It hurt, coming home. In the place she should feel the safest, she felt the most in danger.

Parking behind her parents' gray SUV, Cassandra turned off the truck, unbuckled her seatbelt, and grabbed her bag. Peter followed her to the front door at a respectful distance as Allen helped Julianne up the steps. Her father turned to the bright blue door—her mother's favorite color—and the wreath of autumn foliage wobbled as it swung open. Guiding Julianne through first, Allen turned back to invite them in before continuing into the house. Cassandra and Peter followed, and he took the liberty to shut and lock the door behind them.

As her father hovered at her mother's side, moving with slow, thoughtful steps toward the living room, Cassandra took in the house. It surprised her to find the inside decorated for Thanksgiving already. Little porcelain pilgrims and turkeys littered the hallway table, as well as the dining room to their immediate right. She recognized each decoration. The orange and brown plaid tablecloth. The wooden 'Give Thanks' sign hung by the stairs. The plush squirrel dressed like a pilgrim, bearing a cornucopia in his hands that greeted them into the house.

Her mother had never been one to skimp on holiday decorations. Julianne Clement was known for her cheer during every special occasion. But she was only three weeks from her coma. It didn't seem prudent for a recovering trauma patient to decorate with such abandon.

"Did you do all of this, Mom?" Cassandra asked, running her fingers over the 'Be Thankful' pillow on the couch.

Julianne shook her head as she took a seat, the scars on her face puckering as she smiled at the room. "Oh, no." Her laugh was clearly supposed to sound light and jovial. It fell short, perhaps due to visiting Debbie or the disappointment of having Peter ruin their reunion with their daughter. "Ike, Sandy, and the boys came over last week. They wanted to make sure this holiday was just as special as the rest. We all pitched in."

Cassandra nodded, hearing the unspoken disappointment. Ike, Sandy, and the boys were there for her mother. But not Cassandra.

"That was nice of them," she managed.

"It was, wasn't it?" Allen turned to Peter. "Could I get you anything to drink?"

Peter glanced at Cassandra as though checking to see if he should accept. "Uh, sure. That'd be great, thanks."

"Water? Coffee? Tea?"

"Water's fine."

"Cassie?"

"I'm fine, thanks, Dad."

As Allen disappeared into the kitchen, Julianne suggested they sit and make themselves comfortable. Peter dropped onto the couch, the many

Thanksgiving pillows collapsing around him. Cassandra suppressed a snide grin as she shrugged off her jacket, the leather sleeves too constricting between the heat of the interior and the tightening in her chest.

After resting the jacket across the back of the couch, Cassandra sat beside Peter. The smell of cinnamon and apples warmed the air as Julianne slipped a lighter back into the drawer of the coffee table. Surrounded by blankets and pillows, the atmosphere should have felt comfortable and cozy. Instead, Cassandra's chest coiled tighter still.

"Did you have a pleasant drive?" Julianne asked, the sweetness of her voice as smothering as the room around her.

Peter glanced at Cassandra, replying when she showed no interest in answering. "Yeah," he confirmed. "Cass is a great driver."

The weird compliment took Julianne off guard. "Oh." She glanced at her daughter. "Yes, I suppose she is, isn't she?"

Allen returned, saving them from the small talk. He handed Peter his glass of ice water, turning to take a seat next to Julianne on the loveseat across from them.

"Thanks," Peter said, taking a polite sip before setting his water on the side table.

"Make sure you use a coaster," Cassandra warned under her breath.

As Peter reached for one of the monogrammed coasters from the coffee table, Julianne spoke again. "I am so happy that you came home, sweetheart," she said to Cassandra, her sharp blue eyes bloodshot—the left cloudy from the irredeemable damage done in her accident.

Thinking she should have accepted her father's offer of a drink, Cassandra swallowed around her dry throat. "Of course," she managed. "I had to pick up a couple of things anyway."

The soft laugh from Julianne didn't ring true to her daughter's ears. "Yes, small towns like DeVerre can't provide everything, can they?"

Whether her mother intended the comment to sound as biting as it did, Cassandra felt its cut all the same. "I guess they can't."

"So, you're just in town for today?" Julianne prodded.

"Yes," Cassandra confirmed. "We're going back after this."

"Oh, that's too bad. Did you get to see Ike and Sandy?"

"No."

"Cassie, you really should see about stopping in. The boys love it when you're here."

Feeling the pressure mounting, Cassandra started twisting her ring. "I don't have time, Mom."

"They're your family, Cassandra," Allen charged. "You should always have time for family."

A tense silence stretched out as Peter took another sip of water, and the Clements all stared at each other.

Unable to formulate a strong response, Cassandra dropped her gaze to her hands. Her parents always did this to her—made her feel inarticulate and uncertain. As though the second she stepped under their roof, she lost who she was and the confidence to go with it.

Cassandra knew what she wanted. She knew who she was. She knew what she believed. But being within her family's home, she lost all ability to feel it with the same conviction.

A soft clearing of her throat brought the conversation back into Julianne's control. Her eyes flashed in Peter's direction, then landed fixedly on Cassandra. "I saw Jacob at church the other day. He said you two spent some time together while you were in town last."

Drawing her shoulders back, Cassandra glared at her mother.

"Are you two talking again?" The question was a step too far.

"No, Mom." Cassandra knew her words were too aggressive, but she didn't care. "I'm not *talking* to Jake."

"Why not? You were so good together."

Pressing her lips together, Cassandra tried to think of a way to direct the conversation away from her ex. She'd known Jacob since they were in high school, and her parents had pushed her to date him early on. She knew why from the beginning: Jacob and Isaac were best friends. Jacob's family went to the same church, and his parents had become fast friends with hers. Soon Jacob began showing an interest in Cassandra.

Both families loved the idea of becoming related. They desperately wanted Cassandra to give in and date Jacob. But she felt the pressure was just one more way for them to trap her in Spokane with them.

However, the pressure was also unrelenting. And she did get along well with Jacob. She'd considered him her friend for years. Then they went to college together, and in her sophomore year, he'd finally admitted he liked her. She'd always known. Everyone had. But it wasn't until he'd said it aloud that she realized how much. And after years of pressure, Cassandra gave in. She'd agreed to go on *one* date with Jacob just to see if anything was there.

Their families were thrilled. Her parents stopped pushing her. And, for the first time in her life, she hadn't felt like the problem child.

She and Jacob wound up dating for three months because she was afraid of what would happen if she broke it off. She even thought for a time that things might work out between them. But then she'd told him about her ability to see ghosts as a kid and her desire to learn more about it. Jacob hadn't responded well, telling her that she shouldn't pursue her studies, equating it to witchcraft.

Cassandra broke it off at once.

Neither Jacob nor the rest of her family had given up trying to get them back together.

Fingers practically a vise around her ring, Cassandra glared back at her mother. "I guess there's just some things we'll never understand."

Julianne tipped her head to the side. "I think you should give him another chance, Cassie."

"Julie." Allen set his hand on his wife's, giving her a small shake of his head. "You misunderstand. Cassandra's dating Peter's brother, Spencer."

Peter shifted in his seat, turning to smirk at Cassandra.

Doing her best to maintain her composure, Cassandra kept her chin up, knowing by the sparkle of satisfaction in Peter's eyes that she'd have a long ride home.

"Oh?" Julianne looked between Peter and Cassandra as though he were the culprit upsetting her plans for her daughter's future.

In too deep to back out now, Cassandra crossed her arms. "Uh, yes—kind of."

Peter's smile grew.

"It's new," she grumbled, then pressed on. "But that's not why we're here."

"If it were," Peter cut in, "Spencer would be here, I promise."

Cassandra tried not to grind her teeth.

"Why are you here, Cassie?" Allen asked.

Ready to get the meeting over with Cassandra turned back to Julianne. "I have an important question for you, Mom."

Her mother sat up, wrapping her light pink cardigan tighter around her shoulders. "All right, sweetie, go ahead."

Faced with finally saying it aloud, Cassandra hesitated. She stared past the scabbed-over wounds and into her mother's cornflower blue eyes, looking for any sign that the woman knew—about the Druids, Debbie's "accident," anything—or if she was as oblivious as Cassandra had always assumed. But she couldn't read her mother. And now she wondered if she'd ever known her family at all.

Bolstering herself, Cassandra raised her head. "Are you a Druid?"

There was a single, small flicker in her mother's eyes as her father drew back in surprise. "What are you talking about, Cassandra? Of course, she's not. What a ridiculous question."

Her mother held up a hand to stop her husband. "Al, please."

Mother and daughter held each other's gaze, blue meeting brown.

She knew. She had to. Or she wouldn't have hesitated.

Anger rose within Cassandra. Her mother *knew*. All this time, she'd known, and she'd let her daughter think she was crazy.

"Dear," Julianne said, head angling toward her husband. "Why don't you show our guest the patio? Cassandra and I need a minute."

There was a moment where Allen seemed opposed to the suggestion, but when he met his wife's stare, he nodded. Rising, he waited for Peter, who looked at Cassandra.

"Go on, Pete."

Peter stood, movements tense. He followed Allen to the small yard out back. Julianne's eyes never wavered from Cassandra, even after the door clicked shut behind the men.

A long pause hung between mother and daughter. Each sizing up the other.

Julianne shook her head in disappointment. "It was you, wasn't it?"

Cassandra cocked her head in confusion.

"You did that to Debbie?"

Shoulders caving as though her mother had just delivered a blow to her chest, Cassandra's mouth dropped open. The question was all the confirmation she needed. "Why?" The word hissed out of her. "Why didn't you tell me? Why did you take me away from DeVerre if you were just as involved in it as I am?"

"I'm not." Julianne's voice was sharp and tense. "Did you do that to Debbie?"

"Yes," she admitted. "Yes, Mother, I did."

Tears sprang to the woman's eyes in an instant.

Tears for her best friend.

For the woman who'd tried to kill her daughter.

Irate, Cassandra curled her hands into fists. "Do you know why?"

There was no reply.

"She was going to kill me, Mom. I had no choice."

"Of course you did," Julianne spat. "You always have a choice, Cassandra."

A heavy scoff escaped her. "Didn't you hear me? Debbie was going to *kill* me."

The tears in Julianne's eyes dripped over the edge, trailing down the side of her face and across her chin. But they were no more for her daughter now than before. "I told you to stay here." Her words were tight and impassioned. "I told you to stay with us. But you *chose* to abandon us."

Cassandra tried to pull in a breath, but it caught in her throat. "Are you seriously blaming *me* for this?"

The accusation in Julianne's glare was answer enough.

Shaking her head, Cassandra couldn't believe it. A mirthless laugh left her. "Was I right?" she asked. "Are you a Druid too?"

Her mother's lips trembled as fresh tears came to her eyes. "No."

Sure that there would be no reason for her to lie anymore, Cassandra still doubted the answer. "You're not?"

"No."

"But you knew that Debbie was?"

A single, sharp nod.

Cassandra sighed. "And you . . . you let me live with her? You—you let her into our lives when we were kids?"

"She knew I didn't want any part of it," Julianne said. "And she promised not to bring it into my home."

"But you accepted her as she was," Cassandra accused. "You allowed her to live her life however she wanted. And yet you wouldn't even let me talk to ghosts."

"I didn't want that life for you."

"I wasn't a Druid!" The words ripped through her chest and out of her mouth. "I was a little girl. You made me feel like something was wrong with me because I was different. And all that time your best friend was summoning hellhounds and murdering people."

Julianne's eyes went wide. "How dare you," she hissed. "How dare you assume you know anything! Yes, I knew Debbie was a Druid. Yes, I disagreed with her choices. But she was the only sister I had!"

"And I was the only daughter you had!"

"And you wonder why I didn't want you to have the same life as her?" her mother shot back. "Debbie's parents raised her to be a Druid. So did mine. But I didn't want it, and they respected my choice. They gave me my freedom so long as I didn't stand in their way. So, I agreed."

The tears were flowing freely, streaking her marred face with glittering lines. "Then you started seeing ghosts. A toddler, talking to ghosts. It was unheard of. It was incredible. And they wanted you."

The words struck Cassandra like a slap.

"I begged Debbie to speak on your behalf. I didn't want my daughter to become one of them. I didn't want her to become another sacrifice for their cause. So, she worked out a deal: Your freedom so long as you didn't get in their way."

Hand to her mouth, Cassandra's heart hammered in her chest. Her freedom in exchange for her never knowing the truth. That was the price. If they had stayed in DeVerre, the Druids would have raised her to become one of them. That's what they'd wanted for her. And Debbie had persuaded them to let her go.

"But you're stubborn." Julianne's voice cut through the shame beginning to leak into Cassandra's heart. A snarl tore across her mother's lips. "And you're selfish. And you wouldn't listen to me."

Years of rejection from her parents should have prepared her for the pain, but Cassandra's own eyes watered as her heart tore at her mother's words.

Julianne shook her head. "You went back and began prying into their business. You ruined everything. You and that damn old woman you called a friend."

"What?"

"If you would had just listened, none of this would have happened," she said. "But, no, you're so smart. You know so much better than everyone else. And you don't care who you hurt to be with your precious ghosts."

Cassandra couldn't process it all through the emotions clogging up her mind. "I didn't know!" she insisted. "I had no idea that there was any danger in DeVerre. I just wanted to know who I was."

"And look where it's gotten you." Julianne huffed, the sound breaking through her tears. "You've killed Debbie just like you killed Diane."

That was a knife to the heart.

A horrifying look came across her mother's face then. One of pride at cutting her daughter so deeply. "*You* killed her—your old friend," she said. "Whether you knew it or not, it was your fault. All of this is your fault."

The tears on Cassandra's lashes blurred her vision as she tried to stare through them at her mother.

"If you'd have just stayed home." Julianne repeated Debbie's words back to her.

"What are you talking about?" Cassandra gasped out.

Julianne tugged at the collar of her cardigan. "You broke the deal. You were getting in the way, both you and Diane, and they weren't willing to let you get any closer. So, they gave us one last chance. They told Debbie they would remove Diane *and* you, but there was one final chance to save your life."

Her mother scowled, motioning to her damaged eye. "You did this to me. Just like you killed Diane. This was the price of their deal. They needed to get you away from Occasus—away from DeVerre. And I was their bait."

The truth clouded her mind. "Are you saying . . . ?"

"It wasn't an accident."

Cassandra sat, frozen in shock.

"And here I am—alive but damaged. So that you could live."

The revelation ate at Cassandra. It ripped through her chest and made her body crumple in on itself.

It was her fault.

All of it.

She'd gotten Diane killed and put her mother in a coma. Inadvertently or not, she was the cause of everything that had happened over the past three months.

But she hadn't known. For her whole life, she'd thought her mother was trying to keep her from DeVerre because of her own fear and misunderstanding. Because she didn't support her. Now, she learned it was all to keep her alive.

Yet she couldn't escape the one crushing truth: Her mother had known the truth. She'd lied to Cassandra her entire life. And now she blamed *her*.

Sucking in a long, painful breath, Cassandra turned her hard stare on her mother. "Do you know who the other Druids are?"

Several tense seconds ticked out as more tears streamed down Julianne's face. "No."

"Are you lying to me?"

"No."

"I'll find out if you are."

Julianne scoffed. "You selfish, arrogant child. Everything I just told you, and you're *still* going back there?"

Cassandra stood. "Yes, I'm going back. Because whether you like it or not, I belong there."

"You belong with *us*," she countered. "With your family."

"You're not my family," Cassandra said, surprised at how evenly her voice came out despite how much her chest hurt. "Not anymore."

"They will kill you."

She shrugged. "They can try. But it didn't work so well last time."

Julianne flinched.

Grabbing her jacket, Cassandra drew her shoulders back, glaring down at the woman. "And just so you know, I'm going to end this. We're going to find the Druids, and we're going to remove them. Then I'm gonna build a home in DeVerre. And I'm going to be happy for once in my life."

"You can't abandon your family, Cassandra." Her mother slid to the edge of her seat. "Not after what we've sacrificed for you. Not after what you did to me."

"You did this to yourself." Cassandra slipped her jacket on. "Goodbye, Mom."

CHAPTER SIXTEEN

Peter

The following twenty-four hours were a miserable experience for Peter. After the meeting with Cassandra's parents ended in an abysmal and abrupt departure, she was quiet the entire drive home. The sky turned inky the farther they got from the city. Her seething anger had radiated through the truck, causing Peter to keep his head down and his thoughts to himself. She hadn't even told him what her mother had said. But from the way she glared out the windshield, he knew that it couldn't be good.

Peter had hoped that when they got back to Occasus, the tension would ease. Instead, Cassandra disappeared into her room for the rest of the night. Having met her parents, he couldn't say that he entirely blamed her for feeling the need to decompress. Awkward, stilted conversation had filled his time alone with her dad on the patio. Though the slow-descending sun kept him from getting too cold in his leather jacket, he couldn't help but shiver every so often. And then he'd heard Cassandra and her mother yelling at one another inside the house. Both he and her father had turned around to stare at the doors. Allen Clement had taken a step forward before freezing as though thinking better of interrupting. Neither of them spoke after that. Not until Cassandra had appeared at the door and told Peter that they were leaving.

But the discomfort and silence of the meeting and drive hadn't dissipated even after Cassandra went to her room.

When Peter searched for Spencer, he found his brother in the office as expected, sitting at the large partner desk with his eyes glued to his laptop screen. He hardly acknowledged Peter upon his arrival to the room.

"You working on *Wenzel & Frankly*?" Peter asked, hoping to distract his mind with talk about their book.

Spencer shook his head as he kept staring at the screen. "I'm following up on a lead."

Though disappointed, Peter forced himself to take an interest. "You got a lead?"

"Yeah." He paused. "Well, sort of. I'm following up on Elijah Lawrence's essays."

Peter scrunched his nose. "You mean the missing pages?"

"Yeah."

"We already exhausted that lead, J.B."

Spencer shook his head. "I don't think so." He glanced up at him, blue eyes almost glowing in the reflected light of his laptop. "They're our best bet in figuring out what the Druids want. Or, at least, what it is that they don't want us to know."

Though Peter knew his brother had a point, he wasn't interested in wasting more time researching the essays. They'd spent a whole week trying to find the pages online. There was nothing out there. Just a minimal family tree belonging to the Lawrences and a few theological discussions briefly mentioning their names in connection with Heinrich Schwarz and Martin Luther. It was like the Warden didn't even exist.

"Well, cool," Peter muttered. "Good luck, I guess. I'm gonna go . . . do something else."

Either Spencer didn't notice his sour tone or didn't care because he tossed him an absent-minded grin and turned back to his work.

The rest of the evening they spent separately. Peter let Spencer spin his wheels with the essays and left Cassandra to whatever devices she needed to process the disastrously uncomfortable day. He holed up in his room, writing until his hand cramped and his brain was exhausted. If Spencer had forgotten why they'd come to DeVerre in the first place, Peter hadn't. They were here to get their career going, Druids be damned. He needed a break from the dumpster fire that was their current reality— and what better way to channel his frustrations than through creating monsters for Wenzel and Frankly to fight?

Peter had hoped the morning would see Spencer and Cassandra with clear heads and better moods. But nothing had changed. Over their morning coffee, Cassandra told them about her conversation with her mother. Her usual confidence was gone as she spoke in short, choppy sentences. There was no question that she had little interest in discussing the topic beyond informing them that her mother was not a Druid but was perfectly aware that there were Druids within DeVerre. Otherwise, there was no more information to relay.

At that point, Spencer roped him into helping with research while Cassandra looked over Tom's suspect list. It was an infuriating waste of time in Peter's mind. They'd already looked for the essays. And they'd tried researching the Warden, ending up with the same amount of information Owen had implied they'd find: None.

Between Spencer and Cassandra, the day passed in a colossal failure of research. And Peter was tired of it.

Slipping away the first chance he got, Peter texted Anna. He needed company that wouldn't force him to work. Though Anna replied to tell him that she was on shift a short time later, it didn't dissuade him.

"Want some company?" he texted.

Five minutes later, her text came back. *"Sure!"*

Peter asked Spencer if he could borrow the Jeep before heading to the tavern. Smooth jazz invited him into the golden, glowing atmosphere as the bell over the door chimed. Only five other patrons dispersed throughout the building: a couple having dinner in a far booth and a trio of lumbermen sipping beers at one of the round tables near the front. Knowing the slow night would mean that Anna's shift would be light, Peter couldn't help grinning wider than usual as he approached the bar.

She returned the smile with one of her own as she set a napkin in front of him, then went to work on his signature cocktail. "Just you tonight?"

"Yep," he replied, his mood immediately improving as he shrugged off his jacket and settled onto the barstool. "Mom and Dad are busy working."

Anna laughed, the light catching on her cheekbones. "Spence keeping you busy with the book?"

His shoulder twitched with discomfort as he worked around the truth. "Something like that."

"Are you guys making good progress?"

Pursing his lips, Peter fought against his conscience. "No, not really," he admitted. "Writing a book isn't as simple as it sounds, I guess."

Anna reached over to pat his arm. "Art is never simple," she raised her brow in a knowing gesture, "no matter what form it takes."

"What we do can't be called art, Annie," Peter argued. "Not like what you do."

"How would you know?" Her smile was light and playful. "You've never seen my stuff."

"And have you read our stuff?"

She lifted a shoulder in a shrug. "I've read a couple of posts."

Peter fought the disappointment of hearing that she'd only read a couple in the past month of knowing them. "Then you know that we aren't the artistic types."

"Art doesn't always look the same, Peter. Sometimes it's a masterpiece that will go down in history, and other times it's just something that will change one person's life."

Swallowing a sip of his cocktail, Peter narrowed his eyes at her. "Our serial changed your life, huh?"

Anna rolled her eyes at him even as her smile grew. "I'm not counting the possibility out yet."

He gave her an appreciative nod. "And who's your favorite? Wenzel or Frankly?"

Tipping her head to the side, Anna considered it. "You know . . . I don't know yet. They're both great. I like that Frankly is so cool and knowledgeable, but Wenzel always makes me laugh. Do you and Spencer write them together?"

Peter was surprised to realize she didn't know much about their writing. He supposed he hadn't talked to her much about it. "Oh, uh, no. We each write our own character."

She lifted her chin as she leaned against the bar top. "Which one do you write?"

He smirked at her. "Which do you think I write?"

Her eyes narrowed, and he mimicked her action. They stared each other down for several seconds. A crease formed on her forehead from held-in laughter as her lips pressed together around a smile. Her eyes twinkled like starlight. If Peter had been less brave, he would have dropped her stare. But he didn't want to lose the opportunity to hold her gaze, pretty and comforting as it was. They might be just friends, but he was more than aware that she was one of the most worthwhile women he'd ever met.

Finally, Anna's amusement became too much, and her feminine laughter shook her shoulders before she pulled back. "I don't know," she admitted. "I could see you writing either one."

Another tinge of disappointment met him. "Really?" He didn't know why he added, "Cass guessed it right away."

Anna's smile drooped. "She did?"

He nodded. "Though, to be fair, she has read the whole thing. She and Diane were big fans."

A look of hesitant surprise flashed across her face. Then her expression softened. "They read your stuff before they met you?"

"That's what she said. And since she's kept up with each episode the past few weeks, I don't have any reason to think she's lying."

Another soft laugh slipped out of her, eyes fixed on the counter as she wiped at an invisible spot with a bar towel. "Well, I think that's cool that she reads your stuff. And I'm glad you're all getting along so well. It's great of you guys to take care of her after everything that happened with her family."

Peter sucked in a breath, lifting his brow in wry humor. "Yeah, well, it seems you're the only one who thinks so."

"What do you mean?"

He lifted a hand to brush it off. "People just assume the worst. It's like they think we're teens with no self-control or something."

"Oh." Anna gave him an understanding frown. "Yeah, I get what you mean. But . . . I dunno, I guess, knowing you and Spencer as I do, I just know better than to think that of either of you."

Heartened to hear that someone thought well of him and his brother, Peter lifted his glass in a toast to her. "Thanks, Annie."

She nudged his hand as he set the drink back down. "I gotta go check on these tables. Be right back."

Both tables of patrons cashed out, and Anna was back in no time.

"Well, it looks like I'm all yours," she said, walking around the bar. "At least so long as no one else shows up."

"Lucky me!" He nodded toward the kitchen. "You gotta chef back there looking for something to do?"

"You fancy a sandwich?"

"Always."

She put in his order, then returned to his side.

"All right, so what about you?" Peter asked.

"What about me?"

"We've talked about my *art*," he clarified. "Now tell me about yours."

Angling to the side, Anna's smile turned crooked. "I—I don't really . . . show people my stuff."

"I'm not asking you to show it to me. I just want to hear about it."

Though she took several seconds to stare at the counter, Anna finally nodded. "What do you want to know about it?"

"You said you like to paint, right?"

"Yeah."

"What style of art do you paint?"

Anna's expression grew wistful. "Well, my favorite style is Impressionism. I'm very inspired by Monet and Pissarro and Cassatt . . . and Steer, and Degas, and—well, all of them really." Her laugh was deep and resonant, like the low octaves of the piano that played overhead. "I love how romantic and idealistic it all is. I'm nowhere near as good as them, of course, but it's definitely my favorite style to paint."

Peter knew she was selling herself short. Like she always did. "I bet your stuff is amazing. You're probably the most incredible artist the world has yet to have the pleasure to see."

A soft flush worked its way over Anna's warm brown skin. "That's what Connor says." Her demeanor shifted as soon as the words were out of her mouth, her smile dropping as though she was surprised at herself.

Peter imagined she'd be upset at herself for thinking of Connor after deciding to let him go. He wanted to reach across the bar, take her hand, and promise that it wasn't a sign of failure on her part to still think about him. Not after spending her whole life sure she'd end up with him.

But, in the end, that was the very reason he kept his hands still on the bar top. He knew what it was like to pursue someone who really wished you were someone else. He didn't care to get involved in something that painful again.

Abruptly, Anna perked up and held her hands out toward him. "Do you want to see some sketches?"

Peter felt his eyes go wide in shock. "Huh? I mean, yeah—of course!"

"Great!" Anna hurried to the other side of the bar, near the back. She crouched down to a purse shoved into the corner, then returned with a black, spiral-bound notebook in her hand. She opened to the first few pages. "Here, these—these are my current favorites."

Taking the sketchbook gingerly into his hands, Peter stared at the paper as though viewing something sacred. With her hesitancy regarding her art, he had to assume she didn't show many people. He couldn't understand what he'd done to deserve the honor, but he wouldn't squander the opportunity.

Charcoal and graphite lined the paper in elegant scrolls and strokes. Sketches of intricate florals, beautiful landscapes, whimsical portraits, and ethereal still-life images adorned each page. He turned through them slowly.

"I was right," he said, voice reverent and awe-filled. "These are incredible."

Anna ducked her chin down, that light blush spreading across her face again. "Thanks."

Turning a few more pages, Peter couldn't believe how good each sketch was. So vivid and lifelike despite the monochromatic shades of gray. There was a lightness to each image that made them all more fantastic than reality. Softer, gentler, and more magical.

Peter flipped to the next page, and he felt his lips part in surprise.

"Oh, uh, no, you—" Anna tried to grab the sketchbook back, but Peter pulled it away from her reach.

Unable to contain his smile, his eyes flickered between her and the page. "You drew us?" he asked, pointing to the image.

There, in that enchanting, animation-like style of hers, was a sketch of him and his brother. And it couldn't have been more perfect. Spencer wore his denim jacket, hands tucked into the pockets. His shaggy hair draped over his forehead while he looked over at the sketch of Peter with one of his small, reserved grins.

And there was Peter beside and angled in front of him, wearing a flannel under the jacket that hung on the back of his barstool now. A crooked smile on his face, hair standing on end, notebook in hand.

Peter felt like his smile might split his face in two as he looked at Anna. "Can I have this?" he asked.

Though a hint of embarrassment remained in her own smile, it was clear that she could see his appreciation for the sketch. But she shook her head. "No."

"Why not?"

She shrugged. "Because then I won't have it."

Peter laughed, accepting the sentiment behind her words. "Well, can I take a picture of it, then?"

Though she hesitated, biting down on her bottom lip, Anna nodded. "Sure."

He pulled his phone from his pocket, snapped a picture, and immediately set it as the wallpaper. "Thanks, Ann."

She shrugged. "It was just something silly I drew."

"It's not silly. It's amazing," he insisted.

She rolled her eyes, but joy lit her expression.

"And I wasn't thanking you for the sketch."

Her gaze met his in confusion.

"Thanks for trusting me with your art."

Anna played with her necklace as she held his gaze. There was something about the way that she looked at him that always surprised him. It was as if she wasn't seeing what everyone else did. She looked as though she could see past his bravado and dramatics to the man he always wished people would see. The man he wasn't entirely certain was real.

The chef rang the bell in the kitchen making them both jump.

"Be right back," Anna muttered as she rushed to the pass-through window.

In the few seconds that she was gone, Peter swallowed the unwelcome feelings welling inside him. He smothered the attraction he felt toward Anna as he set the sketchbook to the side. She set his dinner plate before him, the smell of savory roast beef and au jus wafting into the air.

"Thanks," he said.

"Mhm."

Peter picked up a fry absentmindedly as he swallowed down his lingering discomfort. "So, uh—I was thinking. . . ." He scanned the room for something to discuss. His eyes fell on the sketchbook. "Would you be willing to do some sketches for the blog?"

"What? You mean, like, of Wenzel and Frankly?"

"Yeah, exactly!" Peter latched onto the idea, proud of himself for coming up with such a good one in his panic. "It would be super legit to finally have pictures of them. We've had a few fans do some art, but none had near your skills."

"Oh, Pete, I—I don't really share my work with people," Anna said, clearly nervous at the idea. "And I've never drawn anything for anyone but myself before."

"Annie—" He leveled a serious stare on her as he picked up his sandwich. "Your work is incredible. I have no doubt that you'd do just fine."

She reached for the sketchbook, slowly closing it. "I just . . . I don't know."

"Because you don't want other people to see it?"

She shrugged.

"You're too good to hide your art, Ann," he said. "But if you really don't want to do it, I won't push you. I just think you deserve to get some recognition for your amazing work."

Anna didn't agree, but she did give him a grateful smile before returning the book to her bag. Peter was sure to let the topic go as the evening went on. Anna still had a couple of hours left on her shift, and he had no intentions of abandoning her before the night was through.

They chatted about little things and big things. Things that he rarely talked to people about anymore. It was good for him. The evening was such a change of pace from the past several days at Occasus and the heaviness that had settled into their home.

Whatever Spencer and Cassandra were up to, it couldn't be as good as spending time with Anna.

As they got within a quarter of an hour of closing time, the chef—an early twenties-something boy with blond hair—popped his head around the corner of the swinging door into the kitchen to say he was going home. No one else had shown up in the tavern, and Anna didn't hesitate to wave him off on his way.

"Guess I should get out of here too," Peter said, polishing off the final dregs of his second cocktail. "Maybe you can head home a little early."

Though Anna nodded, she glanced through the kitchen window as the back door shut behind the departing chef. She was chewing on her bottom lip when she turned back to him. "Pete. . . ." Her voice was tense and nervous as she stepped closer.

Peter braced himself, uncertain what he might've done but sure that he must have done *something* for her to get this serious.

Leaning against the bar, Anna met his eyes. "Can I ask you something?"

Throat tightening, Peter tugged on his collar. "Yeah, of course."

Her eyes dropped to the counter as her mouth worked around unsaid words. She wet her lips and kept her head down. "Do you . . . will you tell me what happened between you and Ava?"

Blinking a handful of times at the startling question, Peter didn't know what to say. It was one of the last things he'd expected her to ask. "Uh. . . ." He scratched his temple, and a weak chuckle worked its way out of him. "Well, um, she's not super thrilled that Cass is living with us."

Anna glanced at him. "So, you guys had an argument or something?"

"Yeah, but . . . it's fine, Annie. She'll come around."

"Are you sure?"

Peter shifted in his seat. "I mean, I hope so."

The way her dark eyebrows pulled together made Peter worry that he was being far too optimistic. "I've never seen her like this, Pete," she said. "I know my sister can be intense. She's reactive sometimes, but this is different. You're sure that it was just about Cassandra living with you?"

Rubbing the back of his neck, Peter did his best to appear unconcerned by the news. "Ah, yeah, as best as I know." The words tasted bitter on his tongue.

Anna sighed, her shoulders hanging low. "It's just—I don't know. She's not been herself the last week. I thought it must be everything that's been going on in town. You know, with all the deaths and the Merciers' house burning down. Things are *weird*. Honestly, they've been weird since Diane died. And I guess I just assumed that it all upset her. But. . . ."

She took a deep breath, shaking her head as she held his stare. "She's told me to stop hanging out with you, Pete." She scoffed at that. "As though I'm a kid and you're a negative influence or something."

His throat went dry, and he clamped his lips together to keep from blurting out an angry retort.

"And worse," her voice grew thick, as though the words didn't want to come out, "I think something's going on between her and Owen."

He slumped forward.

"There's this weird tension between them and—and I can't figure it out. They never fight, Pete. Literally *never*."

Guilt seeped into Peter's chest. He'd done this. He'd exposed Owen without ever intending it.

Anna shook her head. "I know that has nothing to do with you, but. . . ." She sighed again. "I just don't know what to do. Obviously, I'm not gonna listen to her. You and I are friends, and if she doesn't like it, that's her problem."

She let out an annoyed huff. "I know she doesn't like Cassandra, but . . . I don't understand *why*. And I don't get why she's taking it out on you and Spence."

Peter wanted to tell her the truth. He really did. It was eating at him, tearing away chunk after chunk of his stomach. He could hardly take holding her dark brown gaze with the desperation peering through at him.

It was his mistake that had opened these questions. If he had just kept his mouth shut and let Ava harbor ill feelings toward them, then Owen wouldn't be in danger, and Anna wouldn't have any cause to be truly concerned.

Opening his mouth to reply, Peter paused. Could he tell Anna the truth? Should he? What if she took Ava's side? Would he lose her friendship like he'd lost Ava's?

Another, more frightening thought struck him. What if she took *their* side instead? What if she wanted to help? That would put her in danger. In telling her the truth, not only would he have to reveal Owen's secret, but he'd also be exposing her to a world that could kill her.

Peter shook his head, knowing that he had only one choice.

For as long as Anna didn't know about the spirit world, she was safe. And he would lie to her a million times over before being the one who caused her any harm.

"Annie, I'm sorry," he said. "I have no more answers than you. I wish I did, but Ava won't even be honest with me about it. She just told me and Spence to stop spending time with Cass, and we argued about it. I pissed her off, and now she doesn't want anything to do with us."

Disappointment and a fraction of disbelief drew Anna's expression into a frown. "That's it?"

Peter nodded, guilt ripping through his sternum. "That's it."

A long, terrifying silence hung between them as Anna scanned his face. Peter did everything in his power to remain calm and collected. To not give even a fraction of emotion away besides his apology. And that was entirely genuine.

Then Anna stepped back from the bar. "All right." Her voice was too disappointed for his liking. "Well, I gotta close up anyway."

Knowing that he'd likely put himself in a hole with Anna too, Peter desperately wanted to fix it. He wanted to grab her arm, pull her to a stop, and admit everything. He wanted to let all the secrets and lies pour out and tell her that he was sorry he ever kept anything from her in the first place.

But he didn't.

"Mkay." Peter gave her another apologetic grin. "I wish I could be of more help."

Anna shook her head, brushing off his words with a flick of her wrist. "It's fine. I'm probably being overly sensitive after everything that's been going on."

That kicked him in the gut. "Do you need help cleaning anything up?"

She gave him a wry smile. "No, Pete, it's my job. You go ahead and get home. I'll head out shortly."

"I could stay and give you a ride."

"Go home, Peter," she insisted. "I'm fine."

Holding her firm stare for far longer than he should have, Peter couldn't tell whether her refusal was due to her frustration with him or if he was just reading into the situation.

Peter hopped off the stool and pulled on his jacket. "All right, Annie. Well, be careful going home. It's getting cold out there."

"I brought my coat."

He nodded, backing away. "Text me to let me know you got home safe?"

"Sure."

"Cool. See you soon?"

"See you soon."

"'Kay, g'night."

Forcing himself to turn around, Peter rubbed at the phantom marks on his neck. He hated himself for how poorly that had gone. For lying to one of the best friends that he'd ever managed to make. For keeping secrets and hiding things from her when she was just concerned for him and her family.

Peter felt like a true DeVerrean.

He pushed through the front door, the bell chiming its merry *ring* over his head. It grated against his mood. He pulled the keys out of his pocket as the cold night air seared his skin. After the cozy, golden atmosphere of the tavern, the black sky and silent night air felt lifeless and forsaken.

Slowing to a stop, Peter furrowed his brow as he took in the Jeep. He tipped his head to the side. Something was off. After several moments of staring at it, he finally realized just what it was.

Peter's mouth dropped open as he stared at the flat tires.

Not just flat. *Slashed.*

"What the. . . ." Peter crouched to inspect them.

Yes, definitely slashed.

In disbelief, Peter hurried around the whole vehicle. All four tires lay totally flattened on the macadam.

"Seriously?" He frowned, searching the square. The streetlights cast a yellow haze on the night-blackened buildings. He knew the culprit wouldn't still be at the scene of the crime. Whoever had shredded the tires was sending a message.

Had it been a Druid threatening them? Or was it just a random townsperson angry with them for changing up their routine as Diane had?

Peter's eyes caught on the government building in the center of the square as he scanned the plaza and did a double take.

"No," he murmured, shifting back uncomfortably as he searched the darkness. "Nah, no way."

But there, leaning against the whitewashed brick of the building, stood a man. The shadows clinging to the side of the building obscured everything but the fact that the man was staring right at him.

"Ehhh. . . ." Peter took a step back, unsure whether to leave the Jeep and hoof it home, or to confront the man who was clearly waiting for him.

Peter tried to convince himself that it wasn't the same guy who'd slashed the tires. It could have just as easily been a concerned citizen who'd seen the crime and was waiting to report it to the owner. And he'd chosen to creep in the shadows because it was . . . cooler.

Peter's heart lurched, his breath catching in his throat as the man stood and the shadows around him grew darker.

Chills that had nothing to do with the frigid night air ran over his whole body. He'd seen that happen only one other time in his life: In the Mercier house when the scylla crept out to attack them. His throat tightened as everything surrounding the man turned the same shade of obsidian he'd seen in Cassandra's old room. The shadows stretched to extend across the lawn in the center of Harmony Plaza.

Reaching up to rub his neck, Peter backed away. He expected to see the coiling tentacles of the scylla bubbling out of the darkness again. But what he saw this time was much worse.

A hulking form rose from behind the Druid, too obscured in the shadows for him to catch its details. It looked like a cloak at first, rounded on the top and draping to hover behind the Druid like his own shadow.

But then it moved.

Peter's heart jolted, pushing him into action as he retreated a step.

Several—no dozens of tendrils broke free, disrupting the cloak-like form of the beast's body. It lurched up and over the Druid. The tendrils carried it like some liquid, amorphous tangle of ropes as the beast glided across the grass at an unnatural speed.

Peter stopped staring and bolted for the tavern.

CHAPTER SEVENTEEN

Peter

The bell chimed with an erratic *clang* as Peter crashed through the door. Skin tingling from the icy terror flooding his veins, the heater of the tavern swarmed him with its smothering warmth. A flush spread over his body as he did a quick scan for Anna.

"Pete," Anna gasped, still behind the bar gathering the last of her things as he sprinted across the room. "What—"

Peter grabbed her arms and began pulling her with him toward the kitchen. "No time to explain," he tried not to yell. "We've gotta—"

The lights in the tavern flickered. The jazz music turned to static.

With a sickening *pop*, the room fell silent, and the lights went out.

In the sudden darkness, Peter could just barely see Anna's mouth falling ajar as she stared at the ceiling. "What's going on?"

Heart in his throat, Peter's body began to shake. He looked toward the front door, tension mounting as he caught the slightest movement.

He'd made a horrible mistake by running back in here. A terrible, awful, deadly mistake. He should have run in the opposite direction and led that thing away from Anna. Now she was in far more danger than if he'd just told her the truth a few minutes ago.

But it was too late. Even if they made a break for the back door, the creature would be in the building in seconds. He'd seen how fast it could move. There would be no outrunning it. And nowhere to hide in the open back lot of the tavern.

Adjusting his hold on Anna's arm, Peter yanked her down to the floor with him. They crouched behind the bar next to the rumbling ice maker.

"Pete—"

"Shhh." He pushed her back against the bar and pointed at her face. "Stay here."

"What are you—"

"Annie, please!" He tightened the grip of his fingers on her shoulder and held her gaze. His free hand worked into his pocket, searching. "Something is about to come through that door, and I need you to be absolutely quiet."

Horror and shock spread across her face. "What?"

"*Please*," he hissed. "Trust me."

She looked hesitant but nodded.

Peter returned the nod, then bent over his phone.

He had to be fast. He had mere seconds before that thing would crash into the door. He knew it was a stupid plan, but what else could they do? There was nowhere safe to run that they could reach in time. But sitting behind the bar wasn't exactly the best hiding spot either. The creature would find them and tear them apart—or whatever it did with those tendrils. He hadn't gotten a good enough look at it to guess its preferred method of murder.

Hands shaking, Peter typed a message to Owen: *"Help glass tavern! Anna! Druid!!!"*

Double checking that the ringer was off before shoving it back into his pocket, Peter scooted closer to Anna.

Owen would come. He'd save them. It would be okay.

It *had* to be okay.

The bell over the door chimed again, and Peter wrapped his arm around Anna's shoulder as she looked at him. He shook his head, sure she could feel how his whole body trembled at the memories of scylla and hellhounds flashing behind his eyes.

His throat burned.

The shadows darkened around them, and he feared that any moment they'd burst into more beasts.

A deep hiss met his ears from the far side of the room.

He felt Anna flinch in his arms, and he drew her closer.

Maybe if they were still enough, they could wait it out. Trick it into thinking that Peter had escaped already. It was *him* that it was after, right?

Peter closed his eyes as devastation surged through his chest.

It was *him* that it was after.

He should get up and run. Distract the beast and save Anna's life. Sacrifice himself to keep her alive.

The hissing grew louder and, with it, rose the sound of slithering. Tables and chairs crashed to the floor. The beast was searching, hunting them down in the tavern.

Anna pressed deeper into his side. He squeezed her shoulder as he listened closely, trying to decipher what kind of beast this was. It sounded snake-like, but it had looked little like one when he'd seen it out front—far too large and horrifying with its hulking form.

The sharp, ragged puffs of Anna's breathing roared in Peter's ears. He drew her closer, worried that the creature would hear them. It banged about the tavern, relentless in its search. He knew it would turn the place over as it looked for its prey. And it was getting closer.

Hunched against the back of the bar, the sudden pinch of the handgun in his waistband reminded him that he'd brought the weapon to town. He should have reached for it immediately. But the clip was still in his back pocket, and attempting to retrieve it now could make far too much noise.

Anna's breaths grew louder. Peter reached up to tuck her head into his shoulder to muffle the sound. Her breath was hot against his already burning neck—the phantom bands of the scylla's grip like flames on his skin.

A shroud of impossible blackness fell over the tavern like a hood had been pulled over their heads. He could feel Anna tense in his arms, and he brushed his thumb against her hair. Hardening his jaw, Peter glared at the cabinets against the wall, promising himself that he wouldn't let anything happen to her.

The slithering creature knocked into the other side of the bar, sending the stools toppling. They smacked against the floor with a clatter as the hissing grew to an almost deafening level.

Against the wall, Peter could see the shadow of the beast beginning to hover over them. It was going to find them. It was going to kill them.

Peter's body ached and he held his breath, crouched behind the bar in the eternity of waiting for the creature to strike. His hand slipped to the grip of the handgun. If necessary, he could shove Anna down and out of the way, get the clip from his pocket, and shoot the beast. But would he be fast enough? Could bullets even hurt a being from the spirit realm?

Closing his eyes, Peter scrunched up his face in desperation. He couldn't let Anna die. He couldn't. He had to get them out. But how?

Don't let it see us, he prayed. *Dear God, please, don't let it see us. We can't die right now.* She *can't die. Don't let it see us.*

The hiss grew louder. Instinctively, Peter glanced up.

He immediately wished he hadn't.

The beast's tendrils had wrapped over the bar top like trails of shadow. A massive, angular head came into view, seeking its quarry.

The sight was horrifying. Truly and utterly horrifying.

Peter was sure his heart stopped as he looked up at the beast. He did not doubt Ava's estimation now. This creature could be nothing short of demonic.

As its mouth opened to reveal rows and rows of fangs, a hiss echoed in his ears. It had climbed fully onto the bar, the tendrils that formed its body twisting as it moved. The slitted black pupils centered in its neon yellow eyes sliced the air, searching for them.

Please. Peter clung to Anna as he stared at the beast. *Please, don't let it see us.*

Too afraid to move, sure he'd make a sound and draw the creature's attention, Peter imagined himself as small as possible. He wished he'd been smart enough to find some cubby or closet to hide in. But he hadn't, and the metal ice maker supplied them with no cover. If the beast looked down, it would see them. There was no doubt in his mind.

Peter squeezed his eyes shut. *Don't let it see us.*

The hiss of the beast turned into a growl, and Peter knew it was useless. His fingers burned against the gun's grip. This was the end. It had seen them, and it was about to pounce.

The slithering sound of the beast's tendrils whipped around them, knocking a few more barstools out of place.

Peter opened his eyes, ready to attempt whatever he could to save their lives. But the beast wasn't there.

The hissing retreated, the slithering sound winding to the far side of the bar. Peter chanced a look, catching sight of the beast as it pushed through the door leading into the kitchen.

Gaping through the darkness, Peter remained frozen. How had it not seen them? How could it have missed them?

Heart hammering against his chest, Peter shifted. This was a chance to escape. They had to go. Now! If they could move quickly enough, they could get out the front door and make a run for it before the beast realized they'd been in the building.

Peter took hold of Anna's shaking shoulders and forced her to meet his eyes. He was too scared to attempt words, but he frantically pointed between them, then toward the front door.

Anna clung to the floor, shaking her head.

With an insistent nod, Peter tightened his grip on her. He wouldn't take no for an answer. They had to get out of here. He *had* to save her.

Pulling her up, Peter was grateful that Anna didn't fight him as he rose, ready to bolt for the door even if he had to drag her with him. But neither had taken a step before they heard a shout.

"Hey!" a man called from the far side of the room.

Peter and Anna jumped, seeing the Druid waiting in the shadows. Immediately, his hand reared back.

Dropping Anna's arm, Peter instinctively threw up his hands, as if he could block the incoming arc.

A tremor shuddered from the base of his neck, down his spine, and into his arms as he stepped in front of Anna.

He watched as the black arc flew from the Druid, heading straight for the two of them. But it never found its mark.

A golden field of light burst from Peter's hands, leaving his fingers tingling.

It flew across the restaurant, absorbing the arc and slamming into the Druid, knocking the man backward and into a table.

Anna gasped in shock, and Peter stared at his palms in awe.

Had he really done that? Did he just wield the spirit world and save their lives?

A crash reverberated from the kitchen. They both whirled to see the horrifying beast hurl itself through the pass-through window.

Anna screamed in panic, but Peter threw his hands forward.

The golden light erupted again, his skin buzzing with power as the arc slammed into the beast. It recoiled in pain, its hiss growing angry before it burst into smoke and disappeared.

The chime of the bell drew their attention back to the front door as the Druid made a break for it. The lights flickered on, and a melodious cacophony of jazz hummed to life again overhead.

Peter's hand went to the gun. He was about to rush after the Druid when a shuddering breath behind him yanked his focus back to Anna.

Catching her as her knees buckled, Peter dropped to the ground with her. Anna began to sob, the sound ripping into him. Unsure what to do, Peter held her close and rubbed his hand against her back.

"I'm sorry," he whispered. "I'm sorry. You're okay. It's gone."

Anna's whole body shook in his arms. He couldn't blame her for the response. He should feel just as terrified. He should be a nervous wreck. But he could still feel the tremor running over his skin, the power that had pulsed from him when he'd saved their lives.

A small smile pulled at Peter's lips.

He'd saved their lives!

It was crazy and amazing and frightening all at once.

He was a Wielder.

And he'd saved their lives.

The smile faltered as Anna's tears soaked through his collar, and Peter held her closer. "I'm sorry," he whispered again. "It's gone. It's gone."

~

Peter nearly jumped out of his skin when the bell on the tavern door rang again. But he relaxed once he heard Owen's voice calling their names.

"Over here," Peter said, raising his voice to be sure their friend could hear. He wasn't sure how long he and Anna had sat there. Long enough that her sobs had turned to quiet tears while she trembled. Long enough for his guilt to carve a raw passage down his throat.

Owen appeared around the corner to find them still crumpled on the floor. Dressed in slacks and a button up under his peacoat, he looked like he'd come from some classy event. Knowing Owen, Peter did not doubt that the man had only spent the evening at home with Ava.

Dropping into a squat next to them, Owen rested a hand on Anna's shoulder. "What happened?" he asked, voice calm despite the urgency in his gaze.

"A Druid attacked," Peter explained. "You didn't happen to see anyone running away when you got here, did you?"

"No."

"Too bad." He tightened his grip on Anna's arm. "We need to get Annie home."

She twitched at those words, then pulled away from his touch with slow, lethargic movements. Smeared and crumbling mascara rimmed her bloodshot eyes, the light reflecting off her tear-stained cheeks. She kept her gaze down, her once-wispy curls now matted to her forehead. Peter reached up to brush them back. She flinched at his movement.

Retracting his hand, Peter felt the guilt claw at his chest again. What must she be thinking? He was sure to have lost all her trust forever at this point.

His dark blue eyes shifting between them, Owen edged into Peter's view. "I've got the car out front," he said, holding out his hand to Anna. She took it, and he helped her up.

Peter scrambled to his feet while Anna pulled on her coat and collected her purse from the back of the bar. They moved toward the door together, Anna mechanically turning off the lights and locking the door. Owen hurried her to his silver sedan and held open the passenger door for her.

Playing with the keys in his pocket, Peter watched, unsure what to do. He needed to talk to Owen. He needed to apologize to Anna—for lying and for bringing that beast to her. He needed to get back to Spencer and Cassandra and make certain they were okay. He scanned Harmony Plaza, checking for any sign of the Druid. What if he'd only run to get backup?

The car door closed with a soft *thunk*, and Owen turned back to him. He ran a hand over his blond hair with a grimace. "I know now isn't exactly the time, but we need to discuss what happened," he said. "In detail."

"I'll fill you in as soon as you want," Peter replied, wishing they could discuss it immediately.

Owen nodded, then glanced at the Jeep. He narrowed his eyes. "Did you know your tires are slashed?"

Peter scoffed. "Yeah, I figured that out right before the Druid attacked."

A heavy sigh puffed in a cloud of fog from Owen's lips. "Come on," he said. "I've got to get Anna settled first, but I'll take you home."

Though Peter felt immediate relief at the offer, he shook his head, sure he shouldn't intrude on the family like that. "Nah, that's cool. You need to make sure Anna's taken care of. I can walk home."

"Don't be ridiculous. Get in the car." Owen moved for the sedan as if the conversation was over.

Even as his guilt ripped another layer in his throat, Peter slipped into the seat behind Anna's. The drive to Hope Court was silent. He slumped in the black cloth seat as he tried not to stare at Anna's bun peeking over the headrest. The glow from the lights on the dashboard lit the car's interior with a haunting, ethereal blue.

Peter ran a hand over his mouth and jaw. What had he done? How could he be so stupid? He'd tried to protect Anna by keeping her out of the spirit world's sphere, then brought her face to face with a Druid *and* a beast. And the most freakin' terrifying beast he'd seen yet.

Rubbing his neck, Peter tried to swallow. Their situation was growing worse by the second. He'd thought the scylla and hellhounds were bad. Whatever the hell *that thing* was, he'd take a million scylla before it.

Owen pulled into the driveway and Anna's seatbelt clicked free immediately. She exited the car and walked toward the house, moving like a sleepwalker. As if she was on autopilot.

As Owen opened his door, he glanced back at Peter. "You should come in," he said. "I want to be sure she's settled before we head out again."

Peter followed without hesitation, wanting the same thing.

They climbed the porch steps on Anna's heels as she opened the front door. Owen motioned for Peter to enter before him. Just as he shut the door, Ava entered the living room from the kitchen. Her eyes narrowed upon seeing Peter, but she had no time to speak. Anna dropped her purse, rushing to her sister's side.

Anna's arms surrounded Ava as a fresh wave of tears overcame her. Each one was a gut punch to Peter.

The shock was clear on Ava's face. She peered around her sister at the two men standing by the door. She wrapped her arms around Anna, massaging her back in slow circles. "Shh, shh," she whispered, a kindness in her tone that Peter hadn't heard before.

However, the glare Ava threw his way said she already knew he was at fault.

Peter's shoulders slumped forward. She was right. The joy he felt earlier for saving them soured in his memory. The only reason he'd had to save them was because he was an impulsive idiot.

Owen stepped up to his wife and sister-in-law's side. Though Anna was taller than average for a woman, Ava was much shorter. Owen towered nearly a foot over his wife as he set a hand gently on her shoulder blade.

"What happened?" Ava demanded before he could speak.

Owen took it in stride. "I'm not sure yet," he admitted. "Why don't you take care of Anna? I've got to get Peter home."

Ava's dark eyes flared with anger, flickering toward Peter. She took hold of Anna's arms, drawing her sister back before taking hold of her hand. She looked up at Owen. "Not yet," she insisted. "You two stay here until I can hear what happened."

"Ava, it's almost eleven," he argued. "Let me get him home."

Peter could feel the heat of the glare she gave her husband from the far side of the room. "Owen—" Ava's voice was taut and threatening. "Don't let him leave."

Before he could respond, Ava turned from Owen and pulled her sister down the hall with her.

The room fell silent as Owen stared after the women. He ran a hand over his light, immaculately groomed facial hair. He took a step back, then angled toward Peter. His dark blue eyes locked on him.

Peter knew what was coming. He just hoped they had enough time to get their story straight before Ava returned.

"What happened?" Owen asked, his voice low enough that only Peter could hear.

Taking a single step forward, Peter let the words tumble out. "I was headed home from the tavern and discovered—well, you saw the Jeep. Then I saw this dude creeping in the shadows by the town hall. Out of nowhere, a freaking monster of a beast appears." He kept his voice hushed as he continued. "I freaked out, okay? I ran back into the tavern because the thing charged me, and I didn't know what else to do. I wish I hadn't done it. But I ran back in, and Anna was there, and we hid."

Owen's brow pulled together. "She saw it?"

"Yeah, man." Peter shrugged. "And she saw a whole lot more."

"What do you mean?"

"I mean. . . ." He sighed. "The beast was looking for us and—honestly, I don't know how it didn't see us. We weren't well hidden. But I dunno, I guess—I guess someone was looking out for us."

"Someone?"

He scratched his temple. "God, I mean. I was praying and . . . yeah, I was praying that the thing wouldn't see us, and it didn't."

Owen nodded as though the idea of divine interference wasn't surprising.

"But, yeah, the thing didn't see us, and it went to search the kitchen." Peter grit his teeth before continuing. "I thought it was our chance to get out of there and escape, but . . . the Druid was standing on the other side of the bar. He drew his hand back to throw an arc at us, and I reacted."

"You reacted?"

A dry smile pulled at Peter's lips. "Yeah. I, uh—I guess I'm a Wielder now too."

Owen's lips parted in surprise. "Just like that?"

Peter shrugged again.

"What did you do?"

"I mean, I don't know what you would call it, but I held out my hands, and a freaking wall of gold light blocked the Druid's arc and knocked him off his feet." He raised his brow. "Then the beast came for us, and I killed it. Or whatever happens to them when they're hit with an arc."

Owen's round eyes narrowed on his face as he stepped closer. "That's fast, Peter."

"What do you mean?"

"I mean—" His voice was serious and hushed. "It takes time for people to develop their powers. They don't just start drawing on the essence of the spirit world the first time they attempt it."

Peter didn't know whether to be excited or terrified by that. "What, uh—what's that mean?"

The man studied him as though he were an intriguing anomaly. "I don't know."

A door shut deeper within the house; it snapped Peter's attention back to the moment. "What do we tell Ava?" he asked in a panic.

Owen's chin dipped. He stared at the cream and rust-colored rug beneath their feet. "I don't know," he repeated.

"What do you mean you don't know?" The demand came out in a hiss as footsteps approached. "We have to have a plan!"

Even if Owen had shown a sign that he would respond, he didn't get the chance.

Ava reappeared from the dark hallway, eyes locked on them. The baggy sweater she wore bunched around her arms as she crossed them over her chest. Her braids tucked behind her ears, her appearance was more collected than when she'd left them.

Though Peter would prefer to make the long walk home in the cold rather than stay in the Bernard house facing Ava's wrath, he stood his ground and tipped his head toward the hall. "How's Anna?"

The look Ava sent him was like a gunshot, a piercing and direct tear through his chest. "She's a mess," she said accusingly. "I calmed her down and got her into bed, but I don't think I should leave her for long. Something has really scared her. Care to explain what it was?"

Peter shot Owen a covert glance again, hoping the man would give him a sign. But he received no direction. The man didn't even look at him.

Tossing his arms out to the side, Peter shook his head. "I don't know what you want me to say, Ava."

"I want the truth," she shot back. "I want to know what happened to my sister!"

Peter opened his mouth, but he couldn't speak. Anything he said would reveal too much. But at the very least, he had to try to keep Owen out of it. "This is what I was trying to tell you the other day," he defended. "I was trying to get you to understand that we aren't the only ones looking for the spirit world. And *we're* not your enemy."

Ava tilted her head, her breaths increasing in speed. "You got my sister involved in your devilry?"

Though he wasn't sure he'd ever heard the term used, Peter had no trouble understanding what she was accusing him of. "We're not involved in evil, Ava." He pointed his finger at his chest to emphasize the point. "We are *fighting* evil. And if you would help us, we could do a whole hell of a lot better of a job!"

"What did you do to my sister?" Ava demanded again.

"Ava—" Owen moved to set a hand on his wife's arm, but she jerked away from his touch.

Glaring at her husband, Ava's face passed through three clear emotions in rapid succession. First was her lingering anger at Peter, which had now shifted to Owen. Second was surprise, as though she realized just who it was she was looking at. Third was shock as her full lips parted, and she stepped away from him.

Peter could see the moment coming like a car crash in slow motion.

"Why are you defending him?" she asked.

Owen's calm gaze didn't waver from his wife's face. The dichotomy of the couple stood out in full force in the dim light of their home. They were a picture of balanced contrast—his height against her lack of it, his pale skin against her rich brown, his light features against her dark ones, his peaceful manner against her reactive nature.

They were opposites in many ways, but Peter had never recognized the one thing that tied them together: They loved the other fiercely— possibly to a fault. And as he watched husband and wife about to cross a threshold of no return, he felt he should be anywhere but there.

"Owen. . . ." Her voice faltered as he stared down at her.

Reaching to brush some of her braids over her shoulder, Owen's expression twisted with regret. "I'm sorry, Ava," he said, his voice stronger than Peter had anticipated. "I should have been brave enough to tell you the truth years ago."

Ava drew back from him, shaking her head. "What are you . . . ?"

"What happened tonight was not Peter's fault," he said. "At least, not directly. He and his brother walked into something they had no idea existed. Now, they don't have a choice but to be involved. And in the end, you'll be glad they're here."

"No." Ava's head shook vehemently, her voice broken and in pain. "I don't—no, you aren't. . . ."

Peter pressed his lips together, wishing he could disappear like Gerard and escape the disaster he'd caused.

"I am," Owen confirmed. "I'm a Wielder. I know you don't know the term, but I may as well give it to you."

"No," Ava insisted.

"I can do everything that Cassandra can do and more. And it's my job to ensure the Druids don't take over the Veil of DeVerre."

Ava's whole face twisted in horror. "*What?*"

"I was coming here, married to you or not. And I love you, but I'm a fool, so I lied to you."

She took a step back.

Despite her reaction, Owen didn't hesitate or show any sign of backing down. Peter supposed he'd gone too far now anyway. "I love you, Ava. I do. And I'm sorry that I lied to you. But after what has happened tonight, I can't hide anymore. I have to help Peter, Spencer, and Cassandra find the Druids hiding within DeVerre. And I can't do that if I keep the truth from you any longer."

There was a long silence as the couple stared at one another, each waiting for the other to speak. For the second time that night, Peter felt frozen, terrified that if he moved, he'd alert them to his presence. He held still, waiting for the moment to end, hoping peace would return.

But Ava's lips turned into a snarl even as the tears welled in her eyes. "Get out." The command was a whisper. So different from the way she'd said it to Peter at the library only two days before.

Owen dipped his head, his expression soft and heartbreaking. "Ava—"

"Don't," she snapped, her decision marked by her harsh tone. "Leave. Take Peter back to Occasus and stay there."

Though Owen's face reflected little emotion, Peter felt crushed by her words. Seeing a couple separate was a gruesome brutality no one should ever be witness to. And being the cause of this separation ate Peter alive.

Ava backed farther away until she was in the hall, eyes still locked on her husband. "Get out, Owen," she charged. "And don't come back."

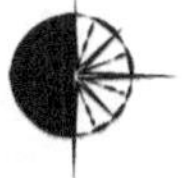

CHAPTER EIGHTEEN

Spencer

Morning light beamed through the windows of Occasus like beacons of hope. Spencer pressed his hands over his uncontainable smile. He'd done it. He'd done the impossible.

The past day and a half, Spencer had researched the Lawrences endlessly. When basic web searches hadn't provided much information, he'd resorted to perusing message boards and forums, diving deep into the theological and academic corners of the internet that often made his head swim. It took over twenty-four hours before the epiphany hit: He didn't need to keep searching the internet.

If Diane's writing habits were like his and Peter's—which Cassandra had already confirmed—then she kept everything. And somewhere in all her things, she *had* to have a record of her trip to Bushmills, Ireland, to visit Elijah Lawrence's church.

After another several hours of searching the boxes they'd taken to the attic weeks ago, Spencer found his answer in the form of a journal labeled: *United Kingdom & Ireland, Summer 1997.* Flipping through the pages,

Spencer had struggled to read Diane's angular cursive handwriting. But when his searching eyes locked on the capitalized *B* of the word "Bushmills," his heart burst into an excited flutter.

Spencer perused the journal as he walked downstairs, attempting to glean any information he could from her notes. Most of the entries chronicled the beauty and majesty of the region and the people she and Liam had met. One such meeting stood out when he saw the name Owen written in her spidery lettering. The familiar first name caught his attention, and he slowed his scan to read about the man.

The couple had met Owen Lewan, a young Irishman, at the town pub where he worked. During their conversation, they informed him of the purpose of their visit to Europe, and the man offered to show them to the chapel.

Spencer couldn't believe his luck in finding the answer so quickly. After weeks of searching, he'd thought it would take him days to peruse the whole journal. Diane laid out their entire visit to St. Thomas Chapel, describing their many meetings with Reverend Colm Cunningham. They'd spoken of Elijah Lawrence, his writings and theological dissertations, and her ability to see ghosts.

Setting aside the journal to read the rest of Diane's notes later, Spencer opened his laptop and searched for St. Thomas Chapel in Bushmills, Ireland. Within less than an hour, he'd found its small, outdated website.

Shaking off the irritation he felt for not thinking of this route before, Spencer clicked the "contact us" page at the top of the website. Despite the time difference, he'd decided to go ahead and send an email last night.

And now, sitting at his desk the following morning, he was glad he had.

Spencer had carefully crafted his message. He took his time to ensure that he effectively detailed their situation without giving anything about the Druids away. Though it was clear from Diane's trip that Reverend Cunningham had been familiar with the spirit world, there was no way of knowing if the man was still in charge twenty-four years later. And Spencer had no interest in stirring up questions that he didn't care to answer.

In simple terms, his email laid-out their great-aunt Diane Larkin's visit to Bushmills in the late '90s. She'd received copies of Elijah Lawrence's essays, but the papers had gone missing after her death. Now, they were hoping to access new copies as they'd meant a lot to her and the book she'd been writing. Spencer thought it was a perfect blend of heartbreaking and nostalgic to make the recipient empathetic to their cause.

When Spencer got out of bed that morning and checked his phone for notifications, he'd ignored all the others when he spotted the reply from St. Thomas. Dressing hastily, he rushed downstairs and opened the laptop to read the email from Reverend Patrick O'Sullivan. The reverend's response was kind and courteous, explaining that he'd recently taken up the post at the chapel from Reverend Cunningham. He said that he'd checked with the prior reverend and that Cunningham remembered Diane and her husband, corroborating all the information that Spencer had given.

O'Sullivan only had a few follow-up questions before he agreed to send the material: What was the subject of Diane's book? Did they want the essays for personal interest or to finish her writings themselves? And would they agree not to share copies of the pages?

Spencer clicked the reply button to write out his response but let the blank box stare back at him as he considered how to respond. He had no problem promising the reverend they wouldn't share the pages. Other than Cassandra and Owen, they had no reason to share them anyway. However, he couldn't figure out how to answer the rest of the questions. Without telling the reverend the full truth—a decision he didn't think would result in the response he hoped for—he'd have to veer close to the unacceptable territory of lying.

Carefully, Spencer crafted his reply: *"Diane never intended to publish her book. She was collecting information about the small town where we live and the ghosts in the area. She found Elijah Lawrence's work and believed it connected to her ability to see those ghosts. I hope to get copies of the essays because, as her heirs, my brother and I find ourselves drawn into her research in ways we never expected. We don't have any intention of completing her draft or making the essays public information. We want to study them and see if they can help us as we work to understand this new world she's brought us into."*

The cursor blinked on the screen a hundred times as Spencer debated his response. Finally, he hit send.

Trying not to panic, Spencer forced himself out of his chair and into the kitchen to make coffee. He took his time, returning an aching ten minutes later to glance nervously at his email tab.

He had one unread message.

Spencer's heart leaped into his throat seeing Reverend O'Sullivan's name on the email. His hands shook, and he nearly spilled his coffee as he rushed to open it. The reverend replied that he appreciated the honesty and was happy to help them however he could.

Scrolling down, Spencer found eleven PDFs attached to the email.

A disbelieving chuckle slipped out of him as he sat back in his office chair. He couldn't believe it. These essays could change everything.

"What are you so cheery about this morning?" Cassandra asked, appearing in the office doorway, her Bible and notebook resting in the crook of her arm, a cup of coffee in her other hand. Anguis padded around her toward Nex, who lay on the floor at Spencer's side.

Smile growing wider, Spencer couldn't help how his chest puffed, knowing what her reaction would be. "I, uh. . . ." He rubbed the back of his neck before motioning to the computer screen. "Well, I found Elijah Lawrence's essays."

Cassandra's face went slack in shock. "What?"

Spencer shrugged.

Practically tossing the books and coffee mug onto the dining room table, Cassandra rushed into the office. She wound around the desk to stand behind his chair, one hand on the back as she leaned down to read the screen, the other hand settling over her mouth. "How did you . . . ?"

"I found the church," he explained, his tone calm as though he wasn't just as thrilled as she was. "And I emailed them."

Cassandra laughed in excitement and wrapped her arms around Spencer's shoulders. "You're a genius!" she said, then pulled away to lean on the desktop. "Have you looked at them yet?"

Chest ablaze from where she'd hugged him, Spencer did his best not to show discomfort at her nearness or the way it electrified his senses. He straightened the collar of his shirt, shaking his head. "No, I just got them now."

"You're amazing," Cassandra said, her eyes locked on the laptop.

Spencer let out an embarrassed scoff. "Thanks," he muttered, clearing his throat. "Here. I'll print them off."

As he downloaded each PDF, Cassandra shifted away from him. The absence of her presence at his side made him equal parts at ease and disappointed. He focused on the essays despite his eyes attempting to drift after her every few seconds.

The printer chimed to life, and the cartridges whirred right as Owen walked around the corner.

Spencer blinked rapidly, taking in the man in his wrinkled slacks and button up. "Owen?"

Standing beside the printer, Cassandra whirled around. Owen tipped his chin up in greeting. "Good morning," he said as though they should expect him to be there.

"What are you—did I forget you were coming by?" Spencer asked, realizing he hadn't heard a knock at the door.

"Ah, no," Owen said, tugging on the tag of a tea bag that dangled over the edge of the mug in his hands. "I suppose Peter didn't get a chance to tell you?"

Spencer and Cassandra shared a glance.

"I was in bed before he got home last night," he said.

"Me too," Cassandra added.

Owen nodded. "Right. I take it he's not a morning person."

Spencer tried to laugh, but the sound was just a puff of air. "Not in the slightest. When did you get here?"

Head dipping, Owen rubbed his palm over the side of his mug. "Last night. It seems. . . ." There was tension in his tone. "It seems I'll be staying with you three for a while."

The only sound was the printer humming in the background, spitting paper out in choppy bursts.

Cassandra stepped forward, mouth agape. "Ava found out?"

He nodded.

Spencer's heart fell.

"She threw you out?" Cassandra asked.

Again, Owen nodded.

"I'm so sorry, man," Spencer said, knowing it wasn't a good enough apology.

Owen gave them a sad smile. "It's my fault. I was arrogant to think that I could keep this from her. Honestly, I'm surprised I made it eleven years."

Cassandra moved to Spencer's side again, her hand resting on the back of his chair. "How'd she find out?"

Peter's head peeked in from the kitchen, a grimace on his face. Dark circles hollowed his eyes, and his wavy hair stood on end. "That'd, uh. . . ." He stood next to Owen, a sheepish expression on his downcast face. "That'd be my fault."

"You told her?" Cassandra exclaimed.

Spencer sent her a disapproving glare for immediately blaming his brother, but Owen held up a hand to interject. "*I* told her," he corrected.

"But only because I was an idiot." Peter tossed Owen a remorseful glance before turning to Spencer and Cassandra. "We need to talk."

Chills raced over Spencer at his brother's serious tone. "What happened?"

Peter's hand brushed his neck, and Spencer recognized the nervous tic he'd picked up since the scylla. "Pete—" He sat up straighter, not wanting the answer he was about to demand. "What happened?"

Shrugging nonchalantly, Peter did a terrible job of making the moment less tense. "I was attacked by a Druid last night."

The words landed on Spencer like a dead body. He felt his shoulders drop as his eyebrows pulled together. But Peter wasn't done.

"And Anna was with me."

"What?" Spencer spared Owen a single glance. "Is she okay?"

"Yeah, yeah, she's—um. . . ." Peter swallowed, more shaken than Spencer thought he'd ever seen his brother.

Rage bubbled within Spencer. It made his jaw tighten, and his hands curl into fists. Someone had tried to kill his brother. "What happened?" he demanded again, the anger cutting into his voice.

Peter flinched at the sound, and his dark eyes narrowed. He drew his head back, chin rising in defiant confidence. "We're fine," he insisted. "We made it out alive, and we're both fine, so you don't need to worry."

Spencer knew better than to admonish his brother. Peter liked to see himself as the protector. The one who kept them safe. He pretended that he was the one who had it together and that he wasn't just as insecure and anxious as Spencer himself.

Any form of rebuke or criticism brought out the worst side of Peter. It was an immediate slap in the face, a suggestion that he was a screw-up, and unable to protect anyone. And he always reacted out of spite to prove his critics wrong. A reaction Spencer directly tied to the days following their dad's death, when Peter began stepping up, struggling to take on the role of caregiver in the impossibly large shadow their father's memory cast.

But Spencer had never been Peter's critic.

Normally, Spencer would do anything to be sure that Peter never felt that sort of self-doubt. He always worked to counter it and disprove it. He let his brother take the lead at every opportunity because he knew he needed it.

Today—when his brother had faced death for a second time in a week—Spencer wasn't about to let Peter's faulty sense of pride get him killed.

"Peter!"

His brother threw his arms out to the side. "I'm alive, aren't I? You don't have to freak out just because someone attacked me."

"Someone *attacked* you, Pete!" Spencer slammed his fist on the desk. He felt Cassandra jump beside him. Owen's brow furrowed, but he didn't interfere. "That's not something you're just *fine* after. You could have died!"

"But I didn't!" Peter yelled back. "I'm here, and I'm alive, and I'm *fine*."

Spencer held his glare, the fury inside of him not yet satisfied.

Peter glared back. "And as it turns out, I'm a Wielder."

Cassandra let out an excited gasp at Spencer's side. She drifted forward, eyes alight with hope. "You are? How?"

He gave her a proud nod before turning back to Spencer. "I don't know. But I saved us, okay? And we're alive. So, you don't need to freak out."

The way Owen's light eyebrows rose said otherwise.

"What?" Spencer asked, directing the question to their sudden housemate. "You don't agree?"

Twisting the string of the tea bag around his finger, Owen pursed his lips. "I'm concerned," he admitted. "The way that Peter managed to wield the spirit world so suddenly . . . it's not common."

Spencer's brows pulled together in confusion. "What do you mean?"

"There are levels to being a Wielder," he explained. "Specific, defined levels. It always starts with seeing ghosts. We call these people

Heralds. They can see the ghosts and creatures from the spirit world but cannot connect directly with them or touch anything beyond the Veil."

Cassandra took another step closer. "Like Diane."

Owen nodded. "The next level is Advocate. They can interact with ghosts and turn them into phantoms. People typically stay in one of those two levels unless they receive training or their abilities are abnormally powerful.

"The third form of Wielder is the Cleric." He turned to Cassandra at that. "Which is what you were a mere week ago. Clerics can reach into the spirit world to summon and control beasts. Most Wielders end at the level of Cleric. But when you wielded the essence of the spirit world in your fight with Debbie, you moved on to a much rarer level of Wielder. You became a Sage, a practice that often takes years of training and a deep relationship with the spirit world to reach."

He stopped and looked at Peter incredulously. "But you became a Sage Wielder right off the bat."

Peter's eyes were wide as he listened to Owen speak. He held his head high, but Spencer could read the alarm in his brother's expression. He knew what his brother was feeling because he felt it himself—heart pounding, thoughts racing, and confusion mounting.

"What does that mean?" Spencer demanded.

With a deep breath, Owen angled toward the table to set down his mug. He tugged on the hem of his shirt to smooth it out, then crossed his arms. "I don't know. I've never heard of this happening. There's a chance the Warden has seen it and chosen not to discuss it openly for . . . whatever reason they thought important. But until I reach out to my friends from Harmony, I won't have any answers for you."

The silence stretched as Spencer tried to process it all.

In less than a month, so much had happened. A hellhound attacked, and they met Cassandra. She'd introduced them to the spirit world and its ghosts, phantoms, and beasts. They'd gained a phantom for a roommate— wherever Gerard was that morning. They'd learned they weren't biologically Collinses and uncovered a plot to keep their heritage a secret. They'd discovered Druids, fought for their lives, and now . . . now his brother was a Wielder with unprecedented ability.

It was too fast.

It was too much.

And Spencer was angry that it wasn't him.

Not that he wanted to see ghosts, tether phantoms, or summon and control beasts. None of that held any interest for him. He didn't care about the connection to the spirit world itself. He cared about his ability—or inability in this case—to protect his brother. To keep him alive and safe and to never lose anyone else he loved.

Cassandra set a hand to her mouth, her other arm wrapping around her waist. Dressed in her typical all-black ensemble, her shadow hovered in his periphery.

Yes, Spencer wanted to protect everyone who meant anything to him. And in moments like this, where he learned that Druids had attacked his brother and he'd had no way to be there for him, he felt incapable of protecting anyone.

"Are there. . . ." Cassandra shifted forward, her eyes locked on Owen. "You said that nearly all Wielders end with becoming a Cleric. What about Sages? Does something come after them?"

A sardonic grin pulled at Owen's lips. "Well, that would be the status of Archsage. It's—" He let out a humorless laugh. "I've never met one; I'll put it that way. Outside of legends, I've never heard of any either."

"What can they do that's different from Sages?" Peter asked.

There was a resigned look in Owen's dark stare as he scanned the three of them, all eagerly listening. "That's mostly classified information," he said. "So, I don't exactly know myself. However, there are rumors that suggest that an Archsage can connect with and, subsequently, control the spirits of others. Therefore, controlling the being themselves."

Spencer's jaw dropped, sure that he had to be mistaken.

"Unbelievable, isn't it?" Owen sighed. "Again, that is a rumor. What they can actually do is beyond my knowledge. If they even exist at all."

The room fell silent once more. Spencer, Peter, and Cassandra exchanged looks of overwhelmed surprise. Someone able to control the spirit—the very being of a person—that was unfathomable. And it sounded far more dangerous and powerful than any human should ever be.

Spencer scanned Peter, hand still at his neck. Heavy shadows lingered under his brother's eyes. Peter didn't carry his usual boyish charm and flippant persona. Instead, he appeared to bear the weight of the world on his drooped shoulders.

Spencer felt his muscles tense, bristling at the thought. "That's all quite interesting." He knew his tone was gruff, but he didn't care. He nudged his chin in Peter's direction. "Back to the issue at hand. What specifically happened last night to cause all of this?"

Sighing, Peter refused to meet Spencer's eyes as he explained. A chill ran down Spencer's spine as he watched his brother recount the harrowing experience. He wondered if he would have thought to pray as a beast sought him in the darkness. Or would he have frozen, too much in a panic to think, let alone pray?

With a heavy sigh, Peter shrugged. "The bell rang, and we saw the Druid run out the door. And that was it."

Several seconds ticked by before any of them could reply. What could someone say about such an intense, near-death experience? How did you accept it or process it? Especially when it was your brother—the person you trusted most in the world—who went through it.

Spencer cleared his raw throat, sure that he wouldn't be able to let Peter out of his sight for the rest of eternity. "You're alive," he managed. "That's all that matters."

Peter's eyes finally drifted to Spencer. There was an unexpected glimmer of fear in his brother's gaze—a look that made him want to get up, find the Druid, and exact his vengeance.

Spencer worked to calm the frantic beat of his heart. "Did you at least get a good look at the guy?"

Peter shrugged half-heartedly. "Kinda. He was DeVerrean, you know? They all kind of look the same." He glanced at Cassandra. "No offense."

She smirked. "You're DeVerrean too, remember?"

A small scoff eked out of Peter. "I guess you're right." He shook his head. "Anyway, I might be able to pick him out of a lineup, but I couldn't tell you who he is. Not without something to reference."

Owen raised his head. "I bet Anna would know him."

Peter stiffened.

"We could give her a call to ask."

"We're not asking Anna anything!" Peter spat.

Owen narrowed his deep-set eyes. "You do realize that this man could be our best shot at finding the rest of the Druids, don't you? If we figure out who he is, we may get some information. But if we can *find* and *talk* to him, we can get all the information we need."

"How?" Peter scoffed. "You think a Druid's just gonna give up and talk to us if we figure out his identity? These people are killers, man! There's no way they'd answer our questions."

"They would if they had the proper incentive," Spencer suggested.

Peter scowled at him. "Really, dude? What are you gonna do? Torture the guy?"

Spencer couldn't deny that the thought had crossed his mind. If it was between saving the lives of his family and letting the Druids walk free, he was willing to do whatever it took. No matter the cost to himself.

Cassandra edged closer, angling across the distance to tap Spencer's arm. Heat tingled along the spot she touched as he raised his head. "I don't think that's necessary," she said, a knowing look crossing her face. "If we can find him, we can take him to Tom."

"You think the judicial system is gonna help us find Druids?" Spencer countered skeptically.

"They don't know that we're working together, remember?" Cassandra leaned against the desk. "If we play our cards right, Tom could convince the guy that he's on his side and find out more information than we ever could."

"So you think the marshal will play double agent for us?"

"I think it's possible. And it's a better option than torture."

Though Spencer was dubious that her idea would work, he liked it better than his own. Yes, he would do whatever it took to protect his brother, but he'd prefer not to take it *that* far. "All right. So, we need to figure out who this Druid is."

Peter crossed his arms, his stance determined. "We're *not* asking Anna."

"I don't see a better option," Cassandra said sympathetically. "I know you want to take care of her, but—"

"No!" Peter shouted, arms swinging wide. "You don't get it! I lied to her, okay? She asked me point-blank what was going on, and I *lied* to her. Then I nearly got her killed! Do you think she's ever gonna speak to me again? I don't."

Though Spencer would have liked to argue with his brother, he knew he couldn't. Not when it came to relationships. They'd always found a balance, Peter and him. He was great at some things, and Peter was great at others. They managed to strengthen each other's weak points. And Spencer was never great with people.

But Peter . . . he lived for people. He was desperate for people. And now he was sure he'd lost one of the people he'd come to think of as closest to him.

Whether he was right or not, now was not the moment to fight him. Not when he was sure that he'd failed yet again.

A tense, sorrowful scoff escaped Peter. "I wouldn't speak to me if I were her."

Massaging the palm of his hand to soothe his tension, Spencer glanced at Cassandra from his seat at the desk. She was already looking down at him with an unreadable expression. But he knew that they were thinking the same thing.

Anna might not talk to Peter, but that didn't mean she wouldn't speak to either of them. One of them might get her to identify the Druid.

"All right," Spencer said, feeling the weight of their situation growing heavier each second. "So, what do we do now? Whatever leeway the Druids were giving us is up. Whether they held off their attack because they were trying to pick us off one-by-one or for some other reason, they made the first play last night."

Owen nodded. "I think you're right. And there's no doubt in my mind they'll try again."

"So, what do we *do*?" Cassandra repeated Spencer's question, her words sharp and forceful. "We can't sit around here researching and hoping we figure it out anymore. Not if they're going to come for us."

"I'm a Wielder now too," Peter reminded them with a shrug. "We could take the fight to them."

Owen held up a hand, a frown twisting his face. "I don't think that's wise. While you and Cassandra may have the abilities of a Sage like me, neither of you has had training. The essence you wield will not be strong enough to have the effect we will need."

"Besides," Spencer interrupted, ready to bring them back to reality, "we don't know who the Druids are. We can't fight them if we don't know them."

"So, what do *you* want to do?" Peter asked. "As Cass said, we can't wait around here anymore."

Dropping his eyes to the desk, Spencer worked his jaw. He knew the action he wanted to take. But he knew he couldn't say it out loud. Not when the other three in the room were dedicated to protecting the town where they would meet their deaths if the Druids had their way.

Yet, there was no doubt in his mind. If it came down to his brother's life or death, he'd leave DeVerre before anything could happen to him. If he had to tie Peter up and throw him into the Jeep, then so be it. He'd abandon this place, the secrets it held, and the dream they'd longed for to keep his brother alive.

Nex lifted his head, suddenly alert. The jingling tags on his collar drew Spencer's attention as the dog stared toward the front of the house.

"What *can* we do?" Cassandra asked, desperation in her voice. "Spencer's right. We need more answers. We can't stay here hoping they'll leave us alone anymore. But we also can't fight someone when we don't even know who they are."

Peter glanced at Owen. "Ava said the answers are in the vault."

Nex stood, edging toward the door while Anguis hopped up beside him. Spencer narrowed his eyes, following their gaze. The dull gray light of an overcast morning hung above the empty lawn of Occasus.

Gerard popped into view, already in mid-stride toward the office. Dark hair slicked back as always, the red tie around his neck the only true color on the phantom. His face wore its usual grimace as he leaned on the doorframe. He tossed the dogs a snarl and scanned the rest of them. "You're all the most ineffective team I've ever met," he said. "Sitting here researching when I've told you dozens of times: *You have to get on the inside*. You have to be a DeVerrean."

"We *are* DeVerreans, Gerry," Peter scowled.

"No," Gerard argued. "Real, secret-holding, self-serving, bastards of DeVerreans. Stop waiting around—if you want answers, *get them*. Burn the whole damn town down if that's what it takes. That is the only way you will get the results you want."

Owen drew his shoulders back, leveling Gerard with a furious glare. "I don't want the results if they have to come at the expense of what I know is right."

The phantom scoffed. "The right thing is subjective, friend. What you call right, I call weakness."

"And what you call right, I call evil." Owen's reply was sharp.

Spencer knew this conversation wouldn't prove fruitful, but he wasn't sure how to stop it. Nor did he think he could. Gerard had been on a warpath ever since Cassandra almost died. And he could understand the feeling. He felt the same fierce sense of protection for Peter.

Gerard's sneer was demeaning as he glared at Owen. "Whatever you think you know about DeVerre, forget it. I've lived my entire life and death *here*. You want this place to be the little slice of heaven the Varons were supposed to create. But it's not. It's a den of liars and murderers. And you'd all know that if you had *real* DeVerre blood in you."

"I don't care what it is to you," Owen returned. "And I don't care what it is to anyone else living here. I've made plenty of my own mistakes. It's why I'm in this house. But I'll do what it takes to make them right. And if I die in the process, I'll die knowing I did what I knew was right."

"Says the man who lied to his wife for over a decade," Gerard spat.

Nex and Anguis began to growl, charging forward through the living room and to the front door, their rumbling turning into fierce barks.

"Dammit," Spencer muttered, leaping from his seat. He grabbed Cassandra's arm and pulled her around the desk toward Peter and Owen. He should have known the second the dogs began acting strange. He shouldn't have let Gerard distract him.

As Spencer stepped to his side, Peter leaned around the corner to look down the hall at the front door. The dogs' furious barking reverberated as they paced before the door. Owen stepped toward the hall, his right hand glowing with an amber rift of the spirit world's essence.

The sight kicked Spencer's heart into overdrive. If Owen thought they were in enough danger to wield the spirit world, then he knew he should be afraid.

"What is it?" Peter whispered.

Owen shook his head.

Cassandra gripped Spencer's arm, angling to stand alongside him. "No offense, dear," she said, her voice tense despite her attempt to be playful. An ashen arc began to swirl around her free hand. "But you're the one who needs the most protection now."

Spencer hardened his jaw, knowing it was true. Even if Peter was brand new to his powers, Spencer was now the only one who didn't have a way to defend himself beyond the physical. And he knew perfectly well that all his karate training and time at the gym wasn't enough to defeat a Druid or their beasts.

As they waited, Gerard stepped up behind them. "I'll check it out," he whispered, then disappeared.

Long, painfully slow seconds passed as they waited for Gerard to return and report. Spencer felt his muscles twitch under the tension as he scanned the house, listening for any sounds. No flickers of movement showed outside the windows. No sounds of entry came from anywhere. The dogs had reverted to their low, angry growls.

Shifting uncomfortably in the stillness, Spencer and Peter leaned closer to one another. Despite the two Wielders holding their arcs at the ready, Peter's hand was empty. He nudged Spencer's arm to catch his gaze, a promise within that one look. He wouldn't let anything happen to him.

Spencer pressed his lips together and gave him a nod, returning the promise. He knocked Cassandra's hand off his arm and turned a hard stare at her. Her hazel eyes narrowed, but he didn't falter under their intensity. "We protect each other, all right?" he whispered. "All of us."

Her gaze softened and she nodded. "All right," she accepted.

"That's sweet," Gerard said, popping back into view. He spoke at his usual level, but a weight in his voice caused Spencer to falter. Gerard's eyes only landed on him briefly before shifting to Cassandra. "But we've got an uninvited guest waiting for us on the front porch."

Spencer, Peter, and Cassandra gaped at him, but Owen wasted no time. He charged to the front door, unlocking it and turning the doorknob by the time the other three recovered enough to hurry to his side.

Owen opened the door, and the dogs rushed out. He froze, staring at whoever—or whatever—was waiting on the other side.

Letting the door fall open, Owen stepped back to reveal the porch.

Spencer's heart stuttered. Cassandra gasped next to him, and Peter slid to a halt, grabbing his brother's arm.

There on the weathered porch of Occasus, a torn and mangled body lay sprawled, dark blood stains mottling his black hoodie and jeans. A man, perhaps Peter's age, with light brown hair matted onto his battered face, stared at the ceiling with glassy, unseeing brown eyes. His chest was still, a slow trickle of blood slipping out of his wounds and onto the floorboards.

It took everything in Spencer to tear his eyes away and scan the horizon for any sign of who had put this man on their doorstep. But all he saw were the open, wrought iron gates to Occasus, the road beyond, and the pine trees surrounding it.

"That's him," Peter murmured, voice hollow. "That's the Druid who attacked us."

CHAPTER NINETEEN

Cassandra

Pure, raw panic seared through Cassandra's body. Her pulse accelerated to a roaring pound as she backed against the nearby wall. Isolation crept into her skin, freezing her to the core. Debbie's betrayal was bad enough. Her conversation with her mother had been a dagger in her gut.

"All of this is your fault." Her mother's voice echoed like a ghost in her head. *"They wanted you."*

It had never occurred to Cassandra that the Druids might want her powers. She'd held no inkling of being innately more powerful than the average Wielder. Why should she? She hadn't known anything about Wielders until just over a week ago. There was no way she could have understood that *this* was why they'd never tried to kill her in the past. They'd let her live because, in the end, what they really wanted was her.

Trembling hands drawing together, Cassandra reached for her ring. They wanted *her*. And why? Because she was just as dangerous as she'd always suspected. *"A toddler, talking to ghosts. It was unheard of. It was incredible."*

For the past two days, Cassandra had grappled with that realization. The understanding she was in over her head in this world of beasts and Druids. Granted with an unforeseen amount of power, she was a commodity so highly desired that someone would kill her rather than allow her to walk free.

When Spencer received Elijah's essays, Cassandra had felt hope for the first time in days. She'd been sure that they could now make headway—that they could save themselves and the town from whatever it was the Druids wanted with the Veil.

But now everything was falling apart in front of them.

As they stood in the foyer looking at the dead body of the Druid on the porch, Owen was the first to recover from the shock, digging his phone out of his pocket.

"What are you doing?" Peter demanded, his hand still gripping Spencer's arm protectively.

Owen's expression was focused as he began typing. "I'm calling Tom."

"What?" Spencer gasped, but Peter didn't wait for a reply.

Cassandra watched as Peter reached across to rip the phone out of Owen's hand. There wasn't a chance for a struggle as Peter's sudden action caught him unaware. Cell in hand, Peter made sure the call hadn't gone through before tossing it to Spencer. "Keep that, would you?"

"Peter—" The steady timbre of Owen's voice did nothing to soften the look of frustration that sparked on his face. "There is a dead man on your porch. We need to call the marshal to take care of him."

"No way," Peter argued. "We call the marshal, and he'll be out here in minutes with his deputy, the doc, and who knows who else to try to figure out who killed the guy."

"Which is what needs to happen."

"It can't," Spencer cut in, his smoky voice eerily calm. He slipped Owen's phone into his back pocket, shoulders straightening. His sharp blue eyes leveled on the man's face as he whistled to signal the dogs, who obediently rushed back in from sniffing the body to stand next to him.

Cassandra recognized this version of Spencer. She'd seen it for the first time after their fight with Debbie. It was the side of him that she knew few people had ever witnessed. A determination that rose in him—one that refused to let whatever fear he felt control him. The side of him that could tackle a hellhound to the ground.

Standing to his full five foot, seven inches—a fact she only knew because they shared the same height—Spencer managed to make it feel vastly taller. "If Tom comes out here, he'll have to start an investigation," he said. "Whether he wants to or not. And that will stop us from doing whatever we have to do to find and destroy the Druids."

Owen pointed to the body across the threshold. "This man deserves an investigation."

"You think it'll be a fair one?" Peter asked, his skepticism loud and clear. "For all we know, the Druids run this town. Whoever killed him, put him here. Which means they're trying to frame us. I'd never suggest we cover up a murder, but . . . we have no clue who the Druids are, man. They could be anyone but us four, Tom, and your family."

"And that's only if we believe there's no chance that Tom could be lying to keep an eye on us," Spencer added.

"So, what do you want to do?" Owen demanded. "Cover up his death?"

Gerard leaned against the living room doorway, close to Cassandra's side. His proximity didn't soothe the anxiety coursing through her veins. "There's not much else you *can* do, friend," he said, his tone haughty.

It hurt Cassandra to admit it to herself, but Gerard was right. The brothers were right. If the marshal came to Occasus to investigate, he would have to investigate them too. And then they really would be part of a homicide investigation as they'd worried about only nine days ago.

Looking over his shoulder at the phantom, Spencer's eyes caught on Cassandra before he turned to Owen again. "We can't risk it."

Owen shook his head. "I won't be a party to that." He held out his hand. "Give me my phone back."

"I'm sorry, man, I can't."

"You *can*," Owen insisted. "You either will or you won't."

Spencer shrugged. "I won't."

The tension between the men grew taut, and a charged silence fell over the house. Three against one didn't seem fair. And though Cassandra couldn't argue with the logic in the brothers' or Gerard's points, she also couldn't stand to see them coming to blows over something the Druids had done to them.

Managing to regain her voice, Cassandra took one step away from the wall. "Spencer."

The men turned to her, but she sought Spencer's attention alone. She gave him one shake of her head. "We can't hide a body."

His brows pinched together for a split second as though trying to figure out if she were on Owen's side or his and his brother's. Then he sighed. "We don't have a choice, Cass."

"There's always a choice," she countered. "Sometimes there are no good options, but there's always a choice."

Spencer didn't respond, but he held her stare. She didn't know whether she'd influenced him or if he was trying to find a way to let her down easily. Peter and Owen watched them with tentative, shifting stares, both men standing awkwardly to the side.

Gerard didn't share their reluctance to speak. He stepped forward to look out the door, dark eyes on the body as he stroked his thick brown beard. "Did any of you take a good look at this man?"

Cassandra knew that she hadn't. She couldn't bear to look at that lifeless stranger dumped on their front porch as a message. The depths of that implied message sent shivers down her spine.

But the other men followed his direction.

"Something catch your eye, Gerry?" Peter asked though he didn't move any closer to the door.

Gerard stepped outside, crouching by the dead body. He pointed to the front pocket of the hoodie. It lay at a strange angle, poking away from the man's chest.

No one moved.

Gerard reached out.

"Don't," Owen called, stepping toward the threshold.

"I'm not going to taint the crime scene." Gerard's low voice rumbled as he ignored the order. "I'm a spirit. I can't leave fingerprints, DNA, or whatever it is your scientists have figured out how to study these days."

They watched as Gerard pulled the object free from the pocket. He unfolded the paper, scanned its surface, and stepped over the body to wave an envelope through the open door. "Looks like you've got a pen pal," he said to the brothers.

Spencer took the envelope as Cassandra and Peter moved to stand behind him in the foyer. Sure enough, in computer printer ink was the address: *The Collins Brothers*.

Without hesitation, Spencer flipped over the envelope and ripped open the flap to pull out a typed letter. They all stared at the page as he adjusted his stance and began to read.

" 'Dear brothers, and Miss Clement, if you're with them. . . .' " Spencer glanced at her, an edge coming into his otherwise flat tone. He cleared his throat. " 'Allow us to formally introduce ourselves. We are the Children of Gaia. And you are in our way.' "

A tingle ran across Cassandra's shoulders and down her arms, her eyes locked on the words as he continued. " 'We have given you ample opportunity to let go of your attempts to discover us, but your self-invitation into our town has reached the end of its welcome.

" 'As you can see. . . .' " Spencer took a deep, shaking breath before he continued. " 'As you can see, we don't value the lives of our own disciples—trapped in this physical cage we call humanity. We value yours even less. But we also believe in fair play. So, this is your warning. You have three days.' "

The air felt as though it had been sucked from Cassandra's lungs as she took a subconscious step away from him.

" 'Three days,' " Spencer read, " 'to leave DeVerre on your own terms. If you do not comply, we will escort you out on *our* terms this Sunday morning.' "

Hovering in the doorway, Gerard looked past the brothers to watch Cassandra. She caught his gaze, then checked on the others. Owen stared at the floor, eyes scanning the rug beneath their feet as though attempting to work through a problem. Peter's hands had formed fists at his sides. He glared at the letter like he could incinerate it with his rage. And Spencer stood still and steady as he read the final lines of the letter.

" 'Thank you for your attention and consideration. Sincerely, the Children of Gaia.' "

Spencer folded the letter with slow, dedicated purpose.

Catching a breath felt impossible as Cassandra watched him, waiting for the explosion she knew was coming from the way his shoulders tensed. He slid the letter into the envelope. His every move was a flame burning down the fuse of his fear. She wasn't sure what would happen when that fuse reached its end, but she knew it wouldn't be good. And she didn't know how to stop it.

Peter grabbed his brother's bicep, a steely look on his face. "Tell me," he whispered. "Tell me what you want to do."

Cassandra's heart stalled. Why was he asking that? Why was he giving him a choice? If it were up to Spencer, they'd leave. They'd forget it all and abandon DeVerre to its devastation.

They'd abandon her.

But how could she ask them to do anything else? They'd never wanted this. They hadn't asked for any of it. Peter and Spencer Collins had come to DeVerre with one purpose: To make a home and pursue their dreams together. And Cassandra had ruined it like she ruined everything else. Their association with her would get them killed like she had killed Diane.

Owen stepped forward, his stance confident. "We have to call Tom."

"Are you kidding?" Peter demanded. "After that letter, you want to bring other people into this mess? They obviously don't know about you or the marshal. We need to keep it that way."

"You *cannot* hide a body."

"We don't have a choice."

Owen's eyes narrowed. "What do you think you're going to do? Dig a grave in the forest, and hope no one finds it?"

The brothers stared back at him with no answer.

"I know this man." He pointed to the body, voice raised for the first time since Cassandra had met him. "This is Robert MacDonald. He was twenty-eight, worked at the Mercier Hardware store, and had a wife. A wife who happens to be Ariel *Guillaume*—the mayor's niece."

Cassandra's finger hurt before she realized she'd been twisting her ring again.

"If they don't already know that he's missing, they'll send out a search party the second they do. And I do not doubt our new acquaintances will be more than happy to send them in Occasus's direction."

The brothers both turned to look out the door as though they expected to see a search party coming up the drive. But the forest remained still and quiet, as though their lives weren't crashing in around them.

"I can take care of it," Gerard said, hand resting on the doorframe.

"What?" The word gasped out of Peter breathlessly.

The phantom nodded at Robert MacDonald's body. "I can take care of him," he repeated. "I'm good at making things disappear. I can get to the lake through the spirit world. It'll only take me a matter of minutes."

A painfully long moment passed as Peter checked with Spencer—who pressed his lips together in their shared, silent conversation—then turned apologetically to Owen. "Sorry, man," he muttered before nodding to Gerard. "Do it."

Rolling his shoulders, Gerard turned to the body. He crouched again, grabbed one arm of the Druid's lifeless body, and yanked, hoisting him onto his shoulders. It was odd to see the phantom make contact with a human. He wasn't supposed to have that ability. But Cassandra knew it was only possible because the man he carried held no spirit anymore. He was an empty shell, a broken jar of clay no longer animated by life.

Gerard stepped off the porch. In the blink of an eye, a flash of dull gray light absorbed him, and he disappeared with the body. His disappearance didn't take the tension in Occasus with him. Owen shook his head in disappointment but said nothing as he looked at the bloody wooden slats. The bizarre thought that they should try to clean them cut through Cassandra's mind, and she grimaced.

"I want to remove myself from this," Owen said, his voice monotone and distant. "I want to refuse to play a role in it. But that'll make me just as guilty as if I'd agreed."

"It's done, man," Peter muttered. "Let it go."

"I can't support this decision."

"We don't like it any better than you do."

With his brow furrowed so deep it looked painful, Owen frowned. "I don't agree with your choice, but I believe we're on the right side of this fight. And we still have work to do. So, yes, I'll let it go. But trust me: I will not stand by if you start walking down the wrong path. If any one of you begins to take *their* path—if I see even the slightest sign that you're taking the Druids' path, I *will* interfere."

Peter sucked in a heavy breath. "Well, dude, you might not have to worry about that," he said, turning back to Spencer.

Still, silent, and dangerously stoic, Spencer stared past the open door of Occasus. There was no clue what was going on in his vivid mind. He gave no sign of the storm raging inside him.

But Cassandra had no doubt it was driving his every oncoming action.

Peter grabbed hold of Spencer's shoulders. "Tell me," he said again. "I promised you before we came to DeVerre that it was up to you. That when you said the word, we would leave. It's your call."

Holding her breath as she waited for his response, Cassandra's lungs began to burn. He was so quiet, so motionless that he could be a statue there in the entryway of Occasus. Standing behind him, she couldn't see his face. But his stiff posture and set jawline told her what she needed to know.

Everyone thought that Spencer Collins was a man ruled by his fear and anxiety. But she'd seen from the outset that was only the surface. It was what people expected from him, so it was what he allowed them to see.

Despite the fear that lingered on the surface, Cassandra had seen the courage deep within Spencer. And he would fight for his brother to his dying breath.

They'd come to DeVerre for a dream—for a promise they'd made one another. And she knew the Collins brothers well enough now to know they were too stubborn to admit defeat.

Before he even opened his mouth, Cassandra knew his answer. "This is *our* home," he said, the words steady and modulated as he locked gazes with Peter. "And they can go to hell."

Peter smiled, pride clear in the twinkle of his brown eyes—the stupidity of their unwavering support of one another damning them to their fate.

"No." Cassandra heard the word slip out more than she felt herself say it.

Owen's brow rose as the brothers turned to look at her. They cocked their heads to the side, confidence exchanged for confusion. Their twin movements and expressions would have made her laugh in any other situation. But now it irritated her as a bundle of panic and tension crept into her chest.

Cassandra forced her hands to her sides. "You have to leave."

Peter blinked, and Spencer frowned.

In the background, Owen shifted. "I'll, uh . . . I'll be upstairs," he said softly, then slipped around the staircase banister to head up and out of sight.

The cold air of the November morning swept through the open door, bringing gooseflesh to Cassandra's skin as she stared down Peter and Spencer Collins. They might be stubborn, but so was she. Her entire life, she'd been fighting others and their opinions. This would be no different.

"Cass—" Peter stepped forward, his voice light as though trying to ease the situation. "You know we can't do that."

Taking comfort in the press of Anguis's body leaning against her leg, Cassandra arched her left eyebrow higher. "On the contrary, the one thing you *can't* do is stay."

An unsure smirk came to Peter's lips. "Come on, that's ridiculous." The humor failed to make it into his attempt at a chuckle. "Of all people, I thought you'd be the last to suggest leaving."

"Why?"

"Because there's still too much we haven't figured out yet." He paused, then motioned toward her. "Too much *you* haven't figured out yet."

Cassandra nodded. "Which is why *I* won't be leaving."

Peter's jaw dropped as Spencer's eyes narrowed.

"You've got to be kidding," Peter insisted.

"They'll kill you if you stay, Cass." Spencer's concern pulled at her briefly before her resolve regained control.

Lifting one shoulder in a shrug, Cassandra did her best to convey her usual poise. Strong, confident, unaffected, and unafraid. "Then they'll kill me," she said. "But first, I'll know the truth."

Shaking his head, Spencer pushed around his brother. His light blue gaze locked onto her, his own obstinance showing in his determined expression. It was one of those looks of his—the kind that inconceivably blended equal parts total feeling and serene detachment. As though he could be both emotionless and fervent all at once.

Cassandra couldn't understand how he did that. Somehow simultaneously appearing passionless while also emitting complete passion in a single moment. It made him impossible to read. And it left her off-kilter, equal parts fascinated and frustrated by the contradiction of the man before her.

"Have you forgotten what I told you not ten minutes ago?" he demanded, inching closer until less than five feet of distance separated them. "We protect each other. *All of us.*"

Cassandra tensed under his charge. She knew this would be the most difficult part of convincing them to leave. Facing the loss of the one thing she wanted more than anything else. Rejecting what Peter had offered her as they drove to Spokane and Spencer was reiterating now: To be a member of a family who would defend her to their dying breath, no matter what. To experience even a fraction of what these brothers gave one another.

Eyes alight with blue fire, Spencer stared Cassandra down. "If you stay, we stay."

Her breath hitched.

Gerard had been so wrong about them. He'd told her she was alone; they could never love her the way they loved one another, he'd said. But here she stood, faced with death, and these brothers—these wonderful, ridiculous, imperfect brothers—demanded she let them stand at her side.

The desire to give in pulled at her. Instinct drew her another step closer to Spencer even as she shook her head. "Don't you get it?" she demanded, the words catching in her throat, making them raw and choppy. "It's my fault."

Spencer and Peter opened their mouths to contradict her, but she spoke over them.

"*It's my fault!*" she repeated, her voice rising. She took another step forward, and Anguis drifted away, his tail tucked as he crept closer to Nex in the hall. "Diane's death. My mother's accident. You two getting pulled into this. Debbie almost killing you. Twice! This Druid attacking you and Anna. Now this man's death and that letter. All of it! *It's my fault!*"

"What are you talking about?" Spencer shot back; his voice was equally as intense, if not at the same volume.

"The Druids wanted me!" The admission brought a rush of tears to her eyes, but she refused to let them loose. Not while she was saving their lives. Not when both of their faces fell in shock, staring at her like she was a new woman standing before them.

Cassandra pressed both hands to her chest, eyes flashing from one brother to the next. "I was different—a child who could see ghosts. I was powerful, and they *wanted* me. But my mother made a deal with them: Remove me from the equation, and they'd let me go. They'd allow me to be free so long as I didn't interfere with their plans.

"And here I am—" Cassandra tossed her hands out to the side with a caustic laugh. "Interfering. And getting everyone killed in the process."

Peter's head dipped as Spencer's determination visibly waned.

The fire of holding back her tears burned in her throat. "Ava was right about me," she whispered. "I *am* dangerous."

Spencer shook his head. "Cass—"

She held up a hand to stop him. "Of all people, you know I'm right, Spencer. You saw what I did to Debbie. I'm not safe. I ruin the lives of those around me. Diane, my mother, Debbie. If I left with the two of you, I'd ruin your lives too."

Peter scowled in the background, but Cassandra hardly noticed as Spencer's fierce stare held hers. He was testing her, she knew, checking to see if she meant it. If she believed what she was saying.

Raising her chin, Cassandra let him study her. She knew he wouldn't find any lie within her words. She had experienced her own destructive nature for almost thirty years. It was high time she admitted it to herself.

She was alone. As she should be.

"Pete," Spencer called over his shoulder, never breaking eye contact with her.

His brother lifted his head. "Huh?"

"Give us a minute, would you?"

"Oh, uh, yeah, sure. I'll be. . . ." Peter motioned to the front door, grimacing at the bloody planks as he stepped outside. Anguis and Nex followed, slipping out just before the door shut behind him.

The entry hall was quiet except for the ticking of the clock in the living room and the occasional rustle of wind outside Occasus's walls. Soft light from the waxing morning filtered through the singular window in the foyer. It lit the right side of Spencer's face while the other settled in a gentle shadow.

Cassandra crossed her arms as she waited for Spencer to speak. He looked more his age in this lighting; his facial hair offset the boyish qualities in his smile and the softness of his features. That was the thing with him, she'd learned—he appeared gentle and mild, but he was far more sharp and cunning than people gave him credit for.

His lips lifted in a soft and knowing smirk. The same smirk she'd seen many times from Diane and Peter—a look that said they understood you better than you understood yourself. But this was different. This was a man she'd begun to develop feelings for. A man she should let walk away and forget her.

Spencer took a breath, and Cassandra tensed, preparing for the argument she knew was coming. His words came out flat, strong, and bristling. "That is the most idiotic thing I've ever heard you say, Cassandra."

The unexpected harshness agitated and unnerved Cassandra. She scrunched her nose in shock. "Excuse me?"

"That's a ridiculous excuse, and you know it."

Cassandra felt her jaw drop.

A taut laugh escaped Spencer. "Seriously?" he pressed. "You want us to abandon you because *you're dangerous*? You remember that you've saved our lives twice now, don't you?"

Feeling trapped under his accusation, Cassandra rolled her eyes. "You remember that if it hadn't been for me, your lives never would have needed saving in the first place, don't *you*?"

He scoffed. "What logic are you using? Cass, you had nothing to do with Diane and our grandfather's adoption. You know that, right?"

She blinked, unsure what his family's history had to do with anything.

"I sure hope you know that. Because unless you're far older than you've said, you weren't even born then."

She sighed, irritated by his mocking tone. "Get to the point, Spencer."

"You had nothing to do with Diane's past, right?"

"Right."

"So, you couldn't have affected her being taken from her family, *right*?"

She pursed her lips.

He waited for her to answer.

"Right," she mumbled.

He gave her a sharp nod. "Which logically follows that Diane would have moved to DeVerre in the '80s, regardless of your existence. Because you weren't born then either, right?"

"Spencer," she warned.

He drew back at her evident annoyance, smirk softening. "Cass, think about it—" His husky voice smoothed over her. "You had nothing to do with Diane coming to DeVerre. She came, and she started disrupting the Druids' plans. *Without you.* They would have killed her whether you ever met her or not."

Cassandra frowned, dropping her eyes to the ground. No matter how right he was, his accuracy didn't deter her concern. She'd drawn them into her search for the spirit world, and it would get them killed if they stayed.

"And," Spencer interrupted her thoughts, "Diane still would have left Occasus to me and Pete, which means we still would have moved here. And we would have died the night the hellhound attacked. Because you wouldn't have been there to save us."

Turning the ring over and over on her finger, Cassandra sucked in a sharp breath. She lifted her gaze to his again, knowing she had to make him see her side. She had to convince him to leave if she wanted them to live.

"It's still my fault, Spencer," she whispered. "Whatever happened with your family, it doesn't matter. I caused this by returning. My mother told me that Diane and I were getting too close to the truth. *That's* why they killed her. If I hadn't come back to DeVerre, she would never have been in danger."

He opened his mouth to argue, so she hurried to cut him off. "I know how important your brother is to you," she said, hoping she'd learned to manipulate them like she'd watched them manipulate each other. She wouldn't let them kill themselves for the sake of their idealistic dream. And if she had to imitate their own underhanded means, she would. "I know that you'd do anything to make him happy. But I also know you'd let him be unhappy if that meant keeping him safe. And that's why you *have* to leave."

A flicker of fear passed over Spencer's face as he glanced toward the front door.

"You will both die if you stay," she whispered. "But you can take care of one another if you leave."

Spencer cocked his head to the side, eyes snapping to hers. "And who will take care of you?"

A sad, sardonic grin came to Cassandra's lips. She reached over to pat his arm. "Oh, don't worry, Spence. I can take care of myself."

As she drew her hand back, Spencer moved too fast for her. His hand shot up to snatch her forearm, sending a jolt of heat up her arm. Her chest tightened but her throat eased, finally letting her take a clear breath.

Spencer's thick eyebrows pulled together. "It isn't just you anymore, Cassandra."

"It's always just me, Spencer." She tugged on her arm, and he let her free. "I've learned to live with being an outcast. That's who I am. People fear what they don't understand. You know what that's like, right? You're afraid of everything. And everyone is afraid of me."

Spencer shook his head, backing away with a deep sigh. He rubbed a hand over his face, then passed it through his shaggy hair. "I hate hyperbole," he muttered.

Cassandra couldn't help but scoff at his unexpected response. "What?"

"You're using a lot of definitives," he said, meeting her glare with an irritated one of his own. "And it's annoying."

Cassandra raised her hands in mock surrender. "My apologies. I'm not a writer like you and your brother."

Resetting his stance, Spencer ignored her reply. He worked his jaw back and forth as he stared at her, eyes roving over her face. Frustration radiated off him. She wondered if he would yell at her. But then he huffed, stepping far too near, holding out his hands as though they could hold all the dark confessions she'd thrown at him. "Listen, Cass, I—I don't think you're right."

"Don't you?"

"No, I don't." He fumbled for words, throwing his hands up in an exasperated shrug and letting them slap back at his sides. "I don't think that no one loved you or that they all thought you were . . . weird or crazy or—whatever it was you felt from them. Maybe some of them, but . . . God, even the Druids saw your value. And you were just a kid!"

A remorseful smile came to his face. "And now? They wouldn't be trying so hard to stop you if they didn't still see it. As far as everyone else goes . . . well, I think they're just scared."

Several heartbeats passed as Cassandra tried to take in his words. "Scared of what?"

"Of you!" He motioned to her as he said it, a laugh escaping from him. "You're right. You're completely right: Everyone *is* afraid of you."

She gaped at him in shock, having expected him to contradict her assumptions rather than affirm them.

His eyes left hers, giving her a momentary reprieve as he searched the wall above her head like it would help him find the words. It must have helped because those startlingly blue eyes drifted back, locking with her dark ones. "Of being less than you," he concluded. "Of risking rejection from you."

The dissonance between his conclusion and hers was impossible to reconcile.

Cassandra shook her head. "That's . . . no one has ever felt that way about me."

"I do."

Cassandra froze, a puff of air rushing from her lungs.

Spencer wet his lips, his gaze steady. "I'm terrified of you."

Unsure what to think or feel, Cassandra felt locked in place. As though his adamant stare had turned her to stone. Her muscles tensed, and her breath hitched as she grappled with his words. There were so many things he could have meant by them. Platonic admiration. General appreciation. Companionable respect. Genial regard. Romantic affection.

The last thought planted the smallest seed of joy in her chest, and she fought a smile. There was no certainty that he was admitting feelings for her. No way to know if he meant the words as a confession of secret interest. It was far more probable that he was admitting that he found her—a ghost-tethering, spirit-wielding anomaly—to be another of the horrifying nightmares that plagued his everyday life.

The soft yellow sunlight reflected in Spencer's cool blue eyes as he shrugged, his next words so quiet that she had to strain to hear them. "I'm terrified that you'll reject me," he whispered. "That . . . that I won't be enough for you."

Cassandra opened her mouth to force an inhale past the constriction in her chest.

"It's why I won't do anything about it."

Her eyes flickered back and forth between his. "About what?"

Spencer swallowed and shook his head, beginning to turn away from her. His hand rose to cover his face, and Cassandra stepped forward to grab his sleeve, pulling the hand away.

"Spencer?" She said it like a demand.

He pulled away, the fabric slipping through her fingers. "You're intimidating, Cass," he admitted. "And even the people who care the most about you are afraid of you."

"Why?" She felt the question sigh out of her, voicing the deeply rooted need to understand her isolation. Desperate to know why she would always be alone.

"Because they're afraid of how amazing you are."

If the rest of the world had frozen there, Cassandra was sure something would have happened between them. She would have spoken up and pushed him to say what he meant. She would have done something or demanded that *he* do something. They would have broken the silence hanging between them, opening a door in her heart that she'd kept locked away for as long as she could remember.

But the world hadn't frozen. And it was the front door that opened, breaking the moment of honesty developing between them as they whirled to face it.

Peter stuck his head in, dark eyes nervously scanning them. "Hey . . . sorry to interrupt, but—" He pointed behind him with his thumb. "We've got company."

CHAPTER TWENTY

Peter

When Peter had said they had company, he'd actually meant *company*.

After leaving his brother and Cassandra to hash it out, Peter stepped onto the porch intending to walk around the property with the dogs. But he'd seen those deep red stains on the weathered floorboards again and grimaced. Hurrying around to the back, Peter snuck in through the kitchen, grabbed some cleaning supplies, listened for two seconds to be sure Spencer was telling Cassandra what he needed to, and headed back to the front to begin his work.

It wasn't easy getting the blood cleared up. But Peter was thankful it hadn't soaked into the slats too much. They remained slightly splotchy, but he managed to get most of it clean before he looked up. He did an instant double take as he spotted someone walking up the road toward Occasus.

Peter's heart leaped into his throat. He rose to his feet, spray bottle of vinegar still in one hand and cleaning rag in the other. The hood of the visitor's thick coat obscured their face. But as he racked his brain, attempting to think of who besides a Druid would be coming to Occasus so early in the morning, he recognized the light blue puffer coat.

Peter's shoulders relaxed, and he stepped forward to set the cleaning supplies on the porch railing. He watched as Anna passed through the hulking gates. His throat constricted despite his initial relief, sure that she'd come to tell him off. To tell him that their friendship had reached its end and that her brush with death had solidified what he'd already known: He'd failed her.

Her tan boots crunching up the drive, Anna met Peter at the bottom of the stairs. They stood several feet apart, staring at one another. He could see an empty, nervous expression on her face across the distance, hands tucked into her coat pockets. Wisps of coiled curls drifted around her cheeks beneath her hood. She didn't wear her typical makeup, as minimal as it usually was. Instead, dark circles and red-rimmed eyes marred her delicate features.

"Hey," Peter managed, keeping his voice light and cautious.

Anna didn't reply but stared back at him. Her dark eyes bored into him as though trying to assess his happiness to see her. Or perhaps she was trying to decide if she was happy to see him.

The cold breeze cut through Peter's thick flannel shirt. "Uh, do you—"

"I want answers, Peter." Anna's voice was firm, so unlike her usual, endearing inflection. Instead of the soft, warm tones he'd grown accustomed to from her, she sounded far more like her sister: hard, unyielding, and tense.

Tugging at his collar, Peter cleared his throat. "Right—yeah. Yeah, of course."

She blinked, waiting for him to continue.

Peter glanced around the grounds of Occasus toward the dogs playing together near the brick fence. "Out here?"

A hint of a grin appeared at the corner of her mouth, but she tamped it down. "I'd imagine this is a conversation that requires sitting down."

"Sure." He took a step back, tripping over the bottom stair. He caught his balance before making a total fool of himself and gestured up the steps. "After you."

Giving him a wide berth, Anna began to walk up the narrow steps to the porch. She scanned the box of baking soda and other cleaning supplies, then glanced at him as she removed her hood.

Peter decided it was best to leave that part of the conversation for later and moved for the door. His hand froze on the cold metal knob, remembering why he'd been outside in the first place. He turned back to Anna. "Let me, uh . . . just a sec."

Hoping that he wasn't interrupting anything too awkward—though he doubted Spencer would have the guts to say anything that would make it uncomfortable to walk in on—Peter opened the door and peeked his head inside.

Spencer and Cassandra jumped away from each other. Though, to his disappointment, he didn't think they'd been all that close in the first place. It wasn't until he'd informed them of their company and panic erupted onto Spencer and Cassandra's faces that he realized how his words had sounded.

"Ah—uh, no." Peter pushed the door the rest of the way open to reveal Anna. "We have *company*, company."

Relief softened their expressions before their eyes narrowed, looking beyond Peter and Anna. The hum of a car's engine met his ears as he turned to follow their stares. A familiar white sedan pulled past the gates.

Anna edged toward the house, lips pressed together in resolve as the car stopped next to Cassandra's truck and Owen's sedan. Peter saw the wire rimmed glasses reflecting the sunlight behind the windshield. Aaron Lambert climbed out of the car, taking in the group before him.

Aaron addressed his sister first. "You're supposed to be at home."

Crossing her arms, Anna didn't waver. "How did Ava find out?"

"She didn't."

"Then why are you here?"

Aaron sighed, shutting the car door with a *thunk*. He stepped toward the stairs, tucking the keys into the pocket of his brown canvas coat. "I'm here to drop off Owen's stuff."

Fighting a grimace, Peter nodded. "He's upstairs, I think."

"He's not at the school?" Anna asked, her voice tremulous as though uncomfortable with his potential presence.

"He said something last night about calling out," he explained.

"I can go get him," Spencer offered.

"That's probably a good idea," Aaron said.

Spencer tipped his chin up, then hurried inside.

A long beat of silence hung in the air as the rest of them waited, eyes shifting from person to person.

"You Lamberts have impeccable timing," Peter said, attempting to lighten the mood.

He failed and didn't bother to try again.

Owen appeared first, Spencer on his heels. As they stepped onto the porch, he gave Aaron a nod before catching sight of Anna. "Good morning," he said to them both. Then he addressed Aaron alone. "I hear you have some things for me."

Aaron appraised him. "I'd also like some answers while I'm here."

"Of course," Owen agreed. "I'll answer whatever questions you have. Both of you."

Peter looked at Anna, wishing he could promise the same thing. But he held his tongue, feeling that the moment wasn't right.

"First, let's get the car emptied," Aaron said. "No matter what you have to say to me, Ava won't accept you back any time soon."

"I know." Owen led the way down the stairs, Peter and Spencer following to help.

"I'll get some more coffee going," Cassandra muttered. "Anna, do you. . . ."

Anna hesitated, then followed her inside Occasus.

Between the four men, they quickly carried the handful of boxes and bags up to Owen's room. It was obvious Ava hadn't sent everything of his, but at least the man would have a change of clothes and his toothbrush, Peter thought.

When Spencer returned Owen's phone and apologized for the earlier tension, he'd given them both a nod. "I understand," he murmured.

They returned downstairs via the back staircase, meeting the women in the kitchen. Cassandra poured a cup of steaming coffee, then handed it to Anna, sitting on the other side of the island. She'd removed her coat, revealing a cream sweater. The two women were in high contrast, Peter thought. Though both were kind, considerate, and attractive in their own ways, he couldn't find many other similarities between them.

Darting around the rest of the men, Spencer helped Cassandra hand out mugs. Owen turned the cup down while the rest of them took one readily.

"So. . . ." Peter scanned the group. Only Anna sat at the island while the rest of them hovered at awkward distances. "Shall we adjourn to the dining room?"

"That's a good idea," Owen agreed, motioning for the rest of them to lead the way.

After several seconds of shuffling around the table, they finally found their places. Anna and Aaron sat together on one side while Owen took the head of the table nearest the office. Peter, Spencer, then Cassandra sat across from the Lambert siblings.

Peter worried there would be another long and awkward pause as they tried to figure out what to say, but Owen took the initiative. "What did Ava tell you two?" he asked.

Anna and Aaron shared a look.

Pushing his glasses farther up his nose, Aaron met his brother-in-law's gaze. "Not much. Only that you'd betrayed her, and she couldn't be with you anymore."

A crease marred Anna's forehead as she turned to look over her shoulder at him. "That's all she said?"

"Yeah."

Anna scoffed, crossing her arms. "She's such a liar," she whispered.

Feeling like he was interrupting yet another Bernard/Lambert family meeting, Peter pressed his lips together, forcing himself to remain quiet.

Owen ran a hand over his well-groomed beard, studying the two of them. "What did she tell you, Anna?"

The young woman shook her head, her ponytail bouncing with the action. "That it was your fault." She met his eyes, a glare of anger within her own. "That everything that happened last night was because of you and people like you."

"People like him?" Aaron's brow furrowed.

Anna nodded, then motioned toward the brothers and Cassandra on the other side of the table. "People like them."

There was an accusation in her eyes as they landed on Peter. He ducked his head. He deserved her anger. It was justified, no matter how much it hurt.

"To be fair," Cassandra spoke up, an unexpected levity in her tone. "Spencer isn't one of us."

"*Yet*," Spencer added.

She patted his hand in a placating, playful fashion.

Aaron scanned the four of them. "People like you, meaning what? What are you?"

"We're called Wielders," Owen replied. "Again, Spencer hasn't come into his powers quite yet, but I'm certain he will soon if Peter is any indication."

Peter glanced at Anna to see her reaction. But she stared straight at Owen, completely ignoring him. "What—what are Wielders?"

Brushing his hand over his jaw, Owen took a deep breath. "It's a bit of an explanation," he said. "And first, I need to assure you that Ava was right in kicking me out. I've lied to her our whole relationship, and I deserve to be where I am now."

"Didn't realize we were that bad of roommates," Peter muttered.

Neither Lambert responded to his sarcasm, but he caught Spencer's smirk and Cassandra's chuckle beside him.

Owen passed him a chagrined frown before continuing. "Both of you need to know I never meant to hurt her. I intended to do the exact opposite. But I was blind and hid who I was in my fear of losing her. And when she found out I'm a Wielder last night, she *rightly* threw me out."

Tipping his chin toward the man, Aaron quirked his left eyebrow. "So, you didn't have an affair?"

A look of horror passed over Owen's face. "No! I would never."

Releasing a sigh of relief, Aaron smiled as he leaned back in his seat. "Okay, cool. Just so long as that wasn't the case, you're all good."

Anna passed him a scowl. "He lied to our sister," she argued. "You're 'all good' with that?"

Aaron shrugged. "How bad a lie could it be, Anna? Unless he's a murderer, an affair is the worst it could have been. And I'll believe that Owen could kill someone in cold blood when hell freezes over."

Having experienced Owen's staunch dedication to the law earlier that morning, Peter did not doubt that his brother-in-law's estimation was correct.

"So, you lied about being a Wielder," Aaron continued. "What does that mean?"

Owen looked to their side of the table, Anna and Aaron following his lead. Peter chewed on the inside of his lip as Spencer shifted uncomfortably between him and Cassandra. After a decade of being out of high school, he felt like he'd been called to the principal's office again for talking too much in class.

With a long, patient sigh, Owen turned back to the Lamberts. "Wielders are people who can connect with and harness the spirit world, utilizing it and its powers within the physical world."

Aaron and Anna stared at him, their dark eyes randomly blinking as they tried to process what he'd said.

"What?" Aaron asked dryly, but Anna set a hand to her lips.

Peter could see the connection click as her eyes grew wide. Whether she understood it or not, she was beginning to get a picture of the truth. How could she not after what she'd seen last night?

Anna's eyes flew to Peter's face though she stayed silent as Owen clarified. "I know it's complicated and . . . unexpected. But the primary thing you need to understand is that this spirit world runs parallel to our own. Through our faith, we can take authority over it and wield it for our purposes. Of course, the *correct* way to wield it is according to God's purposes. But, like everything in this life, many choose to wield it for personal gain."

"Hold up," Aaron cut him off, waving a hand in the air. He scoffed, adjusted his glasses, and leaned forward in his seat. "You're telling me that you're a—a . . . what the heck, man? What *are* you? How do—you can control spirits?"

"I can."

Aaron ran a hand over his buzzed hair, muttering in bewilderment under his breath.

But Peter hardly noticed his reaction. Anna was still staring at him as though seeing him for the first time. "That's what that thing was?" she whispered. "A spirit?"

Peter struggled for words. He hardly felt qualified to explain. But Anna was asking *him*, and everyone else seemed to fade from the room as he held her gaze. "Yeah, kind of. I don't know what that one was in particular, but . . . it was a beast of the spirit world."

Her breathing grew more rapid as she played with the hem of her knit sleeve. "And . . . and Robert?"

Peter blanched. How did she know about Robert?

"He was . . . controlling it?"

Remembering that she'd seen the Druid last night, Peter nodded quickly, hoping to gloss over Robert and his death as fast as possible. "Yeah," he confirmed. "Yeah, he, uh—he was the one who summoned it and sent it to kill us."

A look of fear drew Anna's brows together, and shock crossed Aaron's face as he looked between them.

Realizing the truth of the situation, Peter corrected his statement. "Me," he muttered, staring at the coffee in his hands. "He sent it to kill *me*. And I was stupid enough to bring it to you."

There was a long, charged silence. Anna would either accept his explanation or realize she hated him with the truth. His reactive decision had almost killed her. If she didn't hate him already, he thought she should.

"Hang on," Aaron interrupted. "What do you mean, 'sent it to kill you'?"

Even with his eyes downcast, he caught the movement of Anna setting her hand on Aaron's arm. "It's fine," she whispered. "Peter . . . Peter saved us."

"What are you—"

"Aaron," she interrupted his concerned argument. "I'll explain it to you later."

Before her brother could continue to try and fight her, Anna turned back to Owen. "So, you lied to Ava about all of this," she said. "I understand her being angry. It's—well, I'll admit that I'm angry about it too. We've known you for almost twelve years, and now . . . it's like we've never known you at all."

Owen nodded dejectedly. "I know, I'm sorry. And I'm not proud of the way I handled it. But it was—it *is* my job to be here in DeVerre. Marrying Ava was never—I never anticipated meeting her, let alone falling in love with her."

"Wait," Aaron interjected. "You and Ava met at college in Spokane."

"I had to get my degree so I had a legitimate reason to move to DeVerre. Our meeting was a coincidence."

Peter glanced at Spencer, remembering their arguments in the past about coincidences. He wondered if perhaps his brother was right. Maybe there were no coincidences. Maybe Owen and Ava's meeting was always supposed to happen. But then, the odds of them attending the same college were high. Spokane was DeVerre's closest source of higher education. The two of them winding up there was only logical. Fate might not have played a role in it at all.

"What's your job?" Aaron pursued the subject, a dubious pinch between his eyebrows.

Owen clasped his hands together on the table. "I'm here to determine if there is any danger to the Veil—the lake," he explained. "It's connected to the spirit world. That's why Matthias Varon and the rest of the settlers from Harmony founded the town. Which . . . brings me to another important point: I'm from Harmony, Saskatchewan."

Anna and Aaron gaped at him.

"You said you were from Regina," Aaron charged.

Owen grimaced. "Yes, I—I knew that if I told Ava about my true hometown, she would likely become suspicious of what I knew."

Anna shook her head. "What else have you lied about?"

Owen dipped his head. "Lots of things."

"This spirit world," Aaron said, tapping his thumb on the rim of his coffee mug. "What's the deal with it? Why would it be in danger?"

"There are other people like us," Owen explained. "But instead of looking to protect the spirit world from abuse, they want to use it for their own purposes. They're called Druids, and they want to release the spirit world onto the earth. Robert was one of these Druids. That's why he attacked you and Peter last night, Anna. And he wasn't working on his own. The Druids are upset with us for getting in the way of their attempt to control the Veil. They sent Robert to do a job. And now that he's failed, there's a chance they'll task someone else with the same job."

Anna and Aaron both stared at him in apparent overwhelm. Peter couldn't blame them. He couldn't remember the last time he *hadn't* felt overwhelmed by the new reality of his life.

Twisting the sleeve of her sweater around her fingertips, Anna's expression softened toward Owen. "You're . . . protecting DeVerre?"

He nodded.

"Then why is Ava angry with you?"

"She doesn't understand," he said, sorrow tingeing his voice. "When she was a girl. . . ." He stopped, dark blue eyes flickering toward Cassandra, drawing everyone's attention to her.

Cassandra drew her shoulders back, sitting up straight in her chair. "What?"

Owen smiled at her apologetically. "Do you remember starting school in DeVerre?"

"Yes."

"Do you remember Ava being in your class?"

She shook her head.

He pressed his lips together. "She does. And she remembers you talking to ghosts. She didn't know what they were until your teacher panicked and called your parents. Ava couldn't understand what was happening, young as she was, but she asked her mother about it. Aimee— her mother—explained the spirit world to her then. At least, as best as she could."

"Our mom knows about this?" Aaron demanded.

"She does. All the librarians of DeVerre knew. It was their job."

Peter felt his brow rise. DeVerre and the secrets it held were strange on their own, but the fact that the Lamberts' mother played a role in it now, too, made it all that more complicated. Cassandra had mentioned that Aimee Rayne-Lambert, the previous librarian, had helped Diane to a certain extent. While Ava had no interest in discussing the topic with them, Aimee had spoken to Diane a handful of times, giving whatever information she could—or would—regarding the town. Which, according to Cassandra, wasn't much.

"Aimee never held the same concerns about the spirit world as Ava," Owen continued. "She didn't care to dabble in it but respected its importance. But Ava was horrified by the idea that there was a world out there with the potential for such evil. She's—she's completely wrong about so much of it. Aimee's never had half the facts straight, and I—well, I never could figure out where it all got lost in translation until we talked with Tom. But now I realize it was intentional, ridding the town of the truth.

"If no one is aware of the spirit world, the Druids are unstoppable," he concluded. "That's the point of it all. It must be. They've been working to wipe out everyone who knows anything about the spirit world so their control of the Veil can't be contested."

A chill ran down Peter's spine. It made so much sense. Of course, they'd try to clear their path. And it was no wonder they wanted them gone. They weren't just an inconvenience; they were actively working to thwart their plans.

Owen turned toward Aaron and Anna. "Ava is convinced that the spirit world is evil. It doesn't matter that she came to that conclusion when she was five years old and still afraid of ghost stories. When she learned that the spirit world was real and there was a chance that it could harm her, her parents, and her baby brother and sister, she determined it was the worst thing that could possibly exist."

His shoulders dropped as he sighed. "When I discovered this, I knew there was no way I could be honest with her. Not until I found a way to convince her that her fears were only based on one side of the coin."

Peter ran his thumb along the handle of his mug. There was a fraction of him that felt sorry for Ava. With a brother like Spencer who let his own fear dictate so much of what he did, he could understand the librarian's trepidation. But at least Spencer faced up to his fears. Ava shut down anything that tried to confront hers.

Anna looked at Cassandra, understanding and awe dawning in her expression. "That's why she doesn't like you," she whispered. "She's afraid of you."

A thin puff of air escaped Cassandra, and she glanced at Spencer. "Uh, yeah. It seems like it," she muttered, lifting her mug to take a sip.

Catching Spencer's smug grin, Peter decided to ask him about their conversation later.

"And that's why she threw you out?" Aaron added, looking at Owen. "She thinks you're . . . evil?"

With a shrug, Owen nodded. "Yes."

"Ah, man, this is—this is insane!" He scrubbed a hand over his face. His glasses lifted above his fingers as he rubbed his eyes. His breath puffed as his hand landed on the table with a *thunk*. "Owen, we gotta get this cleared up. You need to explain it to her. If she would just listen. . . ."

They were all quiet as his words faded.

That was the problem, and they all knew it. Ava wouldn't listen. Not when she was so deathly afraid of the spirit world—of the danger it could bring to ones she loved.

Aaron pushed against the table as he moved to stand. "I want to talk about this some more, but I've got Haley's car, and she needs it to get to home from work. Which reminds me—" He snapped his fingers and pointed to Spencer. "You know your Jeep is sitting outside the tavern with its tires slashed, right?"

"Excuse me?" Spencer turned to glare at Peter. "What did you do to my car?"

Peter threw his hands in the air. "Dude, I was attacked by a freakin' Druid. The guy slashed the tires so I couldn't run."

Spencer's hands curled into fists on the table as he lifted his eyes to stare at the ceiling in irritation.

"In that case," Aaron interrupted, "I'll take care of it. I can bring it by tomorrow, and you can explain the rest of this whole . . . whatever this nonsense is."

"Thanks," Spencer said, a genuine sound of relief filling his voice.

"Anytime." Aaron set his hand on Anna's shoulder. "You want me to drop you off?"

Anna looked up at him, lips parting as she hesitated. Her dark eyes drifted over to Peter, and he felt his shoulders slump as Aaron followed her gaze. "No, thanks," she muttered. "I want to stay a little longer."

"All right. But be careful." He gave her shoulder a squeeze as he grinned. "Ava will be pissed if she finds out where you are."

Anna smiled and rolled her eyes. "I'll make sure I'm home before she gets back from work."

He patted her arm before moving to Owen, who stood at his approach. "We're gonna figure this out, man," he promised. "We'll find a way to get Ava on the same page."

Owen returned his smile, though it was nowhere near as hopeful as the younger man's. "I'll walk you out," he said.

The two of them moved down the hall, leaving the rest behind to stare at one another in awkward silence. Peter hated it. After so much time building his friendship with Anna, he'd thought that nothing could push them into this sort of discomfort. It was worse than meeting someone for the first time. At least, then you had a level playing field. But this was like taking a million steps back while still knowing so much about one another. It was miserable, feeling the closeness of friendship twisted into the distance of strangers.

The door shut in the entryway, and Owen returned, his gait slow and steady. He sat beside Anna rather than at the head of the table. "I take it you have more questions?"

Though Anna looked at him first, her gaze drifted back to Peter.

Owen's head drew back, uncertain. "Would you like a moment to—"

"No." Anna interrupted him before he got the full question out.

Peter felt her panic. He couldn't help the disappointed grimace that pressed his lips together. She wanted to ask him questions but didn't want to be alone with him.

"No," she repeated. "It's—it's fine. I just. . . ."

The painful moment stretched on as Anna met Peter's eyes. Her nose scrunched as she shook her head. He could feel the frustration leaping off her. The sense of lingering betrayal.

"Why didn't you tell me?" The question came out in a hushed tone.

Peter pulled in a tight breath, unable to give her a good answer. "I didn't want to get you involved," he murmured.

It was a stupid excuse, especially since he'd brought her face-to-face with a beast.

After several seconds of studying him, she smiled wryly. "Well," she huffed, "I'm involved now. So don't lie to me anymore, okay?"

Peter felt his lips part in awe. Her expression had softened, and he knew she had accepted his lame excuse. Even if it wasn't easy for her— even if it still completely confused her, Anna hadn't written him off. And she was giving him another chance.

"Yeah, of course!" Heart filling with hope, Peter nodded vehemently.

This was good. It was all going to be all right. He may have screwed up a few things, but not all was lost. Sure, they'd started their morning out by covering up a murder and receiving a threat from the Druids, but at least Anna didn't hate him as he'd feared.

And now she knew.

Peter grimaced.

Now Anna knew.

And she was in as much danger as the rest of them.

The Druids were coming for them. They only had three days to figure out a plan: fight or flee?

But with Anna and Aaron now involved, no matter how little they knew, they couldn't leave without them, could they? Would the Druids leave them alone just because they weren't Wielders? At least they didn't know about Owen. If they had, they'd have included him in the letter, wouldn't they? Maybe the Lamberts and Bernards could fly under the radar without the brothers and Cassandra in town.

Suddenly, there felt like far too much to explain to Anna. Too many secrets that he'd been keeping. He wondered how she would react to hearing their lives were in danger. Would she freak out? Would she demand to help them? And what about the rest of it? What about the vault and Diane's murder? What about the fact that they were DeVerreans themselves?

Figuring that was the easiest place to start, Peter cleared his throat. "If, um—I guess I should probably start with the least complicated thing." He sucked in a breath, glancing at his brother, feeling a sense of wonder that this was now the least complicated detail of their life. "It seems that—well, Spence and I aren't Collinses. Not biologically, at least."

Anna's brow furrowed, her mouth dropping open in shock.

"Our grandfather and Diane were adopted, but they were born here in DeVerre."

Her eyes went wide.

Peter attempted a lighthearted smirk. He doubted his success. "We're DeVerrean."

A look akin to disgust crossed Anna's face. "Does that mean we could be related?"

The thought hadn't crossed Peter's mind until that moment. He felt his face twist in revulsion. "Uh . . . I dunno, maybe." He certainly hoped not.

"Wait—" Spencer sat up with excitement. "Anna, you're close with the Frossards, right?"

She blinked a few times as though surprised to see him sitting next to Peter. "Uh—yeah, why?"

A pleased grin spread over Spencer's face. "We have to show you something."

It took less than two seconds for understanding to dawn on Peter. While Spencer rose, he and Cassandra hopped up from their seats with equal excitement. Owen and Anna watched in confusion while the other three moved with renewed enthusiasm.

"This way," Spencer said, motioning for them to follow him to the staircase at the front of the house. He led them up three flights of stairs, straight down the hall on the third floor, and opened the door to the small office at the end.

Light flooded the room from the three windows on the rounded exterior wall. Peter had always thought the room was the coolest in the house. If it hadn't contained Diane's base for genealogical study, he would have turned it into his own tiny getaway. But the corkboard still hanging on the wall covered with black string, random notes, and vintage pictures made him hesitant to change the space or interrupt its sanctity.

The handful of boxes on the far-right side of the room showed that family had been far more important to Diane than any of the Collinses knew. She may not have shown it in the same way they did—by staying together in the same city forever—but she had never forgotten them. Even as she searched for her biological family, she'd kept photos and mementos to keep them close to mind.

Spencer, Cassandra, and Peter stepped to the other side of the tiny desk while Anna and Owen trailed slowly behind them. The light of the late morning sun practically glowed against the wall on the right side of the room.

Peter gestured to the board. "This is everything we know."

Studying the notes and papers on the board, the two newcomers took it in silently. Anna's eyes widened as she zeroed in on the picture and correlating list of Frossard men. Her mouth dropped open as she peered back and forth between the two objects.

"Do you have any idea who that is, Annie?"

Pointing at the image, then at Peter, Anna shook her head. "You're a Frossard?"

Peter couldn't help the laugh that escaped him. "Well, we don't have any proof of that. And Gerard is pretty convinced that we aren't."

"Gerard?"

The phantom appeared in the doorway. "That'd be me."

Anna let out a frightened squeal as she jumped back.

"Gerard," Cassandra admonished.

"What?" He shrugged, leaning against the doorframe. "I've been bored. I took the idiot's mention as an invitation."

Peter sighed, setting a hand on Anna's arm as she gaped at the man. "Anna, this is Gerard, our . . . phantom."

"What!" she gasped.

He grimaced. "Yeah, you can blame Cass for that one."

Cassandra passed Anna an apologetic smile.

"So, we have new friends?" Gerard asked.

"She's *our* friend," Peter countered.

"And what about the brother?"

Owen glared at Gerard firmly. "My siblings are not your friends. I put up with you for Cassandra's sake. But I've begun questioning my leniency with you, so be careful."

Gerard scoffed. "Is that a threat, Master Wielder? Or was it Sage Wielder? All these lovely tidbits of information you keep dropping are starting to blend."

"Just keep yourself in line," Owen warned, turning to the board. "What is this?"

Cassandra gave Gerard one final, concerned glance before stepping up. "This," she pointed to the picture, "is Diane and Phillip. And those are their adoptive parents, Ronald and Helen Collins. This man back here is either Lloyd or Lee Frossard."

"That's not Lloyd," Anna said.

Peter's breath caught with the new information. "You're sure?"

Anna nodded. "Lloyd is Connor's great-grandfather—Alex's grandfather. Alex and Lloyd were close. There are tons of family photos in their house and, I'm positive—" She motioned to the picture. "That's not him."

"So, it's Lee," Cassandra said, smiling at Peter and Spencer.

"I guess so." Anna shrugged. "I can't say I've seen enough pictures of him to know for certain. But Lloyd had a distinct scar on his jaw from a childhood accident. And there's no scar on this guy."

Peter couldn't help himself in his excitement. He wrapped his arm around Anna's shoulders, smiling wide at the board. "Annie, you're a freakin' wonder!"

A light, nervous laugh escaped her. "Thanks."

"What does it mean, though?" Spencer asked, nodding to the board. "It's fantastic to know it's Lee, but if he's not their father, then what good does that do us?"

Peter looked at him, frowning. He had a point. They couldn't ask Lee why he'd taken Diane and Phillip to Norfolk to meet their adoptive parents. The man was dead.

A glitter of light on the wall behind Spencer caught Peter's eyes. He narrowed his gaze against the glare, the wood planks radiating brightly in the warm sunshine.

Anna's voice drew his attention back to her. "Well, if that's Lee, then it would have to be someone the Frossards knew, right?"

"This is a small town, sweetheart," Gerard called. "The Frossards knew everyone."

She glared at him. "Who even are you?"

Peter chuckled as Gerard glowered at her. "I'm the one who can tell you everything that happened back then."

"Not *everything*," Spencer countered.

"Excuse me?"

"If you could tell us everything, then you'd have been able to tell us who Diane's parents were."

The phantom glowered at Spencer. "I'm not here to help you. I'm here to help Cassandra."

"Yeah, but you're not only here to help Cassie," Spencer argued. "You're here to help yourself, and if that means doing her a favor in the meantime, so be it."

"You're gonna want to watch yourself, kid." Gerard's tone was low and threatening. "You might find yourself with more to fear than just your nightmares."

Cassandra stepped around Spencer. "Gerard," she challenged, her tone commanding. "If you're not going to help us, then leave."

"This is a two-way street, Cassandra."

"What's the rush?" she returned, her words clipped. "You're dead, and so is the rest of your family. They're not going anywhere, trust me."

By the fire that instantly burst to life in the phantom's glare, Peter wasn't sure that Cassandra had chosen the right time to pick a fight. Gerard rose to his full height, chin tilted proudly. "Don't say I didn't warn you, Cass," he said and then he was gone.

Discomfort settled into the room after the quarrel, but Peter refused to let it remain. He tapped Cassandra's arm and nodded to the board. "All right, Ann," he said, turning back to her. "Who were the Frossards close to in the '40s?"

"The '40s?" An amused scoff slipped from Anna's mouth. "Pete, how would I know that?"

He shrugged. "You're close with them."

"Well, yeah, with Connor, but—" She motioned to the photo. "Not with his great-great-uncle."

Owen shifted closer. "We know who the Frossards were close to."

"We do?" Cassandra asked.

"Yes. The other founding families. The Varons, the Chapelles, the Garniers. The Raynes, Guillaumes, Sauveterres, Merciers, Ozannes . . . all of them."

"That's a lot of people," Peter grumbled.

"But it narrows it down, doesn't it? We only need to figure out their closest ties in the '40s, and we'll know just who among the founding families the Frossards would be willing to help hide the adoption of two children."

Pushing a hand through his hair, Peter scanned the wall. Was it that simple? Could it be possible that the Frossards had a clear connection to their ancestry that they'd overlooked?

Peter stared at the image of toddler Diane and infant Phillip. He tried to see any connection to the residents of DeVerre. Was there any resemblance to one of the founding families? Their entire lives, everyone always told him and Spencer that they looked just like their dad. And their dad looked just like Grandpa Phillip. But who did Phillip resemble? Not Ronald Collins, that was sure.

Looking at the photo now, Peter wondered how they hadn't seen it years ago. Ronald's dark blond hair and warm olive complexion contrasted with so many of their own genetics. It should have been clear to them all. Peter and Spencer had always stood out in the crowded family photos. Now it was obvious why.

A glare of light beamed off the wall into Peter's periphery. He grimaced at its brightness, glancing to his right once more to catch the same spot shimmering in the low winter sun.

Shaking his head at the abnormal shine of the wooden slats, Peter turned back to the group. "Mkay, so we're looking for some affair gone wrong in the '40s amongst the Frossards' friends?"

Anna crossed her arms, lips pursed as she stared at the board again. "I don't know." Her words were tinged with doubt. "I have never heard about illegitimate children within DeVerre's ancestry. Especially not among the founding families."

"Yeah, well, that's the sort of thing people like to keep quiet, right?"

She laughed. "Have you met the gossips in this town? If a *founding family* member had had an affair resulting in *two* illegitimate children, it would have been all over the place."

On Peter's right, Cassandra scoffed. "They wiped out the very existence of the spirit world," she countered. "You don't think they could handle a couple of kids?"

"Which raises the question of why erasing the memory of these kids is as important as erasing the spirit world," Owen added.

As Peter turned to reply, the flash of light caught his eye again, and he sighed. "What the heck is that?" he demanded, gesturing toward the wall.

"Oh, thank God!" Spencer ran a hand through his hair. "I thought I was going crazy."

Cassandra frowned at them. "What are you two talking about?"

Peter exchanged a look with Spencer, then motioned to the reflection on the wall. "That!"

She followed his direction with her eyes, furrowed her brow, and frowned at him. "*What?*"

Sure that she must be blind not to notice the beam glowing as bright as the sun, Peter turned to Anna and Owen for backup. But they both stared at him, matching Cassandra's confusion. "Seriously? You can't see that?"

"See what?" Owen asked.

Spencer stepped up to the wall. "This." He gestured toward the flash of light, his shadow growing as he approached.

The three of them stared at him like he'd lost his mind.

With a concerned glance at his brother, Peter frowned. "We are seeing the same thing, right?"

"Yeah. I mean . . . I think so," Spencer said, reaching for the beam. "The light keeps reflecting off—whoa!"

Peter gaped at the wall as Spencer leaped back. It had happened so quickly that he wasn't sure he'd seen it. But when Spencer had touched the glowing spot, the wall had immediately changed. For a single second, it wasn't a wall anymore but an old, wooden door with a golden handle surrounded by a stone arch.

And then it was gone, the mundane wall back in place.

Owen took a step forward as Cassandra touched Spencer's arm. "What happened?" she asked.

"What do you mean, 'what happened'?" Peter asked. The alarm of what he'd just seen made his heart beat erratically and the drama of his reaction spike. "There was a—a . . . oh."

Meeting Spencer's bright blue eyes, a slow grin spread over Peter's lips.

A faint laugh slipped from his brother as he returned the elated smile. "We found it," he whispered.

The other three watched the brothers as they edged closer to the wall. Peter lifted his hand, surprised to find it shaking. His fingers brushed the wood, but it wasn't the wall anymore. The door reappeared, smooth and solid under his touch. Inlays of gothic designs arched all over the face. The golden latch glowed in the sunlight. Its black granite surround belonged in a cathedral or castle. And at the top of the arch was a sigil etched on the lintel—the Varon family crest on the gates outside perfectly mirrored above the door in the stone.

It was beautiful.

And it was overwhelming.

They'd done it. Somehow in all the chaos of the last twelve hours, they'd managed one more impossible feat.

They found the vault of Occasus.

Hand sliding down the polished surface, Peter took hold of the handle. His breath caught in his throat, worry that the door would have a lock coming to mind. It was a vault. Surely it would need a key.

But the latch depressed under his thumb, and the door swung wide.

Cassandra gasped behind them. Owen and Anna rushed to their side.

"Is that . . . ?" Cassandra whispered.

"Yeah," Spencer replied, tone almost reverent as they stared past the threshold.

Peter turned to smile at his brother. "Looks like the game's afoot, J.B."

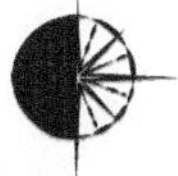

CHAPTER TWENTY-ONE

Spencer

Pulse racing, Spencer followed his brother through the arched doorway into the vault. A tingle ran down his spine as they crossed the threshold. It quickly subsided into a warmth that spread across his back and chest as they walked across the dark navy rug, resplendent golden flowers woven into its design.

Spencer tried to process what he was staring at, the room that he was standing in. But it felt impossible. It was far too much to absorb—too many things for his eyes to land on, so much that drew his attention.

This wasn't a vault, he decided in an instant. It was the most epic library in existence.

Attempting to take a measure of the space, Spencer started where they stood. About four feet away from the door, he and Peter faced rows of bookshelves on their right and left. The spines of the books were aged and intricate. Beautiful leather volumes that gave the air a rich, musty scent.

The low ceiling above them cast a shadow, but beyond the first row of shelves, the room rose much higher, light flooding the space. Giant columns of black granite capped the ends of each walnut bookshelf. Golden and glass sconces flanked little alcoves on the far right and left of the room. Their arched shapes mimicked the door to the vault, and set on the interior, a single granite column that displayed an antique cross on the right and a marble bust on the left.

The rug extended over the wooden floor, and a thin surround of dark granite lined the edges against the walnut baseboards. Spencer recognized the stone within the vault. It matched the archway at the door as well as the granite used on the fireplace surrounds on the floors below them. The decor reflected the rest of Occasus, for that matter: cream walls, walnut trim, and Victorian design. But the opulence within the vault was beyond anything that existed in the rest of their home.

Spencer's periphery caught Peter's step back, angling toward their friends. Cassandra, Anna, and Owen stood on the other side of the door with shock written across their expressions.

"You guys coming, or what?" Peter asked, a thrilled grin on his face.

Cassandra moved first. Her gait was light and relaxed for the first time in days. A smile grew on her face as she neared them and set a hand on Spencer's arm, eyes locked onto the space around them. "This is . . . it's incredible," she murmured.

"Yeah," Spencer agreed.

As Owen and Anna joined them, they moved farther into the vault. Stepping out from under the overhang, Spencer could finally see what the full vault had to offer. Not only did rows and rows of shelves surround them, but built-ins wrapped around the room on a second floor supported by the stone columns. Walnut railings lined the edges, and the telltale signs of a staircase appeared at the back of the room.

Spencer couldn't help the elated gasp that worked out of him. If they'd thought Occasus was the epitome of a writer's perfect home, this made it far more epic by a mile. He couldn't fathom how many books lined these shelves, all bound in brown, red, green, blue, black, and cream leather or linen. It would take far too many lifetimes to read everything within these walls.

When Ava had told them the vault held all DeVerre's secrets, Spencer didn't imagine she had meant *this*. Now he wondered if this vault held the secrets of the entire world.

"This . . . this doesn't make sense," Spencer muttered, turning in a slow circle as he took in the row of opulent chandeliers over their heads.

"What are you talking about?" Peter replied, equally distracted by his inspection of the space.

A fascinating, antique portrait caught Spencer's eye at the end of the far hall of shelves. The rich, saturated colors of its pigments depicted a middle-aged woman, her pale skin a contrast to the deep shadows around her. His gaze lingered on the woman's serious face as he explained, "Occasus isn't big enough for this. And we're on the top floor. Yet this place has its own second story? It's impossible."

Owen ran a hand along a row of books, eyes locked on the spines. "You're right," he said. "This isn't natural."

"What is it, then?" Anna asked, her hands pressed to either side of her face as she examined the space.

"I've heard about places like this, but—well, they're all rumors."

"Like Archsages?" Cassandra asked.

Owen huffed as he turned to her with a small grin. "Yeah." He motioned to the room. "There's a sect of the Warden who believes it's possible to harness the spirit world for creation. That its essence is meant to replicate within us what God can do Himself, connecting us more deeply to Him. As He is the ultimate creator, they say it gives us the ability to create as well."

Spencer turned to him, hearing past the simple words. "To create something from nothing?"

Tipping his head to the side, Owen considered it. "Not exactly. It's said that they're creating it from the spirit. The theory is that some

Wielders found a way to reach into the spirit world and access its very being, pulling it into the world. Thus, creating something brand new within the physical realm."

They all stopped staring at the vault to stare at him.

Owen shrugged. "It seems that the Varons figured out how to bring a part of the spirit world into the physical world and attach it to their house."

"Wait, like. . . ." Peter glanced at Spencer, shifting from foot to foot. "Like a pocket dimension or something?"

"Essentially, yes."

"Dude, that's freakin' cool."

Spencer couldn't disagree as his eyes moved back to their inspection of the room. He leaned his head back, staring at the glowing and massive chandeliers above them. Elaborate molding and medallions covered the vaulted, alabaster ceiling.

As they continued down the center corridor of the vault, Spencer estimated the room to be somewhere around fifty feet long and at least half that wide. Getting closer to the end of the room, he could see the staircase to the second floor in more detail. It curved gently, made of the same walnut as everything else within the room. With the abundant light from the chandeliers and sconces, all the dark wood didn't make the space feel heavy or dim. Instead, it was the perfect blend of welcoming and cozy.

Breaching the last line of shelves brought them to the back of the vault. Straight ahead lay the staircase, a wall of walnut alcoves at the back. To their left was a fireplace, crackling and alive behind a wrought iron grate. Two long leather couches and four elegant wingback chairs made up the sitting area, creating the perfect place to lounge, lost in the world of books for hours and hours.

And to the right, there was a giant desk closely resembling the one in the office on the first floor. The chair that sat on the other side looked like the most perfect spot to write a novel, its light brown leather smooth and plush. Two equally comfortable-looking, navy damask chairs sat on the side closest to them. Papers and books lay across the top of the desk, along with an inkwell, hourglass, and vintage lamp.

Spencer felt like he'd stepped into Wenzel and Frankly's world. They'd studied so much about 1880s New York that all these old-fashioned items and styles clicked in his mind at once. Drawn to the clutter of objects on the desk, he drifted to that side of the room while the rest spread out.

Running her hands along a cream wingback chair, Anna walked through the sitting area. She picked up one of the many books left on the coffee table and began to leaf through it. Owen hovered nearby, still scanning the bookshelves, eyes widening as he began to run his fingers over different spines. Cassandra stepped back toward the alcoves, focused on the antiques within each one.

But as Spencer approached the desk, Peter followed. The pair rounded on either side of the desk to peruse the papers and books, pens and paper clips, sepia photographs, and a singular pair of glasses spread over the surface.

Sharing a look with his brother, they silently checked in with each other before shifting through the clutter, Peter on the right and Spencer on the left. With the massive size of the desk, they both had plenty to search through. Spencer ran across a stack of letters addressed to each of the Varon men. A fancy cursive script signed the bottom of each letter with the name Elizabeth and a strange symbol that looked like a Y but with a third branch rising in the middle. It reminded Spencer of a bird's footprint. He dropped the letters with a mental note to study them later.

Continuing his perusal, Spencer found an open book with a title too long to read in one scan and a scrawling of notes on the papers beside it. Lifting the loose papers, he found a leather-bound notebook hidden beneath them. Absentmindedly lifting the notebook while he scanned the pages in his hand, Spencer struggled to make heads or tails of the notes without the context of the book. So, he set them back down and turned to the notebook, hoping to find something of more interest within its binding.

Opening the cover, Spencer flipped past the empty first page and scanned the tight cursive lines that followed. A couple of lines in, he realized that it was a journal. With the date of 1937 at the top, he quickly surmised it had belonged to either Matthew or Michael Varon. Spencer scanned a few more lines, flipped through a handful more pages, and read two paragraphs before figuring out that it belonged to the latter.

Nudging Peter's arm with his elbow, Spencer motioned to the journal's pages. "Check it out."

"Whatcha got?" Peter peered over.

Spencer raised his eyebrows to indicate the book's importance. "Michael Varon's journal."

"What?" His brother dropped the pages in his hands, hurrying around the desk chair to get a better look. "You sure?"

"Yeah, look—" He pointed to the date at the top of a page in the middle of the journal. "April 9, 1939. And here he mentions talking to his father. Matthew's father died in 1930. There's no way it could have been him."

"He could've been a ghost," Peter suggested.

Spencer tapped another line in the book. "It was a conversation with multiple people. The problem is, I can't tell who these other people are since he's just using their first names."

A sly smile pulled on Peter's lips. "Well, that's why we have a resident expert on DeVerre here with us," he said, turning to the other side of the room. "Annie."

Anna looked up from the book in her hands. "Huh?"

"We need your expertise."

Her eyebrows dropped, dubious at the idea, but she set the book down and headed their way.

Peter's call caught Owen and Cassandra's attention as well, drawing them to the desk. Once they were all huddled around, Peter elbowed Spencer. "Tell her what you found."

"Uh, well. . . ." He lifted the book, though they could all clearly see it in his hand. "I found Michael Varon's journal."

"Seriously?" Cassandra gasped, setting her hands on the desktop.

His expression mirrored the awe in hers. "The problem is, I can't identify the people he's talking about." He turned to Anna. "Do you know the names Everett or Marvin?"

Anna's eyes grew wide. "Oh, uh . . . no."

The hope rising in Spencer's chest deflated. "You're sure?"

"I'm sorry, but—" She shook her head. "I may know everyone in DeVerre at present, but I'm not a historian like Ava. She could tell you, though."

Spencer passed a cautious look Owen's way, the man dipping his head.

Shifting uncomfortably, Cassandra sighed. "Gerard would probably know."

"We don't need Gerard," Peter said. Then his jaw dropped, and he held up a finger. "Hang on."

They all watched as Peter jumped away from the desk, rushing around the corner and back toward the entrance to the vault. He was gone for almost a full minute before he came back, huffing and puffing from his sprint, waving a handful of papers in the air. "Here," he wheezed, handing them to Owen, who stood closest to him.

"What are these?" Owen asked, glancing at the pages.

Spencer recognized them at once. "Diane's list of residents," he explained. "She worked up that list with Gerard's help."

"It's—it's like Gerry is here, but . . . we don't have to put up with his snark," Peter said, still out of breath.

Cassandra smirked at him. "We just get to enjoy yours instead."

Peter gave her a two-fingered salute, leaning forward as he worked to catch his breath.

Moving closer to Owen, Spencer motioned to the pages. "She's got them listed alphabetically by last name."

"That doesn't help much when we're going off the first names," Owen replied, a distracted, studious glint in his eyes as he scanned the papers. "Everett, you said?"

"Yeah."

After a few pages, Owen's gaze drifted to Peter. "These are out of order."

Peter grimaced. "Sorry. I was in a rush."

The man ignored the apology, handing half of the stack to Anna. "Here. We'll find it faster with both of us looking."

They began to scan each page as the other three watched. Spencer was about to suggest they all take some papers when Anna lifted her head, eyes alight with excitement. "I found Marvin," she said. "It's Marvin Garnier. Born in 1903 and died in 1969. The note says that he was the marshal."

"Garnier?" Cassandra looked at Spencer.

Spencer shrugged, thinking it lent extra weight to Tom's information when Owen interrupted. "Everett's a Garnier as well." He showed them the page. "1906-1964. They were close in age, and he also served as a marshal."

"Brothers?" Peter suggested.

"Do you think we should ask Tom if he knows?" Cassandra asked.

Looking through the list once more, Owen nodded. "Probably. But we should see what else that journal says about the Garniers. It would be good to get further assurance of the family's allegiances."

Spencer ran his thumb along the edges of the journal's pages. "I can take care of that."

"And what about the rest of us?" Cassandra leaned against the desk, palms resting again on its surface. "It's great that we found the vault, but we didn't expect it to be this big. Where do we even start?"

With a heavy sigh, Owen let the list of residents hang by his side. "There must be some answers here about what the Druids' plan for the Veil is."

"Something that they want," Peter added.

Spencer's chest grew tight as they all looked over at his brother. He was right. Debbie had said they needed Occasus. And the insinuation had been that it was the vault they needed to access for the next phase of their plan.

Owen shifted from foot to foot by Spencer's side. He wore a wary expression as he looked around the desk at Spencer, then Cassandra, and, finally, at Peter. "I suppose the first question we have to ask," he replied, his voice flat, "is if you three are going to stay or not."

Though Anna's brow furrowed, she didn't say anything as the other three turned to look at each other. The question was valid. Finding the vault did nothing to change the fact that the Druids had given them three days to clear out of Occasus. Or else be forced out.

Spencer held no doubt that the Druids would use violent means to achieve that end.

But looking around the massive library, Spencer knew it wasn't a real question. He hadn't wanted to leave before when they hadn't had access to the vault. Now that they had. . . .

There were hundreds—maybe thousands—of books within the vault. Relics and antiques that certainly held grand significance. And then there was the notebook in his hand.

"We can't leave now," Spencer said. "This is way bigger than we thought. Whatever this vault holds, it can't just be DeVerre's secrets. And if the Druids—or Children of Gaia, or whatever they call themselves—if they're after Occasus because they want access to this vault, it'd be wrong of us to hand it over to them. Even if it means risking our lives."

Peter and Cassandra passed him approving smiles while Owen dipped his head in acceptance.

However, Anna's mouth dropped open as she held up her hand. "I'm sorry, are you saying that these . . . whomever they are—they want to kill you?"

Peter rubbed the back of his neck, a nervous grin pulling at the corner of his mouth. "Uh, yeah," he muttered. "Yeah, they kind of threatened us this morning."

"What?" Anna pressed her hand to her forehead. "Why?"

"Because we're trying to stop them," Cassandra explained.

Releasing a long sigh, Anna took a step back from the desk. "This just keeps getting worse and worse, doesn't it?"

"Welcome to our lives for the last month and a half," Spencer said with a dry grin. But he couldn't help thinking that it wasn't entirely true. Yes, things were getting more and more difficult. When they'd left Norfolk, they hadn't known anything about the spirit world or their uncertain ancestry, and no one was trying to kill them. But they'd also not had their own home, he and Peter had worked dead-end jobs, and they hadn't known Cassandra.

Sure, life was hard in DeVerre. Things were complicated. They might die trying to defend this place. But staring around the desk at his brother, Cassandra, Anna, and Owen, he didn't think he would want it any other way.

Peter may have had to drag him from his lackluster comfort zone, but Spencer was convinced that coming to DeVerre was the best thing that ever happened to them. And if they could get rid of the Druids, it might just be the most perfect place in the whole world.

Spencer drew his shoulders back, glancing at each of his companions in turn. "We have to figure this out. We may not know what the Druids want out of the vault, but right now, that doesn't matter. What does matter is finding whatever information we can that will help when they come for us in three days."

Peter nodded, passing one of his prouder smiles to Spencer. He angled to the woman at his side and brushed her elbow. "Annie, you don't have to help us—"

"Pete—"

"Just listen," he cut her off. "The Druids are going to come to Occasus in three days. They're going to try to kill us. And we're gonna fight them. And while I'd love to have you help us, the more time you spend associating with us, the more danger you'll put yourself in."

Her dark eyebrows lowered.

Peter leveled his most earnest stare on her—the one Spencer knew he rarely wore. "As far as I'm concerned, it's up to you, but . . . I want you to know what you're getting yourself into if you stay to help us."

While they waited for her reply, Anna tucked her chin in thought. Spencer watched her and Peter carefully. They stood closer together than the average pair of friends might naturally. It wasn't their proximity that suggested things were more serious than he'd thought; it was the emotions he could feel in the air between them.

Peter cared about Anna, he realized. More than he cared about most people. Not more than Spencer, but maybe more than Cassandra. Or perhaps he cared for her differently.

It was odd to see. Spencer had watched his brother form crushes and varying levels of attachment to many women throughout their lives. Peter was always looking for someone to date. Unintentionally searching, Spencer knew, but searching all the same. He was desperate to find someone who would love him, someone who respected him. And as much as Spencer loved and respected his brother, he knew perfectly well that it wasn't the type of love Peter wanted—the type of love he needed.

Now Spencer wondered, could Anna Lambert provide that sort of love to his brother?

Anna raised her head again, meeting Peter's gaze. "You saved my life," she said. "It's only fair that I return the favor if I can."

A blend of disappointment and gratitude passed over Peter's expression. Spencer knew the conflict his brother must be feeling—thankfulness for Anna's loyalty conflicting with worry for her safety.

Owen ran a hand over his mouth, watching the two of them with a cautious eye. "So, what's the plan?"

Peter backed away from Anna, turning to Spencer. "What'd'ya think?"

Lifting Michael Varon's journal, Spencer shrugged. "I'll focus on this. If nothing else, it may give us an understanding of what he was studying. And I think getting first-hand knowledge of what was going on in DeVerre in the late '30s and early '40s will help us know who we can and can't trust."

Peter nodded. "Good, yeah, that's smart. Mkay, well, I guess I can read the rest of this stuff on the desk? That way you and I can cross reference it?"

"I noticed some genealogies on the shelf over there," Owen said, motioning toward the fireplace. "Anna, why don't you use it to check against Diane's list."

Peter perked up. "Ooh, and against the marshal's suspect list."

"Good idea. Yes, we'll get that for you too."

Anna looked between them as though they'd asked her to carry the weight of the world. "Okay, yeah."

Owen turned to Cassandra. "I also spotted several books on the beasts of the spirit world."

A look of concern lit Cassandra's hazel eyes.

"Maybe you can study them to see what you can learn about their origins," he explained. "It should help in fighting against the Druids, knowing exactly how to defeat whatever beasts they might think to summon."

"All right," she muttered.

Spencer eyed her, unsure why she was so hesitant to study the beasts. He knew why he would avoid it, but Cassandra wasn't afraid of anything. A book about the creatures of the spirit world couldn't frighten her, could it?

"What about you?" Peter asked, disrupting Spencer's study of Cassandra.

Owen motioned toward the antiques along the back wall, then to the bookshelves. "I'm going to catalog the place. See what I can find and what sort of organizational system they used. If we can get a feel for the vault, we can get a better picture of where to start."

He paused, shifting uncomfortably from foot to foot. "I'm also going to contact a friend from Harmony," he said. Spencer's eyes widened. "He may know something about the vault that wouldn't be common knowledge."

"Hang on—" Spencer leaned forward, hope rising to the surface. "What about the Warden? Couldn't they come to help us? If we had more Wielders here, we could easily beat the Druids, right?"

A hesitation in Owen's expression made Spencer's plan dissolve before it had even fully formed. "The Warden isn't as . . . secure these days."

"What does that mean?" Peter asked.

Owen swallowed, his Adam's apple bobbing with the action. "As in all organizations, there are politics and interests at play," he explained with tension in his usually calm voice. "I've always thought it was idiotic, but . . . the powers that be don't offer the same support they once did."

"Dude, you're being cryptic," Peter pushed. "What are you trying to say?"

Owen sighed. "I'm trying to say that I'm not supported by the Warden anymore."

They all gaped at him in shock.

"After the first eight years of my time here without anything to show for it, they wanted to recall me," he admitted. "As I was married to Ava, they gave me a choice: Return to Harmony to help them there or remain here on my own. I'm still a member of the Warden, but I don't work for them anymore. And like I said, I have a friend I still talk to, but . . . Harmony has problems of its own. Like most Warden towns."

Cassandra crossed her arms. "Why would Warden towns have problems?"

"The spirit world is a divisive subject." Owen tucked his hands into the pockets of his slacks. "People have a hard enough time accepting its presence when they don't know the ins and outs of it. The complications don't get easier the more knowledge you learn."

Spencer glanced around the vault, taking in all the information held within its walls. Things were already complicated. And they didn't have time to debate the merits of the Warden's issues.

With a sigh, Spencer decided to move on. "All right, so we each have our jobs? Owen will figure out what all is in this place and get us organized. Anna will help us figure out the genealogies and connections of DeVerre. Cass will learn about the beasts while Pete and I try to get a handle on what Michael Varon was up to in his final days."

The group exchanged glances, each meeting one person's gaze after the next. It was daunting. And it felt almost useless. If they had to fight the Druids in three days, studying hardly seemed like a practical use of their time.

But Spencer couldn't shake the feeling that something in the journal he held would give them all the answers they needed. That it would explain all the secrets they'd been uncovering for the past several weeks. His fingers practically tingled in anticipation as he felt the urge to crack open the spine of the journal once more and figure out just what had driven Michael Varon to madness.

Peter gave Anna's shoulder an encouraging pat before he moved to Spencer's side. "All right, Columbo, where should I start?"

Scanning the desk, Spencer looked at the numerous books and papers scattered across its surface. His eyes kept lighting on the stack of letters to the right, but he shook his curiosity off, prioritizing the book Michael had obviously been working on last.

Spencer set the journal on the desk, then gathered the notes and stuffed them inside the book. He shut the vintage tome and lifted it to drop it into Peter's waiting arms. "Here. Michael was studying this for some reason. Maybe you can figure it out."

"You got it." Peter began shifting away, but Spencer grabbed the sleeve of his flannel and pulled him to a stop.

He pressed his lips together, eyes drifting to the letters again.

They should prioritize, he knew, but he couldn't help his interest.

Grabbing the stack, Spencer settled them on top of the book. "Give these a look too," he said, pointing his finger at his brother's face. "But only after you've done some solid work on the book."

Peter narrowed his eyes. "You got a hunch there, Sherlock?"

"Maybe," he muttered, then shook his head. "Just . . . check out the book first, okay?"

"Okay." Peter winked at him.

Spencer recognized the amused glint in his eyes. "Pete," he warned. "The book first."

Crooked grin still on his face, Peter backed away. "Don't you worry, Spence. I read you loud and clear."

Sighing, there was little doubt in Spencer's mind that Peter would start with the letters. But his curiosity couldn't help feeling gratified at the thought.

While the rest of them dispersed around the library to begin their own work, Spencer sat in the leather chair at the desk and opened Michael Varon's journal to the first page.

CHAPTER TWENTY-TWO

Cassandra

They'd spent almost the entire day studying in the vault. Even after Peter volunteered to take Anna home before Ava returned from the library, they'd still managed to make a ton of progress.

It was thanks to the impending attack from the Druids, Cassandra thought. That and their excitement to have found something that might help them. Their first real opportunity to find answers. And though she would have preferred to help Spencer and Peter with their research at the desk, she sat on the large couch by the fireplace, taking long, detailed notes as she studied the beasts of the spirit world.

Cassandra twisted her ring at regular intervals during the work. It wasn't that she didn't care to understand how to better defeat the beasts. She saw the merit in it. She thought it was a wise use of their time. But she didn't think she should be the one to do it.

Since she'd discovered the ability to tether Gerard to Occasus, Cassandra had become quite confident in the strength of her power. And when she'd shown up on the porch to find a hellhound chasing the Collins brothers, she hadn't hesitated to intervene despite never before attempting to control a beast. She hadn't questioned if she could do it; she'd known she could. And it had been far easier than she thought.

Knowing how easily the power came to her, a nagging suspicion began to plague her mind after their fight with Debbie. She'd seen how easily her cousin could control the beasts. How simple it had been for her to summon them. And after her mother declared how powerful Cassandra had been since birth, she couldn't shake the realization that Debbie's abilities were likely a mere pittance of what Cassandra herself could achieve with the proper training.

And that worried her.

From the moment Cassandra had learned about beasts, she'd had no interest in summoning one—in discovering what it would be like to control a spirit being that way.

But she knew herself. And she knew that knowledge often made trying impulsive things a given when she discovered herself in a dire situation.

Like controlling a hellhound. Like wielding a rift of the spirit world's essence. Like rending Debbie's soul.

If she knew how to summon, control, and otherwise influence the beasts of the spirit world, what would her spontaneous reflexes persuade her to do when the Druids came for them?

Though the brothers were still hard at work late into the night, Cassandra decided to take a break from the study. The whole day had been more than she could have imagined from start to finish. They'd found the vault, but they'd also faced a new threat from the Druids. She'd fought with Spencer, but he'd practically admitted a romantic interest in her. They'd gained more insight into the ancestry of the brothers and Diane, but Gerard had tested the bounds of their arrangement.

As Cassandra worked her way down the stairs, she paused, replaying the day in rewind. Everything sped through her thoughts until they slowed to a stop at the memory of Spencer sitting at the desk, smiling at her with that proud, excited smile on his face. *"I found Elijah Lawrence's essays."*

Cassandra stared at the steps before her, the carpeted runner soft beneath her feet. How had they forgotten? They'd found the essays and completely ignored them in the wake of Owen's presence, the Druids' threat, and the discovery of the vault.

Rushing down the rest of the steps, Cassandra nearly tripped over her own feet in her panic. She knew it was irrational. There was no reason to be so concerned. But after finding the pages missing from Diane's notes, she couldn't help fearing they were gone again.

Bolting around the corner, Cassandra heaved a sigh when her eyes landed on the printer at the back of the office. The papers reflected the dim moonlight like a beacon. She crossed the wood floor to take them up, pages cold to her touch. As she turned them over, immediate nostalgia welled up in her eyes.

She'd studied those pages so many times with Diane in that very office. They'd talked about what Elijah could have meant, how the essays might affect their lives, and what secrets they held in their old English. It was how they learned to tether Gerard. It gave them their first lead of their time in DeVerre.

Drifting through the office, Cassandra let her hands brush against the back of the desk chair. The seat where Diane used to sit. The one that belonged to Spencer now. They weren't much alike, Diane and Spencer. Yet there was one trait that they did share: their quiet steadiness. The strength and dedication that made Cassandra so drawn to them both.

Cassandra pushed the thoughts down, releasing the chair and moving to the staircase once more. She stared at the essays, the printer ink long dried as she rubbed her thumb against the letters. Unable to fully understand the language, she didn't care to try and read the words now. But she wouldn't let them out of her sight again. Not until she knew what secrets they revealed and what answers they bore.

Returning to Diane's old room—to *her* room, Cassandra felt like the large stack of paper weighed ten times what it should. There was too much. Too much to study. Too much to figure out. Too much to do. And too much for her mind to work through in one night.

After securing the essays in her bag with the rest of Diane's things, Cassandra forced herself to go about her nightly routine. She moved with mechanical, rote lethargy as she brushed her teeth in the elegant, gold and marble bathroom of the master.

Cassandra stared into the mirror, wondering at the vacant expression on her face. How could she look so calm and unfeeling with so many worries coursing through her head? How did she go about mundane tasks such as her nighttime routine, washing her face and methodically applying her regimen when her heart felt as heavy in her chest as it did now?

The cool thread of Gerard's knock at the back of her mind pressed in just as she flicked off the lights to the bathroom. The whisper of his request nagged at her conscious. Though she had little interest in talking to him after her day and his earlier outburst, she allowed his entry. Pulling the bathroom door shut behind her, Cassandra looked up to find Gerard sitting on the chair at the far side of the room.

Moving to close the curtains over the numerous windows, Cassandra spared him a single glance. "Is there something I can help you with?"

Gerard watched her, arms crossed over his chest. He always looked the same—locked in the exact moments before his death, with no sign of the wounds he'd suffered. She'd asked how he'd died once, but he didn't know. *"However, it happened,"* he'd explained, *"they snuck up on me from behind."*

Pulling loose the red tie around his neck, Gerard tipped his chin up at her. "I wanted to apologize," he said, his voice monotone and dull, like he was bitter at having to apologize at all. "I was angry earlier and . . . I was out of line."

Cassandra let the strap of the woven, navy curtains drop free, almost smiling at the reluctance in his voice. "Yes," she agreed as she met his dark stare. "You were."

The phantom worked his jaw back and forth. "As I admitted."

"So, that's it? You're just going to admit it and expect me to be okay?"

"You made a deal with me, Cass." There was no malice in his tone. Just fact. "And you're going back on it."

"I'm not."

"You're choosing them over me."

Pulling in a deep breath, Cassandra tossed her hands in the air. "What do you want me to do? I tried to find answers. Everything keeps pointing back to the Druids. And right now, they are the very people threatening my life. If I'm supposed to help you, I need to stay alive, right?"

Gerard's hands fisted at his sides. She had him, and he knew it. If she died, Gerard's tether dissolved. He would revert to his ghostly form, alone and without any hope of becoming corporeal again.

His eyes flashed a deeper shade of brown when he looked up at her. "I want you to know, Cassandra," he said, voice quiet, as if he was going to great efforts to manage his next words. "You've been kinder to me than most people in my life. Maybe kinder than anyone, aside from my Kristina."

Her eyes narrowed at the mention of his late wife. He never talked about her. He'd only spoken of her once—to tell Cassandra what he wanted from her. To establish their deal. Hearing her name now made Cassandra aware that he was far more serious than she'd anticipated.

"I won't forget that," he continued in her stunned silence. "But I won't let you forget what you promised me either. Nor where my priorities lie."

Cassandra swallowed through the tightness in her throat. "I know. And I want to find answers for you. I truly do. But I don't know what to do besides what I'm already doing."

Gerard gave her a firm nod, the emotion still playing in his voice as he spoke. "So long as you understand me. I will do whatever it takes to have my justice."

"I want that for you too. I swear."

"Good." He stood. "Goodnight, Cassandra."

She barely got out her "goodnight" in reply before he'd disappeared. Per her rules, she knew he wasn't in the room anymore. She'd made sure that he couldn't enter anyone's room without making himself visible, as a matter of peace of mind more than actual concern that he'd care to creep out of view.

Running her hands along the black satin of her nightclothes, Cassandra tried to center herself to the moment. She needed to clear her head and regain some semblance of calm. She was desperate for rest after the emotional strain of the day.

Cassandra climbed under the heavy blankets and tucked herself amongst the fluffy pillows. The sheets were cold against her bare arms, but she turned off the light on the nightstand and snuggled deeper beneath the depths of the blankets. Her breath warmed her face under the covers, creating an immediate, humid cloud that smothered her senses.

Closing her eyes, Cassandra gave herself thirty seconds. That was all she would allow herself. Thirty seconds to think about everything that weighed on her.

The Druids. The vault. The beasts.

Gerard's threat and apology.

The dead body they'd hidden.

Their new allies among the Lambert siblings.

Spencer and that maddening, infuriating smirk he'd given her. The way he'd stared through every wall she put up with those piercing blue eyes of his. His steady voice as he'd told her that it wasn't just her anymore. How wonderful those words felt to hear. His irritation at her insistence that it wasn't the truth.

Cassandra heard herself let out a soft, scoffing laugh at the memory of his frustration as he muttered, *"I hate hyperbole."*

She smiled, thinking how cute he'd looked with his brow furrowed and jaw tight in anger. She wondered if it was a problem, enjoying how irritated she'd made him.

Twisting her ring, Cassandra opened her eyes, staring into the blackness under the covers. Had he meant it? Or had she just assumed the meaning of his words? He might hold no interest in her at all. Perhaps he thought of her like a sister, the way Peter did, and that's all he'd meant.

She shouldn't care. Not now, when their lives were on the line.

But as she lay under the blankets, hiding from the rest of the world, Cassandra allowed herself to pretend everything else had faded from existence. It was nice—pretending that her most complicated problem was whether or not a boy liked her. Like she was back in high school or college when her biggest struggle was figuring out what she wanted to do with her life. Did she want a boyfriend? What major would she choose? Would she ever see ghosts again?

The simplicity of those inconsequential problems was like a distant daydream. And, for the moment, Cassandra let herself rest in the ease of worrying about Spencer and his confusing words. She mused over the way he'd begun acting like his normal, reserved self around her once Anna and Aaron had arrived. She fretted over the fact that even if he was interested in her, he had shown no sign that he wanted to pursue her.

The heat under the blankets grew stifling, and Cassandra pulled her head free, the cold night air sending immediate tingles of relief across her cheeks as she rested against the pillow. "How stupid," she whispered to herself despite the smile that grew across her face. "Thinking about a boy this way. You better get your act together, Cassandra. You're a grown woman. And you have Druids to fight."

But snuggled under the blankets, Cassandra's thoughts drifted back to Spencer, hoping he was thinking about her too.

~

Cassandra sat in the same spot she'd vacated the night before, studiously reading about the beasts again. The group had agreed that they wouldn't take anything outside the vault's unnatural four walls. Not even into the rest of the house. Not when they didn't know which of the items the Druids wanted.

All of them were back at work, Gerard with them this time. He'd apologized to the rest that morning—particularly to Anna for his poor first impression—and offered his help. "I know DeVerre and its people," he'd reminded them. "And if that vault has been closed since Michael Varon's death, I was alive during the last days it was accessed. I guarantee that I could be of use to you."

Though there had been some hesitation from the brothers and lots of it from Owen, they'd all agreed that things would go more smoothly if they had his help. Spencer had frequent questions about the names he came across within Michael Varon's journal, and Gerard's knowledge would make his studies far easier.

Now, Anna sat across from Cassandra, perched on the other couch as she referenced the lists of suspects and residents against the genealogies. She'd kicked off her cute, tan ankle boots and sat with her knees in the air, the rosy pink of her socks in high contrast to the black that Cassandra chose to surround herself with. In fact, everything about the young woman was practically her opposite, she thought.

Anna wore bright, cheerful colors in feminine cuts and styles. They shared dark hair and eyes, but even those features weren't truly similar. Not with the way Anna's black-brown hair curled into tight spirals that drifted, light and ethereal, around her face like there was a constant breeze. Her perpetually smooth brown skin gave her a regal look no matter how much or how little makeup she wore.

Anna Lambert was the epitome of refined, Cassandra thought. And she felt sorely lackluster—and quite frankly, old—next to her.

The sound of muted laughter came from the far end of the room, and Cassandra turned to see Spencer snickering as Peter said something to him. A bead of jealousy rose in her chest, seeing their lighthearted banter and being on the outside of it. Only two days after Owen's arrival and having Anna around more, Cassandra already felt removed from her closeness with the brothers.

Rolling her eyes at herself, Cassandra tried to read once more. Then a sudden exclamation from Peter drew the gaze of both women this time. They stared over, expecting some revelation from the brothers, but Spencer only laughed as Peter slugged his arm, a sour grin on his face.

The brothers returned to their work, still chuckling, and Anna followed suit. But Cassandra watched for a moment longer. Just long enough that Spencer caught her.

He passed her a small smile. One that said he wasn't sure if she was looking at them because they'd made too much noise or just because she'd been looking. His sharp eyes darted to the journal in his hands for a second before flickering back up and then back down again.

Tucking a few smooth, dark waves behind her ear, Cassandra turned back to her book, a wry smile in place. Whatever Spencer had intended to say the previous day, she was convinced she understood. He was interested but not enough. He was too terrified of her and her rejection. And his fear would always keep him from making the first move.

Turning the ring around her finger, Cassandra furrowed her brow, reviewing his perplexing words again. He'd claimed he wouldn't pursue her because she was intimidating. But not just to him; to everyone.

Glancing back toward the brothers, zoned in on their studies once more, Cassandra wondered if he could be right. She didn't think it was likely. After all, he'd only known her a month, and she'd spent her whole life compiling data that said otherwise. People weren't afraid of her because she was great; they were afraid of her because she was different. They either chose others over her or tried to control her to make her into what they wanted her to be, leaving her with the distinct impression that she was some broken, faulty version of a human. A creature as unlovable as the beasts in the book on her lap.

Irritated by her own insecurities, Cassandra grabbed the notepad sitting beside her and shoved it between the book's pages. She shut it with a *thunk*. Anna looked up as Cassandra stood to shift over to the wingback chair.

"Can I ask you a question?" she asked, keeping her voice low enough that no one else would hear.

Anna raised her brow, pulling her feet beneath her. "Sure," she said, dropping the lists into a heap in her lap.

Drawing her eyebrows together, Cassandra wondered if it were stupid to ask.

She huffed. Of course, it was stupid. Almost as stupid as using her crush on Spencer to distract her from her worries last night.

But she refused to let it stop her from asking. "Am I intimidating?"

There was a second of confusion in Anna's brown eyes before she let out a thin laugh. "Right." She smiled, nodding as though she understood. But she didn't say anything else, continuing to chuckle.

Cassandra didn't join her laughter.

Anna's jaw dropped. "Oh, you're serious?"

"Yeah," she assured her, wishing she'd never asked the question now.

"Oh," Anna repeated. She reached up to play with her necklace—as dainty as its owner. "I'm sorry, I didn't—I thought you were joking."

"No."

"Huh, well. . . ." Anna bit her bottom lip, staring at the coffee table as if for help. When she turned back, there was a nervous glint in her eyes. "Yeah, you're *really* intimidating."

Wrapping her arms around herself, Cassandra leaned forward. "Really?"

Anna nodded as though it should be obvious.

"Like . . . intimidating in a good way or in a bad way?"

She thought about it. "In a good way. Like, in an, 'oh my gosh, she's super cool, and I want to be her best friend,' kind of way."

Cassandra couldn't help grinning as she wondered if that was just an example or if it represented the younger woman's actual feelings.

Ducking her head at the compliment, she tried to figure out how to take it. "Thanks," she finally muttered.

"Sure," Anna replied with a sheepish smile. "Why do you ask?"

"Uh. . . ." She glanced up at Anna, trying to decide how honest she could be. She couldn't tell her the truth, could she? They weren't that good of friends yet.

But then, Anna had just admitted to wanting to be best friends. And she didn't think she'd ever had someone be so upfront about their desire to be her friend. Anyone besides Peter, at least.

Smiling at the thought, Cassandra rested her arms on her thighs as she sat on the edge of her seat. "I just didn't ever think of myself that way," she whispered. "I always thought people didn't like me because I was different, and that was why they stayed away from me, but . . . well, yesterday Spencer told me that—that I intimidated him. And that he thought I intimidated pretty much everyone. Which was the *real* reason they stayed away from me."

Cassandra noted how Anna's eyes darted toward the desk over her shoulder. The young woman scooted closer, keeping her voice hushed. "To be honest, I think he has a point. I know that some people might not realize it, but . . . you come across as super confident, Cassandra. And that freaks a lot of people out. Most people are afraid to be friends with someone as confident and independent as you. They see it as a reminder of how imperfect and insecure they are."

Frowning, Cassandra shook her head. "I'm not perfect either. And, trust me, I'm not as confident as you think."

A bright smile lit up Anna's face. "Well, obviously," she said as though they were discussing something inconsequential. "No one is as confident as they seem. We all know what fears and flaws we have, and we experience them every day of our lives. We're perfectly aware of how insecure we are. But no one else is.

"You may not feel it, but you strike people as self-sufficient and sure of yourself. As though you don't need anyone. As though you could take or leave the rest of the world because you know who you are and what you want. And that's a scary thing for people." She shrugged. "Because it makes us feel like we'll never be good enough for you. As though we'll never matter to you."

Cassandra didn't know how to take Anna's words. She felt as though she should be grateful and devastated all at the same time. Hearing how people perceived her was illuminating in equal parts rewarding and discouraging.

Spencer was right. People *were* terrified of her. But not at all for the reason she thought.

Or, she corrected, at least not for people like Anna. After the conversation with her mother, there was no doubt in her mind that her family viewed her as the dangerous monster she'd always imagined. But the image Anna described suggested that her family was in the minority. While a few feared her because of who she was and what she could do, far more feared her because of the persona she chose to portray. Because they were drawn to her, yet feared she'd push them away.

Cassandra had learned to put up walls, expecting that people would disapprove of and dislike her. She protected herself from them because she couldn't stand the rejection. By pretending she didn't need them, she defended against the hurt that came from the feeling that they didn't want her.

But in just a few words, Anna had shattered that perception. She'd made it completely clear she'd like nothing more than to be her friend. And she wasn't the only one.

Though she didn't allow herself to turn around, Cassandra angled her head back Spencer's way. *"It's why I won't do anything about it,"* he'd said.

Anna leaned in, her smile curious. "Are you . . . ?" The question died as Cassandra met her eyes. Anna tried again. "Are you and Spencer . . . ?"

Forcing out a laugh, Cassandra shook her head. "No."

"No?"

"No," she assured her. "We're not."

"Oh."

Cassandra couldn't help smiling at the frown that overtook Anna's whole face. "Don't look so disappointed," she teased. "There's always time."

Lifting a hand to her mouth, Anna laughed. "So, you *are* interested?" she whispered behind her fingers.

Wondering if this was the first time she'd ever participated in "girl talk," Cassandra couldn't help the sense of connection that welled up in her heart. "Have you seen the guy? Of course, I'm interested."

A little snort of humor came from Anna.

Feeling she'd done an adequate job making a friend, she tapped Anna's hand. "We'd better get back to work," she said, voice still low. "Thanks for being honest."

"Thanks for asking."

Cassandra was about to get up when she realized she had more to say. "I never felt that way about you, by the way."

Anna tipped her head to the side.

"That I didn't need you or that I had no interest in being your friend. To tell the truth, I don't feel it about anyone. I just . . . I don't know how to let people . . . get close, I guess. I don't know how to say that I'd like to know them."

The kind smile that Anna gave her was encouraging. "I understand. It can be hard to be open with people. Not everyone is like Peter."

Cassandra laughed. "Thank God for that," she joked. "I love the guy, but he can be a handful."

Anna played with the papers on her lap, tossing a sidelong glance the man's way. "Yes, he really can."

What a pair they were, Cassandra thought. The way Anna studiously avoided eye contact with her, she didn't think she should ask about the woman's relationship with Peter. She was curious but doubted she would take it as lightheartedly as Cassandra had taken her inquisition on Spencer. But she also didn't feel right about abandoning the young woman to the sway of whatever thoughts she'd unintentionally stirred up.

Nudging the papers in Anna's hands, Cassandra caught her attention again. "You finding anything?"

"Uh, no," Anna admitted. "Not really. I mean, I'm making connections and everything, but . . . I don't know enough about DeVerre's history and ancestry to be of much help. Like, I know the names and family lines and everything, but I have no clue if they're significant."

Pressing her lips together, Cassandra nodded. She knew exactly what she meant.

"Are you finding anything?" Anna returned.

Cassandra glanced at the books she was supposed to be studying. "Sort of. I now know about six different types of beasts, plus a lot of folklore about them. So that's something. But I don't see how any of this will do us much good."

"What do you mean?"

"We have two days left." She felt her pessimism growing as she gave the vault a scan. "Two more days to get this figured out. And we don't even know what we're looking for. How are we supposed to find anything in all of this?"

Anna nodded, matching her gaze as it passed around the room. "I wish Ava were here," she whispered. "She's a genius at this stuff. *And* she knows everything about DeVerre."

She had a point, Cassandra had to admit. Ava had known about the vault before any of them. Even if she was against the spirit world, she clearly had the information they needed. And if they could get her on their side, there was a chance that their task might not be as impossible as it felt right at that moment.

But Ava wouldn't help them. If she'd separated from her husband due to her misunderstanding of the spirit world, there was no chance they could persuade her to help them here. Not even if it meant saving their lives.

Cassandra turned her ring thoughtfully. Was that true? Would Ava sacrifice her husband's life just because he'd lied to her? She couldn't imagine that she would. Not with the way that people like Anna and Owen admired her so much.

Ava wasn't cruel, she knew. She was afraid. And fear made people do crazy things.

Pushing herself out of her seat, Cassandra gave Anna's hand another pat. "Keep up the good work." She stepped around the chair. "I've got to go check on something."

There were questions from Anna and the brothers as Cassandra excused herself, but she managed to convince them she would be right back, avoiding the demand to take a bodyguard. She slipped past the corridors of bookshelves where Gerard and Owen worked together, cataloging the books while they discussed the history of DeVerre. Then she hurried down the stairs, only stopping by her room to grab her jacket, bag, and keys before she was out the door and in her truck, pulling through the gates of Occasus.

Following the path onto Harmony Plaza, Cassandra glanced to the right. The two parking spots in front of the police station sat vacant—Tom and Hunter both out searching for the missing Robert MacDonald. The marshal had called Spencer yesterday evening. Just as Owen suspected, the town was in an uproar about the mayor's nephew-in-law's absence. But the call was not out of suspicion or a demand for what they knew—it was out of concern.

"This might mean they're killing again," he'd warned. "Like Jess, Taylor, and Brendan's deaths. I'd lay low if I were you. And I'll keep you updated on what I learn."

The brothers and Cassandra all felt a tinge of guilt at the marshal's evident trust in them. He clearly didn't think they could be involved in any way. They were allies now; if there was something Tom needed to know, he expected that they would have told him.

Squelching the lingering guilt, Cassandra caught sight of the dark green Jeep still idled at the tavern. Aaron knelt next to it, changing the tires. He'd called earlier in the day to update Spencer on the estimated return of his prized possession. She couldn't help the dry grin that tugged on her lips as she parallel-parked on the opposite side of the square. The poor guy would be distraught until he got it back.

Cassandra stepped from the truck, intent on her task. She marched right up to the library door, grabbing the handle to yank it open. It wasn't until she stepped inside, the scent of spiced, ginger tea and plant life instantly surrounding her, that she felt the full force of her decision. What was she doing here?

She blinked, staring at the bookcases in front of her. Plants dangled over their sides, giving the library a dangerous, wild atmosphere. It was so different from the library in Occasus—the vault they only knew about because of the woman who ran this one.

Steeling herself, Cassandra curled her hands into fists and pushed through the maze of bookshelves. It was a ridiculous design for a library, she told herself. None of the shelves lined up correctly. They were all different sizes and staggered through the room, forcing you to walk in a zig-zag pattern to the back, where their overseer sat like a queen surveying her kingdom at the large table.

A book lay open before Ava, the woman's long braids hanging around her face like a curtain. She was the opposite of her younger sister in so many ways. Where Anna was refined and sweet, Ava was sharp and aggressive. Abrupt. Indifferent. Disinterested.

Intimidating.

Just like Cassandra.

Ava looked up, a glare in her eyes. "What are you doing here?"

Unable to stop herself from laughing, Cassandra motioned back toward the front door. "I asked myself that exact question when I walked in here."

One of Ava's thick eyebrows lifted in a callous appraisal. "I hope you gave yourself a good answer."

Realizing this was the first time since her return to DeVerre that she'd actively sought out Ava's company, Cassandra felt herself confronted with what she imagined Spencer had meant when he'd called her terrifying the day prior. This woman—the one who despised her for no reason but that she threatened the world she strove to keep under her control—was terrifying to her. Strong, clever, and cunning, she could outtalk most people—including Peter—and she never backed down.

How was Cassandra supposed to make any difference coming here? Why *had* she come here? She shook her head, tossing her arms out the side in a shrug. "I came to apologize."

That caught the woman off guard. Ava sat there, frozen, as she glared at her. Steam rose from the cup of tea beside her, the only movement in the room as Cassandra waited for a response that never came.

Seeing she'd have to keep the conversation going, she continued. "I'm sorry," she said. "I didn't realize that my presence here was causing you so much trouble."

A scowl came to Ava's face. She leaned back in her chair, arms wrapping around her stomach. Her gray and blue flannel bunched around her shoulders, hanging loosely over a white tee.

Cassandra sighed. "And I know that what I can do bothers you. I know that you think it's wrong. That it's evil. But do you really think that Owen could be part of something like that?"

Anger flared in Ava's eyes. "Don't you dare talk to me about my— about *him*."

"Why not?" Cassandra shot back. "He didn't *want* to lie to you, Ava. He was doing what he thought was right."

"You're wasting your time." Ava leaned forward, resting her arms on the table. "You realize that, don't you? Of all people, do you think *you* are the one who will convince me to help you? That what you're doing is just fine? To take back my husband even though he lied to me for over a decade?"

She had a point. What Owen had done was wrong. But he also had a reason. One that Ava would never listen to, which was the exact reason he'd done what he'd done in the first place.

Cassandra met Ava's aggressive stare with a compassionate one of her own. "I'm sorry," she said again, but for a different reason. "I didn't realize that I'd done this to you."

A look of absolute shock made Ava's face fall slack. Whether her expression was due to her confusion or to rage was indecipherable.

Cassandra continued before the woman could recover. "I grew up with them," she explained. "And I didn't know they were ghosts either until our teacher figured it out. I just thought—I don't know what I thought. But I didn't know what they were. And I didn't know where they came from."

"But you do now."

"Yes," she admitted. "And I know that it isn't what you think it is."

Ava gave her a bored glare, but Cassandra held up a hand to stop her before she could start an argument.

"I'm not here to debate the merits of the spirit world with you, Ava."

"Why are you here?"

"To apologize."

"Congratulations, you just did."

"*And* to ask for your help."

The woman didn't even give her the satisfaction of a scoff but turned away with a smug smile.

Cassandra returned the smile. "I know. Ridiculous, right? Why would I ask the woman who hates everything I am for help?"

"Why, indeed."

"Because you're the only one who *can* help us."

"And I won't."

Pressing her lips together, Cassandra nodded. She'd expected it would be difficult. But she refused to give up hope.

Cassandra stepped closer to the table, digging into the bag that hung at her side. She pulled out the stack of papers and set them down with a gentle *slap.* "Read them," she said. "Maybe they'll change your mind; maybe they won't. But they'll give you some perspective on things I'm quite certain you don't know. And beyond that. . . ."

Ava glared up at her as Cassandra pulled in a long breath.

A wave of desperation washed over Cassandra as she felt the weight of everything they now faced crashing into her. She drew her shoulders up in an exaggerated shrug as she passed the woman a sad smile. "I don't want you to be unprepared."

Ava's deep skin blanched. "Unprepared for what?"

"We're not doing this for ourselves, Ava." The words came out hushed. "None of us. It may have started that way, but now. . . . If things don't go well for us . . . well, then you'll have what you wanted, and we'll be gone from DeVerre. But you need to know what will remain without us here to stop it."

Her dark eyes narrowed as though unsure if she believed her.

Cassandra took a step back. "*Someone* needs to know. And I don't think that this town will be safer in anyone's hands than your own."

Ava didn't reply. Nor did she move to reach for the essays.

Taking that as her dismissal, Cassandra nodded to the woman. She'd done what she'd come to do. If nothing else, there was now a backup plan. Someone who would recognize the impending danger within DeVerre that might pick up where they left off. Someone who wouldn't let anyone take her town from her.

Cassandra turned to start back through the maze of books when Ava's sharp words brought her to a halt. "They won't listen to me, anyway."

Looking over her shoulder, she caught the way Ava folded her arms back over her stomach, her chin dipping toward her chest.

"So, whatever it is you think I could do to warn them, I couldn't even if I wanted to."

Shifting to face Ava, Cassandra watched her. "If anyone could, it would be you."

Ava scoffed. "I've never been able to do anything in this town." Her words were taut and rigid. "No one has ever listened to me. Not Sam. Not Tom or Alex. Not Diane. Not Peter or Spencer. Not even my own husband."

The hurt and fear that laced the woman's voice made Cassandra's heart jolt with compassion. She knew what Ava felt. She'd felt the same her whole life.

While she'd been busy trying to understand who she was and what made her different, everyone else had pushed her away, insisting that she should just try to be normal. Urging her to forget everything she believed in so strongly.

And though they were different in many ways, Cassandra realized she had far more in common with Ava than their ages alone. They were both isolated and solitary in their identities—in whom they believed themselves to be and in what they believed to be true.

"I don't think you're right," Cassandra said. She knew she was repeating Spencer's words but wasn't sure if it was because she needed to hear them again or because they were what Ava needed to hear herself. "They may not have appeared to be listening to you, but . . . there's more at play here than you realize. And if you would listen to the people who love and care about you . . . you might find that *they* were listening more closely than you think."

Ava didn't respond, but she didn't react with the disgust Cassandra expected from her either.

Taking it as a sign that she'd done just enough to convince the woman to give the papers a chance, Cassandra nodded toward where they lay on the table. "Give those a read, would you? They might explain some things."

Her eyes flickered to the pages and then up to Cassandra.

"I'll let myself—"

"I'm pregnant."

The abrupt confession made Cassandra trip over her feet as she stepped back. "What?"

Ava gaped as though just as surprised by what she'd said. "I'm . . . I'm pregnant."

Cassandra nodded, still processing through the news. "I—I heard the first time. Why, uh . . . congratulations?"

"Thank you."

The women stared at each other in stunned silence.

Cassandra twisted her ring, waiting for Ava to explain the point of her admission.

Shifting in her chair, Ava pulled her flannel around her. "Owen doesn't know."

Cassandra waited.

"No one knows."

She wanted to ask why she'd told her, but Ava tucked her chin, a haunted expression across her face.

"It's our third," she whispered. "I lost the first two. This is the farthest I've ever gotten."

Cassandra's heart dropped.

So, this was why Ava had reacted with such fear over the past few months. She was protecting the child she thought she'd lose. The future she feared she'd never get.

And then she'd discovered that her husband had spent the last decade lying to her.

"Ava—"

"Don't," she demanded, though the softness in her voice surprised Cassandra. A hush that sounded a lot like exhaustion. "I don't want your pity or apologies. That isn't why I told you."

"Why did you tell me?"

Ava shrugged. "I don't know."

Tipping her head to the side, Cassandra hoped she wouldn't have to prod to get a better answer than that.

"My whole life," Ava's tone was quiet, almost a hiss, "I have done everything I could to keep my family safe. My baby brother and sister. My parents. My husband. I would do anything to protect them. *Anything.* But this town seems determined to tear everything I love to pieces."

Cassandra looked at the plush rug under her boots. She knew that feeling far too well. Everything and everyone she loved seemed to come to ruin within DeVerre's boundaries.

"I won't let my child die."

There was nothing Cassandra could say to that. Nothing that would make the truth any less fearful or brutal. No way she could promise the woman she'd never lose a child again.

The sound of a chair scraping against the carpet and onto the wooden floor beneath drew Cassandra's eyes back up as Ava stood. The woman set her hands on the table, leveling a furious glare at her. Despite her tiny frame and short stature, she made the posture look more threatening than most people twice her size could. "What did you mean?"

Cassandra shook her head, confused.

"What did you mean, I need to be prepared? That something will remain when you're gone?"

The realization that it had worked—that her warning had been successful—sank deep within Cassandra's chest. Ava was listening. For once.

Raising her chin, Cassandra met the woman's fierce stare with one of her own. "We're not alone," she said. "And believe me when I say we're not the ones you should be afraid of."

Peter

When Cassandra returned to the vault after her disappearance, she'd rounded the corner, marching straight toward Peter and Spencer. "Hey," she said, resting a hand on the back of Peter's chair.

"Where've you been?" Peter asked, leaning back to look up at her.

"I had an errand to run."

Spencer narrowed his eyes. "You're not supposed to go out by yourself."

A dry smirk lifted her lips. "It's sweet of you to care, dear, but I'm fine. You guys know where Owen is?"

The brothers shared a look. Spencer frowned as Peter furrowed his brow at her suddenly improved demeanor. Since the meeting with her parents, Cassandra had been sulking. Peter didn't like it, but he also didn't feel there was much he could do if even Spencer had failed to cheer her up.

Peter turned back to her. "Yeah, he just got started upstairs. But we made a deal, Cass. We can't protect you if you sneak out."

She gave his cheek a taunting pat. He jerked away, but she was already heading for the stairs. She took them two at a time, calling out for Owen.

Sitting on the far side of the room as they discussed the genealogy of DeVerre, Anna, Aaron, and Gerard watched her approach. Aaron's introduction to the phantom had thoroughly wigged him out, but he'd come to accept the arrangement in short order. Having dropped off the newly tired Jeep, Haley would come pick Aaron up after her shift at the tavern. It was thanks to Haley that no one knew what had happened at The Glass Tavern two nights ago.

Haley had worked the morning shift after the attack, texting Anna immediately upon seeing the overturned tables and chairs. Without hesitation, Haley had taken care of the situation, promising that she would clean up *and* cover any of Anna's shifts until she was feeling up to working again.

Owen walked into view as Cassandra reached the top of the stairs. "What's up?" he asked, notebook hanging open in one hand, a pen in the other.

"Could I talk with you for a minute?" Cassandra pointed over her shoulder. "Down in Occasus."

Her words made Peter share another look with his brother.

After a slight hesitation, Owen agreed, and the two hurried down the stairs. Owen dropped his notebook and pen on the side table next to Anna, and they headed down the center aisle of the vault out of sight.

"What the heck is that about?" Peter whispered across the desk to Spencer.

Spencer shrugged, sinking lower into his chair. His eyes returned to the pages in Michael Varon's journal. He'd been fixated on the thing since they'd found it, already discovering that Diane's theory about the final Varon held far more validity than they'd thought. It turned out the man knew about the Druids and was working to uncover them with the help of the Garniers and a young woman named Seraphine.

That, coupled with Peter's research on the book they'd found lying open on his desk, told them that the man had also been studying the spirit world in far greater depths than either brother could quite understand. The book was titled: *Introductory Dissertations & Epistolary Selections on the Ether Beyond, for the Attachment of the Called Upon Prophets*. If that hadn't been enough to make Peter's head swim, it was a giant, thousand-page volume that weighed about fifteen pounds, and its author, Dr. Eugene Faulk, was more challenging to understand than any of the papers from Liam's research on its own.

But Michael Varon's notes made the thing a fraction easier to understand. Peter had concluded the book was a collection of essays and letters about the spirit world, either written by Dr. Faulk himself in the mid-1800s or assembled from Heinrich Schwarz, John William Lawrence, a guy named Robert Sheraton, some lady named Ariane Valente, as well as a Gabriel Varon, and a bunch of other people that he'd never heard of. It was all quite intriguing and equally confusing.

As Peter flipped through his research notes, Cassandra reappeared, walking over with her usual confidence. She took the seat next to Peter, smiling at the brothers.

Staring at the aisle, Peter waited. But no one appeared. "What'd you do with Owen?"

She settled into her seat. "He has a visitor."

"A visit—" Peter cut himself off, staring across at Spencer.

His brother looked just as confused, eyebrows raised high on his forehead.

"What the heck, Cass? You disappear, then you get all cryptic on us? What's the deal?"

Cassandra adjusted the collar of her sweater, a smug grin on her face. "It's not really any of your business at the moment." She nodded toward the journal in Spencer's hands. "You finding anything interesting in there?"

Peter held up a hand to stop his brother from replying. "You can't do that."

"Do what?" she asked.

"Change the subject like that."

Cassandra sighed. "I know you're very curious, but you'll just have to practice patience. I'm sure they'll join us soon."

Spencer leaned forward, dropping the journal on the desk. "Come on, Cass," he prodded. "You disappeared on us. It's only fair that you tell us what you were up to."

"How do you know my disappearance has anything to do with Owen's visitor?"

"So, you're saying that someone just happened to show up to visit Owen when you got back to the house?"

Cassandra shrugged, though her amused grin said she enjoyed teasing the brothers.

Peter shook his head, the heavy book restricting how well he could adjust in his seat. "What're you up to, Cass?"

"Nothing, anymore."

"Cassie," Spencer prompted, drawing their attention. He stared directly at the woman, an unusual glimmer in his bright blue eyes.

Peter watched, incredulous. He could have sworn his brother was flirting the information out of their friend.

Narrowing her eyes, Cassandra noticed it too. She smirked at him, shifting to cross her legs. Her arms draped over the arms of the chair as she scanned him.

Certain that he was now a bystander to Cassandra's method of flirtation, Peter suddenly felt he should excuse himself. He didn't want to get in the way of their budding . . . well, whatever it was they were figuring out. But he also didn't have much interest in sticking around to watch it.

Spencer backed down first, drawing back in his seat as he dropped her intense gaze. Peter could have sworn that he saw a flare of red creeping along his brother's collar. "You're the worst," he muttered.

"Flattery will get you nowhere, darling," she replied without sharing his embarrassment.

These pet terms she'd begun using with Spencer made Peter's eyebrows pinch as he looked between the two of them. Something had happened. Something that had made Spencer equal parts more and less comfortable with Cassandra while making her more candid with him. And it could only be due to the private conversation they had a couple of days ago.

Peter reminded himself to ask his brother about it later. "Well, if you won't tell us what you've been up to," he said, "then at least tell us what you've figured out about the beasts."

"All right," she agreed, angling in her seat, so they were both in her sightline at once. "There are twelve kinds of beasts, apparently. I haven't gotten through all of them yet, but I think I found the one that attacked you and Anna the other night."

"Oh, yeah?" Peter's heart thrummed against his ribcage at the thought. He fought against the tightening in his throat, not wanting to show how the memory haunted him.

"It's called a hydra."

"Wait, wait." He held up a hand, recognizing the mythological beast. "Big, multi-headed thing that grows more heads when you cut them off?"

"More creatures from Greek mythology?" Spencer added.

She passed him a glance. "Where do you think they got the inspiration for their mythologies? The spirit world has been around since time began. I assume that means there have been Wielders since then too. Whether or not they knew what they were, people were seeing these creatures and forming stories around them."

Peter shook his head. "That's not what this was, though," he insisted. "It looked nothing like a hydra."

"What do you mean?"

"It had—I mean, yeah, it had like a million serpent-like limbs, but they weren't, like. . . ." He held up his hands as he searched for the words to describe the tendrils of darkness. "They didn't have *heads* on them. They were just arms or something. It had *one* singular and *very* creepy head."

"That doesn't matter," she countered. "This book is just giving a name to what probably has some other name that we'll never truly know. Two separate descriptions don't make something any less the same. The way you'd describe Spencer versus the way I'd describe him would certainly give a different impression to someone trying to create a sketch or a written description based off the information we conveyed. But that wouldn't make the subject of our description anything other than Spencer."

The subject she spoke of edged forward to lean against the desk. "So how does the book describe the monster—the hydra?"

She looked toward the intricate ceiling as she recalled the information. "Serpentine . . . fluid, and . . . ever-evolving." She turned back to them. "It said that they're known for speed and the ability to alter their form to fit within whatever space needed. They move in an almost flight-like pattern, limbs carrying them across space like propellers."

The image was too vivid for Peter. "Yep," he muttered. "That's the one."

Spencer looked about ready to pass out. "So, we've got hellhounds, scylla, and hydras. What else?"

"Well, like I said, there's twelve of them, and I didn't get to read the whole thing yet, so—"

"Hey—" Owen popped his head around the corner, and the three of them jumped. He pointed at Peter. "Could I borrow you for a second?"

Glancing at Cassandra and Spencer before replying, Peter frowned. "There's an awful lot of secret meetings happening right now," he mumbled, closing the book on his lap.

"They're about to end," Owen assured him.

"Fine." Peter handed the book to Cassandra and stood. He followed Owen around the corner into the hall of bookshelves. "What's up?"

Owen pointed ahead of him. "I just need your help really quick."

"Why is everyone being so freakin' cryptic?" He threw his hands in the air just as he caught sight of a shadow on the other side of the door to the vault. The light from the windows silhouetted the figure, making the details hard to decipher. But when they drew near the entrance, he caught the cascade of braids over her shoulder.

Gaping at the woman in shock, Peter nearly tripped over his feet.

Ava rested one hand on the door frame though she made no move to enter the vault. Instead, she was scanning the massive room before her eyes fell on the pair walking toward her.

"Peter," she greeted, her voice flat as they approached.

"Ava," he returned, instantly nervous at her presence within Occasus.

She glanced at Owen, then turned back to Peter, her expression softening. "I wanted to tell you that I'm sorry."

Peter thought his brows had flown off his forehead the way they soared upwards.

"While I'm . . . not thrilled about the circumstances," her dark eyes and the firm set of her jaw confirmed her reluctance, "I realize now there are certain things of which I wasn't aware. Things that you tried to tell me about, and I refused to listen. I'm not saying that I'm any more . . . *accepting* of your opinions or choices."

Peter watched as fury lit her glare. He almost took a reflexive step backward.

"But I'll be damned before I let *anyone* take my home from me."

Realizing that he was still gaping at her, Peter clamped his mouth shut and swallowed. "Okay," he mumbled lamely. "What, uh—"

"I want to help you," she explained without him having to finish the question.

Scratching the back of his head, Peter tried to reconcile the woman's change. He glanced at Owen, the man's face a blank mask. It hit Peter in an instant. She hadn't taken him back. Not yet, at least. She may have listened to his side, determining that they weren't in the wrong, but neither had she accepted that they were totally in the right.

Peter understood that Ava wasn't joining the team; she was granting them the temporary benefit of her knowledge to take back control over the town.

Either way, Peter decided it was a victory for them. And they'd be stupid to refuse her help.

"Yeah." He tossed his hands to the side. "Yeah, of course, we'd love your help. That's what we've wanted this whole time, Ava."

She gave him a sharp nod. A strange, almost apologetic furrow pulled down her brow. However, she made no move to enter the vault.

Owen stepped forward. "Could you invite her in?"

"Huh?" Peter looked up at him in confusion.

"She can't get in."

"What are you talking about?"

Ava went to put her arm through the doorway and into the vault, but it stopped abruptly as she tried to cross the threshold. Her palm pressed against an unseen barrier. "It appears your vault doesn't permit uninvited visitors," she explained.

Peter stared at it, wondering at the others who'd joined them in the vault. When they'd first entered, it had been him and Spencer. Then Cassandra, Owen, and Anna walked in right behind. Had they invited them into the vault? He supposed that he had.

Then in Gerard's case, Peter and Spencer had spoken with the phantom before they'd entered the vault that morning. The man had given his apologies and offers of help, at which they'd decided that they could use all the help they could get. So, they'd accepted the apology, thanked him for the offer, and Peter had said, "Well, then, let's get inside and do some work."

Finally, Aaron showed up with the Jeep and asked if he could get more answers that afternoon. As Peter had answered the door, he'd said, "Sure, man. Come on upstairs. We're all in the vault, so you may as well join us."

As offhanded as the invitations were, they *had* been invitations.

"Uh—right, yeah." Peter waved a hand in Ava's direction. "Come on in."

Instantly, Ava's hand flew past the place where the barrier had held it steady. She glanced wide-eyed at Owen before stepping through onto the luxurious floors of the vault. Her eyes never stopped moving as she took in the space.

Peter turned to Owen. "I don't understand," he said. "How is it that I'm the one who can let people in?"

"It's your house," Owen said as though it should be obvious. "When the Varon estate fell to you, the ownership of the vault came with it. And I don't think it's just you. As Spencer owns 50% of the estate, I'd guess that he has the same authority. You're just the one who takes the initiative."

He couldn't argue with that. Spencer always let Peter take charge of those sorts of things: introductions, invitations, social meetings, everything.

Ava continued to scan the vault, though her wary expression said she was listening as Owen continued, "I'm presuming it's why you and Spencer were the only ones to see the entrance."

Pressing his lips together, Peter considered that. "Then why didn't we see it before? We'd searched this whole place for days. Shouldn't we have seen it?"

He shrugged. "You weren't Wielders yet."

"But Spencer isn't—" Peter's mouth dropped open, the idea springing into clarity in his mind. He took off down the hall. "Spence!"

His brother was standing behind the desk as he barreled around the corner. "What?" he asked, a look of concern on his face.

A huge smile split Peter's face as he hurried around the desk, grabbing his brother's shoulder. "Dude!" He gave him a shake. "You're a Wielder!"

"What?"

"Owen just said so."

"But . . . how would he know that?"

The couple came around the corner with a notable distance separating them. Ava's gaze drifted longingly behind her at the dozens of shelves they passed, but Owen kept moving, the dispassionate expression painted on his face clearly an effort to tamp down his disappointment at the rift between him and his wife. He joined them at the desk. "I don't know for sure," he contradicted. "But I assume it's true. I don't see how you would have discovered the vault otherwise."

But Spencer didn't seem to hear the explanation as he stared at Ava, glancing at Cassandra and then back. He didn't get a chance to voice his surprise as Aaron and Anna bolted up from their couch at the sight of their sister.

Ava turned at the sound of Anna's gasp. She raised her thick eyebrows, lips pursed. "So," she muttered, her steady voice heavy with irritation. "My whole family is more loyal to the Collins brothers than they are to me."

Anna looked shamed, while Aaron just looked nervous, as if they were the younger siblings trusted to handle themselves alone and had broken a family heirloom.

Ava scoffed. "It's fine."

Peter didn't think it sounded fine. And by how she and Owen avoided looking at each another, he was certain he was correct.

The discomfort didn't lessen even as Anna rushed over to hug Ava, Aaron following casually behind. The Lambert siblings conducted a hushed and lengthy discussion about how they'd become part of this investigation. No one asked if Ava had taken Owen back, the signs clear as he stood separate from the three siblings. When the trio turned back to the group, they sat down to bring her up to speed.

First, they introduced her to Gerard. And while she didn't seem to immediately disapprove of the phantom as her husband had, she did act wary of the idea of his presence in general. They updated her on the cause of Debbie Mercier's condition, Tom Garnier's allegiance, and all the other information they'd collected over the past month.

After explaining the attack at the tavern, the subsequent threat, and their studies in preparation to defend their home, Ava dropped the hand she'd been holding over her mouth as they spoke. Her jaw set and her eyes implacable as she took in the information, she spoke firmly. "The library is closed tomorrow. I'll spend the day here getting this place figured out." She turned to Owen, her gaze no less fierce. "Will you show me your notes and the layout?"

"Of course." He held her stare unflinchingly.

Her nod was sharp. "Once I understand this place, I can help you all determine the best direction for your study."

"You don't think we're studying the right things?" Peter asked, feeling attacked by her presumed role of authority.

Ava smirked at him. "I have all the family lines of DeVerre memorized. The genealogical research that Anna, Aaron, and Gerard are doing is a waste of time. It wouldn't surprise me to discover that your book of essays is too. At least when it comes to fighting Druids."

Though he felt like she'd knocked him down a peg, Peter couldn't fault her logic. Ava knew far more than she'd said. They'd always known that. And having her on their side made winning this fight feel far more possible.

While Owen gave Ava what was sure to be an awkward tour of the vault, the rest of them got back to work. She'd reassigned Anna to set up the resident lists for her to overview later while she asked Aaron and Gerard to bring her all the books they could find on Druids within the vault. Cassandra was back to reading her book on beasts on the couches with Anna while Peter and Spencer sat at the desk, dumbfounded.

"Did Ava just become the new leader of our group?" Peter muttered.

Spencer grunted an unintelligible reply before clearing his throat and sitting forward in his chair. "Am I a Wielder?"

"Oh." Peter realized they'd dropped that conversation prematurely. "Yeah, I mean . . . it seems like it."

"But how? I didn't do anything."

"You found the vault."

"*You* found the vault."

Peter rolled his eyes. "I pointed it out, but you'd already noticed the light radiating from off the handle yourself. It wasn't just me."

"What if you're wrong?"

"Why would I be wrong? And why would it matter if I was?"

"Pete," Spencer's voice was tight, "if we go into Sunday thinking that I'm a Wielder and I'm not . . . I'll be a liability."

With a grimace, Peter supposed his brother had a point. "Yeah, well . . . even if you are a Wielder, you may not be like the rest of us."

Spencer tipped his head to the side in confusion.

"You might not be able to wield arcs," he clarified.

"Right." Spencer rubbed a hand over his face. "Right, that could be a problem, couldn't it?"

Peter saw the panic starting to rise in Spencer's demeanor as he stared off into space. "But," he added quickly, "why wouldn't you? If I figured it out on the first try, surely you will too. You've always been a faster learner than me anyway."

"That's just because you don't pay enough attention when someone's teaching you."

"Well, I didn't have anyone teach me how to be a Wielder. And neither did you."

"But you figured it out first."

"Because I had to," Peter insisted. "Look, out of the two of us, I would have put money on you figuring it out before me. And you're a black belt, dude. You'd be ten times more dangerous than me as a Wielder, even if you couldn't wield arcs."

None of that seemed to encourage his brother.

"Plus," he grinned, hoping to distract him, "you're the one with a Wielder girlfriend. If anyone's gonna pick it up quickly, it'll be you."

Spencer glared at him.

Peter smirked. "I wouldn't be surprised if you're one of those Archsages, or whatever, in no time."

"She's not my girlfriend."

"You sure about that?"

"Pete."

He shrugged. "You two seem to be getting awfully flirty these days."

Spencer leaned back in his seat, lips smashed together as he lifted the journal from the desk and began to read again.

Peter wanted to push the subject. It was fine if Spencer was nervous or even simply embarrassed. He'd always been overly cautious when it came to dating and relationships. But Cassandra wasn't just some woman. She was their friend and their roommate. And Peter really liked her. He didn't want his brother screwing up a good thing just because he was too scared to make a move.

But Peter also didn't want to be the one who screwed up whatever was growing between the pair either. So, he relented and picked up his own book to study. Ava hadn't assigned him another task yet, so he kept on with the monotonous tome, praying that something in it would make sense. But the contents were too heavy and theological for him to truly grasp any of the concepts involved.

After several hours, Aaron joined the two of them at the desk. "I've gotta head out," he said, tugging on his heavy jacket. "I wish I could come back and help you all tomorrow, but I've got work pretty much all day, and I promised Haley that I'd spend the night with her at the tavern since she's picking up Anna's shift."

"Right." Peter patted the man's arm. "Appreciate your help. We'll, uh . . . see you Sunday?"

Aaron shifted uncomfortably. "Yeah." He glanced between the two of them. "For sure."

But there was nothing sure about it. Not when Sunday morning would bring a fight for their lives.

"I, uh. . . ." Aaron ran a hand over his buzzed hair. "I want to offer my help. . . ."

Peter glanced at Spencer in the wake of the unfinished sentence. Aaron wanted to offer his help . . . but what could he do? He wasn't a fighter. He was a mechanic. And Peter knew perfectly well that neither he nor his brother blamed the guy for feeling like he had nothing to contribute to keep them safe.

"I have a rifle," Aaron offered. "And a handgun. It's not smart to live in the middle of a forest without some form of self-defense against bears, wolves, and . . . other things like that, you know? I could . . . I could—"

"It's cool, dude," Peter assured him. "These aren't bears or wolves that we'll be fighting. And I'd rather not have you tied up in all this when . . . when people start dying, you know?"

Aaron didn't look convinced. In fact, he seemed upset. "I want to help."

"We don't even know when they're coming, Aaron," Spencer cut in. "The best way you could help us is by being with Owen to ensure that Anna, Ava, and Haley are safe while we figure this mess out up here."

"I won't be with the rest of them," Owen said, rejoining them on the bottom floor of the vault, Ava just behind him. Cassandra and Anna drifted over from the couches, Gerard hanging behind as he flipped aimlessly through a massive genealogical book.

Peter frowned in Owen's direction. "What are you talking about?"

"I'll be here," Owen clarified. "With you three."

"Come on, man. You've got a family that needs protecting."

He raised his brows. "And I won't be able to do that on my own. Without you three to help us, DeVerre will fall into Druid hands. So, my priority is making sure you all stay alive."

Ava stepped up to stand at his side. "Besides, we'll be here."

"What?" Peter gasped.

She motioned toward Anna and Aaron. "The three of us, and Haley, will be here in the vault when the Druids arrive."

"What—how—why *on Earth* would you think that's a good idea?"

"Because they can't get in here. This vault is the safest place in DeVerre."

The reasoning was sound. Still, Peter didn't like the idea of them waiting in the vault while the rest of them fought the Druids right outside. "And what happens if they kill us all?"

The weight of the question fell upon the room leaving only the crackle of the fireplace roaring in their ears.

"They can't get in here while Spence and I are alive," he concluded. "But if they kill both of us, then what happens?"

There was another silence in which Spencer let out a low scoff.

They all turned to him.

"If we die—" Spencer nodded across the room. "The house falls to Cassandra."

They turned to her.

"Oh, God," Cassandra whispered, the words a desperate prayer for help. She pressed her hands to her face in shock, covering her mouth and cheeks. "That's what they wanted."

"What?" Anna asked at her side.

Understanding dawned on Peter. "That's why they sent the hellhound after us," he realized. "They were trying to kill us so the house would fall to you. And the vault with it."

Cassandra, Spencer, and Peter shared concerned looks. The Druids had been planning this—preparing to kill the brothers—for far too long.

"Okay." Peter nodded, trying to come to terms with it all. "Okay, yeah, so . . . we already knew they wanted us dead. So what? If they kill us, the house falls to Cass, and they won't kill her. That's good."

"Pete," Spencer muttered. "They'll make her let them in."

"I won't." Cassandra's voice was hard.

"They'll *make* you, Cass."

She shook her head. "I'll die first."

"Then what?" Spencer argued. "If you die, what good does that do us? We don't even know whom the house will fall to after you."

"Next of kin," Ava said.

A thread of uncomfortable silence stretched through the room.

"Who is . . . ?" Peter prompted.

"Well, as she's not married, has no children, and I'd presume, no will of her own—" Ava shrugged. "Typically, her closest living relative would inherit. I believe both of your parents are still living."

"Yes." The word gasped out of Cassandra.

"Then, it'd fall to them."

"It can't."

"It would."

"No," Cassandra insisted. "If it falls to them, it falls to the Druids."

Ava raised her brow. "Your parents are Druids?"

Peter stepped forward, thinking he might have to intervene with the growing intensity in the room.

But Cassandra didn't appear to share in the frustration as she twisted the signet ring she wore. "No, but . . . my mother. . . ." She sighed. "My mother and Debbie made a deal with the Druids—my life in exchange for my absence in DeVerre. When I returned . . . well, that's what got my mother involved in a car accident that nearly ended her life. They wanted me gone so they could kill Diane."

"And they wanted us dead," Spencer added, "so the house would fall to you."

Cassandra nodded. "It seems that way."

"Then," Peter said, bringing the conversation back to the point. "The vault *isn't* the safest place in DeVerre unless Spence and I are alive. Because once the two of us die, Cass's life will automatically be forfeit. And then it's just a matter of time before the Druids get Mrs. Clement up here to invite them inside."

"Unless I write a will of my own," Cassandra countered.

"Do we have time for that?" Spencer asked.

"How hard is it to write a will?" She stepped over and grabbed a piece of paper and a pen from the desk. Leaning down, she scribbled out a few lines. "There. 'I, Cassandra Clement, being of sound mind, hereby declare this to be my last will and testament. Upon my death, I leave everything I own to Owen and Ava Bernard in equity.' How's that?"

Everyone turned to Owen and Ava as though the two of them had the answers. The couple looked at each other, the unresolved nature of their marriage adding a charged energy to their hesitant glances.

Ava shrugged. "Technically, it's legally binding even if she doesn't get it filed, as long as she and two witnesses sign it."

Owen nodded. "I'm not sure the spirit world would care if it's legally binding, anyway. If she has declared intention to leave the house to someone else upon her death, I'd imagine the spirit would override the physical."

"But just to be sure. . . ." Ava turned to the three at the desk. "Cassandra, sign it. Peter and Spencer, sign it as witnesses."

The trio did as ordered and turned back to her.

"Now—" Ava flashed them a satisfied smile. "The vault really is the safest place in DeVerre."

CHAPTER TWENTY-FOUR

Peter

It had been Spencer's idea—calling their mom. He'd always been the better son, though. Thoughtful, respectful, and obedient. But the joy that filled Mallory Collins-Powell's voice when she answered the phone made Peter's heart erupt with bittersweet emotion.

They weren't going to tell her the truth, they'd agreed. There was no reason to call and inform her that they were thirty-six hours away from fighting a mysterious cult of Druids who were intent on ending their lives. Fourteen years ago, when Peter and Spencer had promised to care for each other after their dad's death, they'd also promised to take care of their mom. To be sure that she was happy and never saw the brokenness that had settled into both of their lives with the loss of their father. They knew that she couldn't handle it. Not while she carried a broken heart of her own.

And they weren't about to break her heart again, knowing that her only children's lives were in far greater danger than any they'd ever written into their stories.

So instead, they asked about Norfolk, their stepdad Ben, and the Collinses. They listened to her bright, cheery voice through the speaker on the porch of Occasus as she rambled for several minutes, both of them smiling as she laughed at all of Peter's joking interruptions. Peter and his mother had always been two peas in a pod. Not only did they share their dark eyes, but they also shared their personalities—energetic, playful, and passionate. She never got upset with him for talking too much or going off on weird tangents because she did the same herself. And they were both wildly protective of Spencer.

When she'd asked them about DeVerre, they kept their responses neutral. Yes, the house was amazing, and they were very grateful for the chance to own it. No, they couldn't wait for her to see it either. Yes, it would be strange being apart for Thanksgiving for the first time. Maybe she and Ben could come to stay with them for Christmas. Yes, Mom, they were making friends. No, neither of them had a girlfriend yet. "Though Spencer—ow!" Peter exclaimed, stopping mid-sentence as Spencer punched his arm.

"What was that?" Mallory asked, suspicion raising her tone.

Peter rubbed his arm as Spencer glared at him. "Nothing," he mumbled.

Mallory wasn't convinced. But she let it go, clearly trusting that her sons would tell her when there was news that she needed to know.

Guilt left Peter's body feeling hollow as they said their last "goodbyes" and "love yous." He didn't like lying to their mom. Especially not when there was a possibility this was the last time they'd ever speak to her.

But he tapped the screen and ended the call anyway.

Peter slumped back in the vintage porch chair, staring across the lawn of Occasus. The faded grass was almost amber in the sunset. Purple and orange painted the cloudy sky, the sun's last light barely making it over the pine trees surrounding their home.

They'd come out to the porch to escort Ava and Anna out as the two of them headed home together. Peter didn't want to let them out of his sight with the threat of danger hanging over their heads, but Ava insisted they'd be fine and would return in the morning to work in the vault once more.

When Spencer had the idea to call their mom, it made sense to stay on the porch. Owen and Gerard were working in the vault, but Cassandra had offered to make dinner. In want of privacy, they'd grabbed their new coats and braved the cold.

Now Peter shivered, and he crossed his arms to deaden the chill that numbed his fingers. Turning to Spencer, he caught the rigid tension in his brother's jaw as he stared at the wrought iron gate. Nex sat contentedly at Spencer's side, muzzle resting on his master's knee.

Peter couldn't help the wry grin that came to his lips at seeing the dog's attachment to Spencer. Both dogs loved him from the moment the brothers had arrived at Occasus. And they'd hated Peter.

But the dogs had grown used to Peter over the past month and a half. Or at least, they were indifferent to him now. They no longer growled or snapped at him, allowing him to coexist in their space with a detachment that said they found him acceptably non-threatening. However, that didn't mean that Peter had any interest in giving them an affectionate pat on the head anytime soon.

"Hey," Peter said, breaking the silence, "I know it's probably really stupid to be concerned about this, but. . . ."

Spencer turned to him, eyebrows raised curiously.

"Don't we have an episode of *Wenzel & Frankly* due this Sunday?"

A disbelieving scoff puffed out of Spencer; a moment later, it turned into a full-fledged laugh. Peter joined his amusement at the ridiculous notion that four hundred readers were expecting an episode while the two of them were about to walk into a fight for their lives.

"I finished my edit two days ago," Spencer said as his laughter faded. "It's scheduled to release at 10AM."

"Cool."

"Mm."

The phone on Spencer's armrest lit up with a text notification, and they both glanced down at it. Peter frowned at the name on the screen. "So," he met his brother's eyes, "you're talking to Danielle now?"

Spencer cleared his throat, then gave a small shake of his head as he slipped the phone into his pocket. "She's been wanting to come by and see the dogs."

"The dogs, huh?" Peter replied, doubtful.

"Yeah. She watched them while the will was in probate."

"Sure."

"What?" Spencer demanded, glaring at him.

"Nothing."

"Oh, don't do that. If you have something you want to say, say it."

Peter shrugged, seeing it as his opportunity to get the answers that had eluded him for the past two weeks. "Okay, fine." He held Spencer's challenging stare. "You're not allowed to date Danielle. She could be a Druid like Robert for all we know."

The bitter smirk pulling on the corner of Spencer's mouth gave Peter no doubts of his brother's irritation. "First off," Spencer said, voice flat and acerbic, "you don't get to tell me who I can and can't date. Second, I have no interest in dating anyone, let alone Danielle."

Peter screwed up his face, equally as disgruntled as Spencer. "Well, *that* better not be true."

"I thought you just said—"

"You're supposed to date Cass."

Spencer's head whipped around to the window behind them as though Cassandra would be able to hear them all the way from the kitchen. When it was evident she was nowhere in sight, he turned furiously back to Peter. "Look, you gotta cut that out," he ordered. "If you keep saying stuff like that, she's gonna start thinking that I like her. And then things will get awkward, and she won't want to work together anymore."

"She lives with us, Poirot," Peter said. "She's our friend, not our co-worker."

"And I'd like to keep her as a friend."

Peter narrowed his eyes. "Then you might want to stop flirting with her. I think you're sending mixed signals."

Spencer ground his teeth together, sucking in an impressively intimidating breath. Nex yawned and settled at Spencer's feet as though bored with their conversation.

"What happened between you two the other day?" Peter prompted, watching his brother closely.

Rolling back his shoulders, Spencer turned to the yard instead of answering.

"Dude, if you guys want to be a couple, it's no big deal," he insisted, trying to give him the encouragement he needed. "We're all waiting for it to happen anyway."

"What?" Spencer gasped, jaw dropping.

Peter shrugged, pleased with the reaction. "Annie and I have been expecting you to make a move for weeks now."

Slowly, Spencer began to nod as if understanding was dawning on him. "All right," he murmured. "All right, fine. If we're gonna talk about Cassandra and me, then we're gonna talk about you and Anna."

"So, you admit that you and Cass are a thing?" he asked, attempting to deflect.

Spencer ignored his quip. "What's up with you and Anna?"

"Nothing."

"Yeah, right."

Peter pressed his lips together and began adjusting uncomfortably in his seat. "Nothing is going on."

"You've had a crush on her since we moved here. Now, even though you almost got her killed, she's on the team and working surprisingly hard to keep you alive. You're telling me that's nothing?"

Still squirming, Peter shook his head. He leaned forward, arms on his thighs. He didn't want to talk about this. He'd intentionally ignored working through it himself for the past week. There were things that Spencer didn't understand about his relationship with Anna. Things that Peter hadn't foreseen when they'd started growing close. Things that he hadn't anticipated when he'd worked up that ill-fated crush on her during their first weeks in DeVerre.

But, Peter supposed, if anyone could help him figure out what to do about Anna Lambert, it was his brother.

"Nothing's going on, Spence," he admitted, surprised at how empty his own voice sounded. "I'll be honest, I kind of thought something might happen, but . . . it's the same as ever. I'm the friend, not the boyfriend."

Spencer took in his sudden change in demeanor. "What if you're wrong?"

"I'm not."

"What if she changes her mind?"

Peter shook his head. "I don't want her to. I'm . . . I like Anna, but . . . she chose Connor a long time ago. A guy who couldn't be more opposite of me. And the idea of trying to take his place in her life . . . it feels like a mistake."

"A mistake, how?"

Swallowing the lump in his throat, Peter stared at his hands. "Do you remember Beth?"

Spencer scoffed. "How could I forget? She was your worst girlfriend."

"We were never official."

"She still led you on before dumping you when her ex came back."

"Exactly," Peter said, eyes locked on the porch railing before him. His gaze traced the faded grain of the wood as he spoke. "I know what it's like to date someone else's girl. And it doesn't feel good—always being in the shadow of a man who isn't even in the room. I don't have any interest in competing with a ghost."

Spencer was silent, listening as Peter knew only his brother could. Taking in both the words he was saying and the ones he wasn't.

"It doesn't matter what she says or that she's trying to let go. Anna's not over him," he continued. "And she won't be for some time. If she ever is."

Spencer gave a weighted exhale.

And somehow, Peter felt as though everything came into sharp focus with the sound. He looked over to meet Spencer's attentive gaze again. "I don't want to be someone's second choice."

Spencer nodded and clapped a hand on his shoulder. He didn't say anything, but he didn't have to.

Pulling in a deep breath, Peter slapped Spencer's knee. "It's too cold out here," he said, moving to stand. "We should see if Cass needs any help."

~

Peter was the last to wake, as usual, and was, by extension, the last to the vault the next morning. Owen read in the wingback chair on the far side of the sitting area while Ava went over the genealogy notes with Anna on one of the couches. Aaron and Haley were supposed to join them late that night to stay in the vault with Anna and Ava—though Peter didn't think anyone had fully explained the situation to Haley yet.

Tossing a greeting in their general direction, Peter moved to join Cassandra and Spencer at the desk. The dogs lounged at their feet.

Peter took the empty seat next to Cassandra and set his mug on the desk. "You guys working on the same stuff as yesterday?"

"Mm," Spencer murmured but didn't look up.

Cassandra, however, turned to him with a sigh. "Yeah. And it's getting old. There's only so much you can read about beasts before everything starts to sound the same. They're made of shadow. They hate light. They're violent and dangerous and laser-focused on their tasks until they complete them. It's boring."

"Huh," Peter muttered, glancing over his shoulder toward Ava. The rudimentary information reminded him of their conversation in the library and her troublesome accusation about the beasts.

Turning back to Cassandra, he nodded to the book. "Anything in there suggested that they're, oh, I dunno . . . demons?"

Cassandra's eyebrows rose as Spencer looked up from the journal.

"Just curious."

Tapping her thumb against the pages, Cassandra pursed her lips. "Technically? No."

The tension in Peter's throat eased instantly.

"I could see how some people would assume that they're demonic, though," she added, reversing the effect. "They certainly have similar qualities, and . . . I mean, I got my Bachelor's in theology, and as I had a particular interest in studying ghosts, demonic influence and how demons may make their appearance in our lives came up fairly often in my research.

"Some of the things I've read *could* sound similar to what they're describing in this book," Cassandra conceded. "However, I also get the feeling they're not the same."

Peter and Spencer shared a questioning look.

"What makes you say that?" Spencer prodded.

Cassandra rested her arms across the book's open surface. "It's pretty clear to me that these beings don't influence the natural world—our world—without being summoned. A Wielder *has* to let them through the Veil. Everything I've ever read about demons suggests that they're already present. Like angels are. It doesn't seem they're part of this spirit world we're harnessing. Or, at least, not in the same way."

Her theories somehow managed to reassure and unnerve Peter all at once. "Do you think Owen would know for sure?"

"I doubt it," Spencer muttered, his eyes drifting beyond the two of them. "Seeing as how he suggested that Cass study beasts to help us fight the Druids, I'd imagine he doesn't know much about them, to begin with."

"Fair point."

Cassandra pinched the bridge of her nose, releasing a long sigh. "I feel like this is a waste of time," she whispered, her voice just loud enough for the two of them to hear. "We know enough about the beasts now to know they can be destroyed by two means: arcs or light."

"Or fire," Spencer offered, a distracted sound in his voice.

She passed him a knowing look. "Right. So why am I reading this when there is so much more to figure out?"

"I know what you mean." Peter gave the massive volume awaiting him a dismissive glare. He didn't feel like picking it back up. And he had to admit that he thought Ava was right the previous day. He didn't see how it would help them fight the Druids.

Spencer flipped a page in the journal. "You two could check out those letters," he suggested, his eyes narrowing on a line.

Remembering the letters that Spencer had given him on their first night in the vault, Peter snapped his fingers, then pointed to Cassandra. "I forgot about those. I gave 'em a once over but didn't want to waste too much time. Michael had a lady pen pal."

"Oh?" Cassandra's dark eyebrows arched high with interest. "You think he was writing love letters?"

"No," Spencer cut in.

"No?" Peter asked.

He pointed to the book. "He had a thing for Seraphine."

"What?" Peter leaned forward in interest. "Dude, that's huge! Why didn't you share before?"

"Because we know it didn't work out. There are no records of Michael Varon marrying anyone, let alone Seraphine."

Cassandra tipped her head to the side. "Maybe because she caught him writing love notes to this mysterious pen pal?"

Spencer didn't look convinced. "He likes her," he argued. "A *lot*."

"What are you trying to say, Matlock? They were having an affair?"

"Not . . . not exactly."

"Not *exactly*? How about generally?"

Spencer scratched his forehead nervously, ruffling the waves of hair lying there. "I'm currently reading his entries from 1937. The journal spans to his death, but he wrote most of them before early 1939. Anyway, he and Seraphine haven't talked much until the past few entries because she was trying to throw the Druids off or something. But they've been getting to spend way more time together because no one's paying attention to her anymore. And. . . ."

"And what?"

Glancing at the journal, Spencer's ears grew pink. "He just kissed her."

Peter snorted. "Way to go, Michael."

Cassandra smirked, a playful glimmer in her eyes. "You mean Michael Varon was chronicling his love life?"

"No," Spencer said, then paused. "Well, I mean . . . kind of. Just stuff about Seraphine. As I said, he likes her a lot."

"That's too bad." Cassandra sighed, then swatted Peter's arm. "Let's read those letters and see if they'll give us anything else to go off of."

Though Peter wanted to hear more about Michael Varon and what happened with the woman, he knew Spencer would have to read more before he could tell the rest of the story anyway. He hopped up, grabbed the stack of letters from the desk, and hurried to follow Cassandra toward the fireplace. Anguis followed them.

"Here." Peter gave Cassandra half of the stack. "I'm not sure if they're in any particular order, but we should probably figure that out first."

There were about twelve letters total. Some were double-sided and multiple pages in length. It didn't take long to organize, but reading the tiny, looping script was difficult. And with only one-sided correspondence, it was equally difficult to get the full context of the conversation.

However, Cassandra grabbed Peter's arm as she started on her third letter. "What?" he asked, looking up from his own.

She didn't answer him but looked across to the others. "Owen."

The man lifted his head from the book he was reading.

"Didn't you say that the Varons were following a prophecy?"

"Yes." His lifted tone was curious. "They were originally in Paris when one of their closest friends told them they needed to journey to Nova Scotia and make their way across the continent."

"And in 1884, they got the next bit of the prophecy, right?"

"Right. To come to DeVerre and protect the Veil."

Cassandra grinned, eyes alight with excitement. She held up the letter. "It was this woman," she said. "Elizabeth. She was the one who told them to come here. And she was in contact with the Varons the whole time."

Ava sat up straighter on the couch across from them. "The last of the Varons died in the '40s. If she'd been in contact with them the whole time, she would have written them letters for fifty-six years."

Peter doublechecked the dates and names on the letters. "She was. This one is the first one—to Matthias Varon in 1883."

"And this is the last," Cassandra said, holding up a letter from the bottom of her stack. "To Michael Varon in early 1940."

Peter stared at the letters. They all had the same handwriting and signature, so there was no doubt the sender was the same. "This lady must've been old."

"And they're all prophecies?" Owen asked.

Peter thumbed through a few of his. "Not necessarily. Some are just simple conversations. You know, 'how are the kids,' 'mine are fine,' 'did you figure out that weird rash.' Stuff like that."

Cassandra narrowed her eyes as though she doubted the accuracy of the last line.

Waving his hand to brush off the made-up conversation, Peter continued. "The point is, whether they're prophecies or not, this lady was important." He lifted the top letter. "Important enough that she's the reason DeVerre was founded in the first place."

Owen nodded, running a hand along his light beard. "What did you say her name was again?"

"Elizabeth."

"No last name?"

Peter and Cassandra shuffled through the letters together. He looked at her when they'd both checked their stacks, but she shook her head. "Nah, but . . . well, there's this weird marking next to her name on all of them," he said.

Owen held out his hand. "Can I see that?"

Peter passed a letter to him.

The man stared at the page for several seconds before Ava extended her hand without a word. Owen hesitated but relinquished the letter to her. Her dark eyes narrowed on the bottom of the page. "I know that symbol."

"You do?" Peter exclaimed.

She nodded, still staring at the signature.

"Do you know what it means?" Owen asked.

"No, I . . . hmm." She turned to Anna. "Do you remember the necklace that Mom wore?"

Anna nodded. "Of course."

Ava showed her the letter. "This is the same symbol, right?"

Peter felt the blood drain from his face. "Your mom is Elizabeth?"

Ava frowned at him. "No. That wouldn't be possible, but. . . ."

"Maybe they're related?" Cassandra said, looking at one of the letters in her own hands. "Why else would she wear the same symbol?"

"I don't know." Ava tapped her fingers along the back of the letter in thought. "My mom inherited that necklace from her father. Technically it was a ring, like the one you wear, Cassandra. It was too big, so she wore it on a chain. She promised to leave it to me one day. She said it was a gift to the Rayne family when they came to DeVerre."

Anna looked down at the letter in her sister's hand. "This is the one from 1883, right?"

"Yes."

Anna's eyes flashed over the page, her finger tracing the lines. "There." She pointed, then read aloud: " 'I've enclosed a package for

Yvan as a thank you for his help. Please be sure he gets it and knows that. . . .' I can't read that name. Is it Cora?"

Ava shook her head. "No, it's. . . ." She narrowed her eyes. "Corva."

"Corva?" Peter repeated, a tingle running along his spine. "Who's that?"

"I don't know."

Anna resumed reading with the corrected information. " 'Please be sure he gets it and knows that Corva sends her regards. There is a future of great value in his lineage, and they shall change the tide.' "

The sisters shared a look.

"We're Yvan's lineage," Anna whispered.

Ava hesitated. "We don't know that it means us."

Owen shifted uncomfortably in his seat. He scanned his wife and sister-in-law with a nervous and enlightened gaze. Then he turned to Cassandra. "What does the last letter say?"

"Huh?" She gaped at him, pulling her attention away from the sisters. "Oh, right. Um. . . ."

They all watched as Cassandra pulled the yellowed letter from the stack. Peter peered over her shoulder, heart roaring in his ears. This was getting weird. Even for DeVerre. Prophecies, lineages, and coincidences that linked Anna and Ava to the spirit world in ways they'd never known? He didn't like it.

Cassandra lifted the letter. " 'Dear Michael,' " she began. " 'I hope this finds you well. . . .' Hm, she's just greeting him . . . asking about his father . . . giving regards from mutual acquaintances. Ah! 'I regret that my time has come to an end. This will be my last letter to you as I will die within the month.' "

Peter frowned, reading the lines with her as she said them aloud.

" 'Please take heed of these last words as this is the. . . .' " Cassandra's voice caught as Peter felt his heart stutter. " 'This is the end of it all. Do not fear but remain steadfast in the truth as we pursue what is beyond this veil together.

" 'The age of the Varons is coming to an end in your town of glass. A day is swiftly approaching that will force you to make a choice.' " She sucked in a sharp breath before she continued. " 'To protect either your family or the truth. Only one will remain, and the other must perish. I have no doubts that you will make the right choice, my child. Your father raised you rightly, and though many have sought to bring your family to ruin far longer than your lifetime, do not think they will have succeeded. Not even as they wipe your very name from their records. The Varons will fade, but they will rise again more powerful than ever.

" 'Corva assures you that the finality of the Varon line within DeVerre will last for not a century but will—with your absolute devotion to the truth and to the guardianship placed upon your shoulders— resurrect to restore that which was stolen from you.' " Cassandra glanced first at Peter, then at the others. " 'The Children of Gaia—these Druids of old—will not hold your town forever. When the harvest is ready, they will be cut down and separated, like tares from wheat. Your own blood will restore the cracks that have marred the surface of the glass. And they will establish a future that . . . that will. . . .' Oh, God help us."

Peter gaped over her shoulder at the rest of the line.

"What?" Ava prodded.

Owen sat with his hand on his chin, and Anna stared at them with wide eyes as Peter shifted in his seat. Cassandra just kept shaking her head, unable to continue, so he picked up where she stopped. " 'They will establish a future that will set the spirit world free.' "

Cassandra nearly dropped the letter, and Peter grabbed it from her before it could fall to the floor. He held it up to Owen. "Didn't you say that the *Druids* wanted to set the spirit world free?"

"Yes," the man confirmed.

"So why would this Elizabeth woman suggest that the Varons would want that?"

"I don't—"

The sound of a chair toppling on the far side of the room interrupted, drawing their attention as Spencer stood abruptly. Nex jumped away from the falling chair behind him. Spencer lifted one arm into the air as if calling for their attention, eyes still locked on the journal in his other hand. His face had turned as white as a ghost's.

Peter stood, sure that it couldn't be good. "Spence, what—"

"He married her."

They all stared at him, but Peter knew what he meant. As their eyes locked on one another, he knew what his brother was going to say. He could feel it in his gut. Even as Spencer took his time, walking around the desk to join them.

Peter took a step forward, nodding to confirm that he knew the truth.

Spencer let out a disbelieving laugh. "Michael married Seraphine in secret," he said. "And she had their first child in April of 1938. A daughter they named Diane."

Cassandra started, shifting to the edge of her seat. Expressions of shock and understanding flashed across Owen, Ava, and Anna's faces.

But it didn't surprise Peter. Somehow it solidified what he'd already known.

"Their first child?" he prompted, just to be sure.

Spencer hesitated, looking at the journal. "I haven't gotten that far."

"Look," he ordered.

Lifting the book, Spencer began flipping through the pages.

Cassandra twisted her ring anxiously, moving to stand next to Peter. "1940," she said. "Phillip was born in October of 1940."

Some might find it strange that Cassandra knew their grandfather's birthday better than they did, but Peter knew that Diane had told her everything about her life. She'd told her everything about the two of them too. Sharing the date of her own brother's birth was a given.

The pages furled under Spencer's thumb, the *whoosh* of paper the only sound in the room as they all held their breath to hear it confirmed. He grabbed the book more firmly in his hand, flipping back two pages before he resumed scanning its lines.

Peter stepped around Cassandra, headed for his brother.

Spencer looked at him, blue eyes bright with hope. He held the journal out for Peter to see as he pointed to the lines. *"It is my deepest regret,"* it read, *"being a distant father. But it is the truest joy to know I now have a son as well as a daughter. Our sunshine, Diane, and our new ray of light, Phillip."*

Lifting his gaze, Peter couldn't help the sense of importance that flooded him. The weight of a name—of a family sworn to protect the Veil—was like a mantle worn across your shoulders. It gave you purpose. It gave you significance. And it changed everything about who you were.

Peter scoffed as he reached over to pat Spencer's cheek. "Would you look at that, Sherlock?" He smiled at his brother. "We're Varons."

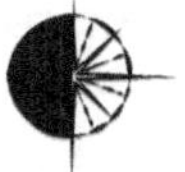

CHAPTER TWENTY-FIVE

Spencer

"We're Varons."

When the words left Peter's lips, it was as if a key turned inside Spencer's chest, unlocking a door long held shut. He felt a tremor roll from his shoulders to his arms and down through his fingers. They were Varons.

Beyond his brother's shoulder, Spencer watched as Owen and Ava stood. Anna stayed in her seat, looking no less in awe. But it was Cassandra who held his attention. He watched the way she stood, the backlighting of the fireplace radiating in a glow around her. She looked at him and his brother as though seeing them for the first time.

"We're Varons," Spencer repeated.

Cassandra's eyes locked with his, and he wondered what she felt at this new revelation. He knew how he felt. Whole. Complete. Like the part of him that he'd always thought was missing had suddenly returned to him.

How odd it was, Spencer thought, that an ancestry he knew so little about could give him that.

But for the first time since his father had died, Spencer felt confident. He felt secure, knowing who he was. The world could crumble around him; it wouldn't matter. They were Varons, after all. DeVerre was their town. It was their home. It was their birthright. And he wouldn't let the Druids take it from him.

Owen stepped around his chair, round eyes growing to almost twice their size. "You're sure?"

Nodding, Spencer offered the journal to him. "The dates all line up. Diane and Phillip were Michael Varon's legitimate children, but he didn't raise them because he feared what would happen if the Druids found out. When he and his wife discovered her pregnancy with Diane, they decided to convince the town that a man had taken advantage of her, but she wouldn't reveal his name out of fear of his retaliation. They kept their relationship a secret from everyone but his father."

"That's so sad," Anna whispered.

Spencer couldn't disagree.

Ava crossed her arms, glancing at the genealogies on the table beside her and then back to Spencer. "You said Seraphine, right?"

"Yeah," he confirmed. "That's all I have, though. He didn't give a last name or anything."

"I don't need it." She gestured to the book. "Seraphine was the town secret herself. It isn't surprising that she chose to live like that. She'd been living in the shadows her entire life."

"What do you mean?"

"Back in 1914, while he was still at university, Lloyd Frossard had an affair with a young woman in Spokane and got her pregnant."

Spencer's heart skipped a beat.

"She didn't want the kid, terrified the scandal would ruin her life, so he agreed to take full custody. He sent the child back here to DeVerre for his parents to raise as a 'distant cousin's mistake.' He was only twenty or so and didn't have a family of his own, so he managed to keep it a secret from the majority of the town. But he didn't fool *everyone*. My great-grandfather worked out the conditions of Seraphine Frossard's birth and detailed it in our private records, despite the town's official genealogies' ignorance of it."

Peter's mouth dropped open as Spencer tried to catch his breath. "Seraphine *Frossard*?" he managed.

Anna stared at Peter like he was a whole new person. "You're related to Connor."

With a scowl, Peter drew his shoulders back. "Well, I *don't* like that," he grumbled. "You're positive she was a Frossard?"

Ava nodded.

"It would make sense," Gerard interrupted, appearing on the balcony above them.

They all stared up at him.

"Where've you been all day, Gerry?" Peter glowered.

"I've been around," he replied with a bored tone. "Reading and the like. But it explains all of Diane's research. Why Lee took the children to the Collins family. Why they let them go in the first place. If she was a descendant of the Frossard line, they'd want to be sure their blood was safe."

Cassandra dropped onto the couch with a heavy sigh. "It's why they were allowed to live," she whispered.

"What?" Peter asked.

"They were part Frossard," she explained. "They didn't want to kill their own family."

Spencer gestured to the journal. "But their mother was a Frossard too. What happened to her if they didn't let her keep her kids?"

"She died," Ava said. "Seraphine Frossard's grave marks her death on December 21, 1940."

"Two days after the death of Michael Varon and his father," Gerard added.

"That's awfully convenient," Peter mumbled.

"So, they killed her? Why?" Spencer asked, but the pieces came together as the words fell from his mouth. Running a hand over his face, he saw the rest of the puzzle fall into place. "The Frossards are the Druids."

Anna's face erupted in panic as the rest of them turned to stare at Spencer.

"I knew it!" Peter exclaimed, a sardonic smirk coming to his face.

"Oh, shut up, you did not." Cassandra rose again and moved closer to them with an intense stare set on Spencer. "We know that the Sauveterres are linked to the Druids. That much we have proof of. What proves that the Frossards are Druids too?"

Motioning to the journal, Spencer couldn't help the humorless laugh that came out of him. "She was working against her family, Cassie," he explained. "It's why she and Michael kept their relationship a secret. He never listed them by name, but he mentioned that her family was the cause of everything. It was her family they were fighting to bring down, and that was why he admired her so much. He called her the bravest woman in the world—willing to fight against family while still living amongst them. She was a double agent."

"And it got her killed," Cassandra surmised.

"It seems like it."

Owen lifted a hand to point at the journal. "Did Michael say who the leader of the Druids was?"

"Yeah. Seraphine's father."

Owen gave a single, solid nod. "Lloyd."

Anna dropped her head into her hands, and Ava turned to wrap her arm around her sister's shoulders. "If Lloyd Frossard was the leader of the Druids in the '40s," she said, voice sharp and protective as she held her sister. "Who's inherited the role?"

"His son?" Spencer offered.

"Which one?" Ava asked.

No one responded.

She sighed. "Lloyd had two sons: Wallace and Bill."

Still no response.

"Which was older?" Owen suggested.

"Wallace."

"Probably him, then."

Gerard scoffed from above them. "You clearly don't know your DeVerrean drama." He scanned them all with his cutting, dark gaze. "Wallace Frossard and his father never got along. He and I were close in age, so he was around my crowd quite a bit. He didn't like how demanding and narrow-minded his father was. His father didn't like how disrespectful and foolhardy his son was. Lloyd usurped the rights of the firstborn and passed everything onto the younger son."

Ava let out a hum of thought. "So, the leadership got passed to Bill. Which is a problem."

"Why?" Spencer asked.

Her arm tightened around Anna. "Bill died in 1995, which means that . . . the leadership of the Druids would have been passed to *his* son."

A small groan came from Anna. "Bill was Alex's father," she whispered. "Connor's grandfather."

Peter looked like he'd been punched in the gut as he turned to Spencer.

At a loss for how to help his brother, Spencer began flipping through the journal again. "Michael mentioned several names in association with Seraphine's family a while back. I can find them, and we can figure out exactly who the Druids are."

"Good." Owen nodded. "Then we can hand the list over to Tom and he can take care of it."

Spencer pulled his brows together, but Peter took the initiative. "Your moral code is inspiring, dude, but think about it for half a second." He crossed his arms, leveling him with a stare. "How fast do you think one marshal and his deputy can round up who knows how many Druids by tomorrow morning?"

Drawing his shoulders back, Owen looked ready to fight them. "We aren't doing this ourselves."

"I'm not suggesting we do," Peter argued. "But we can't leave it to Tom to do it on his own either. Yes, we figure out who the heck all these Druids are. But then we call Tom and have him join us in taking them down *tonight*."

"Tonight?"

Spencer understood his brother's plan in an instant. "We can't wait for them to come here," he agreed. "We know who their leader is: Alexander Frossard. There are four of us, plus Tom. If we go to the Frossards' tonight, we can take down their leader. Then we take care of the rest of them over time. But if we wait for the marshal to handle it alone, they'll kill us before he gets the chance."

"Four of you, huh?" Gerard called above them, a snarky thread in his tone. "You sure you're ready to face a Druid untested, kid?"

Glaring up at the phantom, Spencer didn't flinch. "I'm a Varon," he reminded him. "And this is *my* home. They drove us out once. Now Pete and I are here to take it back."

While the rest of them were quiet in the tense silence that followed, Peter slapped Spencer's chest with the back of his hand, a grin on his lips.

Spencer felt the tremor rising within him. He was ready to find the Druids and reclaim his home.

Owen huffed, scratching his forehead as he shrugged. "Varons," he mumbled. He tossed Peter a look of recognition. "It makes sense now."

"What does?" Peter asked.

"A Sage Wielder on the first try? I should have guessed you were a Varon then."

Cassandra shifted next to them as though wary of standing too close to two men who might be bursting with so much power that they could explode at any second. "So, what's our plan?" she asked, eyeing them cautiously.

As Spencer puzzled at her sudden discomfort, Owen answered her question. "We do what they said. I'll call Tom and tell him to meet us here as soon as possible. Then, once we figure out our plan, we take down Alex."

"Are you . . . ?" Anna's words faded as she stared up at them, her eyes drifting to rest on Peter. "Are you going to kill him?"

Peter looked like a deer caught in the headlights as he rubbed his hand along his jaw and struggled for words. "Well, uh . . . I mean, I—I don't— I dunno. Only if, uh . . . only if we have to, I guess."

The downtrodden look on Owen's face told Spencer that he thought they *would* have to.

Anna shook her head. "He's Connor's dad," she whispered. "What if . . . ?"

Peter's whole face lost color, and Spencer didn't think any of them needed to hear the rest of her question to know what it had been.

What if Connor was a Druid too?

Spencer had never met the guy. From Peter's description, it wouldn't be far-fetched to think of him as a villain. For Connor to have been best friends with Anna Lambert for almost twenty years, though—so close that a kindhearted, caring person like her could fall in love with him—surely he couldn't be all bad.

"We'll figure that out later, Annie," Peter whispered back, voice devoid of emotion. "We just gotta take care of the first step: regaining control of DeVerre."

Drawing his shoulders back, Peter turned to Spencer and set a hand on his arm. "Read the rest of the book, yeah?" he suggested. "Figure out who might still be working with Alexander, and we'll work out a game plan with Tom when he gets here."

Spencer nodded, seeing his brother's need to feel like he was doing something. To have a task to distract him from what was coming. "I could use someone to cross-reference names and dates for me," he said, hoping to give his brother something constructive to do.

Peter scanned the rest of them in thought, thumb brushing the side of his nose. "Right, that's a good idea," he muttered. He swatted Spencer's arm. "Cass'll help you."

Certain that his brother had misunderstood his intentions yet again,

Spencer pressed his lips together and looked at Cassandra. She was twisting her ring, brow furrowed as she stared back at him.

Gesturing for her to follow him, Spencer sighed. "Let us know if you need anything."

~

The hours crept by as they continued their studies. Time moved strangely within the vault. With no windows or clocks beyond their phones or watches, it was as though the world could stop around them if they wanted it to. If they tried hard enough.

But the illusion wasn't real, and time moved on without asking for approval.

They'd called Aaron and told him not to come over as plans had changed. Then Owen called Tom and informed him that they needed his help. Spencer still wasn't convinced that involving the marshal was a good idea, but desperate times demanded unprecedented trust in even the most unexpected allies.

The town was in a panic with Robert MacDonald's disappearance, Tom had told them, and he'd been working hard to find the man and pull together a search party. He didn't want to leave the station too early, fearing he'd arouse suspicion if he abandoned the case. So, when he took his first steps into the vault, dusk was already on the horizon.

While Owen, Peter, and Tom strategized at the fireplace, Ava and Anna continued working on the genealogies with new information in mind. Gerard disappeared before the marshal arrived to maintain his secrecy. Though, Spencer didn't see the point much anymore.

When Peter invited the marshal in and explained all their news, Tom's mouth fell slack. "You're Varons?" He scanned both brothers— Spencer behind the desk and Peter at his side. "Looks like the Guillaumes are in for a rude awakening."

"What are you talking about?" Spencer asked.

Tom scoffed. "The second this town finds out you're Varon descendants, there will be two responses: The ones who supported the Varons back in the '30s and '40s will transfer their support to you. And the ones who didn't will want to kill you. Either way, everyone is going to see your presence here as a claim for DeVerre."

The brothers stared at him in concern.

Ava crossed her legs as she leaned back on the couch. "He's right. And once you remove the Druids, you can count on the townspeople demanding that you take leadership."

"Eh. . . ." Peter grimaced as he looked down at Spencer. "That's not . . . that's not really our thing."

With a snide grin, Ava raised her brow. "You're a member of one of the founding families." She shook her head, then corrected herself. "Of *the* founding family. You don't have a choice anymore."

Spencer and Peter frowned.

Cassandra smirked as she tapped her pen on the desktop. "Look at it this way," she teased. "If one of you becomes mayor, you won't have to worry about losing the house to me anymore."

"I'm twenty-six," Spencer argued. "I'm not old enough to be a mayor."

"Actually, within the state of Washington, the legal age of election is eighteen," Tom offered. "So, either of you *could* take the job."

Peter gave a dramatic shiver at the thought. "On that pleasant note—" He tossed a hand toward the couches. "Shall we get to work?"

And there they'd huddled for the rest of the afternoon. While the others were concluding their plans to pay Alexander Frossard a visit, Spencer and Cassandra were working through the final few pages of the journal. He'd wound up sitting on the same side of the desk as her so she could see the names as he found them. They'd discovered far more than he'd have liked. The names of the Frossards and Sauveterres were expected, but their list also included the MacDonalds, Laflammes, Guillaumes, Dumonts, and even a few Alaries.

They'd counted a minimum of twenty names listed within Michael's journal. And Spencer was sure that couldn't have been all of them. But if there were twenty Druids within DeVerre in the '30s and '40s, how many more were there eighty years later?

As Cassandra wrote down the name of her own grandfather, Keaton Sauveterre, Spencer watched the way she chewed on her lip. Some of her dark hair hung over her shoulder, casting a shadow on her face that defined the sharp lines of her cheekbones even more. The small hollow that typically only appeared when she smiled, showed now as she worried her bottom lip.

Though they'd already known Cassandra's family was amongst the Druids' ranks, Spencer didn't like how close the relationship came. It made him uncomfortable, imagining she should have been one of them. If her mother and Debbie hadn't intervened, she really *would* have been the enemy Ava had alleged.

The idea sat like a lead weight in Spencer's stomach. Going up against the Druids was frightening enough. Going up against Cassandra? That was downright insanity.

While they'd waited for Tom's arrival, Owen had joined them at the desk. He'd run a hand over his trimmed beard, eyeing Cassandra cautiously.

"What's up?" Spencer had asked.

Owen glanced at him but turned back to the woman at his side. "I feel the need to warn you," he began.

Spencer and Cassandra drew their shoulders back in surprise, sharing a nervous look at the man's ominous tone.

"Warn me about what?" Cassandra asked.

Owen moved to sit on the edge of the desk. "I'm concerned," he admitted, keeping his voice low, "about your abilities."

Though she faced Owen, Cassandra's dark eyes flickered toward Spencer. He did his best not to show his shock at the man's words, but he couldn't help his hand flexing to release the tension rising in his chest.

Cassandra's chin rose in defiant confidence. "Because my powers are stronger than they should be?"

With a single nod, Owen confirmed it. "Yes."

"Hang on," Spencer interrupted, holding up his hand. "You said the same thing about Peter just two days ago."

"And at that point, I was equally concerned about his sudden burst of power," Owen replied. "But that was before I knew you were Varons."

"How does that change anything?"

"Varons are always powerful. More than anyone else."

Spencer tried not to let his chest puff too notably, hoping his own powers would come through when they needed it most. "So why should Cass's power be any more concerning?"

"For the same reason that Peter's was before this revelation of your heritage." Owen leaned forward, his dark blue gaze overwhelming in its intensity. "No one makes these leaps this quickly. It's one of the reasons I was willing to consider the idea of Cassandra being a Druid. With little to no training, she managed to tether a phantom and control a hellhound. Speaking to ghosts is one thing. Advocates pop up all the time. But Clerics take training nine times out of ten. And Sages?"

"It's impossible?" Cassandra concluded for him. "And since I'm not a Varon, it's problematic."

Spencer glanced at her, throat tight in anticipation of the answer to his next question. "Do we *know* that you're not a Varon? At least in some way?"

She smirked at him and reached over to pat his hand. "Don't worry, darling," she teased. "I've been studying my ancestry for the past week to find the Druids in my line. There wasn't a Varon in sight."

He couldn't help his instant relief.

"Which is, indeed, problematic," Owen added.

"Why?" Spencer demanded. "Because she's powerful? Shouldn't we be thankful for that?"

"It's not that simple, Spencer," she whispered, smoothing over his instant defense of her. Then she met Owen's stare. "I know. And I'm just as concerned as you."

Owen's stance softened at her admission. He nodded. "I'm glad to hear it. But I'd still like to warn you: Be careful about when you choose to access the spirit world. The longer you draw on its essence, calling forth an arc, for example, the more danger you put yourself and the rest of us in."

Spencer's jaw tightened as Cassandra's eyebrows pinched together. "What do you mean?" she asked.

"The more you wield the essence, the more you open yourself up to the spirit world and *all* its influence," Owen explained. "And that makes it far more likely for you to give into its pull. Especially someone like you."

"Give into its pull, how?"

He shrugged. "That depends on the Wielder. Some draw even greater power into their arcs. Others begin to call on the power of the Veil itself. And others start to open portals and summon forth beasts."

Cassandra's dark eyes dropped to the notebook in her hands. Spencer could practically feel the tension of her fingers gripping the pen in her hand on his own tight shoulders. He wanted to reach out and take her hand, to reassure her that he didn't fear what she might do. He knew that no matter what, she'd only do what it took to save their lives. Just as she had when she'd destroyed Debbie's soul to rescue them.

Spencer swallowed past the dryness that leaped into his throat as he returned to the present, still staring at the hollow in her cheek. Even after Owen had left, her nerves remained, and she'd grown distant as they'd studied the journal.

Turning back to the book in his hands, Spencer pressed his lips together and forced down his concern for her. "Um," he muttered, flipping through the remaining handful of pages left. "I think that's probably it."

Cassandra glanced at him. "Probably?"

"I can handle the rest myself," he said. "I don't think he's going to name many more from how he's going on right now."

"What do you mean?"

Spencer fingered the edge of the page, the paper scraping against his skin. "Well, he's . . . he's talking about how scared Seraphine is now. She told him that she overheard her father discussing the Druids' plans and that they were in danger. He wrote that he knows they're going to die and . . . he's preparing for it."

"Oh." Cassandra smoothed down the front of her sweater.

"It seems like these last few pages are part of one entry where he's . . . basically he's processing how he feels about dying."

"I see."

They sat silently, and Spencer wondered if he should say something. He wanted to promise her that he wasn't afraid of her power. That it didn't concern him the way it so clearly concerned her and Owen. But he couldn't get the words out.

After their conversation the other day, Spencer only felt capable of putting his foot in his mouth as he had then. He knew he'd screwed up, being so honest with her. He couldn't believe the words that had almost tumbled out of him. The admission would have ruined everything between them.

Spencer hadn't lied to Peter. Not really. He did like Cassandra as a friend. And he wasn't interested in a romantic relationship with her. But only because he was too afraid of losing her if he screwed it up. He couldn't risk damaging the amazing friendship they'd already built after just a month of knowing one another. He found her to be the most incredible woman he'd ever met, but he couldn't risk it. It was too soon. And he wouldn't lose her before he'd even had a chance to know her.

But the other day had almost ruined everything. He already felt the awkward distance that had grown between them. He feared that if he spoke up now, the words he'd kept at bay in the foyer of Occasus would burst free, destroying every good thing about their relationship in their wake.

Rising, Cassandra laid the papers on the desk. The weight of Owen's warning curled her shoulders down. Her gaze averted from his even as she turned to leave. And Spencer knew he couldn't stay silent anymore. Not when they were about to face the Druids.

Cassandra couldn't hold herself back because other people were afraid of how strong she was.

Keeping his voice low so as not to draw the attention of others, Spencer hurried to speak before she could move away. "Hey, Cass?"

She halted no more than a few inches from the desk. "Yeah?"

"I just. . . ." The words died as she met his gaze. He didn't like the way she did that to him—rending him speechless with a solitary look. He wondered if she even knew she had that sort of effect.

It was infuriating, really, and he felt like an idiot for it.

Spencer forced himself not to falter under her direct stare, swallowing past the lump in his throat. "I'm sorry," he said, the words unexpected to his ears.

Cassandra's sharp brows pulled together as she tilted her head. "You're sorry?"

Shifting in his seat, Spencer tried to understand the meaning of his apology. Was he sorry? "Yeah."

"For what?"

That was an excellent question, Spencer thought. What *was* he sorry for?

For finding her attractive? Not really. That was a compliment to her character and beauty more than anything.

For the mess they were in? Sort of. But he didn't have any more control over that than she did.

For Owen's warning? He certainly didn't appreciate their friend convincing her she was dangerous. But he had to wonder if it wasn't Owen alone who'd given her evidence to support the idea.

Spencer pressed his lips together, resolved in his response. Yes. He was sorry that she thought of herself as a danger, as though she were a problem or an outcast from the world. And he feared that he'd contributed to that misconception of herself.

"I think. . . ." Spencer sighed, ran a hand through his hair, and tried again. "After our conversation the other day, I owe you an apology."

Cassandra backed up and took a seat on the edge of the desk.

"I know I said some kind of . . . harsh things." Spencer worked not to stumble over his words as she smirked at the understatement. "And I just—I wanted you to know that I didn't intend them to—to sound like I . . . I didn't intend them to be hurtful. So, I'm sorry if they were. I just wanted you to know that you're not alone. And that you matter to us."

Her expression lightened as though his words were softening her. But the discomfort didn't fully disappear.

Spencer took a deep breath, preparing to fix the last bit of damage he'd done. "And I just want you to know that I disagree with Owen. I don't want you to interpret anything I said the other day to mean that I think you're dangerous. Because I don't. I think you're amazing."

Her lips twitched and her eyes narrowed.

Spencer blanched, hearing the insinuation in his words. "Not that I— gah, sorry." He hurried to get his point across to her, holding his left hand out in the air as he tried to clarify his position. "That came out wrong."

"It did?"

"Yeah, I—I—I'm not trying to. . . ."

The glimmer in her eyes blended amusement and confusion as she watched him panic.

Spencer ran a hand over his face. "I'm sorry, I feel like that came across wrong. I didn't mean to suggest that I—I'm not trying to say I have an interest or anything. I just—I just want you to know that I think you're great."

Cassandra's smile deepened, the hollow growing on her right cheek. The glint in her eyes grew into a playful shine. "Let me see if I understand," she replied, her voice pitched as low as his. "You're saying that despite the fact that you find me intimidating to the point of being afraid of how *amazing* I am—that you're terrified of not being enough for me, I believe is how you put it. . . ."

She let the thought linger as she scanned him.

Spencer didn't like how she was using his words against him. But he refused to drop her accusatory stare.

Her brows lifted as she completed the question. "You don't have an interest in me?"

He opened his mouth to confirm it, but nothing came out.

Cassandra's smirk turned into a soft smile. "Hm . . . that's too bad." She clucked her tongue against the roof of her mouth as she slid off the desk. "I hoped you did."

As she took a step to move away from him, Spencer felt his hand shoot out on its own accord. His fingers wrapped around hers, keeping her in place. The tremor he'd felt pulsing through his limbs earlier returned, her hand so soft and warm in his. The signet ring on her finger cut into his palm, but he wasn't aware of anything other than her hazel eyes staring down at him.

A dare hung between them, goading as they waited to see who would speak first, demanding they break the silence and say they meant it. Really, truly meant it.

Cassandra's smile fell, her head angling toward him. "Spencer?" she prompted with a whisper.

Sure that he heard the invitation within her voice—the request to hear him be absolutely honest with her—Spencer swallowed past the dryness in his throat. He tightened his grip on her hand and rose to say it face-to-face.

But he didn't get the chance.

"Sorry to interrupt you all," Gerard said, suddenly appearing at the base of the stairs.

Everyone in the vault jumped, but Spencer was sure no one startled as much as him. He yanked his hand away from Cassandra's as though it had burned him, and he practically leaped onto the desk in his rush to pull away.

"What the hell?" Tom exclaimed from the far side of the room.

"Sorry, marshal, we don't have time to explain." Gerard leveled a glare at Cassandra and Spencer. "Seems your plans are going to have to wait."

"Why?" Peter asked.

But Spencer could already see the answer in the phantom's piercing expression as Gerard spoke again. "The Druids are here."

CHAPTER TWENTY-SIX

Cassandra

An icy chill tore through Cassandra's veins. The Druids had come for them.

Everyone stood throughout the room, nerves and anxiety etching each of their faces.

"But it isn't Sunday," Peter insisted.

Gerard nearly growled at Peter. "Clearly, they don't care. They passed through the gate less than a minute ago. They were moving to surround the house."

"Then we don't have any time to lose," Spencer said, stepping around Cassandra. His arm brushed hers in the process, but she didn't let herself enjoy it even after the way he'd held her hand moments ago. "How many were there?"

"I didn't stick around to count."

"And you can't give us an estimation?"

Gerard shrugged. "Maybe around a dozen or more."

A dozen or more. Cassandra twisted her ring. That estimation didn't do them much good. With Owen, Peter, Spencer, and her defending Occasus as Wielders and Tom functioning as a gunner, they could probably handle twelve, though likely with a bit of difficulty. But more? That would change the odds entirely.

Tom's hand rested on the pistol at his side. "This isn't what we planned for."

"But it's what we're facing." Owen gestured for Spencer and Cassandra to join them.

Anguis and Nex followed on their heels.

"All right," Owen said, eyes downcast in thought. "It appears we're going to have to face what we'd hoped to avoid. If the Druids are here, they intend to force you three from Occasus."

Peter edged to stand beside Cassandra and Spencer.

"What if they're just here to ensure you leave by morning?" Anna offered. "We could play like we're all here helping you pack up, and you could still go take down Alex."

Peter shook his head, giving her a sad smile. "That's not why they're here, Annie."

Tom tapped his fingers along his belt. "She could be right."

"Even if they were," Cassandra interrupted. "They wouldn't let us drive out of town without an escort. And how would we explain your presence here, Tom?"

"We don't have time to discuss this." Owen's voice was firmer than usual. "If they're surrounding the house, they're preparing for an attack, and we don't have time to sit around perfecting a plan. Tom—" He turned to the marshal. "We'd appreciate your help in this, but this will not be the type of fight you're accustomed to. The Druids won't use weapons like that gun you carry. They'll wield the spirit world's essence."

"They'll what?" The marshal gaped at him.

Knowing they didn't have time for detailed explanations, Cassandra raised her right hand, a trickle of power thrumming across her skin as the grayish ivory flash of a rift rippled around it.

Tom jumped back in surprise while Ava and Anna stared at her. She recognized the struggle between awe and worry in their faces. She'd felt it herself the moment she'd first brought forth a rift by a mere act of will.

"We call them arcs," she clarified.

Owen watched her as though he wished she wouldn't have accessed her power so readily, but she didn't particularly care. The time for caution had ended; action was all they had left.

"Arcs hit the soul," Owen explained. "Not the physical form."

"Though it hurts like hell to get hit," Spencer added. "And your body sort of stops working for a minute."

Remembering how Debbie's arc had sent Spencer flying back to land with a heavy *thud* on the floor before he lay there like a dead man, Cassandra let the rift dissipate. She'd felt utterly helpless at that moment. Alone and useless as the Collins brothers lay dying.

The memory flickered away as Cassandra stared at the two of them standing side by side before her now with wavy brown hair, strong shoulders, and ready stances. A small grin crossed her lips. They weren't the Collins brothers anymore—they were the Varon brothers.

Setting a hand on each of their shoulders, Cassandra leaned closer to Spencer. "Don't you worry," she gave them each a teasing glance, "I'll be there to keep you both safe and sound."

Peter smirked at her. "We can protect ourselves this time, Cass."

"Have you met us?" Spencer's elbow tapped gently against her ribcage. "We'll always need Cassie to save our lives."

Warmth rose, spreading through Cassandra's chest. They could do this. They *had* to. Whatever the rest of the world thought of her, Cassandra knew these brothers were her family. The only people she'd ever truly trusted beyond Diane. And she wouldn't let anything touch them. Not while she was still breathing.

"You're running out of time," Gerard warned.

Owen nodded. "We have to assume they'll enter the house."

"If they haven't already," the phantom added.

"I think we need to sweep the place to be sure they can't sneak up on us." Owen gestured to the brothers and Cassandra. "You three stick together. Varons or not, you two have had little to no experience fighting Druids or wielding essences. Cassandra, you take the lead. I'll take Tom with me."

"They're coming for the vault, right?" Peter asked. "We could just make them come to us."

Owen shook his head. "They'll wait us out."

He had a good point. There wasn't any food, water, or even a bathroom within the vault. They could manage for some time within its protected walls, but it couldn't last for more than a day or two at most.

And while they weakened within its walls, the Druids would be ready to take them down once they stepped outside.

"So, we take the fight to them," Spencer concluded.

"Tom and I will clear the second floor and make our way to the back of the house," Owen suggested. "While the three of you head to the first floor to barricade the front door."

Cassandra disliked the idea but knew it made the most sense. Even though Owen's abilities were much more developed, the three of them were capable of three times his power's strength. Plus, Tom was practically a liability rather than an asset in this situation.

Turning to the marshal, Cassandra tipped her chin toward him. "If it comes down to it, are you going to be all right with shooting people you may know as family and friends?"

Tom shifted uncomfortably, but he nodded. "I know what I'm up against. I'll do whatever I must to make my town safe again."

"Pretty sure it's their town now," Ava remarked, nodding to the brothers.

While the rest of them took that in, Ava moved to take hold of her husband's arm. He looked down at her in surprise. "This is not a reconciliation," she said, direct as always. "But as you're about to risk your life, you need to know something."

Cassandra shifted between the brothers, sure she knew what Ava was about to confess. She tugged on their sleeves, drawing them back a step.

Husband and wife stared at each other, the separation between them unnatural.

"You're not allowed to die," Ava demanded.

Owen gave her a sad smile. "I promise I'll do my best not to."

"No, Owen," she returned. "*You're not allowed to die.* Because I won't raise our child alone."

Peter and Spencer shared a look, before turning to Cassandra. She continued slowly drawing them backward with her. Anna held a hand to her cheek, edging away from her sister and brother-in-law to give them space. Tom and Gerard just avoided looking at the couple altogether.

"You're pregnant?" Owen gasped.

Ava nodded. "A little more than three months."

"What?"

"You're not the only one who knows how to lie," she said, then began to step away. But Owen didn't let her go.

He reached out, wrapping one arm around her waist to lift her onto her tiptoes as he bent down to kiss her full on the mouth.

Spencer's jaw dropped. Peter's eyes drifted to the ceiling, his fingers tapping against his thighs. But Cassandra couldn't help smiling smugly at the couple. They were both stubborn and idealistic. And they were perfect for each other.

Owen pulled away, releasing her completely. "This isn't over," he said firmly. He stepped back and looked at Anna. "We'll be back in a bit. Take care of my wife."

Anna nodded, still shocked, as Owen turned on his heel and walked toward the entrance of the vault. Tom followed, ready to be free of the awkward moment.

Still gripping the sleeves of both brothers' shirts, Cassandra started to follow. "See you soon," she called to Anna, who had moved to Ava's side, both sisters staring in awe after Owen.

"Be safe," Anna eked out, her eyes lingering on Peter.

Anguis and Nex bounded forward to catch up with them, and Spencer broke free of Cassandra's grip. "Hey." He held up a hand to them. "No, you're staying here."

The dogs stared at them with knowing amber eyes, their animated, wiry brows drooping in concern.

Cassandra's heart melted, but Spencer remained strong. "Stay," he ordered.

Both dogs sat, watching as he began to back down the hall.

Then Spencer turned, brushed a hand against Cassandra's arm, and guided her and Peter down the center hall of the vault. The carpet was soft, absorbing the sound of their footsteps as they neared the door.

The deep orange light of dusk flooded through the large windows as they stepped into the third-floor room. The light burned Cassandra's eyes, the sunset beaming into its namesake. Occasus was Latin, meaning sun-setting or end. The home was meant to be a rebirth for Diane, an end to her questions and a beginning of answers. But she'd gotten none of that.

Yet here Cassandra stood, flanked by the nephews who had managed to uncover all those answers Diane had searched for after only a month and a half of entering DeVerre. The sunset might not have come in Diane's lifetime, but it was here now. And in the end, her quest led to the rebirth of the Varon family.

When Cassandra had heard the truth of their ancestry—when they'd revealed Diane as Michael Varon's daughter—she felt it in her gut. And she couldn't help the overwhelming sense of sadness that her closest friend in the entire world had lost her family all because of the Druids that threatened them. From the sounds of it, Michael and Seraphine would have been loving, caring parents. Ones who would have supported Diane, fostering goodness and happiness in their daughter's life. And maybe, if the Varons hadn't become extinct in DeVerre for eighty years, they could have stopped the Druids long ago.

Catching the twitch of Spencer's hand mere inches from hers,

Cassandra couldn't help her regretful smile. If the Varons had never left DeVerre, these brothers wouldn't be here today. In fact, Cassandra might not be there either. Her own grandfather had been a Druid. It was a miracle she hadn't become one herself.

She supposed she should thank her mother for trying to protect her in her twisted way. If she hadn't lied to Cassandra, she never would have returned. She would never have found the brothers running from a hellhound, and she would never have found the family she'd always wanted.

Peter grabbed the handle of the vault's door, slowly pulling it shut behind them. It latched with a *click*. And then it faded from view.

Fumbling with the hem of his shirt, Peter nudged Spencer's arm. Spencer looked down at the item his brother proffered: the small black handgun, snug in its holster.

"Just in case," Peter muttered.

Cassandra watched nervously as Spencer accepted the gun, taking a second to slip it into his waistband. She didn't like the idea of him going into the fight with his powers untested. And she wasn't sure a gun would be much better at keeping him safe against beasts.

"I can see them," Tom said, standing in the shadow of the far window, gun in his hand. The light had dimmed to almost nothing, only the faintest brown glow on the horizon shone amongst the blue-black of night. He gestured carefully to the lawn. "Your friend was right. They're pressing in. Slowly, but they're headed for the house."

Cassandra's heart rate kicked up. "They haven't entered yet?"

"Doesn't seem like it."

"I wonder why they're being so cautious," Spencer muttered, edging closer to the windows.

Tom extended a hand to halt him. "Stay back," he warned. "If they see movement inside, they'll know where we are. Our best bet is to catch them as they enter."

Owen moved for the exit. "They probably hope to catch us unawares," he suggested. "Thinking that if they can sneak up on the house, we'll be unprepared."

"They're probably also concerned because they see my car out there," Tom added. "To attack while I'm here means that they will make themselves known to me."

Following Owen out of the room, they passed through the lightless hall toward the staircase.

"If they see your car," Cassandra kept her voice low, "they'll be suspicious of your presence already."

"I doubt it," he countered. "They probably think I'm here to investigate Robert's disappearance."

Cassandra felt Spencer tense beside her, and she did her best not to react herself. They'd chosen to keep the arrival of the Druid's body on their porch to themselves, and she didn't think that now was the time to bring it up. "Why would you investigate us for that?"

"Because no one in town trusts you," Tom explained, and she felt her muscles relax—though only a fraction—at the lack of accusation in his tone.

"And what about Owen's car?" Peter asked. "You think they'll question his presence?"

"I doubt it," Tom said. "Everyone in town knows that Ava kicked Owen out. And that he wound up here."

"I imagine the speculations are running wild," Owen grumbled as they stopped on the second floor. He held a finger up to his lips as they scanned the hallway.

The house was dark. They'd spent the whole day in the vault, forgetting to come downstairs to turn on the lights. The late evening cast a soft blue luminescence onto the cream-colored walls of Occasus. Shadows hung in every corner, causing the dark wood to look almost black in the twilight. Her bedroom door hung ajar to their right as did Peter's a handful of feet away. All the other doors rested tightly shut.

It was haunting in the silence, knowing the Druids were creeping up outside. There was a chance some of them had already made their way in. They all held their breath as they moved slowly about their tasks, cautious not to make a sound.

The cold thread of Gerard's presence notified Cassandra of his proximity—somewhere downstairs—but she knew he wouldn't be much help beyond reporting in or keeping an eye out. As a phantom, he couldn't very well combat a living being. And per her rules, he couldn't hurt anyone either. Unless he managed to see something they didn't, he was more likely to be a distraction rather than a help.

Pulling in as silent a breath as she could, Cassandra reached behind her to take hold of Spencer's arm. She edged around Owen, leading Spencer with her. With her free hand she summoned the spirit world's essence, the arc tingling as it spiraled between her fingers.

But Owen waved a hand at her, shaking his head.

Cassandra startled, freezing in her path toward the staircase. "What?" she mouthed, afraid that he'd seen movement.

Owen held his hand aloft, signaling her to wait as he listened to the floor around them. When nothing happened, he leaned closer. The blue shadows lining his face made him look as ethereal as the rest of the house. He gestured to her hand, reminding her of their earlier conversation. "Not yet."

The rift extinguished at Cassandra's side as Spencer stepped closer behind her. His hand landed on hers where she'd gripped onto his forearm, his warm touch reassuring. But she didn't heed his comfort now.

Giving Owen an understanding nod, Cassandra secured her promise as she backed away to the staircase.

She didn't question Owen's warning. She was just as convinced as he that she needed to practice caution. Spencer may trust her, but she didn't trust herself.

After her mother's honesty, Cassandra didn't have any doubts left.

She was an anomaly of unexpected proportions. The brothers were Varons, but she was something else. Something so powerful that the Druids wanted to either control her or kill her.

Cassandra knew her tendencies. And now she knew the untamed power she could wield and the acts that power made possible. If it came down to it, there was no telling what she'd do to protect Spencer and Peter. Whether it required her to summon beasts, channel the Veil, or tear down the whole of DeVerre to its foundations, she wouldn't hesitate.

The look on Owen's face said he understood her acknowledgment. He gave her an encouraging smile, passed the same to the brothers behind her, then motioned for Tom to follow him to the back staircase. While the men moved swiftly and silently down the hall, Cassandra turned to Peter and Spencer.

They watched her with worried expressions, whether from knowing what they were about to do or because Owen had admonished her, she didn't know. But they didn't have time to waste. Not while the Druids were within Occasus's gate.

"Come on," she whispered and turned to the stairs.

But Peter cut her off, a hand on her shoulder. He held up a finger, pointed to himself, then raised it back up, signaling them to wait as he took the first step down. Never before had Cassandra noticed how loudly the stairs in Occasus creaked. She grimaced with every step that Peter took. It was like each ounce of weight placed on their warped boards produced another loud whine that pierced the air like the cry of wraiths in the night. Yet all remained still as he edged down, peering around the corner before he motioned for them to join him.

The creaking increased as Cassandra and Spencer descended behind him. She flexed both hands, ready to summon forth a rift the second she saw any sign of trouble.

On the porch, she could see the faint yellow glow of the exterior lights. But the interior of Occasus was covered in gloom. The windows taunted her as she scanned the yard for Druids. She didn't see any through the nearest panes, but a flash of movement caught her eye in the living room.

Heart leaping into her throat, Cassandra sighed in relief when she realized it was Gerard standing in the room. He gave her a shrug confirming the house was empty. Then he disappeared once more.

As the sky deepened to a darker shade of blue, so did the house around them. The entry hall was a horrifying corridor, allowing an attack from all sides. They were vulnerable from the living room, the dining room, or the front door.

Peter led the way through the house, focused on the living room windows. Spencer's hand brushed Cassandra's shoulder blade and arm as he slipped from behind her to peer into the dining room. She kept her eyes to the right toward the entrance of Occasus.

Any second now, she thought. Any second and the Druids would burst through the house. They'd knock down the door with the might of a hellhound and scores of the other beasts she'd studied.

Cassandra tried to remember them all. Twelve, right? Each distinct and specifically animal-esque in its form. But none quite like any natural animal on Earth. Nothing their world could ever truly recognize.

Would the Druids even enter themselves? They didn't need to. Not if they summoned enough beasts to come after them.

The thought thudded into Cassandra's chest as the shadows around them darkened. Her pulse quickened as the flashbacks of her fight with Debbie caused her hands to shake. Was it the shift to night or the Druid's approach that caused the black to deepen so ominously?

The sound of a grunt from Peter drew Cassandra's attention. She jumped, thinking that he'd seen something. But his low exclamation was due to a tap on the arm from Spencer. He motioned back to Owen, who stood in the kitchen doorway.

Owen shook his head.

No sign of the Druids back there.

He held up a hand.

Stay.

Two fingers to his eyes.

Keep a lookout.

The trio nodded, but then Owen's eyes widened, and a sharp rap behind Cassandra sent them all jumping back in panic. They whipped around to see a woman knocking on the window right next to the door. Cassandra was ashamed to admit she'd yelped as Spencer and Peter grabbed her arms, yanking her between them. Her hands lit up with rifts as the woman waved at her.

Immediately, Cassandra recognized her. Light brown hair, crystal blue eyes, and those sharp eyebrows that matched her own. "Well, hello there, Cass," she called through the window.

Cassandra stared at the woman in shock. "Rene?"

Rene wiggled her fingers in another wave. "How's it going, cuz?"

Blinking at the appearance of Debbie's daughter, Cassandra's heart began to beat an erratic rhythm. "You're a Druid?"

"Of course I am," Rene said, her voice hostile, eyes flaring angrily. "I'm my mother's daughter, after all. And as we're blood, I'm here to offer you one final courtesy. We'll let you live, Cassandra. All it'll take is walking out of this house and DeVerre forever. If you ever come back, the deal is up. But you'll get to live your life and forget any of this ever happened."

Spencer's hand tightened on her arm, and Peter's shoulders drew back, but the brothers remained silent.

Bolstered by their presence, Cassandra snarled at Rene. "Not a chance."

A glint passed through Rene's eyes. The same glimmer of anger that had coursed through her mother's eyes in the moment she'd grabbed Cassandra's throat. Just before Cassandra had shattered her soul.

"Very well," Rene said, backing away from the window. She raised a hand as she turned her chin back, calling out to the yard behind her. "It's time for a party, everyone."

CHAPTER TWENTY-SEVEN

Cassandra

Now, Cassandra was sure the shadows really were growing darker. And it was in no way natural.

Holding her arms out to the side, Cassandra felt the tingle of the spirit world's essence rising over her skin. "Get ready," she whispered to the brothers.

Peter stepped away, a golden arc of light already erupting around his right hand. "Oh, I was born ready, Cass."

"Let's hope so," Owen called from the kitchen.

Spencer hovered at Cassandra's side, his breathing growing ragged as they both stared at the door. His hand went to the gun at his belt. As unconvinced of its use on creatures of spirit as she was, seeing it in his hand gave her a sense of reassurance.

The shadows lengthened, signaling the impending taunt of beasts. Even after days of study, Cassandra still didn't know how summoning beasts worked. Either the Warden didn't understand the process or didn't care to teach it. She'd convinced herself they couldn't just spawn the creatures inside someone's home, though. And she certainly hoped that was true.

But as the corners of Occasus turned to the deep, shrouded color of obsidian, she recognized the signs. And within the blink of an eye, her fears proved founded.

Out of each corner of the doorway, two hulking creatures unfolded from the shadows. Huge, lanky limbed beasts with two branch-like protrusions on their long-snouted heads. They were antlers—Cassandra knew from her studies—those protrusions that scraped along the ceiling of Occasus. And these beasts—deer-like creatures with humanoid bodies—were called wendigos.

Cassandra raised her hands to slice through the air in front of her. Rippling energy tickled across her skin as the essence raced forward in streaks of deep gray to strike the lumbering creatures. The thunderous *snap* of gunfire rang in her ears as Spencer double-tapped the trigger.

The wendigos moved close, and Cassandra took a reflexive step back. The bullets impacted, barely indenting the beasts' shadowy forms. The arcs sliced across the chest of one and nicked the shoulder of the other. They both recoiled at the essence's touch, but only the one who'd taken the full force of the hit seemed to sustain any real damage.

And that was almost worse in Cassandra's mind as its response was to rear back its angular head and let out an ear-splitting bellow.

On instinct, Cassandra lifted her hands to cover her ears, but Spencer grabbed her shoulders, yanking her back as the wendigo slashed at her with both of its clawed hands. She was immensely grateful for his interference as those claws sliced the air like knives, their long, spindly digits narrowly missing her.

The less injured wendigo followed up the attack, but Cassandra was ready for it. She lifted her hand, sending a blast of energy into the air around her like a shield. A guttural rumble came from the beast as its hand slammed into the arc.

She and Spencer retreated, his one hand still clutching onto her to help keep her upright as they ducked the wendigo's advance. Absently, she wondered why Peter wasn't helping her when she caught a golden burst of energy to her right.

"I could use some help here," Peter called.

Cassandra couldn't spare a second to see what was assailing him—wendigos or otherwise—but shoved Spencer backward as she ducked under another swipe from their attackers. They crashed into the wall. The gun rattled on the floor, knocked out of Spencer's grip from the impact. "Kind of busy," she yelled back.

A gunshot boomed from the back of the house. Tom's muted curse echoed with it. Sure that the marshal and Owen were dealing with an onslaught of beasts at the back, Cassandra didn't question that their attackers far outclassed them in the fight. An untold number of Druids waited outside the house. They didn't even need to enter the fight themselves. They could send in monster after monster to do the job for them.

Throwing forward another, more concentrated beam of her arcs, Cassandra aimed for the injured wendigo. It struck the beast fully in the face, eliciting another, even more blood curdling scream of pain before the creature erupted into smoke.

It was a victory, a small one. But she didn't have time to enjoy it as the other wendigo immediately slashed down at her.

Cassandra tried to leap out of its reach, but the tips of its razor-like claws caught her forearm. The initial impact felt like a needle piercing flesh. But then a flash of fire whipped across her arm as the skin tore.

A strangled cry ripped from her as she stumbled backward, crashing into Spencer. His arm slipped around her waist, twisting her away from the wendigo's immediate range and behind him. She grabbed onto his arm to stop him from taking the front. Even if he was a Wielder, he had no experience and, therefore, no real protection.

Her concern proved unnecessary.

A flash of deep bronze light burst from Spencer's hand. It flew straight at the wendigo. An instant surge of energy pulsed through Cassandra's fingers. She gripped his arm as she watched an arc three times the size of any she'd ever wielded envelope the wendigo's whole form. The power of Spencer's arc tingled up her hand and into her arm. The beast didn't even get the chance to send out its pained bellow before it burst into dust.

Cassandra gaped at the cleared entry. She turned to Spencer. He gave his hand a momentary inspection, glanced at her for a split second, then released her to step to his brother's side.

Freed of their assailants, Cassandra finally got to see what Peter was up against. The flashes of gold light arcing from his hands barely kept a mass of scylla at bay. Their tentacles flew through the air at him, their sickening *slurps* sounding as though they were sticking to the air with each attack. But Peter ducked around their attempts, thwarting their advances with his glowing arcs.

Arcs as large as the one that Spencer had just produced.

With Spencer now at Peter's side, the brothers made short work of the scylla clogging up the living room's floor. Gold and bronze energy twisted together to disintegrate the shadow creatures they fought.

Cassandra's arm tingled at her side, and she reached to grip it, expecting to find it covered in the viscous trickle of her blood. Instead, she stared down to see the shreds of her torn sleeve, damp despite the restored, unmarred skin of her forearm.

With a gasp, Cassandra realized that Spencer had healed her even as he'd protected her.

But she didn't have time to appreciate it.

Tendrils snapped around Cassandra's legs, yanking them out from under her. She landed on the ground with a *whack*, the back of her head narrowly missing a concussive meeting with the floorboards. Her body went numb as her eyes watered from the pain, and the tendrils slid her down the hall toward the dining room.

As her vision cleared, Cassandra found herself staring at a hydra, looking dead into its slitted, neon yellow eyes. The creature was as horrifying as Peter had described. The slithering of its snake-like limbs danced in the air around it, holding it aloft in a manic sort of hover. Sharp fangs of black barred at her in its horrifying maw, primed to strike.

Panic trickled down her chest like droplets of water. Her hands flew out in front of her—whether to defend herself or simply to stop the beast from coming nearer she didn't know. And perhaps it was due to this indecision that only a faint blip of energy managed to drift through the air at the beast.

The arc did little but annoy the hydra as two more tendrils sprang forward to snap around her wrists, lifting her off the ground as it drew her closer.

Amber glittered through the air in a cloud against the hydra's back. It hissed in rage and pain, dropping its hold on her to twist around and face its attacker. Owen.

Landing with a softer *thump* the short distance to the ground this time, Cassandra rolled onto her hands and knees to clamber up. They were under attack on all sides, and she refused to drop out of the fight in her rising panic. She couldn't hear Tom's gunshots or cursing anymore, and she hoped that didn't mean the worst for the man.

As another cloud of amber energy slammed against the hydra, the monster's screeching cry cut through the air. It crumbled into dust. Owen ran toward her, a streak of blood across his shirt. Knowing it was either his or the marshal's, Cassandra sucked in a sharp breath.

"Are you okay?" she asked as he reached her side.

Owen didn't reply, staring over her shoulder as he raised his hand. Spinning as he sent out yet another arc, she could have cursed herself for being negligent. Behind her, two more wendigos had risen to fight the brothers along with a new pair of hydras. The horror of each beast tightened her throat, but she refused to let fear take hold.

Arcs of gold, bronze, amber, and gray tore through the air at all the beasts. A wendigo and a hydra evaporated in an instant with Peter and

Spencer's attacks. The other hydra disintegrated from a shared blow of Cassandra and Owen's arcs.

The remaining wendigo struck out at Spencer, who was nearest the beast, but he disintegrated it with an instant flash of energy.

Sure they had yet another creature to face, Cassandra whipped around to find it.

Quiet stillness met her.

All four of them kept a sharp eye on their surroundings.

"Where's Tom?" Spencer whispered to Owen.

"Upstairs," the man replied, his words hushed. "One of those antlered things practically tore apart his shoulder, so I sent him back to the vault."

"Shit."

"That's what Tom said."

"Why aren't there more?" Peter asked, voice tight and eyes focused.

The shadows lengthened, and Cassandra caught movement at the kitchen door. "There are."

Tendrils slithered around the doorframe as another hydra slipped through, its angular head hovering in the center while its limbs drifted fluidly. Twice the size of the others, its tendrils wrapped up and around the doorframe to pull it into the room. Knocking lamps and paintings from their homes and shoving furniture out of its way, it began to make its way toward them.

"We can't stay in here," Owen commanded as the brothers rushed forward to take the lead. "They'll keep sending beasts in and wear us down until we can't fight anymore."

The rumble of heavy growls vibrated through the air to their right in the living room. Cassandra turned to see a pack of six hellhounds preparing to charge. Owen was right. There was no chance they could survive if they stayed in the house like this. Not when the Druids had an endless supply of monsters to send in after them.

Leaving the hydra to the brothers, Cassandra turned to the hounds. These, at the very least, she could handle.

Raising her hands, she snarled back at the hounds as three of them charged her. She stood her ground as they rushed forward, tossing rifts of gray at each one in succession. One, two, three. They howled, tearing apart into smoke.

Owen's amber arcs melded with hers to take down the remaining three beasts.

Hand on the lock of the front door of Occasus, Owen called her name. "Cover me."

Arcs ready at her hands, Cassandra watched as Owen twisted the lock and yanked the door open. Without waiting to see what lay beyond, she let the rifts fly. And she found herself immediately thankful that she had.

Two Druids awaited them right outside the door, their own hands raised and their eyes closed as a shadow of darkness hovered around their forms. She could only assume they'd been summoning more beasts. But her arcs slammed into their chests, causing them to stumble and drop their hands. Owen shifted around the door and blew both of them back with a barrier-like arc of his own.

As fast as she could, Cassandra turned to grab the brothers' collars as they fought off more hydra climbing through the room. She tugged.

She wasn't strong enough to do much more than startle them into action, but they shuffled backward, sending a handful of brightly lit arcs at the onrushing hydra. Following Owen outside, Cassandra rushed through the doorway, ready to handle whatever Druidic forces awaited them on the porch of Occasus.

Owen tossed another Druid back and into the porch swing to their right. Cassandra found another to their left near the chairs and table. The two Owen had knocked off the porch before began to rise from the gravel drive.

Recognizing one of them as Rene, Cassandra opted to mark the woman as her focus. Her family, her fight.

Without waiting for Rene to clamber all the way to her feet, Cassandra unleashed a dark gray flare of energy at her.

It went wider than she'd intended, only catching Rene's left arm. But the woman gasped in pain as the man at her side raised his hands.

Expecting to defend an arc from him, Cassandra sent a defensive blast through the air. No arc came, though, and the energy fizzled out before her like smoke from a wick.

Instead, shadows bubbled up from the earth beneath the Druid's feet. A writhing mass of movement scurried and shifted around his feet, rolling and transforming into a beast whose name Cassandra couldn't remember. The creature began as a hoard of mice-like beings that melded into one another, growing as they merged to become massive rats. They then twisted together to rise into one giant rodent-like beast that grew to Cassandra's height with slavering jowls and wild, neon eyes.

Refusing to let the beast scare her into inaction, she threw out two more arcs. One at Rene and one at the rat-like monster. Her cousin had her eyes closed, shadows pressing around her to create her own beast when the arc connected with her sternum. She cried out in pain, the shadows softening as the blow drove her to the ground. The rodent-like beast took the hit with equal displeasure but not with quite as much pain.

It bounded toward Cassandra at the bottom of the stairs while its master helped Rene to stand.

Cassandra shot two more arcs at the rodent, one only grazing its ear as the other missed entirely. The thing was faster than she expected.

Backing quickly up the stairs, Cassandra tripped. But Peter was there, catching her arm as he sent a golden rift over her shoulder. "You good?" he asked with a smirk.

Surprised at his good humor, Cassandra managed to return his smile as the beast disintegrated. "Thanks to you, yeah."

"Anytime, sis."

"Shut up."

He squeezed her arm and pushed her upright. "Let's clear these people off our property, mkay?"

Together, Peter and Cassandra descended the steps and rushed forward past the vehicles, charging Rene and her Druid friend. They were both raising more beasts, but she and Peter were faster. Gray and gold knocked into the pair, halting their summons. Rene dropped to her knees from the force of Cassandra's arc while the man rolled across the ground from the intensity of Peter's.

The man twitched as Peter rushed to his side and grabbed his collar, hand alight with a rift. "I wouldn't try anything if I were you," he threatened as Cassandra reached Rene's side.

Hands glowing with the ashen light of her rifts, Cassandra crouched next to Rene. She could hear Spencer and Owen back on the porch. She knew she needed to move quickly.

Staring into Rene's angry eyes—so like Debbie's, despite their icy color—Cassandra held her glare, unflinching. "How many of you are here?"

Rene gave her a disappointed grin. "You gonna kill me, Cass?"

"If I have to."

"Mm, you best do it, then. Because unless you plan on betraying your boyfriends and handing Occasus over to us, you'll need all the help you can get."

Cassandra set a hand on Rene's shoulder, the arc rolling and pulling itself apart to hover around her hand. "I will do it, Rene."

The woman scoffed. "Oh, I don't doubt you, Cassandra. Not after what you did to my mother."

Feeling her jaw tighten, Cassandra worked against the guilt tapping at the back of her brain. The memory of Debbie's look of shock when her hand had hit her chest. The way the woman's knees gave beneath her. The glassy stare in her eyes as she lay with the flames crawling higher around her.

She didn't want to do that again.

Rene smirked. "You're more like us than you think. You could join us, you know? Forget these idiots. Who are they, anyway? Help *us*." Her hand shot out and grabbed Cassandra's right wrist.

With a fierce, painful twist, Rene showed Cassandra the back of her hand. The Sauveterre crest stared back at her—a lush tree, budding with life set behind the gothic S. The moonlight glinted off the silver ring on Cassandra's pinky finger, mirrored by another on Rene's own hand. "Help your *family*."

The word smacked Cassandra across the face as she realized how ridiculous it was. "You're not my family." She ripped her hand free. "They are."

Rene huffed. "Kill me, then. Like the murderer you are."

"Fine."

Cassandra's hand hit Rene's chest like a shove. The immediate look of pain and shock that had crossed Debbie's face was now mirrored in her daughter's. Fire ripped through Cassandra's body as she felt Rene's soul tear apart under her hand. The woman's eyes went glassy as she fell back to the dirt, lifeless despite the survival of her physical form.

Her hand tingling and her chest searing from the pain of what she'd done, Cassandra stood. She caught Peter staring at her as the Druid in his grip kept looking back and forth between her and Rene. His breathing escalated as he began to try scrambling out of Peter's grip.

Tightening his hold, Peter turned away from Cassandra to fix a glare on the Druid. "Calm down, would you?"

"Are you gonna do that to me too?" the Druid demanded, a notable shake in his voice.

"Not if I can help it."

Cassandra's chest felt hollow as the wound of destroying a second soul tried to patch itself up. Staring down at Rene, she wondered if Peter thought she'd been too callous. But what else was there to do? Rene had made it clear: kill or be killed. And she wouldn't stand by to let anyone take her family from her.

"Hold still." It was clear Peter was struggling to keep ahold of the Druid as the man fought to break his grip. "God, I wish I was Spencer," he muttered. "Spence!"

"Busy!" came his brother's call.

Realizing how long they'd taken with Rene and this other Druid, Cassandra turned to see Owen and Spencer fighting more beasts, in addition to the same two Druids who'd been on the porch when they'd first arrived. Neither looked any more subdued.

Gritting her teeth, Cassandra knew why. Owen wouldn't hurt them. Not enough to take them down. And he was going to get Spencer killed in the process.

Gerard had seen a dozen or more Druids out here. They'd only fought four. So there were a minimum of eight more somewhere on the property. They didn't have time to play nice. Not when their lives were on the line. Not when the Druids wouldn't play by the same rules.

"Peter!" Cassandra knew her voice was sharper than usual. But this was no time to flinch away from action he needed to take.

He looked up at her, understanding already in his dark eyes before she said another word. He gave her a nod, then nudged his chin toward the porch. "Help Spence. I'll be right behind you."

Cassandra could see it in his hardened stare. He wasn't going to let anyone hurt his brother.

The Druid saw it too.

The man scowled and struggled harder against Peter's grip, managing to wrench himself free. His shadow darkened as he pulled away, the long tendrils of a hydra appearing as it stretched out behind him. But Peter was ready.

A wall of golden light rammed into the man, sending him flying to roll limply across the ground. His shadow and the hydra he'd begun to summon went dormant beneath his body. By the unnatural way he sprawled out, half on the gravel and half on the grass, she had no doubt he was dead. Whether his demise had come from a shattered soul like Debbie and Rene, or the sheer impact of Peter's arc, she didn't know.

Releasing a ragged breath, Peter turned from the man and rushed forward to grab Cassandra's arm as he hurried for the porch. "Come on," he muttered.

Cassandra glanced over her shoulder at the dead Druid, feeling guilty for pushing Peter to become this man. It was one thing for her to kill these people. This mess was her fault, to begin with. But for her to drag Peter and Spencer into the violence was another story altogether.

As they reached the porch, amber and bronze arcs cleared off another half dozen hellhounds and other shadow beasts Cassandra didn't have time to process and name. But the Druids were already summoning more from the far side of the porch.

While Owen prepared to fight them off, Spencer didn't wait. He charged across the weathered boards toward the Druids. Expecting to see them defend themselves with arcs, instead, they only drew forth more beasts from the spirit world as he neared. The realization hit her that these Druids didn't know how to wield arcs. They weren't Sages like the rest of them. It almost made her feel guilty.

But either Spencer didn't notice, or he had no qualms about the unfair advantage. He dropped to the floor, sliding under the reach of a freshly summoned wendigo, and hopped up in front of the two Druids. Both hands lit with the glowing essence, he sent an arc straight at one man's chest—knocking him back over the porch railing—and connected a fist right into the other man's jaw.

The Druid's head snapped back from the force, and he went limp as he fell to the ground, the beasts crumbling around them.

With a flicker, the porch light came back on.

Peter and Cassandra ascended the steps together as Owen straightened his collar.

"That wasn't it, right?" Peter muttered as Spencer approached. "Gerard said a dozen."

"Maybe they decided four deaths was enough," Owen suggested, a grumble in his tone that Cassandra didn't appreciate.

Spencer shook his head. "I didn't kill either of them. I hit the one hard enough to knock him out, and the other one—" He glanced over his shoulder. "I think he's just recovering."

Eyeing Spencer with interest, Cassandra couldn't help admitting to herself that his charge had been particularly impressive. "You can knock people out with one punch?"

He shrugged.

Peter rolled his eyes. "Why do you think I wanted him back there with that guy?" He thrust a hand in his brother's direction. "Spence is a black belt."

Sure that nothing could have been more surprising to learn about the man the world perceived as the sweet, reserved Collins brother, Cassandra smiled. "And here I thought you couldn't get more attractive."

Spencer's brow lifted, but she didn't give him time to acknowledge her statement as she turned to scan the yard. "There's more of them out there."

As if in response, the night sky shifted to a darker shade. It was as if a cloud hovered over Occasus, more and more shadows encroaching on its grounds. A chill raced down Cassandra's spine as she searched the darkness for any oncoming Druids or beasts.

Feeling Peter and Spencer step up to her side, Cassandra allowed the energy to course back through her veins. The essence floated around her hand, weaving in and out of her fingers like a dance. "Owen," she called behind her.

There was a hesitation then his flat tone came to her ears. "Yes?"

"No more pulling your punches."

He sighed. "Cassandra—"

Whipping around, she glared at him. "I get that you have ethics. But when it's between the life of your friends and the life of the Druids attacking them, you have to set those ethics aside. Got it?"

Owen's dark stare narrowed on her as though trying to decide if her motives were pure enough for him. Was her dedication to the brothers a just enough cause to become a killer? She wondered if it was fair of her to ask of him. They might be his friends, but they weren't his family. Not like the women upstairs were.

But saving Peter and Spencer wasn't just about keeping the brothers alive.

Spencer tapped her arm. "Cass, they're coming."

She caught Owen's gaze flickering to survey the yard before her, but she had more to say. "If you want to raise your child in this town," she charged, her fierce words drawing his attention back, "without the threat of Druids in it, then you'll let go of your scruples and save our lives."

A flicker of anger passed over his expression, but Cassandra didn't wait for a rebuttal. Perhaps her manipulation was cruel. But it was the truth. And she wouldn't let his qualms get in the way of keeping these brothers alive.

Her confidence was short-lived as she turned around to see the yard of Occasus shrouded in black. Like pitch poured out to cover the grass. The porch light began flickering behind them, and she heard Owen take a step closer as she continued to scan the yard.

As the porch light pulsed irregularly, Cassandra couldn't be sure that the Druids hadn't managed to dim the moonlight as the world around them turned to shadow. It was as though they'd pulled a curtain around the gates of Occasus, blocking out all hope and life, bringing with them only monsters of horrifying, infernal form.

The light went out, and a shudder escaped Cassandra as beasts of all descriptions rose to stand among the Druids scattered across the lawn. She tried to count how many there were, but the beasts blended in with the humans making it hard to decipher. She managed a count of at least fourteen men and women, along with what she could only guess to be twice as many beasts.

Standing on the steps of Occasus between the Collins brothers with Owen flanking their back, Cassandra felt like dropping under the weight of what they had to face. They'd gone against four Druids, and it had already taxed them so much. How would they face this sea of attackers standing before them now?

The rifts around her hands flickered and died out.

"All right, Pete," Spencer muttered, scanning the lawn. "You got a plan?"

Peter snorted as he took a step forward, shoulders held back proudly. "Yeah, Frankly," he replied, far more confident than he should have been. He raised his voice. "I'm thinking that we ask these fine folks to leave our property, knowing that if they don't, we'll be forced to remove them."

The shadows only grew thicker and the beasts larger.

On the left, Spencer angled in front of her. "I don't think they're getting the message."

Peter shrugged. "Can't say we didn't warn them."

In any other case, this display of arrogance—this suggestion that two brothers could take on more than ten times their number—might have struck Cassandra as ridiculous. A joke. But these weren't just any brothers.

Correcting her earlier doubts, a slow tingle spread across Cassandra's hands as the rifts reappeared. She stood with the Varon brothers at her side and Owen at their back. What couldn't they face together?

"This is your last chance," a Druid called out, a man with a rumbling voice somewhere to their left. "Get in your cars, leave DeVerre, and we'll let you go."

Peter glanced back at Spencer, his dark eyes drifting to Cassandra, then settling back on his brother. He smirked at them. "Sounds like a bad deal to me."

Both of them returned the sentiment and stepped up to stand beside him.

The next moments were pure chaos. Beasts surged forward in a tangle of shadow and smoke and terror. A wall of death that came to tear them apart. Most of the Druids remained behind the wall, controlling the beasts and summoning more even as the current crowd rushed them. But a small number of the Druids charged in alongside the beasts.

Rippling black rifts tore through the air in front of the five Sage Wielders who burst ahead of the ranks of the Druids. Arcs of the spirit world's essence rippled and coalesced, aimed at the four of them. No matter how powerful Peter and Spencer were already, neither they nor Cassandra had had much training. And remembering Owen's hesitation, a spark of worry nagged at her brain over the odds that weighed in favor of the Druids.

There wasn't time to dwell on such concerns. Not with the onrushing horde pressing in on them. The Druids and their beasts surrounded and outnumbered them.

Peter and Spencer sprang into action first. It struck Cassandra that both of their rifts were reminiscent of one another's; Spencer's held a darker glow and a beige ring of light, while pure white edged Peter's.

Their arcs lit up the night, clashing against the black surrounding them. A cacophony came from every angle. A fiendish symphony of beasts' growls, hisses, howls, and less identifiable sounds. Cassandra didn't have time to consider the best means to bring down these beasts and Druids. There was no strategy they could play within this game.

The only choice was to fight for survival.

Leaping into action, Cassandra found herself locked into a brand-new experience of life. She'd combatted hellhounds and other beasts, yes. She'd fought Debbie and killed twice now. But this was something she'd never thought she'd encounter.

Every decision was impulse. The world seemed to slow and speed by at a simultaneous and incomprehensible rate. One second, she was defending against a scylla, and the next, she was ducking under the attack of a beast the size of a panther. The following moment she was face-to-face with a Druid.

The woman—somewhat familiar to her, though she couldn't place the name—flung a black arc of energy at Cassandra. Managing to get a hand up just in time to send out her own arc to deflect the blow, she hadn't been as fast as she needed to be. The shield of gray light knocked the Druid's arc off its original course for her chest but managed to strike her left bicep.

Her arm went numb as the contradictory burn of flame and ice shot across her skin. Cassandra gritted her teeth and returned the attack with her good hand as the other arm hung limply at her side. The Druid blocked it but didn't bother attacking again as three more beasts surged around her, headed straight for Cassandra.

With her useless arm still sending spikes of pain into her shoulder, Cassandra retreated rapidly as she willed forth a barrier-like burst of energy like the one she'd seen Peter wield. An ashen gray wall flew ahead of her, though it wasn't the same grand size that his had been. She scowled sardonically, thinking that the brothers managed to usurp her in power without even trying. She was supposed to be dangerous. Some overwhelming source of power that the Druids were desperate to possess. And she couldn't come close to what the brothers had already managed to produce.

Pins and needles tingled in her arm, signaling the start of returning sensation. Cassandra edged closer to Spencer and Peter, who were holding off a swath of beasts and Druids far better than she'd done. She decided it would be smarter to stick close to them. More power meant more protection as well as better attacks against the Druids. She might not be as strong as the brothers, but she could defend them while they took down the more difficult creatures.

Owen closed in, too, his amber rifts dropping beast after beast. She supposed he'd found a way around his aversion to killing the Druids. But she knew it couldn't last.

On and on, they fought. Whether it took minutes or hours, she didn't know. But she was growing tired, and they'd only managed to take down two of the Sage Druids who had assailed them up close.

There were too many. Too many beasts and too many Druids. And even Peter and Spencer's arcs dimmed as the darkness pressed in.

They were wholly surrounded, Cassandra realized as she blasted a scylla's tentacle off her leg. The Druids had driven the beasts to encircle them. To box them in on every side, encasing them in a dome of darkness.

The four stood back-to-back, trying to defend themselves from the onslaught. And they were all growing weaker by the second. Their hope darkened with the depth of the night around them.

Spencer took down a massive beast that Cassandra didn't even try to recognize—its form twisted and mangled. Then a streak of black energy struck his side, and he doubled over as his knees buckled.

"Spencer!" Both Peter and Cassandra yelled together.

Attempting to take advantage of the undefended opening, a Druid rushed in, more beasts at its back. Peter leaped over his brother's agonized form. He grabbed the Druid's dark collar in one hand and clutched onto the side of his face with the other. The Druid screamed in pain before falling limp in Peter's grasp.

Cassandra could hear his heavy, angered breathing as he took down half a dozen beasts. She felt the same rage building in her. But the knowledge that it wouldn't stop tempered the emotion. This was a never-ending tidepool of beasts. One wave crashing in on them after the other.

And when Owen cried out against the wendigo that shoved its claws deep into his gut, Cassandra knew it was useless. They couldn't fight off these beasts or the Druids controlling them on their own.

What do I do? Cassandra sent up a panicked prayer as she blasted more of the beasts back just as another crashed in to take its place. *How do I save them?*

Her arms tingling with the swirl of gray rifts around them, Cassandra fought on. She stepped back to dodge a hydra's tendril, almost falling over Spencer as he tried to stand. He caught her, his hand on her back. At the base of her spine where his palm rested, the tingle of energy spiked.

A vision flashed before Cassandra's eyes as the tingle soared across her body. She saw a clear, singular image: *Two round, soft brown eyes stared at her, small, close-set orbs, covered in shadow—hazy as though hidden behind a veil. They blinked and shifted—suddenly piercing and ice blue, still shrouded in darkness and mist.*

Then it was gone.

Cassandra's throat went raw as she came back to reality and face-to-face with a hellhound the size of her truck. Spencer shoved her out of the way, sending a bronze burst of energy into the beast. She lost her footing, dropping to roll across the ground before staggering to her feet. By saving her, Spencer had failed to save himself. The giant hound was too strong for his weakening arcs. Despite its howls of pain, it charged, its impossibly-large jaws ripping into his shoulder and chest.

If Cassandra had ever considered such a scenario, she would have sworn that the horror would have crippled her into inaction. But as Spencer grit his teeth, eyes squeezed shut in pain, she couldn't hear his scream. Not over the roar of rushing wind that rose around her. Not as every nerve in her body lit up with that chilly tingle.

It shot up her spine, meeting her shoulder blades and tearing through her arms.

A jolt of energy unlike anything Cassandra had ever experienced shook her body as the essence ripped out of her.

There was a split second of absolute, total, resounding silence.

Then, like an explosion, a light ruptured the air around her.

Peter

They were about to die. Peter knew that for sure.

No matter how hard he'd worked for his entire life to make sure that Spencer was safe and cared for, he'd failed. Tonight was proof of that. He'd done nothing but screw it all up. And now they were going to die for his mistakes.

It had been Spencer's guttural shout of pain that alerted him to their total failure. He looked over to see a hellhound's sharp canines clamped entirely over his brother's right shoulder, ripping and tearing through the bulk of his chest. Peter had been defending Owen, who lay bleeding out on the gravel of Occasus's driveway, but he abandoned the man to rush for his brother. The pebbles crunched under his feet, his hand rising to attack the hellhound.

And then, light.

It slammed into Peter and everything else within the vicinity. Knocked backward—along with the beasts and Druids—from the collision, he rolled across the gravel, the small, sharp pebbles cutting into his skin. He brought himself to a halt, regaining control as he looked up, his mouth dropping open as he stared in awe at the scene before him.

A bright rift of light had torn open around Cassandra. Massive and glowing, an ashen gray portal with an ivory halo rippling around the edges surrounded her. Beyond the halo, a gray-tinged image loomed behind her. Peter could see a faint image of trees reflecting in the lake, the water smooth as glass. Cassandra stood, her arms held out to the side, a look of pure focus and serenity on her face. A look that said she was in total control.

With a twist of her wrists, a hundred flashes of light burst through the portal. The beasts around them snarled and whimpered, recoiling away from the light. A loud, collective gasp erupted from the Druids controlling them. Someone yelled, but Peter couldn't hear what they said, his gaze too fixated on the transformation of these beams of light to pay any attention to the panic of the Druids.

The flashes Peter had first thought to be arcs, he realized were nothing of the sort. They morphed and glittered, shifting in front of his eyes as they sailed past him on bat-like wings, growing as they moved. Whatever their names, they were creatures from the spirit world, beasts of light rather than shadow.

As the glowing, ashen creatures attacked the beasts and Druids, Peter turned back to Cassandra. The portal was gone, but the creatures remained as she stood with her hands extended and eyes closed. Heart in his throat, he knew she was wielding them. Controlling them just like the Druids had controlled their own beasts.

But these were nothing like the beasts he'd seen before.

Peter watched as the bat-like creatures harried the shadow beasts, which swiftly turned to smoke and dust in the wake of their attackers. Unlike the shadow beasts, these light creatures weren't horrifying at all. They were spectacular. Beautiful, if odd, in their formation. Beings of enticing and captivating creation. And extremely deadly.

A few Druids stood their ground, working to create more beasts and fight the newcomers. But the light creatures made short work of them.

The rest of the Druids—Peter counted six—ran out of the gates of Occasus, glancing over their shoulders in panic and fear as they fled. He wondered if Cassandra would send her beasts to hunt them down. But once they'd cleared all threats from the grounds of Occasus, the glowing creatures circled back, ignoring the ones who'd escaped into the forest beyond their property.

Like a cloud of swirling bats, the creatures encircled the four of them—Peter, Cassandra, Spencer, and Owen. They became a pillar of light around them, streaks resembling shooting stars. The creatures grew smaller with each second, closing in. Two broke free from the spiral. One drifted toward Owen, landing on his chest before bursting into a flare of light.

Peter jumped but watched as the trickle of blood seeping from Owen's gut halted its flow. He narrowed his eyes to be sure he wasn't crazy just as Spencer gasped beside him.

Whipping around, Peter watched as the second creature dropped onto Spencer's shoulder. His brother shook from shock and blood loss as the bat-like creature flapped its light gray wings. It rested on his shoulder, staring at him as if waiting. For what, Peter couldn't guess.

Spencer's eyes flickered between Peter and Cassandra as though unsure of the creature's delay himself.

But they didn't have to wait any longer. The creature flared brightly and sank into Spencer's shoulder. He released an instant sigh of relief.

The cyclone of creatures spun around them with increasing speed as their coil tightened. They grew smaller and smaller, spinning faster and faster before dimming to a pinprick of light that struck Cassandra's sternum.

She sucked in a sharp burst of air, dark eyes going wide.

Then she dropped.

~

It was too much to unpack in one night. Too much to deal with or process after all that had occurred. Cassandra summoning and wielding beasts. Owen almost dying. Spencer almost dying—again. The fourteen dead Druids in their yard.

Peter had moved through the whole experience like a zombie. He'd helped Spencer check himself for damage first. But the light beast had fully healed his brother. There was no sign of the hound's bite marks apart from the holes in his shirt. Though Spencer said he still felt them.

Rubbing his neck, Peter could relate.

With just the two of them left conscious in the yard, Spencer suggested they pull Owen into the house together. They got him into the foyer. Then Spencer went outside, crouched down, and lifted Cassandra in his arms. He carried her up to her room as Gerard popped in to follow, like a hovering father.

Once Spencer had returned, assured that Cassandra was safe in her bed, he helped get Owen onto the couch in the living room and agreed to sit with him while Peter went up to fetch the others from the vault. To say that leaving his brother alone was difficult would have been an understatement. Peter kept glancing around, doublechecking to be sure there were no Druids or beasts that had managed to escape their notice.

But after bolting the lock on the door—useless when doors didn't deter beasts—Peter forced himself up the staircase in the darkness of Occasus.

Opening the vault and facing their friends on the other side was a harrowing experience all on its own. The fear and concern on Ava and Anna's faces, and the pain in Tom's, made everything he'd faced that night feel far, far worse. Tom's injury had put them all on edge, despite Ava managing to staunch the bleeding.

Anguis and Nex brushed against Peter's legs for the first time since they'd met him, and everything in him wanted to drop to the rug and rest his head on his knees as he hyperventilated.

He didn't let himself do that either.

Instead, he accepted Anna's hug for a far shorter time than he would have liked before turning to take care of Tom's shoulder. Not entirely certain what he was doing, he attempted to duplicate what Owen had done for him. To his surprise, the wound in Tom's shoulder closed, the man gaping as the skin freshly fused together. Upon his success, Peter took Ava to her husband. Despite the couple's tension and Peter's assurances that Owen was all right, she tore down the stairs to sit at his side.

As much as Peter wished he could take a seat himself, he and Spencer went with Tom to show him the bodies of the Druids. He managed to name them all: several Frossards, a handful of Dumonts, and a mixture of Guillaumes, Alaries, MacDonalds, Sauveterres, and Merciers. All the names they'd already had on their list.

"Well," Tom said, hand on his pistol as he looked around the yard. "Guess this confirms it. We've found our Druids."

Spencer crossed his arms. "Unless there are others."

"What do you mean?"

"There were six who got away," he explained. "They could be from other families, and we just don't know about them yet."

"And there could be more," Peter added. "Just because they sent these twenty after us doesn't mean there aren't others. They probably thought it would be enough."

"It *was*," Spencer muttered.

"It was *almost* enough," he corrected. "They won't take chances next time."

Under Tom's guidance, they decided to cover the bodies with old sheets but otherwise leave them as they were. "I'll have to get the mortician up here tomorrow to take care of the rest."

Peter pulled his brows together. "Will there be an investigation?"

Tom gave a single emphatic shake of his head. "I was here. I saw those things. What you did was self-defense, and I can corroborate that."

The three of them scanned the bodies littering Occasus's landscape.

"Gotta admit, though," he ran a hand over his mustache, "I'm kind of surprised you managed to come out of this alive."

Though he didn't say it, Peter was surprised himself.

"What's next?" Spencer asked. "Alexander wasn't here tonight, and we know there are at least six other Druids out there still."

Tom motioned to the bodies. "Leave all this to me. We'll handle the appropriate legal proceedings in-house and ensure that the Druids are taken care of. The state doesn't need to get involved. In the meantime, the most important thing you two can do is prove to the people of DeVerre that you're the good guys. Go to church in the morning. Once the townspeople hear about this disaster, they'll appreciate that your first instinct was to seek the house of God, if nothing else. We'll figure out the rest tomorrow afternoon."

Peter shared a hesitant glance with his brother. The idea of sitting in the chapel next to the family and friends of the fourteen Druids that lay dead on their lawn made his throat tighten. The people of DeVerre might not know the truth yet, but they would soon. And he feared what they'd do once they found out.

"What if there are Druids there?" Spencer asked, his voice flat.

"They probably will be," Tom admitted. "But, as you said, they won't take chances next time. And an attack in the middle of the town reveals them to *everyone*, not just you two."

"Us four," Peter corrected. "Cassandra and Owen fought with us. They'll consider us all the same."

Excusing themselves, Peter and Spencer moved back into Occasus while the marshal remained outside to call his deputy and keep an eye on the bodies.

As senseless as it seemed, Peter knew that the marshal was right. No matter what knowledge they had, they needed to convince the innocent people of DeVerre that they were protecting them. When it came time to reveal everything to the townspeople—which would likely occur way sooner than Peter would prefer—they needed as many on their side as possible. People who would stand up against however many Druids remained.

Even if it would be difficult to walk into church after having faced down death—after having caused death themselves—they had to do it.

There had been several points in the fight when Peter felt his conscience flagging him down. Reminding him that life was sacred. But with each life he'd been forced to take, he'd counted the cost. And with the price of each one, he realized that it wasn't remorse he felt. It was peace. While there was sorrow for life lost, there was also a firm assurance that whatever choice he'd made, he did it to protect the lives of his family, friends, and the whole town of DeVerre. It was worth it all, no matter the internal damage it caused.

Tom and his deputy kept vigil on the porch throughout the night. The young deputy, Hunter, arrived at Occasus with wide eyes and a nervous twitch as he scanned the yard. But he listened to Tom with unflinching loyalty, allowing Peter and Spencer to attempt to sleep with some semblance of confidence.

While Ava stayed with Owen in the living room, Anna took the spare bedroom at the back of the second floor. Once she'd disappeared inside, the brothers stood in the hall silently.

Peter looked at Spencer, his whole being exhausted. It was hard enough dealing with the weight of everything else. But having watched his brother be almost torn to shreds by a hellhound was something he didn't care to remember.

Peter gripped his brother's shoulders, pulling him in for a hug. He felt like a teen again, promising to take care of his little brother after their dad's death—both mourning and scared and ill-equipped to take care of anyone. But Peter held his brother tight, swearing to himself that he would never let his brother near the brink of death like that again.

~

Waking the next morning to arrive at church on time was almost impossible, but they managed. Ava and Anna left early—without Owen, who still lay passed out and recovering on the couch. While Anna hesitated to go, Ava understood when Peter explained the plan: Earn the town's good graces before revealing that there was a cult in its midst trying to take over. She took her sister's hand and pulled her out the door, dark eyes sharp as she said, "We'll see you at church."

Now they stood in the foyer, preparing to leave. Spencer zipped up his heavy coat, Cassandra slipped a scarf loosely around her neck, and Peter glared at Gerard's scowling form, hovering in the corner. "If you've got something to say, Gerry, say it," he commanded.

"I don't like it," Gerard grumbled, eyes on Cassandra. "You nearly died last night. You shouldn't be going out, rubbing their failure in their faces."

"We don't have a choice," Cassandra said, a lack of conviction in her tone as she kept her gaze downcast. "We need this town to believe us when we tell them the truth. And you know as well as we do that they won't if they don't see us as DeVerreans too."

"That's no reason to risk your lives," he spat.

Spencer stepped around Cassandra, effectively blocking her from Gerard's view. "We're not going to let anything happen to her," he vowed. "We're going to church and coming straight back here. Then we'll figure out our next move."

Gerard's glare was ice cold. "Your next move should be getting her out of here. Getting her somewhere safe."

Peter tossed the Jeep's keys across the room to Spencer. "Get the car started, would you?"

Spencer nodded, then opened the door and turned to Cassandra. She hesitated for only a second before stepping over the threshold before him.

Glancing at Owen's sleeping form on the couch, Peter turned back to Gerard. "I know you don't like my brother and I much," the phantom scoffed at the obvious statement, "but by now, I would think that you could understand that we care about her just as much, if not more than you do. We'll keep her safe."

Gerard's dark eyes swept over Peter's face, but he didn't speak.

"In the meantime—" Peter gestured toward the living room. "Would you tell Owen where we are if he wakes up? I don't want him to freak out."

Gerard gave a firm nod in agreement.

"Thanks," Peter muttered. He was about to move for the door when he thought better of it. "For everything, I mean. I know you've got your own agendas and plans, but you've helped us figure things out. And you saved us last night. Your warning—it was the only reason we knew the Druids were out there in the first place. They would have ambushed us otherwise."

The phantom's dark brown hair hung around his sharp face, creating jagged edges in his already severe features. The mustache on his thick beard twitched, but he didn't speak or smile or show any sign that Peter's words had affected him. Instead, he dipped his head in acceptance.

Seeing that was all he would get, Peter gave him a quick salute, then stepped outside of Occasus, pulling the door shut behind him. In the wide circular driveway, Tom and Hunter's identical cop cars sat next to the Jeep. And farther up the drive was a large white van that resembled an ambulance.

Earlier that morning, Tom had informed the brothers that he and his deputy had taken the night to collect photographic evidence and anything they could see as pertinent to any criminal or civil case should any family members of the deceased attempt to press charges. Then the pair had moved the bodies, laying them out and covering them with a tarp to protect them against the snow that began to fall in the early morning.

Now, Gabriel Chapelle—the reverend's brother and town mortician—was helping the cops to load the bodies into his van so he could take them back to the funeral home and prepare them for burial. The sight caused Peter to shudder, and he pulled his scarf tighter around his neck as though it were the cold that shook him to his core.

Peter watched a moment longer as the three men worked. Gabriel looked a lot like his brother, but his reddish-tinged hair had a darker tint. They'd had just a few moments to talk with the mortician at the start of the day, but Peter was surprised that the man showed no apparent concern at the situation that had occurred within Occasus's grounds. In fact, he'd remarked on its fortuitous nature.

"We should talk," Gabriel had said. "It seems we have common interests."

Paranoia running high, Peter hesitated to interpret that as a good thing. He worried the man was a Druid working to create an "in" with them rather than another hidden Wielder like Owen or a Warden-supporting town member like Tom. But he decided to trust the marshal and deputy to take care of both the work and the mortician until they returned from church.

Peter tugged on a pair of gloves as he marched down the porch steps to the Jeep. He felt rather foolish, wearing so many extra layers when Cassandra had only donned her leather jacket and thin scarf. But it was November, he reminded himself. And it was snowing.

Hopping into the front passenger seat of the Jeep, Peter shut the door. "Ready to go?"

Spencer set to work at once, putting the Jeep in gear to back up, then pulling around the drive. Cassandra sat in the back seat with her chin tucked as she stared at her bare hands. Peter had noticed the emerging of this black mood of hers when she'd risen that morning. He'd seen how she looked at him and Spencer, her gaze cautious as she approached them like she'd done something wrong.

As they pulled through the gates of Occasus, Peter reached back to swat Cassandra's knee. The low melody of the CD hummed through the stereo. Cassandra's gaze rose reluctantly to his. "You all right back there, kid?" he asked, eyebrows lifted in a prompting gesture.

With a heavy sigh, Cassandra shifted to the edge of her seat. "I think I should probably explain myself," she whispered.

Peter frowned, but Spencer beat him to the reply. "You mean you should explain how you saved our lives for the—what is it, Pete? The third or fourth time now?"

Hearing the tempered intonation of Spencer's words, Peter caught on to his brother's plan. "I've lost count, to be honest, J.B."

"Mm, me too."

Cassandra rolled her eyes, but a faint smile tugged on her lips as she leaned forward to rest her elbows on the back of their seats. "No. I want to explain what happened."

"You mean the beasts you summoned?" Peter asked.

She hesitated, the smile nearly gone as she twisted the ring she wore. "Yeah."

"Not sure it needs explaining."

"Me either," Spencer agreed. "It happened. You defeated an entire army. Enough said."

"But I summoned beasts," she said as though they should see the problem. "And wound up killing . . . *several* people."

"Cassie," Spencer said as he glanced at her through the rearview mirror. He'd bundled up just as much as Peter against the biting cold and snowfall. His thick brows almost reached the knitted cap he wore over his shaggy hair. "How many times do we have to tell you? You saved our lives. What is there to explain?"

She stared back at him through the mirror, her whole expression softening in hope.

Spencer smiled at her. "If you think we're ever letting you leave us, you better think again."

As Cassandra ducked her head in appreciation, Peter reached over his shoulder to pat her hands, which hung between the seats. "Like I told you—" He gave her a wink. "I always wanted a sister."

Though she narrowed her eyes at him, she didn't say anything. And even if Spencer heard the connotation of his joke, his brother showed no sign of disapproval.

Despite the lingering tension that burned in his throat after their harrowing night, Peter turned back to the road ahead of them as they took the bend that turned Whitehill back into Trinity, satisfied with the group's return to camaraderie. They passed Haven Boulevard and Hope Court on their left, the rooftops of each house beginning to turn white in the snowfall. Gentle snowflakes drifted down from the heavens to settle onto the windshield, melting the instant they met the glass. Though it had only been snowing for a few hours, it almost fully covered the dying grass.

The season was changing and DeVerre along with it.

Peter smiled at the thought. DeVerre was changing. The fight for their home was only a start, perhaps, but it was a good start in his mind. One that signified the end of the Druids' reign and the return of the Varons.

They pulled into the church parking lot, full of cars and people making their way into the building. The three of them hurried inside, Peter and Spencer both shivering from the cold. There was a pile-up in the main entry as people removed their winter wear, and Cassandra laughed at the brothers as they waited their turn to be away from the frigid doorway.

Soon they took their seats near the back of the sanctuary, where Danielle had invited them to join her again. However, this time, Spencer sat between Peter and Cassandra. And Peter noted every extra glance or subtle smile his brother sent Cassandra's way. He couldn't help the smug grin on his face, sure that their budding romance was proof that miracles could happen.

As they sat there, Peter caught the conversation of those around them.

His heart began to beat nervously again. Several empty seats made the pews look decidedly sparse, and the gossips of DeVerre were never idle. Already, the news of Gabriel Chapelle joining the marshal and deputy up at Occasus this morning had reached the townspeople. Peter could hear them questioning why certain members of the congregation hadn't made it to church. But once Reverend Chapelle stood up to begin the service, the muttering faded.

When Ava and Anna slipped in late, there was another uptick in chatter, the congregation eyeing them as they tried and failed to stealthily join Aaron and Haley in their usual seats. Peter passed Anna an encouraging smile across the aisles which she returned with a bashful one of her own.

After his conversation with Spencer two nights ago, Peter had felt off-kilter with Anna, as though recognizing his true feelings had created a rift between them. He liked her. He cared for her. But he didn't want to be with her. Not when he'd so clearly be the second best—the one she only accepted because Connor wasn't smart enough to love her back.

Peter's eyes caught the golden heads of Alexander and Giana Frossard at the front of the church. Anna's love for Connor wasn't as simple as he'd once thought. Not after everything they'd learned. The man she loved was the son of a Druid—the son of the leader of the Druids. And Connor might very well be a Druid too.

Gaze shifting between Anna and the Frossards, Peter realized that everything had changed. Each relationship in DeVerre was about to be pulled apart and inspected in a new light. Brothers, sisters, mothers, fathers, lovers, friends. There would be division within all the families of DeVerre. And it would be up to Peter and Spencer to manage it all.

Everything had changed, all because of one revelation: They were Varons.

A tense grin pulled at Peter's lips.

Not just Varon. Also Frossard.

Whether or not Ava and Tom were right—regardless of whether the town desired to have a Varon in control again—he and Spencer had work to do in DeVerre. It was their job to finish what their great-grandparents had begun. Michael and Seraphine had been working to save their home from the Druids. Eighty years later, the task had fallen to their great-grandsons.

And they would do it.

For the rest of the service, Peter watched the Frossards. He only allowed himself to interrupt his vigil by scanning the crowd for other Druids, attempting to deduce who might be evil enough to murder for the sake of power over the spirit world. He watched for any sign of aggression. Any flinch or tick that spoke of a threat.

Peter tensed at every hand raised to cover a cough or scratch a nose. He flinched when people adjusted in their seats, crossing their legs or stretching slightly. His eyes flashed to his side when Danielle tucked some hair behind her ear.

His heart ramped into overdrive, pounding between his ears. What if they were wildly underestimating the Druids? What if every other person within the church was one of them? What if just by stepping inside the building, Peter had sealed the deaths of everyone he loved when they attacked?

From that thought on, Peter was on edge. He felt like he was Spencer the way he kept fidgeting—knees pumping up and down as he clasped his hands in fists between them.

Spencer noted the behavior, elbowing him at one point. He leaned over and whispered, "Chill out."

Peter gave him a nod but failed to follow through.

When Sam finally prayed the last prayer, asking they be taught to "see the unseen," Peter hopped up from his seat before anyone else, pacing out into the cold air to clear his head. He knew it was dumb. He was probably putting a target on his back by showing how unnerved he was to be in a room with an unknown number of Druids out to kill him and his family.

His family.

Peter scoffed, running a hand over his face. Was that what had become of Cassandra? What about Owen, Ava, and Anna? Aaron and Haley? Had he come to see them as his family? Were they just as important as Spencer?

Shaking his head at the foolish thought, Peter shoved his hands into his jeans pockets. No—no one was as important as Spencer. They all mattered to him; he'd do what he could to protect them. But if it came between them and Spencer, he'd choose his brother every time.

The door to the church opened, and Peter turned, expecting to see the onrush of DeVerreans coming his way. Instead, Anna slipped through. Her light blue coat looked like a robin's egg, immediately flecked with snowflakes.

"Hey," she said, stepping over to him.

"Hey."

She had her hands tucked into her coat, the coils of her hair puffing up as she shrugged in the winter chill. "You okay?"

Sighing at the confirmation of his earlier concern, Peter wondered how many others in the service had noticed his agitation. Or had it just been Anna? Had she been paying particular attention to him? "Uh, yeah," he told her, kicking some snow off his boots. "Yeah, I just . . . I'm picking up some of Spencer's paranoia, I think."

She smiled at him, a tender look of compassion in her eyes. "I think that's pretty understandable these days."

He returned the smile but dipped his head down, unsure what else there was to say. He had nothing to add. It *was* understandable. They were in over their heads here in DeVerre. And this was only the start.

Anna tapped his arm. "Hey, so, I know it's probably weird," she said, voice low though no one else was around. "Considering last night and everything, but—well, I wanted to invite you, and Spencer, and Cass to join us tonight."

Raising his brow, he looked up at her. "Us?"

"Ava, Aaron, Haley, and me. And I don't care if Ava's mad at him, Owen's gonna be there too."

He tipped his head to the side. "Sounds like a family affair."

She smiled coyly. "Which is why you should be there."

He chuckled, rubbing a hand along the back of his neck as he shivered in the cold. "Wow, uh—thanks."

Anna gave him a happy nod.

"What's the occasion?"

She pressed her lips together, twisting side to side. Peter recognized the playful behavior; he may not have been successful in his past relationships, but he knew the signs. Anna was flirting with him.

He felt his neck go warm, unsure how to take the revelation.

Anna gave him an embarrassed smile. "It's my birthday."

The church doors opened while Peter stared at her wide-eyed. People poured out of the church, talking and crunching through the snow. Anna had to shift closer to Peter to get out of the way, and he backed up to keep a healthy distance between them.

"Wow," he repeated, scratching the back of his head. "Well, happy birthday. That's—that's cool. Thanks for the invitation."

Her smile faltered at his obvious nerves. "Thanks. So . . . you'll be there, right?"

Rushing to clear up his lapse in manners, Peter nodded. "Yeah, of course! We wouldn't miss it, Annie. You know that."

"Great!" She turned bashful again. "Cool, yeah, it's—it's kind of a big one."

"It is?"

"Quarter of a century and all that."

Peter raised his chin, confirming her age for the first time. Twenty-five. He'd been close in his guesses. Not that much younger than Spencer.

Managing a laugh, Peter gave her arm a tap. "Practically over the hill, huh? We definitely can't miss it then, can we?"

As though the clouds had parted, Peter felt the tension in his chest ease as Spencer walked out of the church with Cassandra at his side. Anna's family followed—Ava, Aaron, and Haley. The group walked over to the pair, and Spencer held Peter's coat out to him.

"Thanks," he said, pulling it on. He felt strange not being able to wear his leather jacket, but with the encroaching cold weather, he'd had to say goodbye to it for the season.

He motioned to Anna as the group circled up. "Annie just invited us to her birthday party."

"It's hardly a party," Anna argued.

Ava slipped her arm through her sister's. "Are you saying what I have planned isn't party enough for you?"

"No," she insisted. "It's just—I mean, it'll just be us having dinner and playing games. That can't really be called a party."

"When's your birthday?" Spencer asked.

"Today."

Spencer and Cassandra both gave their immediate salutations to her. Her light blush and smile showed Anna's appreciation of the fuss.

"You'll all be there, then?" Aaron asked, arm around Haley's shoulders.

"Yep," Peter promised.

"Cool," he said, then dropped his voice. "Then you can tell me what the heck happened last night."

Peter, Spencer, and Cassandra all shared a glance, but Ava shook her head. "Huh-uh, no one is talking about any of that stuff tonight," she insisted. "We're celebrating Anna's birthday. Everything else can wait."

Aaron didn't appear concerned by his sister's insistence. "Whatever," he muttered, turning back to them. "I'm glad you're alive."

"Me too," Haley added, her voice hushed.

Though Peter supposed it shouldn't surprise him that Aaron had told his girlfriend about their predicament, it did. But if everything went right over the next few days, all of DeVerre would know. And he thought that would probably be for the best.

"All right." Ava pulled away from Anna. "We've got to get home. I've got a *party* to decorate for. See you three later."

They all said their goodbyes. Peter and Anna were a bit more awkward than all the others as she went to give him a full hug while he'd intended to only go for one of the side-variety. The trio watched the family walk away to their respective vehicles, Cassandra and Spencer chuckling together.

Peter glared at them. "Can we get going? It's freezing out here."

"Hang on." Spencer tipped his head back toward the chapel. "I want to show you guys something."

Cassandra and Peter looked at each other but followed him down the path and around the corner of the building. He led them through the snow that blanketed the earth and to the graveyard, surrounded by its wrought iron fence.

"What are we doing here?" Peter asked, brushing a hand through his snow-damp hair.

Spencer motioned for them to follow as he walked to the fifth row of plots. He led them down to the fifteenth headstone before coming to a stop. "There," he said, gesturing to the grave.

Looking down at the plain marker, Peter saw why his brother had brought them there. " 'Michael Varon,' " he read. " '1914-1940. Virtus, devotio, et cor.' "

"Courage, devotion, and heart," Spencer translated. He gestured to the rest of the row. "It's on all the Varon headstones."

"A family motto?" Cassandra suggested with a sly grin. "It fits."

The brothers gave her appreciative smiles.

Spencer tucked his hands into his coat pockets. "I thought it'd be nice to see them," he said. "Honor their memory since Diane never got the chance."

Peter clasped a hand onto Spencer's shoulder. "It was a good idea."

He grinned and stepped back. "Come on, then."

They returned to the outside of the rows, headed for the back.

"I checked with Sam before we left the chapel," Spencer explained.

"He didn't know Seraphine's name, but he knew the timeline and layout of the cemetery well enough to give me a general idea. Row eight or nine, he thought."

It took a few minutes of searching, but they found her. Seraphine Frossard, 1915-1940. Nothing more was engraved on her simple headstone. A smattering of other families and names that Peter didn't recognize as having any familial relation surrounded her. It clearly conveyed that, unlike Michael's grave, their great-grandmother was buried without any family, not even other Frossards nearby.

"Diane never got to see this," Cassandra muttered. "She remembered her, and yet she never knew her name."

Spencer shifted and pulled a hand from his pocket. "Here," he said to Cassandra, holding out his fist.

She looked at it, then up at him.

"I thought . . . well, Diane can't honor her mother's memory," he explained. "But you can."

Cassandra extended her hand to take Spencer's offering. He placed a small picture frame on her palm. It held a drawing of a baby girl, one with Seraphine's signature at the bottom.

"I found it on Michael's desk," Spencer said.

Peter smiled as Cassandra ran her fingers along the twisted edge of the frame. It was tiny, not much bigger than her palm. But its sentiment was more meaningful than most things.

Crouching down with care, Cassandra set the picture gently along the edge of Seraphine's headstone. The snow glinted against its surface. The memory of a daughter who never forgot her mother.

When Cassandra stood, she was chewing on her bottom lip, clearly fighting back the tears. "Are, uh . . . are you guys ready to go?"

Peter didn't think his brother could have done a better job of wooing Cassandra Clement if he'd tried. But Spencer appeared not to notice, tipping his head toward the exit. The trio walked through the snow, quiet and content.

The gate squealed as Spencer closed it behind them. He pulled his beanie further over his ears. Cassandra huffed as he pulled his gloves on next.

"What?" Spencer asked.

"Nothing," she said, a hint of teasing in her tone. "You're just adorable all bundled up like that."

Spencer bumped his arm against hers. "Hey, I didn't grow up in this frozen wasteland like you, okay?"

"It's the first snowfall," Cassandra exclaimed. "You guys realize it gets way colder than this, don't you?"

"Speaking of—" Peter nodded to Spencer as he pulled on his own gloves. "Did you get my scarf from the hook inside?"

Spencer narrowed his eyes in thought. "I didn't think you were wearing a scarf."

"It's freakin' cold out here, man. Of course, I had a scarf."

Cassandra smirked. "Says the guy who walked outside without a coat fifteen minutes ago."

Peter tossed her a frown. "I was in a rush."

"Well, go get it then," Spencer suggested as they rounded the corner toward the front of the chapel. All the other vehicles had gone, leaving the dark green Jeep standing out amongst the white contrast of snow.

Peter motioned to the vacant lot. "I can't get in. Everyone's gone."

"The church is never locked," Spencer explained.

"Oh. Really?" With a shrug, Peter broke away. "Be right back, then."

"We'll be in the Jeep."

"Cool," he called over his shoulder. "See you in a sec."

With a light jog, Peter neared the church doors. He grabbed the handle, pulling hard against the heavy door, and slipped inside. Darkness enveloped the empty chapel, only the light from the office to his right still on. He heard a couple of men speaking—Sam must have had a post-service meeting—and hurried to find his scarf so he didn't disturb them.

Peter made it to the wall of coat hooks, hand already on his scarf, when one of the voices registered, loud and clear in his mind. A deep and heavy tone that often handed out far too much snark for a dead guy. But he didn't have enough time to ponder how the phantom could be so far from Occasus as he listened in on the conversation.

"I told you," Gerard said, "if you want to get rid of them, you have to come at them with everything. Not send a handful of your pathetic lackeys."

Peter gaped into the darkness as the other man replied. "And I told you," the man's smooth voice cut through the air with a finesse that he didn't recognize, "Varons or not, those boys aren't a threat. They're just an irritant."

"So why the fight?" Gerard demanded. "Why try to kill Cassandra?"

"You know we wouldn't have killed her."

"Your people damn well tried last night."

"They know better than that, Gerard."

Peter held his breath, sure he should get out, but knowing he'd stumbled into something that changed the course of everything yet again. Gerard was helping the Druids. He had to tell Cassandra. And Owen, so they could break the phantom's tether to Occasus.

His eyes went wide.

Occasus. Gerard had access to the vault. And if he was working with the Druids. . . .

Peter had missed some of the conversation as the revelations hit him, but he jumped back in as the stranger spoke, ". . . they've bumped up the timeline, that's all. It isn't ideal, but now we have the information we need, and the Vessel is returning later this week, so we'll be ready to go. Just be sure *you're* ready to do your part."

"Don't worry," Gerard replied in a low growl. "I've been waiting for this moment for over seventy years."

This week. They had a manner of days until the return of . . . the Vessel?

"What the hell is a Vessel?" Peter mouthed to himself.

Before he processed that the men had stopped talking, the door to the office opened, and Alexander Frossard stepped out.

Peter froze, hand on the wall beside him. He remained as still as possible, hoping the man would head for the front door without looking around.

He wasn't that lucky.

Alexander did a double take when he saw Peter standing there, but he didn't hesitate like Peter had.

The second the doctor's eyes locked on him, his hand lifted, and an arc of pure obsidian black cut through the air toward him.

Peter pushed off the wall with one hand, the other flying up to send his own arc forward, but it was too late. Whether Alexander Frossard's arcs were faster than the other Druids' or Peter had just been too slow, he would never know. The dark shadow of energy slammed into his chest, knocking him flat on his back as his whole body went numb.

Pain rushed through his veins, causing his muscles to go rigid and his breath to escape him. He couldn't move. He couldn't even get his brain to listen to his command to get up. To run. To cry out and get someone's attention.

Spencer and Cassandra were just outside in the Jeep. They were so close, and they could save him. But he'd been inside for less than two minutes. They wouldn't start getting concerned for another handful, at least.

"Well. . . ." Alexander stepped across the wooden floors of the chapel. "It seems one of my thorns has decided to present itself for some pruning."

Peter tried to move. He tried to breathe. But nothing worked anymore.

Crouching, Alexander Frossard reached out and grabbed the collar of Peter's coat in both hands. "Hm," he murmured, pulling him up to study his face. "Now, which one are you, again?"

Unable to do anything else, Peter returned the favor, taking in all the details of the man. He looked a lot like his son, an air of sophistication and perfection making him irritatingly good-looking. Blond hair, sky blue eyes, a strong jaw, and an indefinable charm in the tilt of his smile.

"The older one, I think," Alexander said, then sighed. "What should I do with you?"

The numbness was beginning to dissipate from Peter's body, but he still couldn't get his brain to function, and his limbs were slack. It was as though he were paralyzed. He couldn't even speak.

"Ah, yes," the Druid leader said, a cruel glint coming to his eyes. "While you haven't been kind enough to invite me into your home, allow me to welcome you to mine."

Peter's stomach leaped into his throat as it felt like the world had suddenly dropped out from beneath him, the Druid clutching tightly onto his coat as everything went black.

Peter & Spencer will return
in book four of Archives of the Warden

Also Available from V. K. Dixon

ARCHIVES OF THE WARDEN
Lake of Glass
Vault of Stone
The Raven's Cry (Coming 2024)
Book Four (Coming 2025)
Book Five (Coming soon)

WARRIORS & MAGES
Fire & Night (a serial novel)
Book Two (Coming soon)

Looking for more?
Follow the QR code below for:
The Family Trees of DeVerre,
a novella of Gerard's backstory,
and more!

Newsletter: vkdixon.substack.com
Instagram: @v.k.dixon
TikTok: @vkdixon

Peter's Nicknames for Spencer

& where they come from:

J.B. — Jessica "J.B." Fletcher, mystery writer and amateur sleuth *(Murder, She Wrote; television show)*

Sherlock — Sherlock Holmes, consulting detective with Scotland Yard *(Sherlock Holmes stories by Sir Arthur Conan Doyle)*

Poirot — Hercule Poirot, private investigator *(reoccurring character in Agatha Christie's mystery novels)*

Columbo — Lieutenant Columbo, police lieutenant and homicide detective *(Columbo; television show)*

Watson — Dr. John H. Watson, assistant and confidant of Sherlock Holmes *(Sherlock Holmes stories by Sir Arthur Conan Doyle)*

Matlock — Ben Matlock, defense attorney with a knack for solving the murders himself *(Matlock; television show)*

Frankly — Dr. Charles Frankly, ex-doctor turned private investigator *(Wenzel & Frankly serial by Peter and Spencer Collins)*

Glossary of Terms & Names

Aaron Lambert — *[Lam—bert]* — Middle of the three Lambert children; boyfriend of Haley Roux; mechanic

Aimee Lambert — Mother of Ava, Aaron, and Anna; previous town librarian; descendant of Yvan Rayne

Anguis — *[An—gwis]* — German Wirehaired Pointer under the care of Peter and Spencer Collins

Alexander Frossard — *[Fros—sard]* — *aka 'Alex'* — Doctor in DeVerre; husband of Giana Frossard; father of Connor Frossard

Allen Clement — *[Klem-ent]* — Father of Cassandra Clement; lives in Spokane

Anna Lambert — Youngest of the three Lambert children; bartender/waitress and artist

Arthur Wenzel — *[Wen—zuhl]* — Private investigator of the online serial *Wenzel & Frankly* written by Peter and Spencer Collins

Ava Bernard — Oldest of the three Lambert children; wife of Owen Bernard; town librarian

beast — A creature summoned from the spirit world to work on behalf of a Wielder

Benjamin Powell — *aka 'Ben'* — Step-father of Peter and Spencer Collins; second husband of Mallory Collins-Powell

Brendan Descoteaux — *[Des—co—toe]* — High school student; boyfriend of Juliet Chapelle; third victim of the hellhound attacks

Cassandra Clement — *[Kuh—san—druh]* — *aka 'Cass' or 'Cassie'* — Best friend of Diane Larkin; Wielder

Charles Frankly — Ex-doctor and private investigator of the online serial *Wenzel & Frankly* written by Peter and Spencer Collins

Connor Frossard — Prior best friend of Anna Lambert; medical student

Danielle MacDonald — Member of Anna Lambert's Bible study; waitress at MacDonald's Diner; mega-fan of *Wenzel & Frankly*

David Collins — Late father of Peter and Spencer Collins; mechanic for the United States Navy

Debra Mercier — *aka 'Debbie'* — First cousin of Cassandra Clement's mother; descendant of the Sauveterre family; Druid

DeVerre, WA — *[Deh—Vair]* — Small town in northeastern Washington State

Diane Larkin — Late great-aunt of Peter and Spencer Collins; left the brothers her estate upon her death

Druids — *aka 'Children of Gaia'* — A cult of Wielders intent on releasing the spirit world upon the physical world

Elijah Lawrence — Son of John William Lawrence; reverend and theologian from Bushmills, Ireland, in the early 1600s

Franklin Alarie — *[Uh-lar-e]* — Older brother of Gerard Alarie; suspected murderer and Druid

Frederic Chapelle — *[Sha—pell]* — Original reverend of DeVerre; cousin of Matthias Varon

Gabriel Chapelle — *aka 'Gabe'* — Mortician; younger brother of Samuel Chapelle

Gerard Alarie — Phantom from 1950s; tethered to Occasus by Cassandra Clement

ghost — The lingering spirit of a dead Wielder with unfinished business in the physical world

Giana Frossard — *[Gee—ah—nah]* — *aka 'Gia'* — Friend of Anna Lambert; wife of Alexander Frossard; mother of Connor Frossard

Haley Roux — *[Rue]* — Girlfriend of Aaron Lambert; friend and co-worker of Anna Lambert

Harmony, Saskatchewan — *[Suh—ska—chew—on]* — Original hometown of the founders of DeVerre, WA

Heinrich Schwarz — *[Hiyn—rick Sh—warts]* — Mentor of John William Lawrence; co-founder of the Spiritualists

hellhound — Hound-like beast from the spirit world

House of Occasus — *[Oh—kay—sus]* — Diane Larkin's home, left to the Collins brothers; previously built and owned by the Varon family

Hunter Durand — Deputy in DeVerre

hydra — *[hi—druh]* — Snake-like beast from the spirit world

Isaac Clement — Older brother of Cassandra Clement

Jessica Calderon — *[Call—der—on]* — aka *'Jess'* — Distant relative of Thomas Garnier; second victim of the hellhound attacks

John William Lawrence — Theologian, co-founder of the Spiritualists, and founder of the Warden

Julianne Clement — Mother of Cassandra Clement; cousin of Debra Mercier; descendant of the Sauveterre family

Juliet Chapelle — High school student; daughter of Samuel Chapelle; girlfriend of Brendan Descoteaux

Lee Frossard — Town veterinarian in the early 1900s; brother of Lloyd Frossard

Lloyd Frossard — Town doctor in the early 1900s; grandfather of Alexander Frossard

Mallory Collins-Powell — Mother of Peter and Spencer Collins; remarried to Benjamin Powell; lives in Norfolk, VA

Matthew Varon — *[Vair—en]* — Previous mayor of DeVerre; father of Michael Varon

Matthias Varon — Founder of DeVerre

Michael Mercier — *aka 'Mike'* — Husband of Debbie Mercier

Michael Varon — Great-grandson of Matthais Varon; last of the Varon line

Nex — German Wirehaired Pointer under the care of Peter and Spencer Collins

Owen Bernard — Husband of Ava Bernard; substitute teacher for DeVerre School; freelance article writer for online publications; originally from Harmony, Saskatchewan; Wielder

Peter Collins — *aka 'Pete'* — Older of the two Collins brothers; writer

Phillip Collins — Grandfather of Peter and Spencer Collins; brother of Diane Larkin

phantom — A ghost that has been tethered to a specific location in the physical world

Porthaven, ME — Small, Warden-run town in the state of Maine

Rene Mercier — Daughter of Debra and Michael Mercier; second cousin of Cassandra Clement

Samuel Chapelle — *aka 'Sam'* — Reverend in DeVerre

Sandy Clement — Wife of Isaac Clement; sister-in-law of Cassandra Clement

scylla — *[sky—luh]* — Cephalopod-like beast from the spirit world

Serene Verlice — *[Ver-lis]* — Character in the online serial *Wenzel & Frankly* written by Peter and Spencer Collins; inspired by Cassandra Clement

Spencer Collins — *aka 'Spence'* — Younger of the two Collins brothers; writer

spirit world — A parallel world that exists alongside the physical world

Taylor Ozanne — *[Oh—zawn]* — Farmer; first victim of the hellhound attacks

Thomas Garnier — *aka 'Tom'* — Marshal in DeVerre

Tony MacDonald — Owner of MacDonald's Diner; town councilman; uncle of Danielle MacDonald

Travis Mercier — Son of Debra and Michael Mercier; second cousin of Cassandra Clement

Veil — Specific locations around the world where the boundary between the spirit world and the physical world is thin

The Warden — An organization of Wielders dedicated to protecting the spirit world from the control of the Druids

wendigo — *[when—de—go]* — Deer-like beast from the spirit world

Wenzel & Frankly — Serial historical-fantasy blog written by Peter and Spencer Collins

Wielder — A human with the ability to wield the spirit world

William Larkin — *aka 'Liam'* — Late husband of Diane Larkin; writer; researcher of history and theology

Yvan Rayne — *[Ee-vahn Rain]* — Original record keeper in DeVerre; the Lambert siblings' ancestor

Acknowledgements

Where to begin? I am beyond grateful to so many people.

Publishing my second novel, I have to say I am overwhelmed with how many relationships I've made over the past year of this journey. So first, thanks to you, dear reader. You are the whole reason I write these stories. I hope you find them as entertaining, silly, and wonderful as I do.

As always, thank you to my husband, Josh. You truly are a champion, listening to my rambles. (And I'm so sorry for the near constant spoilers.) I can't imagine what I'd do without you cheering me on. You really are my biggest fan.

To my family and friends: This hermit of a writer appreciates how much you love and care for me. I could never thank you enough for the way you've cheered me on as I've pursued this dream of mine.

To my amazing editor: Britt, you are my sanity. Thank you for making me a better writer, for turning my words into readable stories, and for always encouraging me. I don't know what I'd do without you.

To my lovely beta readers who saw all the plot holes and helped me make this sequel worth reading: Alexandra, Brooke, Emma, Erica, Kaydte, Lydia, Molly, and Serenity, you guys are heroes!

To my social media community: You all make me feel so loved with your support and feedback. I couldn't be more grateful for all your shares, reposts, and messages. This journey wouldn't be the same without you.

And finally, to God: These are the stories you've place in my heart. I aspire that every word written would fit your purposes more than my own.

About the Author

V. K. Dixon writes fantasy and romance novels filled with found family, lasting love, and unique magic. She believes that the extraordinary gives us a deeper desire for the things beyond us; for the things of God. Faith, art, and community are her guiding values as she pursues the vision on her heart.

Currently, V. K. and her husband, Josh, live the life of the nomads as they each build their careers and seek out their long-term home. They dream of living by the sea with two dogs, at least one cat, several kids, and a table large enough to host uproarious dinner parties.